Crush on

Mr. Bad Boy

LILLYCOOLEST1

Lilly Purdon

Crush on Mr. Bad Boy

First published 2012.
First published paperback 2017.

Copyright © 2012 Lilly Purdon
Cover image & design © 2012 by Lilly Purdon
Published by Lilly Wan Purdon

Copyright © 2012 Lilly Purdon
All rights reserved.
ISBN 978-154-993-867-2

This is a work of fiction. Names, characters, businesses, places, events and incidents are either the product of the author's imagination or used in a fictitious manner. Any resemblance to actual persons, living or dead, or actual events is purely coincidental.

Crush on Mr. Bad Boy

TO

MOM, DAD, PETER, & GRANDMA
FOR TEACHING ME HOW TO FEEL.

ANYONE WHO IS READING THIS FOR BELIEVING
IN SOMETHING I'VE CREATED.

C O N T E N T S

Chapter 1 NERD

"Rosaline Arlene Winnefred!" Layla, the Queen Bee AKA the school's bitch, snarled out mockingly as I opened my locker. Her obnoxiously high pitched voice pierced through my ears.

Layla Cleo Star was the most popular girl in school. She was completely gorgeous with her chocolate brown eyes, dark hair, and perfectly tanned skin. You could say she was the most beautiful girl you had ever laid eyes on, and I would have to completely agree with you. Physically, she was perfect. However, her personality was opposite.

Apparently, if you got on her good side, she could be one of the sweetest people ever.

Somehow I managed to get on her bad side. Don't ask me how. The moment she heard my name, she hated me. Her half smirk which had potential to turn into a smile, turned into a scowl instead.

Since that day? I was doomed.

She made it her mission to make my life a living hell, and succeeded.

Her favorite hobbies seemed to be: making me suffer, gossiping, and cheerleading- oh and did I mention? Making me suffer.

My best friend Jaxon claimed he believed she preyed on the weakest just for the thrill of domination. But personally, I had no idea why.

The cheerleaders around her giggled at the scene before them as she stood in proudly in the middle.

She faked a gasp, "has the nerd gone mute?"

According to everyone, I was the typical nerd. Braces, glasses, unfashionable clothes, good grades, and being painfully shy made my reputation the way it was.

The person who forced me into getting braces was my step mother, Cleo. Cleo wasn't the type of step mother someone would want. She wasn't physically abusive, but her harsh words were quite cruel and could destroy someone's confident in a blink of an eye.

She was a child psychologist, and worked part time for the local newspaper; writing articles about 'Raising Your Child Right!' I was her ongoing social experiment. She gave me zero tips on being confident, made me go shopping at all the wrong places, and convinced me to wear glasses just for the purpose of protecting my 'sclera'. Of course, I only wore my glasses when I knew there were risks nearby.

Since she married my father, she seemed to take me under her wing, and transformed me into an utter geek, just for experimentation. I had a feeling that she too, wanted to see me suffer.

As part of the usual routine, I decided to ignore Layla. I grabbed my books from my locker before shutting it as softly as I could, not wanting her to react more negatively. I spun the lock twice to make sure it was fully locked, so I wouldn't get any more nasty surprises from any of my tormentors. When I looked up, I saw them all smirking at me like they knew something I didn't. I tried to step around them, but they all blocked my path.

"You think you can ignore me?" Layla questioned daringly. Her presence was stressing me out. I knew it was best if I stayed quiet and let her do all the talking.

"You can't ignore me no matter what! No one ignores me! If you don't want to have any trouble for the rest of the year, I suggest you start respecting people who are better than you."

'As if that would make a difference.'

I bit my lip nervously, avoiding eye contact. Glancing down and my watch, I knew I was going to be late if I didn't get to my next class within the next minute. We only had 3 minutes for hall passing time.

"Now I suggest you apologize!" she said, holding her head up high.

I sighed. "Sorry."

She scrunched up her face. "You call that an apology?!"

I looked up at her. I already apologized, what else could she want?

"Don't look at me like I'm nuts!" Her frustrated face was bright red.

Someone cleared their throat impatiently behind the cheerleaders. I tensed when I saw who it was. It was Axel. He was standing right behind Layla, and his face was filled with pure annoyance. Layla stood there, staring up at him like she was hypnotized. He pushed straight passed her and started walking my way.

Once Layla realized what was going on, she fixed her cheer skirt and batted her eyelashes sweetly in his direction, but he didn't even glance back. The only guy who refused to look at her for that matter.

I looked down at the floor the moment he walked passed me. The feeling was uncontrollable. I felt a whole zoo in my stomach. My heart was pounding so hard against my chest, I felt like I was going it was going to fly out of my chest any moment. I looked up at his back when was a few feet away. And as he walked down the hall and out of sight, I felt utterly shattered.

There was no hope for a girl like me.

Axel Storm Spencer, known as the school's 'bad boy' that everyone feared. On the popularity pyramid, he was the only one who stood above Layla. He wasn't your typical bad boy; there was something special. He didn't seem to have any friends, or at least from what I knew. He was sharper than a needle, but he didn't participate at school. The only way he passed school was through his exams. He could be scary, but he had his sweet moments where he would stare out into space, deep in thought.

His personality was absolutely fascinating.

I had gotten my hands on a couple of essays he had written

on different pieces of literature, and his interpretations were beyond creative, and were written with a sense of defiance. The interpretations themselves were pieces of art to me. He was a puzzle I strived to solve, as I admired him from afar. As if his intelligence wasn't enough, he looked like a Greek God to me. His perfect blonde hair was the shade of sand, giving a sense of optimism, his eyes were emerald green, hypnotizing me from afar, and his body was muscular, highlighting how fit he was.

Axel was perfect. At least he was to me. So perfect, he was untouchable.

My crush began in middle school. It would sound cliché if I said it was love at first sight, but it was true. He had gotten in a fight with some 8th graders while we were in 6th grade, and his face was coated in blood.

Peculiar? Definitely.

I strived for the freedom he had.

I would dress a little more girly just for him to notice me, (from the terrible selection Cleo gave me), I would get more beauty sleep to look prettier, I tried expressing myself more in front of him, but of course, he never did notice me.

I was a nerd, he was bad.

I was soft, he was tough.

I was quiet, he was loud.

I held my tongue, he said anything he wanted to.

There was no way we would've worked.

Opposites never seemed to attract in my world.

"Quit day dreaming." Layla huffed from behind me. "You're everything he doesn't want in a girl."

I felt as if someone took a piece of shattered glass and stabbed it straight into my chest. Layla seemed to know what nerve to hit every single time. I turned to face her. She had a knowing smirk on her face. He was my secret, and the last person I wanted to know was her.

I decided to play dumb. "Who?"

She rolled her eyes in annoyance.

"She's so stupid." One of the cheerleaders said.

"I know!" Another one replied.

"She doesn't even understand English!" another one commented.

"Totally!" Another agreed.

The bell suddenly rang. I felt myself start to shake. I was already late to class.

"Look who's late to class!" Layla sang.

"She's so scared, she's shaking!" Another cheerleader laughed.

"Never had a tardy before, Little Miss Nerdy?" Layla snarled.

They parted a way for me so I could get to class. I sprinted forward and tripped on someone's foot. All my books and papers scattered all over the floor.

"Oops!" Layla giggled.

I collected my assignments from the ground quickly before rushing to class. After a few minutes of sprinting like a mad man, I finally reached my class. I entered the room panting heavily like I was just running from a bunch of thugs.

"Miss Winnefred!" Mrs. Meisty, my History teacher called out while adjusting her spectacles.

"I am so sorry-"

"Tardy!" She interrupted me. "You're lucky this is your first tardy otherwise you'd get a 15 minute after school. Grab a tardy pass and get to your assigned seat."

I sighed in relief, relieved I didn't get a detention. "Yes ma'am." I knew better than not to obey her orders. She was one teacher who gave out detention slips faster than you could say the word 'shit'. I rushed to my assigned seat. Right when I was about to reach my seat, I tripped on someone's foot and fell flat on my face.

The whole class erupted into laughter.

I looked up to find Matt McCartney grinning evilly at me. Matt McCartney was that typical school football player. He was Layla's best friend and had joined her in her mission to make my life a living hell. "Nerd," he snickered.

"Dork," someone else said.

"Ugly dork." Another person corrected.

"Shut up!" Mrs. Meisty hissed at everyone. I got up and picked up all my books. "And Rosaline."

"Yes ma'am?" I asked politely.

"Try not to die before we start class."

With that, the class erupted into laughter again. She didn't stop the class from laughing this time. Instead, she went to her computer and started setting stuff up for our lesson. I frowned at every single person laughing at me.

I ducked my head down low and slumped into my seat. The humiliation seemed to increase for me every single day. Last week didn't seem this bad. The comment about being ugly seemed to get to me quick.

I knew I wasn't the prettiest girl, but I couldn't have been *that* ugly, right? Pale skin, dull blue eyes, and blonde hair. I was nothing compared to Layla look wise, but personality wise, I knew I could beat her by a long shot.

~*~

"You're beautiful and everyone knows that." One of my best friends Kasay attempted to cheer me up.

Kasay was one of those punk type girls. Everything in her wardrobe was black. She had ear length jet black hair that reminded me of Snow White's hair. She was pale and had over 3 pounds of eyeshadow on every day. She never left her bedroom without makeup on.

Her grey eyes were eerily hollow and she had piercings on different parts of her body except on her lips and tongue. 'The best kissers don't have them.' She once said high on cannabis.

She also had quite a reputation with the guys. Most of the guys at school called her the 'Blow Queen' or 'Freebie'. She

"It's a long story." He replied.

"I've got time." I pressed further.

He turned to me with a blank expression. "I'm not in the mood, Rosie."

I knew he was just making up excuses to avoid the touchy subject again. I decided not to press further since Axel was standing only a few feet away from our table. I knew he'd never give in and tell me. I suddenly felt the urge to talk to Axel.

Before I knew it, I was walking straight to the lunch line. I had no idea what I was doing, but I knew I couldn't stop now. My feet carried me to the spot right behind him. I felt myself start to panic. My palms started sweating and my heart pounded crazily against my chest.

I heard someone call my name, but I didn't know what to do. I was frozen in my spot. What if I tried talking to him and he blew me off? I was just another nerd after all. I was as attractive as a drooling llama, so why would he ever want to talk to me?

I bit my lip nervously. I didn't have a clue what to do and all I could seem to hear was the pounding of my heart through my ears. How was I supposed to know what to do when the hottest guy on earth was standing right in front of me with his back to me?

I stared at his perfect broad shoulders and the way his perfect blonde hair seemed to glow in the sunlight shining in from outside.

Maybe I should've said hi.

Maybe I should've made myself look good.

Maybe I should've cleaned up better.

Maybe I should've changed my reputation.

Maybe I should've made sure prepared myself better.

But no, I couldn't wait to just be near him.

And I hated myself for that.

What if he thought I was just another horny teenage girl looking for some fun? My mind was screaming for me to run, but my heart was yelling for me to take a chance and talk to him. A chance like this came once in a lifetime.

The line moved forward. I took a step forward, following him. He was next in line to get his lunch. I bit my lip harder until I drew blood.

A decision that could change my life…

~*~

Chapter 2 LOSER WITH A CAPITAL 'L'

There he was, standing right in front of me in line.

I felt like a little girl in elementary deciding whether or not to talk to her little crush. My heart was hammering against my rib cage frantically. As corny as it sounded, I felt the whole zoo in my stomach.

I knew I was a love sick puppy, but I just couldn't help it. During the summer, I found his social media profiles and got some photos of him. I was just randomly surfing the internet to kill time, and somehow I ended up on his profile. It was either fate, or my stalker senses deep down inside.

I tapped my foot impatiently, trying to decide whether to tap his shoulder or not. It was now or never.

Time's running up Rosie, time's running up.

I took in a deep breath before lifting my index finger up slowly. Right before I could tap his shoulder, a voice interrupted me.

"Well, well, well, look who it is. Little Miss Rosaline Loser Winnefred!" she laughed, making an 'L' with her fingers on her forehead. Her voice sent me chills down my spine. Of course she would be here to ruin one of my brave moments.

I shifted uncomfortably as the whole cafeteria silenced. All eyes were on me, making me feel exposed. I glanced at where Axel was standing, but luckily, he wasn't paying any attention at all. I tried to play it cool like him and ignore her too.

"Bitch, don't pretend you don't hear me," she growled, threatening me.

I knew I was stupid not to obey her, but you know what they say, *'Love is blind'* so therefore, I paid no attention to her. I stood there, staring at his masculine back and the back of his head. I stared at his the way his perfect blonde hair was styled.

I bit my lip nervously, wondering why Layla hasn't tried anything so far yet.

"Did you hear what I just said?!" Her tone was even more threatening now.

I was pissing her off with every second I was ignoring her. My heart was in frenzy. I didn't know whether it was because the head cheerleader yelling at me, or because the hottest male specimen ever was standing right in front of me.

I took long steady breathes to calm myself. Suddenly, I felt ice cold water being dumped on my back. The whole cafeteria erupted into laughter. I squeezed my eyes shut as Layla poured a whole bowl of soup on my head.

I opened my eyes slowly, feeling more embarrassed than ever before. Everyone was laughing at the display of the nerd getting soup dumped over her head. And unfortunately, the nerd was me. I didn't even bother to look up, because I knew I would be facing the embarrassing crowd.

I glanced at Layla, to find her already smirking evilly at me. She stood there proudly with her 'cheerleader friends' standing right behind her. I turned around to see if Axel was still there, but he was gone. It was like he vanished in thin air.

I felt relieved that he was gone. Looking on the bright side, at least he wasn't there to see me get humiliated. I don't know what came over me, but hot tears started sliding down my soup-covered cheeks. I didn't bother to wipe them away, because they wouldn't be able to see them anyway.

The tears blurred up my vision, and before I knew it, my feet carried me to the girl's bathroom as fast as they could. I ran straight to the girl's bathroom and locked myself in one of the stalls. Not bothering to wipe the seat, I sat down and let the rest of my tears run freely down my face.

I leaned my elbows on my knees and covered my face with my hands. I hated myself for not standing up to her and for letting her humiliate me. Even if I tried to stand up to her, she would always find a way to put me where I belong anyway, so why bother?

Axel. Axel is why you should bother.

I ignored my inner self for a moment. My inner self was blinded by emotions. "Shut up feelings, just shut up for once!" I growled at myself. I sat there for what seemed like forever.

A part of me was telling me I should've listened to Layla in the first place. If I had just obeyed her, none of this would've happened. But another part of me was yelling at me and telling me to fight back.

"Love is stupid, love is blind, and I'm in love with a stranger who doesn't even know who I am," I laughed with no humor.

I had no plan of escaping that stall anytime soon. I wasn't ready to face the outside world yet after the incident. I thought I would never be able to face the outside world ever again. All the faces of classmates laughing at me getting humiliated.

The teachers might've tried to prevent bullying, but they never tried hard enough.

"Tell an adult, they'll help you."

Well, from my experience, adults couldn't do shit about bullying. From the day she started her mission to break me down; no adult had backed me up or had been on my side.

Out of all the people she could've picked on, she picked me. And I had no idea why. Maybe it was because I was an easy target, or because my face annoyed her. But from what I knew, I had never done ANYTHING to her. From the moment she heard my name, she had never thought twice about hurting me.

She had moved here when she was 12, and that was when I met her. It was the first day of school when I first saw her. The only thing I did was introduce myself to her, and before I knew it, I was an instant target for her. And the funny thing was there were wimpier people out there like me, but she never spared a second glance at them.

20

"Rosie! Rosaline! Winnefred!" Kasay's frantic voice filled the bathroom.

I sniffed away some tears and kept quiet.

"Rose, is that you?" She asked.

I whimpered quiet, hoping she didn't hear me, but that chick had super hearing when it came to finding someone.

"I know it's you..." She trailed off softly.

I was in no mood to deal with anyone, so I stayed quiet. I looked up at the stall door in front of me, debating whether I should open it or not.

"Can you come out?"

I shook my head in reply even though she couldn't see. I just couldn't trust my voice to speak.

"We were so worried when you left the cafeteria. Jaxon dragged me all around the school like a ragged doll trying to find you," she said. "First, we went to the computer lab- no luck. Then we went to the upstairs science lab, no luck there too. We searched some empty lockers, but you were nowhere to be found."

She chuckled. "Jaxon actually thought you got stuck in one of those lockers. You know how panicky he gets when things don't go his way. Drama queen!" she laughed.

A smile crept up on my lips as I imagined Jaxon with disheveled flaming red hair and crazy hazel eyes.

"He doesn't know you as well as I do though." She said snottily. "I told him you'd be in here, but he wouldn't listen. He said you wouldn't hide in here since you don't like places infested with bacteria."

I imagined her shaking her head on the other side of the door.

"The idiot has less brain than all your stuffed animals' combined," she snickered. "So are you going to come out here nicely or do I have to kick the damn door down?"

I got up from the toilet seat slowly before opening the stall door. Right when I opened the door, she pulled me into one of her killer hugs.

Her hugs were called 'Killer Hugs' for a reason. Every time she pulled me into a killer hug, I always seemed to hear a few of my ribs crack. She squeezed me so tight; I felt a lack of oxygen in my lungs. After a few minutes of oxygen debt, she finally let me go and ruffled my hair with her bacteria infested hands like I was a little kid.

"No offense but you like shit," she stated. "Let's get you fixed up."

"I'm not skipping school," I stated.

"Why not? It's just a few classes-"

"Kasay, no." I stared her straight in the eye.

After a few minutes of us staring each other down, she finally gave up and sighed.

"Fine, I'll get you a hoodie from Jaxon."

She slipped out of the bathroom for a few minutes before she came back in with a back hoodie with 'Drama Club' in yellow bold letters on it.

"Cover up," she threw the hoodie at me. I failed to catch it so it fell to the floor. "I thought you had afternoons off."

"Depends on the day, but usually I have mornings off." I corrected her as I picked up the bacteria infested hoodie from the ground.

"Lucky bitch."

If she only knew how shitty I was feeling inside...

~*~

"First off, you've got to get rid of those stupid braces." Kasay paced around my room. "Didn't you get them like five years ago?!"

"Six years ago," I corrected her. "They're not stupid, they're actually helping me."

"Your teeth are already straight," she snorted. "They were straight before your stupid step mommy came along."

22

"Not the point."

"You're right. The point is you've got to get rid of those damn braces!"

"I can't just walk up to a random Orthodontist and tell them to remove my braces! My step mother is best friends with all the Orthodontists in town! Heck, she's somehow best friends with every single adult."

"Pussy."

~*~

After I kept the hoodie on all day long and avoided everyone we decided to come back to my house. My step mother was up in the study working on who knows what while my non-existent dad was traveling in some part of China trying to do business.

Kasay had cleaned me up. She made me shower and wash my hair, and she straightened my hair for me. She put on some light makeup on me for no reason and decided to pick out a skirt I had never worn for me to wear.

She said I was picture perfect, except for my braces. Me having braces was the 'only reason' I was still nerdy, because they made me look like I was 12. That's why the only guys who seemed to look at me were freshmans. Her idea was to fix me up and make me 'pretty' so I would no longer get bullied.

"You should just tell her you want your braces off!"

"I've told her before!"

"Well, you obviously haven't nagged her enough about it."

"If you were in my position you wouldn't either!"

"She's just using you!" she pointed out before shaking her head sadly. "She's experimenting on you like a damn lab rat."

The words stung. Even though I knew it was true, I refused to admit it. She had to at least care for me. But Cleo had never shown any affection towards me.

I had never wanted a step mother in the first place, but my dad wanted someone to care after me. He was pretty desperate after my mother left us. He went on multiple dates with women until he found the one 'fit' to take care of me.

"Do you know the feeling?" The question slipped out of my mouth before I could stop it.

"What feeling?"

"The feeling you get when you're dying for someone you notice you, but they don't even know you exist." I stared out into space.

She tilted her head to the side. "You mean a crush who doesn't notice you?"

I shrugged, "something like that."

"I haven't had a crush since elementary," she admitted. "Crushes are called that for a reason. They leave you crushed."

I sighed hopelessly; there was no hope in the situation. Axel would never notice a girl like me. I was merely a shadow. I had no one to go to for advice besides Kasay. Jaxon wouldn't be the right person to go to since he'd probably say something like

'If he doesn't notice you, then he's an asshole and he's not worth it.'

No one understood my situation. I was stuck in between failure and failure.

"Who is it?" Kasay questioned.

"Who's who?" I asked.

"Who's the guy?"

I decided it was best to play dumb. "What guy?"

She narrowed her eyes at me. "You can't play dumb with me. I know you like the back of my hand."

I still played dumb, "I honestly don't know what you're talking about."

"You're a horrible liar." She shook her head.

"I seriously have no idea what you're talking about," I lied again, attempting to sound smooth.

"No need to be shy. I'm your best girl friend!"

24

"Did you hear about the costume dance this year?" I asked, trying to change the subject.

"I know exactly what you're trying to do." She gave me a flat look. "You can't run away from the subject."

"I actually think I can."

"Just tell me already."

"No."

"Why not? Please?"

"No."

"Pretty please?"

I didn't reply.

"Pretty please with a cherry on the top?"

"Of course!" I beamed.

"Really?" she asked her voice filled with hope.

I gave her a dry look, "no."

"Tell me who the lucky bastard is!"

"There is no lucky bastard!" I snapped at her.

Only an unfortunate guy who has stolen a nerd's heart by accident...

"Rosaline, is that you?" My step mother called from her office.

I rubbed both my temples before shutting my eyes.

I officially hated my life.

~*~

Chapter 3 A WALKING JOKE

"Yes mother! I'll be right there!" I hollered back.

"Just tell her about the braces-"

I interrupted her before she could finish the sentence, "she won't approve."

"Who cares if she approves or not?"

"She's my step mom and my only guardian present right now, she has the right to tell me what to do," I sighed.

"Not in my book." Kasay looked me straight in the eye. "You're her puppet."

I glared hard at her, "get out."

"Are you on your monthly or something?"

I glared at her harder before she finally threw both her hands in the air. "Don't kill me, I'm too young to die, I'm leaving."

And with that, she left. I felt bad for snapping at her, but she had no right telling me what I was.

I sighed as I made my way downstairs. I hated how controlling my step mother was, but I couldn't do anything about it. Deep down inside, I knew Kasay was right, but I wouldn't dare say that to anyone.

"Rosie," my step mother greeted coldly with a smile. "I have great news to tell you," she beamed. "I have been offered a new job with Mr. Spencer, and I heard he goes to your school." My ears perked up at the name. Mr. Spencer? Did she mean Axel? I covered up my curiosity by keeping my shoulders sagged. "No congratulations?" she questioned. Her voice was as cold as ice.

"Congratulations," I mumbled gloomily.

"That's more like it." She replied snippily. "So how was your day?" the question I dreaded came out of her mouth. When I didn't reply, she sighed. "Let's go talk in the study."

I followed her into the study and slumped into her 'patient' chair. She sat at her desk, observing every move I made closely. "You had a bad day." She stated.

"No shit," I grumbled.

"What was that?"

"Nothing ma'am."

"Tell me, what happened." I shook my head in reply as I stared at the empty space between us. "That wasn't a question, that was an order." She snapped. "Now tell me what happened."

"I'm tired."

"Then go to bed early."

"No, I'm tired of being like this." This time, I stood up and stared down at her ice cold chocolate brown eyes.

"Like what?"

"Like this!" I gestured towards my body.

"Don't raise your voice at me." She stared me straight at the eye. "And I don't see anything wrong with the picture. There's nothing wrong with being the way you are."

"I don't want to be this way," I gestured towards my geeky clothes.

"You don't want to be yourself?"

"This isn't myself!"

"Don't raise your voice," she growled. "We shall work through this together."

I groaned out of frustration. "You've said that every other time I came to you with this problem. I don't want to be viewed as the school's 'nerd' anymore!"

Her lips pressed into a firm straight line. "How can I help?"

"I want to remove my braces."

"Why?!" she gasped in shock.

I felt like screaming in her face. I had just told her exactly why. I stared down at her before storming out of the study. I didn't want to be this way anymore. I wanted to have a social life instead of locking myself in my bedroom on a Saturday night reading cheesy romance novels, I wanted to feel confident with how I looked, and I desperately desired his attention.

It pissed me off how everyone looked down on me. I had to change.

~*~

"I never thought this day would come," Kasay said. "So who's the lucky bastard who got you so hooked?"

"What do you mean?" I furrowed my eyebrows together.

"You couldn't have just decided you wanted to change. There must've been a specific reason, and I have this feeling it's a guy."

"It's for no one but myself," I replied confidently.

"That's a lie," the girl snorted. "I know a guy is behind it all. I mean, you would never do ANYTHING behind your mother's back."

"Step mother," I corrected her. "And can't I make decisions on my own? I'll be in a college far, far away from this sad town soon."

"You know she'd kill you if she heard you talking about going to college far away, right?"

"I could care less. Once I'm out of school, I'm out of here and I'm never looking back."

She sighed sadly. "I wish I were like you. I wish I could just go far, far away, but my mom would murder me before I reached the front door. Plus, my family's broke."

"You could get a scholarship," I suggested.

She snorted out loud. "Scholarship my ass, I barely passed elementary."

Jaxon came running up to us as we entered the school doors. He stopped in front of me, panting heavily with his hair filled of sweat. "R-Rosie" he panted, leaning both his elbows on his knees.

"What is it?"

He held up his index finger, telling me to wait as he tried to catch his breath. Whatever he was trying to tell me must've been urgent. Once he finally got his breath back he got up into his normal standing position again. "What are you going to be for Halloween?" he asked.

I stared blankly at him. Was he serious? He ran all this way just to ask me that? "That's all?"

Kasay started giggling like a middle school girl on crack. Jaxon glared at her as she walked away cackling like a dying hyena. I turned back to Jaxon and cocked an eyebrow at him. "You came all this way just to ask me what I'm going to be for Halloween."

"That makes me sound nuts." He frowned. "I was just wondering if you wanted to coordinate this year." In the past years, we had coordinated on Halloween costumes before.

In 3rd grade he was Ron while I was Hermione. In 4th, we were Siamese twins, let me tell you one thing-that costume was so uncomfortable. (Especially when we had to use the bathroom.) In 5th grade he was Peter Pan while I was Wendy. Freshman year, we were both zombies.

"So what's your answer?"

I just shrugged. I didn't really want to coordinate with him this year. "I guess we could..."

"Perfect!" he grinned. "So what should we be?"

I just shrugged. "Invisible people like we are in school?"

He rolled his eyes at me. "How about Bella and Jacob?" he wiggled his eyes at Bella.

"How about no? I don't want to have a piece of paper stuck to my face the entire day."

Kasay didn't get my joke, but Jax did.

"She's still hot."

As we both entered the building, I saw a large banner hanging down from the ceiling reading:

"COSTUME DANCE OCTOBER 19TH"

"So have you changed your mind about going to the costume dance this year?" he asked hopefully.

All I could do was shake my head. "You know how I feel about school dances."

"But this is our last year here."

I shook my head again. "I'm not going."

"This year could be different."

"I highly doubt that."

He sighed sadly. "There's always hope, Rosie."

"Not for me." I mumbled under my breath as I headed straight to my locker. Jaxon and I exchanged our goodbyes before he headed off to class. Of course, I had free periods in the morning so I headed straight for the library.

As I stepped into the library, all heads snapped in my direction and all small chitter chatter stopped. All eyes were on me. I ducked my head low and made my way to my favorite spot farthest away from everyone, but I noticed someone had already taken my favorite seat. I cursed lightly and slipped into a section of shelves no one ever visited and made myself home there.

As soon as I was out of sight, small chatter was heard from everyone again. I started reading a cheesy romance novel about a bad boy and a nerd who fell in love. I knew things like that never happened in real life, but deep down inside, I had a little flame of hope.

The intercom switched on before the voice I hated most filled the whole damn school. "Good morning Jordan High Jaguars!" Layla greeted on the intercom in her annoying high pitched voice. "Are you ready for some good news?"

Everyone in the library cheered. I glared at the wall. I thought you were supposed to be quiet in a library. "First of all, this is anti-bullying week. So I would like everyone to help stomp out bullying!" More people cheered. Was she serious? She was possibly the biggest bully ever, yet she still dared to talk about stopping bullying.

"We are also having an all school costume dance on the 19th! Tickets are available now, don't forget to come!" When

"I'm not addicted," Axel cut him off. "Addiction is the uncontrollable physical or psychological *need* for something. I don't need them, and I can stop whenever I want to. But I want them, and I don't want to stop."

"Drugs and alcohol only hurt you" the man said. "And it's a waste of money."

"If it's a waste of money, then why do you snort up lines every time you get home from work?" There was a moment of silence before Axel continued on. "And from the last time I checked, you still have student loans to pay off," more silence, "and mortgages."

Two hands grabbing my shoulders from behind made me jump. I dropped my novel which echoed through the halls. "So your new hobby is stalking now too?" Kasay asked from behind me. I spun around and glared at her.

"You scared me!" I hissed at her.

"You weren't the only one I scared." She peeked around the corner and snickered, "that old teacher would be in so much trouble if we snitched."

"Well we aren't going to snitch on that poor guy," I peeked around the corner, but Axel was no longer there. The only person who was there was the old teacher. "And I'm supposed to be going to the office, so if you excuse me." I started walking away from her, but she grabbed my upper arm.

"That was actually me trying to get you out of this hell hole," she explained. I turned back so that I was facing her and raised both my eyebrows at her. "Before you ask why I didn't make it less embarrassing, I had no choice." She threw both her hands in the air. "Layla was the only one announcing shit in there and that was the only way."

"Great, now I'm going to be the top gossip for the next three days."

"Weeks," Kasay corrected me.

I rolled my eyes. "Thanks a lot."

"So do you want in or not?"

"For what?"

"Getting your braces removed."

"Of course."

"Then follow me."

"I just can't skip my afternoon classes."

She rolled her eyes at me, "meet me in the school's parking lot after school."

It was finally time to change.

~*~

"Tell me if this hurts," the young dentist said.

If I were to be factually accurate, he was no dentist. He was a college student that Kasay 'conveniently' shared bodily fluids with. Sure, it was illegal, but that never stopped Kasay from anything.

He had introduced himself as 'Rex'. He was quite an intelligent guy, really. He had graduated high school with a 4.5 GPA and he was now a medical student. I had to make sure I knew his background before I let him even look at my braces.

"Don't hurt her Rix!" Kasay grabbed his arm as he was trying to remove the wire from my brackets.

"If you stop clinging to me I won't" he laughed nervously, "and my name is Rex, not Rix."

"But braces hurt, don't they Rix?" I didn't know whether her calling him the wrong name was intentional or not, but in my book it was hilarious. "Is there a way to numb the pain?" she questioned. I imagined the question coming out of Axel's mouth. I pushed back my thoughts about Axel.

"I have some painkillers over on the coffee table," Rex replied.

Kasay let go of him to go search for the painkillers. He successfully removed the wires from my brackets without putting me in any pain. My friend came back with a large bottle filled with painkillers. "So do I just shove them down her throat?"

34

"I can't take those," I pointed at the painkillers in the bottle.

"Yes you can" Rex said.

"I can, but I won't." There was no way in hell I was taking some mysterious painkillers from a college guy's house. But before I knew it, Rex had pinned me down to the couch as Kasay painfully shoved painkillers down my throat. Kasay held my nose and clasped my mouth shut to try to make me swallow them.

I struggled for them to let go, but they refused. After running out of oxygen, I finally swallowed the damn pills. Kasay let go and beamed down at me. "Now that wasn't hard, was it?"

"Dirty work done babe, now we've just got to find a way to get these brackets off." Rex flipped through the textbook beside him.

"Thanks for helping Rix."

"It's Rex."

"Whatever, Rix."

After a while, my mouth started to feel dry and numb. My eyes became droopy and I lost focus of everything. Everything around me felt so weird. "I don't have the equipment to get her brackets off..." Rex trailed off.

"We could always improvise."

"G-Guys." I stuttered sleepily. "I-I fe-feel weird."

"Rix honey, did you misplace something?" Kasay asked him confusingly.

"How many painkillers did you give her?" he asked.

"Honestly?"

He nodded for her to continue.

"I have no clue." She admitted.

Both their heads snapped in my direction as the whole world seemed to spin out of control. And I suddenly realized how I had left my cheesy romance novel on the ground at school before I blacked out.

~*~

"Dude, please take care of her for us." Kasay's voice rang through my ears.

"Take her home." Jaxon's sleepy voice replied.

"Please, we can't let her mom see," she begged.

I tried to correct her, but my mouth wouldn't open.

"Is she drunk?!" Jaxon gasped.

I tried to open my eyelids, but they were too heavy.

"I wish." Kasay sighed sadly. "But no, she overdosed on painkillers."

"What?!" Jaxon panicked. "How?! Who?! When?! Where?!"

"Calm your tits redhead." Kasay said calmly.

"She threw up so she's fine." Rex replied, his chest rumbled beside my head when he spoke.

"And who the hell is this?!" Jaxon yelled.

"Dude chill-"

Jaxon being the drama king he was wouldn't let Rex explain himself. I felt him snatch me out of Rex's arms. "Both of you leave, now." Jaxon growled as I heard the door slam shut. "I'll have to talk to those idiots later." He said to himself.

I felt myself being carried up a flight of stairs before I was placed onto a soft comfortable surface. I tried to get up or to say something, but my muscles refused to move. Where was all your energy when you needed it? I felt a pair of lips on my forehead before I heard the door shut.

~*~

The sound of a shower running made my eyes fly open. I scanned the room I was in immediately. Blue walls filled with Broadway posters, piles of clothes folded neatly in different spots of the room, scripts set neatly on a desk beside a large mirror. I relaxed, knowing I was in none other than Jaxon's bedroom.

The shower suddenly stopped. A pale guy with flaming red hair and hazel eyes stepped out of the bathroom with only a towel wrapped around his waist. His flaming red hair was wet and clung to his forehead. He had an impressive set of abs-

"Done checking me out?" Jaxon asked playfully.

I shook my head, still staring at his abs before nodding. "No-I mean yes- I mean-" I stopped myself. What was I going to say...? I searched my brain for an intelligent reply, but none seemed to pop up. "I wasn't checking you out."

"Now you're blushing." He laughed. I covered up my flaming cheeks with my hands. I had to admit, he had changed a lot since the last time I saw him shirtless. "Do you still have a headache?" he asked in a motherly tone. I never knew guys could act motherly until Jaxon asked that.

He cocked his head to the side, making some water rip from his flaming red hair. "What are you thinking about?"

"Huh?"

He shook his head with a smile on his lips. He grabbed a random t-shirt and slipped it on. I turned around and let him put the rest of his clothes on. "I'm done, you can look now." I turned back to fully dressed Jaxon. His expression suddenly changed when I bit my lip. "Rosie?"

"Yeah?"

"Smile."

So I did.

Chapter 5 HALF NUDE

Jaxon's face when he saw my teeth was priceless. He looked so shocked at first, but then he composed himself and took in a deep breath. "Rosie."

"Yes?"

"I have two things to ask you." I nodded for him to continue. "The first thing is: where are your braces?"

"I-I got them removed."

He nodded calmly. "And the second thing is: what the hell did they do to your teeth?"

"What do you mean? All they did was remove my braces…" I trailed off, running my tongue over my teeth to make sure.

"That's not all they did." My eyes widened at his statement. I hadn't checked my teeth after they had taken off my braces… "You might want to look in the mirror." I didn't need to be told twice. I turned ran to the mirror beside his desk and looked in it.

I almost died of a heart attack when I saw my teeth. My teeth were pink, as in the damn color pink. The color I highly disliked, PINK. I had no idea how they did it, but all my front teeth were pink.

Jaxon came up from behind me and threw an arm around my shoulder. "Pink doesn't really suit you."

I just stared at my reflection in shock. "How?!"

"Don't ask me, ask that emo friend of yours or her college sex partner."

"I'M GOING TO MURDER BOTH OF THEM!"

"If the cops question me, I won't say a thing," he promised.

"HOW COULD THEY DO THIS TO ME?!" I sprinted to the bathroom and grabbed a toothbrush and toothpaste. No matter how hard I tried scrubbing my teeth, it wouldn't come off.

"I've seen you pissed before, but not this pissed." He said as he watched me amusingly.

38

"I HATE PINK!" I screamed.

"Blue would suit you, you know?" Jaxon teased.

"Shut up."

"You love me." He smiled.

I sent him a death glare.

"You love me for who I am, and for who I am is the guy who never shuts up."

"You're an asshole…" I muttered.

He gasped. "You did NOT just call me an a-hole."

"How about we rewind the tape and watch that again? Yes Jaxon, I just called you an asshole." I walked back into his bedroom and threw myself on his head hopelessly. How did they manage to turn my teeth pink in the first place?! I thought that was factually impossible."

He sat on the bed next to me, making it dip and wrapped his arms around me. "It'll probably wash out soon enough."

"How the hell did they though?!"

He just shrugged. "I have no idea. I just noticed your teeth when you woke up." He patted my head like a child. "So what do you want to do now?"

"Get the stupid pink off my teeth, go home and snuggle into my bed and lay there forever until I grow old and die."

"Are you sure?"

"Sure about what?"

"About snuggling into your bed?"

I gave him a flat look.

"I'm kidding."

I ignored him and shut my eyes.

"You're not falling asleep on me. Nope, not going to happen." He hauled me up into a sitting position. "Go take a shower, you smell like dog shit on a hot summer day."

"You and your comparisons," I snorted sarcastically. "One day all your fancy sentences will come back and bite you in the ass."

He didn't reply as I got up and went to the bathroom. I stripped all the clothes off my body and got into the shower. I let the hot water run down my body as I hummed a melody. It was one of the most relaxing moments I have had so far.

But of course like every other great moment, it had to end. When I got out of the shower, I realized there were no clean clothes around. In fact, there were no clothes at all except Jaxon's. I grabbed a towel and wrapped it around my body. I called for my best friend multiple times, but there was no response, so I decided to slip out of the bathroom in only a towel.

I held my towel tightly. I was incredibly insecure with people seeing my body, since no one had ever seen me in a bikini before, besides Jaxon of course. The last time he saw me in a bikini, we were only 11. It might've seemed weird, but that was who I was.

Kasay had tried convincing me into wearing a bikini, but I refused. She said I had a killer body and I'd look hot in a bikini. I stepped back into his bedroom and grabbed a t-shirt lying on the ground. But right when I sniffed it, I literally died. It smelled so disgusting.

I went through some of the other clothes in his bedroom, but they were too dirty, too wet, or too smelly. Overall, they were all disgusting. That boy had not a piece of clean clothing in his bedroom. I didn't want to take the risk and try to put any pieces of clothing in there on.

I stuck my head out of his door and called his name, but there was no reply. I tip toed through the empty hallway and tried opening his parent's bedroom. Sure there must've been some clean clothes in there. But with my great luck ^note my sarcasm^ the door was locked.

"Jaxon," I called his name again, but there was no reply. I took a deep breath and tip toed downstairs. I made sure I was extra quiet just in case there were any guests downstairs. I wouldn't want them thinking there was a random half-naked girl creeping around.

I looked in the kitchen, but there was no one. I sighed in annoyance. Where the hell was my best friend when I needed him? I went into the basement to search for some clothes, but I had no luck. Karma was never on my side.

After I searched pretty much the entire house, I slumped onto his couch. I threw my head back and sighed tiredly. When I opened my eyes, something outside caught my eye. My clothes were all hanging on a line outside along with some other clean clothes in his back yard.

If only I could go out there without being seen... I got up and snuck out his back door. The moment I opened the door a blast of cold air hit me like a slap in the face. I shivered, hugging the towel closer to my body. It must've been about thirty degrees something since it was still early in the morning. And there I was wrapped in a towel. Boy was I clever...

I took in a deep shaky breath.

"Run Rosie run!" I sprinted towards the clothes line.

With my first step, I tumbled down a short flight of stairs and landed in a puddle of muddy icy water. I got up quickly and ran straight for the clothes line. There were goose bumps on every inch of my body, but I refused to go back inside without my clothes. Right as I was grabbing my clothes from the line, I heard a window open.

"Dude, there's a naked chick outside!" Someone yelled. My head snapped in the familiar voice's direction. Matt McCartney had his head hanging out of his window pointing straight at me. My eyes widened in fear. This was going to make the school's paper front page.

"Holy shit!" a blonde popped stuck his head out of the window too as he grinned ear to ear. "I guess today's our lucky day bro!" he slapped Matt's back.

I grabbed my clothes quickly as two other guys stuck their heads out of the same window. I was so screwed.

The guys were all gawking and pointing at me as I collected all my clothes and ran back inside. "Hey, I didn't get your name!" Matt yelled as I slammed the back door. I clutched all my clothes to my chest, panting like I had just ran a marathon.

After a few minutes of me leaning against the door shaking, the front door flew open revealing Jaxon. "What the hell happened to you?!" he slammed the door and rushed over to me.

"M-M-My clothes were gone and I-I c-c-couldn't find you and a-any clean clothes s-so I looked and f-found them outside. Then M-M-Matt and his buddies-s saw me half naked." I stuttered because I was shivering from the cold.

"And why are you covered in mud?" he raised an eyebrow at me.

"T-Tripped."

He pinched his nose bridge before looking up at me again. "Go put on some clothes then we'll talk."

~*~

"I'm so sorry we turned your teeth pink Rosie, I really am." Kasay apologized for the thousandth time.

I scoffed.

"I really am, it was just-"

"I know, I know," I sighed. "My braces were 'invisible'-" I quoted with my fingers. "So your partner pulled some witchcraft and turned my teeth pink, because he said it was the normal thing to do. This is the fifteenth time you've tried to explain-"

"Sixteenth," she corrected.

"Doesn't matter."

"So am I forgiven?" She asked hopefully.

"Of course not."

"Why not?!"

"You turned my teeth pink with god knows what, dumped me at Jaxon's place without making up an excuse for my stepmother, Matt and his buddies saw me running outside half naked covered in mud-"

"That was actually your fault you didn't wait for Jaxon," she interrupted me rudely.

I glared at her. "Not the point." I huffed before I continued. "I almost freezed to death running outside to get my clothes, and I fell in a frozen muddy puddle-"

Rex interrupted me. "No wonder your hair looks better." He cocked his head to the side. "You look better with dark hair."

Kasay turned to me with a mysterious grin on her face as Jaxon looked between us confusingly. "Oh god," I muttered. Whenever Kasay had that look on her face, she was planning something evil in her head. And this time, her evil plan had something to do with me.

~*~

Chapter 6 JAXON'S NEIGHBOR

We suddenly heard someone knocking on the front door. "I'll get it!" Jaxon called out as he jogged to the door.

"Hello, Smith." Matt's tone was threatening.

All our heads snapped in the front door's direction. Matt stood there, tall, strong, and proud with his cronies behind me. His brown hair was disheveled and he had his cocky signature smirk on his face.

Behind him stood Trent- a silly and at times an annoying blonde who pretty much hung out with everyone, Justin and Dustin- the identical twins who nobody could tell apart, and last but not least Ricky. Ricky was the one I dealt with the most, and the one I had the most hatred for. Sure, I hated Matt, but with Ricky it was on a whole other level.

Matt looked over Jaxon's shoulder over to us, trying to find something- or might I say- someone. "Where's the chick?" Matt questioned.

"What chick?" Jaxon furrowed his eyebrows in confusion.

"The hot chick." He replied, still searching for that someone.

"What hot chick?"

"Don't play dumb with me," Matt said in such a threatening tone, shivers ran up and down my spine.

"The one who ran half naked across your backyard," Trent said.

Jaxon glanced at me through the corner of his eye before returning his attention to the jocks. "I really don't know what you're talking about," Jaxon lied smoothly.

Matt stepped forward, closing the gap between him and Jaxon. "Oh I think you do."

"We all saw her!" Trent exclaimed.

"Maybe we should just leave." One of the twins suggested. I couldn't tell whether it was Justin or Dustin. The other twin nudged him, telling him to shut up.

"Look," Matt started. "I know you're hiding a really hot half naked chick in here, and I want to know where and who she is." He flashed a fake smile.

"There are no other chicks in here besides from us," Kasay gestured to me and her.

Ricky stepped out from behind the other guys. "Hey there, babe" Ricky cooed as he stepped around Matt and brushed passed Jaxon to get to me. He stood there right in front of me, eyeing me up like a juicy piece of steak.

I once thought Ricky was the perfect guy for me... but boy was I wrong.

I gave him everything I could- at least I gave him a lot of things I'd never give anyone else. I let him copy my homework, I spent time outside of school hanging out with him, heck- I even went to watch stupid action movies with him, but he still wanted more. He wanted more than I could give him.

When I didn't give him what he wanted most, he dumped my sorry little ass.

He seemed so sweet, so fun, so loving at first, but his true colors finally showed. His lips were dripping such sweet honey, but he stung me like a bee. He dumped me for a girl who would spread her buttery legs for him.

Then he ended up joining Layla in tormenting my life since I refused to give in. Both him and Layla did the same amount of damage to me. The funny thing was, those two actually dated once, but Layla broke it off because he cheated on her too.

I did one thing I never thought I'd have the courage to do. I flipped the bastard off. He faked a gasp. "Damn you've grown a backbone," he laughed. "Since you're so confident now, wanna' fuck?"

I tried to walk away from him, but he grabbed my upper arm roughly. "Not too fast, Kitten." I turned around so quickly my head ended up smacking his chest.

"Let. Her. Go." Kasay growled.

"What are you going to, Little Punk?"

"This," she said as she kneed him in the balls. He groaned out in pain and fell to the ground. All the jock's eyes went wide as Ricky cupped his groin and cried out in pain. Anger flashed through the jock's eyes except one of the twin's eyes. The twin was the only one who looked like he felt Ricky got what he deserved.

I knew they could make my life hell, even though it was bad enough already. Matt stared at me coldly. "Get em'."

~*~

"Matt's your neighbor and you never freaking told me?!" I yelled at Jaxon.

"Well you never asked me!"

"Cut the crap guys!" Kasay cut in.

"Or what?!" Jaxon and I asked in sync.

"You guys argue like a married couple," Kasay laughed. Jaxon's cheeks flushed bright red before he excused himself to the bathroom. Since Rex left after the jocks tried chasing us; that left only me and Kasay. "You're going to that dance."

"No I'm not."

"You are."

"I'm not."

"I'll buy your ticket!" she offered.

I still refused.

"Come on Rose."

"You know I don't do dances."

"Live a little."

"That saying never ends well," I replied.

"Well, I could make you go."

"How?"

"You won't like it…"

"Just tell me."

"You're giving me no choice but to-"

"To what?!"

46

"Just let me finish!" she snapped. "You're giving me no choice but to step over your head."

"What's that supposed to mean?"

She answered by pulling out her phone and tapping on it like a pro. She put her phone up to her ear and waiting for it to ring.

"What are you-"

"Hi Cleo, this is Rosie's friend, Kasay." She said into the phone. My eyes widened in shock. She did not just do that.

"Stop-" Kasay covered my mouth with her hand. I licked it, but she didn't even flinch.

"Yes, I would like Rosie to go to the school dance-" Kasay said as she ran away from me with her phone up to her ear.

"Kasay! Get back in here!" I chased her down the stairs and into the basement. Before I could step foot into the basement, she slammed the door in my face and locked it. I banged on the door over and over and used the most colorful language I had ever used in my life, but she continued on talking to my stepmother about the dance.

I finally gave up and slumped against the door, exhausted from all the events. Luckily this was the weekend and I had time to rest. "What's going on down here?" Jaxon asked as he walked by.

All I could do was point at the basement door since I was too exhausted to reply. He gave me a questioning look before trying to open the door I was leaning against. The door was locked, so he couldn't open it.

He put up his index finger telling me he'd be right back before tip toeing off. A few minutes later, he came back with a key in his hand. He inserted the key in the hole and opened the door. I of course, fell backwards and landed on the first step going down. Kasay was fast asleep on the washing machine, clutching onto her phone.

I rolled my eyes at the sight before me. Kasay would pull something like that. My phone started vibrating and ringing in

47

my pocket. I pulled out my phone and on the street it read 'CLEO' in bold letters. I answered the phone, preparing for the worst.

"Hello?" I said to the phone.

"I need to talk to you. Come home now, because it's urgent." She ordered icily before hanging up. What a bitch.

~*~

Chapter 7 MAKE ME

"Let me guess," Jaxon held his chin like he was thinking. "She wants you to come home so she can force every little detail of your day out of you."

"That too, how'd you guess?" I asked sarcastically.

"Well it's not really hard since she pretty much controls your life." He said as he hugged me from behind. I wiggled out of the hug and turned around so that I was facing him. His perfect red hair was falling over his hazel eyes. There was an emotion in his eyes and I couldn't tell what it was.

"I should go." I backed away from him.

"Want me to take you home?"

"It's fine, I'll walk."

"I'll walk with you," he offered.

I chuckled nervously. Something about him was a little off. "It's okay, I'll walk alone."

He chuckled along too. "No, I want to walk you home."

He was starting to make me feel uncomfortable. "I want to walk alone." He frowned at my statement. "I need some time to think."

"You can't walk home alone. Matt and his gang are still out and about."

"I'm sure they've given up, I can walk alone."

"No you can't. I won't let them hurt you."

"That's very sweet of you but my house is less than a mile away. I'll manage."

"But Rose…"

I rolled my eyes and laughed. "I'll be fine you old-"

"Codfish," he finished for me.

"So now you're finishing my sentences now too?"

"That's what best friends are for," he grinned. The unknown emotion in his hazel eyes was still there, but I shrugged it off. ~*~

"But Cleo!"

"You want to change, I'm giving you a chance to change!" she said sharply. "You're going to that dance no matter what."

"But I don't do dances!"

"You do now." She glared down at me.

"There's no point in going," I sighed. "I'll just end up alone like always."

"You won't be along, Kasay accompany you to the dance."

"But knowing her she'll probably ditch me the moment we get there-"

"You are going and that's final." She interrupted me. "Besides, it will help with your pathetic social skills."

The words cut me like a newly sharpened blade.

"How am I supposed to go when I don't have a costume?" I asked.

Of course, my stepmother always had a plan. "You're going shopping this afternoon."

"But-"

"I could get you a date if you really want one." She interrupted me again.

"No thanks, I'd rather go alone."

"Fine, but I do know one thing." A small cold smirk appeared on her face. "I do know you have your eye on someone."

I froze up immediately. There was no way she could've known-

"I don't know who it is." She said. I sighed in relief, but she wasn't done. "But I'm sure I'll find out soon enough." I fiddled with my fingers on my lap. "Whoever it is, he must be going."

I rolled my eyes at her. I knew Axel never did that kind of stuff. And these were the reasons why:

1. He called dances 'Assholes Seizures Night'.
2. He got in way too much trouble.

3. He hated pretty much everyone at school.
4. He'd never wear a lame Halloween costume.
5. He claimed to be 'too cool for that bullshit'
6. School spirit to him was like a llama taking a shit, it didn't matter.

There was a whole list of reasons, but to list them all out would be a waste of time. But I knew for a fact, that he wasn't going to show up to the dance.

"You're going shopping right now." She stated, waving her hand in dismissal.

"I'm not going out with pink teeth!" I shook my head. "That'd hurt my reputation even more."

"Darling," her ice cold eyes met mine. "You don't have a reputation to maintain."

Her words stung, but I didn't show it. "I'm not going to the dance."

"I think you don't understand me." She pressed her lips in a firm line before continuing. "You are going to the dance no matter what."

"But-"

"I don't care if you're sick, you're on your monthly, or you're dying. You are going to that dance. You asked for help, and I'm giving it to you."

"Why do you want me out of the house so bad?" I questioned, making her tense up.

"I don't." she replied in a clipped tone. "I'm just helping you."

I looked at her suspiciously. I was certain she was hiding something, but I decided to drop it. "I'm not going to that dance." I stood up from my chair and slammed both my fists onto her working desk. "You can't make me."

~*~

"I regret challenging that ice queen." I grumbled to myself.

I was currently at a random store in town trying to find a costume for the dance. Kasay was helping me- but if I were to be factually accurate, she was the one doing all the work while I stood there like a mannequin complaining.

"You know, I could use a little help here." She said as she went through racks and racks of costumes.

"You're the one who got me in this shit," I pointed out. "So you're doing the work."

She sighed while shaking her head. "You're a real pain in the ass sometimes."

I grinned at her. "I know."

"This year's dance will be huge." She said as she picked out costumes. "I heard even Axel might be going."

"Axel Storm Spencer?"

"Yeah," she nodded. "The guy whose initials spell 'ass'."

"But he doesn't do dances…" I trailed off.

"That's what everyone thought, but the rumors say differently."

"Rumors are rumors." I shrugged.

"The rumors also say he's going dressed in costume."

"Axel and costumes don't mix."

"Unless his costume consists of a leaf." She snickered, "or nothing at all…"

A picture of Axel with only a leaf covering his private area popped up in my head. Even though the image was worth drooling over, I shook my head to try to get it out of my mind. "There's still no way he's going." I stated.

"You know there is."

"Get back to work."

She rolled her eyes and continued searching. After she found about 20 different costumes she thought were fit for me, she rushed me to the fitting room and made me try every single one on.

1. Pirate

2. Mermaid
3. Princess
4. Vampire
5. Killer
6. Zombie (Which I actually considered, but she changed her mind and said I'd never find a guy like that)
7. Alien
8. Duck
9. Hamburger
10. Cocktail (don't ask)
11. Robot

And the list went on. I gave up once we went through all of the costumes. "I think you looked good in the cocktail one." She said. "What do you think?"

"I hated them all." I replied.

"Let me go get you some more costumes-"

"No, I'm not trying on any more," I stated. "Let's go home." I tried to leave, but she blocked the exit.

"Let's make a deal. You try on one last costume and I'll leave it there."

I thought about it. "What if I say no?"

"Then your stepmother will find you a costume-"

At the mention of my stepmother, I agreed to it, "deal."

She disappeared from the dressing room and came back with an odd looking costume. I couldn't tell what it was. "Since you're such a pain in the ass, I decided this would match your personality."

"What is it?" I got the costume from her.

"Try it on and you'll see." She handed me a halo and dark feathered wings that came with the costume.

I did what she told me and tried it on. The costume fit me like a glove made just for me. It was a black sleeveless dress that came up above my knees. It hung onto what little curves I had and made me look good. I put on the wings and the halo.

I spun around in the mirror to get a full view of it. The dress showed off my back and down to my waist, but unlike other dresses, this one didn't seem slutty or too revealing. This one seemed elegant. I looked at the price tag and almost choked. The price was beyond high.

"Get your ass out here so I can see how you look!" Kasay banged on the dressing room door. I opened the door slowly and looked down at the costume. Her mouth fell open in shock. "You do have a killer body."

"How does it look?"

"It looks fucking sexy on you girl!" she yelled. "So how do you feel about it?" she questioned.

"I actually kinda' like this one." I admitted.

A Cheshire cat grin appeared on her face. "I knew you would love-"

"But," I added. Her grin faded immediately. "The price-"

"Do something for yourself for once. Cleo spends your dad's checks on herself all the time, once for you won't hurt."

She was right, but I still had other concerns, "everyone will know it's me."

She held up her index finger before she rushed off. A few moments later, she came back with a half face mask in her hand. "This will match both your dress and your heels." She chirped happily. I smiled along before I realized something.

"Wait- heels?! Who said anything about heels?!"

Chapter 8 BRAND NEW ME

Have you ever felt completely new?

Like after a shower or after some sort of treatment? Well, feeling new felt like a newly plucked chicken.

"Stay still," Kasay hissed as she tore a waxing strip off my leg roughly. I screamed in agony. "Gross, I can't believe you have never shaved." She scrunched up her face in disgust. "You're lucky your hairs are pretty much invisible though."

She tore another waxing strip off my leg, making me scream again. "THAT HURTS LIKE FUCK!"

She tore another one off my leg. "Only I'm allowed to swear."

"But it hurts so bad!" I panted, gripping the edges of the bed I was on.

"Beauty hurts, get used to it," she huffed. I screamed again when she tore the last waxing strip off my leg, "suck it up."

I glared at her. "I never asked for your help."

She just shrugged as she went back to look for another torture device. "We're doing your eyebrows next."

"What?" I got up into a sitting position.

"Or do you want to do them tomorrow?" she questioned.

"Can you just not use any more torturing equipment on me?" I begged.

"If you want to be pretty, then you've got to go through the pain they go through."

"Layla goes through this?" I asked in disbelief.

"Of course! How do you think she gets her smooth legs, her perfect eyebrows, and her magnificent downstairs-?"

"I don't need every single detail," I cut her off before she got more explicit.

I didn't know being the hottest girl in the school meant lots and lots of torture. I thought the popular people were just born perfect. Guess I was wrong… To magazine beauty, there's pain behind it all… and tons of retouching.

Maybe I didn't want to be popular if it was going to cost pain and suffering.

Deep down inside, I knew I didn't want to become popular. I didn't want guys kissing my feet, begging for a date with me, nor did I want to have fake friends around me.

But one thing I knew I wanted was Axel.

I wanted no one else's attention, but *his*.

Since I had set foot on Earth, he had never spared me a glance. I was invisible to him. I blended into the crowd too much, but Layla didn't seem to think that. I was noticeable, but in a bad way. Something in the pit of my stomach told me I should try talking to him, but there was no way in hell I would ever do that.

I would never be able to work up the courage to go up to him and start a conversation. Heck, I didn't even have the nerves to tap his shoulder. Maybe if Layla hadn't interrupted, I might have been able to get his attention somehow, but then I probably would have acted like a complete retard in front of him.

I hated myself for being in love with a guy who knew absolutely nothing about me. No matter how I tried to look away, or how I tried to block him out, my little crush never seemed to fade. Even when I was with Ricky, a small part of my heart was still beating for Axel.

Axel was the complete opposite of me. He got in fights, did drugs, drank alcohol, was violent, got in trouble 24/7, couldn't stand authority, and failed every single subject.

Looking back, I still wander why I went out with Ricky in the first place. Even though he was a gentleman and made me feel wanted to a certain extent, I still had feelings for the guy who didn't have a clue who I was. Ricky bought me gifts, walked me to my classes, carried my books, said the sweetest things to me, and acted like the perfect boyfriend… but I couldn't seem to fall in love with him.

"Rose!" She yelled, pulling me out of my thoughts. "Quit daydreaming."

"I do what you want."

She snorted out loud. "No you don't, you do everything your stepmother wants." She corrected me.

I glared hard at her.

"You're wasting time, I have to do me after you." She sighed.

"That sounds so wrong." Jaxon commented as he barged into my bedroom.

Kasay looked up from what she was doing. "Get out."

"Can't a guy come visit his best friend?"

My two best friends were the most stubborn people on the planet. If they were to get in an argument, World War III would start. Kasay was a violent bad ass, while Jaxon was an overdramatic drama geek. I couldn't imagine if those two were to get married…

"I said get out." She repeated herself. "I need to finish her up."

"Kasay, you're saying the dirtiest things today." He shook his head while chuckling.

"Dirty minded drama queen," she grumbled.

"I don't have a dirty mind," he stated all serious. "I have a sexy imagination." He winked. That was something I would imagine Axel saying to someone…

"That's what they all say," she rolled her eyes,, before turning to me. "All guys are the same."

"Who told you to try them all?" Jaxon asked sweetly.

Kasay clenched both her fists. "Get out, now." Jaxon laughed as he exited my bedroom. Kasay shook with anger. She was glaring hard at her torturing equipment. "That was a low blow."

After a few minutes, she cooled off. "Your best friend is an asshole." She stated as she grabbed my upper arm.

"Wait- what are you doing?"

"Next step to changing your reputation is changing the way you act."

~*~

"I can't do it!" I gave up and slumped onto the couch.

"Of course you can! All you have to do is sway your ass from left to right."

"First of all, I don't want my new nickname at school to be 'Slutty Rosie'. Secondly, I have no ass! Plus, I don't to get attention for that-"

"BULLSHIT! You know damn well you have an ass, and you've gotten attention for it before. Remember you dancing? All eyes were on your ass-"

---*Flashback*---

In a room full of drunk people, I was the only sober person. Ricky had tried getting me to drink some, but I poured it into a nearby pot of plant. Ricky's hands were running up and down my sides, feeling what little curves I had. He leaned down so that his mouth was by my ear. "You're barely dancing."

"I don't dance." I replied in his ear.

"You're dancing tonight. No excuses."

"But I don't want to embarrass myself," I frowned.

"You won't," he assured me, but I didn't feel so sure. I had embarrassed myself before multiple times that night.

He lifted my chin up so I was looking up at him, but I refused to meet his eyes. But once he got my chin in a firm grip, it was hard not to look into his mesmerizing grey eyes. His eyes reminded me of the clouds on a rainy day. Sure, his eyes might've been pretty, but Axel's were prettier, even from afar.

"I can't dance."

"Yes you can. If you tried you could."

"Ricky, I seriously can't-"

"Yes you can," he said. This time his voice was harsher.

I furrowed my eyebrows together. "Why do you want me to dance so badly?"

He sighed, pinching his nose bridge. "Don't tell anyone, but I kind of made a deal with the guys." I didn't know whether to be mad or what. "I'm telling you because I trust you." He made me melt right there. "Please, just get up there and dance. I'll be right there watching you the whole time to make sure you're okay."

I blinked twice. He gave me a quick peck on the lips that made me almost shrivel up. He smelled like strong vodka and cigarettes. He beamed down at me. "Now get up there and show them what you've got."

I took in a deep breath before nodding. He dragged me out of the dancing area into the basement where most of his friends were. "Hey bitches!" he hollered, getting everyone's attention. "Time to turn up!" All the guys cheered along with him. I gulped nervously. There was no way I could dance in front of all of them.

The music was even louder down in the basement. Ricky gave me a small shove towards the pool table. I froze when I felt all eyes on me. All the drunken teen's eyes were glued to me, the fragile nerd who didn't know how to dance. Someone shut the music off which left us in silence.

"You're seriously going to let a middle school girl dance?" one of the guys scoffed.

"I'm a junior," I protested.

"Doesn't look like it to me." He snorted before turning to my boyfriend. "Rick, I put 20 bucks on this chick to grind on the pool table. Are you fucking around with me by letting this little girl embarrass herself?"

"First of all, she's not a little girl, she's our age." Ricky said in a low voice. "And trust me, she can do this."

"I'm killing you tonight if I lose my 20 bucks." The guy threatened.

"I have 120 on her, so I think I'll die without your help if she can't." Ricky replied before turning to the crowd around us. "Who wants to see her get her grind on?" He asked the crowd. Most people cheered while the rest yelled rude perverted stuff at me.

Loud music started pumping through the speakers as Ricky lifted me up and placed me into the pool table. I closed my eyes and let the music get the best of me.

After attempting to dance, I tripped on one a cup and ended up face planting the ground. People around me cheered for my suffering, and I was stepped on my some drunk dancers. I got up and hid in the bathroom for the rest of the night. After all, it was a night no one would remember...

---End of Flashback---

I snapped back to reality when Kasay shook my shoulders. "I saw it on video, you were incredible! Every single guy in there got a boner!"

I swatted her hands off me. "It was a mistake!"

"You were incredibly-"

"I fell off the pool table and got a concussion."

"Do it that again and you'll get every guy's attention!"

"There's no way in hell I'm repeating anything from that night."

"Do it for me."

"No!"

"For Jaxon."

"No."

"For yourself?"

"How about no?"

"Who would you do it for?" she asked, giving up.

The only person I'd do it for was Axel. But then again, I wouldn't him to see me all wasted and acting like a complete slut in front of strangers.

I lied "no one."

"There must be someone out there."

"There's no one out there."

"You're lying." She narrowed her eyes at me suspiciously.

"How am I lying by stating the truth?"

"There's someone-"

"Nope," I interrupted her, popping the 'p'.

She kept her eyes narrowed on me. "I know when you're lying to me."

I fiddled with my fingers as I looked at her with a straight face. "I'm not lying. Quit accusing me of things."

"There's someone you're hiding from me." She sucked in her bottom lip as she thought hard on it.

"I'm hiding absolutely nothing." I crossed my fingers on both hands behind my back.

"Just admit it already," she sighed. "I'm too lazy to pry it out of you."

"There's nothing to admit."

"Quit playing dumb!"

"I can do what I want."

"As long as your stepmother approves." She added, making me glare at her. But of course, she just ignored my glare. "At least give me a hint."

"Of course not!" I scoffed.

"Not even a little one?"

"You don't seem to know what 'no' means." I glared at her. "No means negative, impossible, and it also means leave me the fuck alone in my book."

"Come on," she groaned. "What harm could it do?"

I thought hard about it. What harm could it possibly do to me? It's not like she was going to find out who it was from one little hint. "He's a blonde."

"Time to go through my book of blondes!" She chirped excitedly.

~*~

Chapter 9 A NIGHT TO REMEMBER [PART 1]

Friday October 19th 4:00 p.m.

A loud knock on the door interrupted my dream. I groaned loudly and buried my face deeper into my pillow. Cleo yelled something from the other side of the door, but I just ignored her. "Rosaline Arlene Winnefred! Get up now!" she ordered, but I ignored her and drifted off into sleep.

Cleo knocked on the door impatiently again before trying to opening it, but I had locked it before going to sleep. "I told you there shall be no locked doors in this house!" she snapped. "Meet us downstairs in ten minutes or else you're grounded for five months!"

Another voice spoke up. "It's okay Cleo. We'll get it done upstairs" Kasay replied.

"Who gave you permission to call me Cleo?" my stepmother questioned. "Call me Mrs. Winnefred."

"Yes, Cleo" Kasay snickered before banging on my door.

"Go away!" I yelled back.

"You shall not talk to your stepmother that way!" my stepmother warned from the other side of the door.

"She wasn't talking to you." I could imagine Kasay rolling her eyes.

"I'm still on the other side of the door-"

"Just save us the trouble and let me in Rosie!" Kasay interrupted my stepmother to talk to me.

"Why do you even want to come in?" my voice was muffled from the pillow.

Someone cleared their throat on the other side of the door. "Did you seriously forget about the dance?" Kasay questioned.

I sprung out of my bed immediately. I ran to my mirror first and checked my teeth. Luckily, they were all back to normal.

Then, I let Kasay in before shutting the door in my stepmother's face again. Kasay locked the door so Cleo couldn't come in before turning to me with a grin.

"Let's get you freshened up!"

~*~

After about three and a half hours of hair coloring, hair pulling, skin scrubbing, nail painting, prep talks, and makeup, she finally finished. Throughout the whole thing, she didn't allow me to look in the mirror at all. "Can I look now?" I whined.

"Almost..." she bit her lip and studied everything she had done to me. She made me close my eyes again and applied some lipstick to my lips. "That's what you were missing!" she said once she was done. "Go see yourself in the mirror!" she shooed me off.

I rushed the mirror and let a gasp out in shock. The girl standing the mirror wasn't me. She had wavy chocolate brown hair, gorgeous ice blue eyes, pale skin that made her eyes stand out even more, bright red lips and high cheekbones.

Kasay handed me the costume and left the room with a smug expression. I put the costume on quickly and looked in the mirror. The costume was perfect, just how I remembered it. I was so busy staring at myself in the mirror. I didn't notice Kasay had snuck up behind me.

"He'll love you..." she whispered, staring at my reflection too.

I jumped at her voice. "Who?"

She just smirked. "Whoever the lucky guy is." She turned back and packed up all her torturing equipment. She reached in her bag and handed me a dance ticket. "Keep it safe," I accepted the ticket from her.

"Do I have to pay you-?"

"Nah, Cleo already paid me." She grabbed all her stuff and headed out the door.

"Wait! Where are you going?" I asked.

She turned back to me. "Home, I'll be back." And with that, she left.

I sighed after she left and headed downstairs. I tried to get some food, but she wouldn't allow me to have any. She was afraid I would make a mess and Kasay would have to redo my makeup. I mentally rolled my eyes at her; she treated me like a three year old.

I waited till 6:30 p.m., but Kasay still hadn't showed up. I paced around the living room waiting for her to arrive, but the longer I waited, the more nervous I got. I texted her multiple times, but she didn't reply. My stepmother just sat there on the living room couch waiting patiently for Kasay to arrive.

My phone suddenly buzzed. I pulled out my phone and checked it. It was a text from Kasay, saying she was grounded and couldn't make it. My palms started to get sweaty and my heartbeat increased. Maybe if I just threw up on my costume that would convince my stepmother not to take me-

"You're still going to the dance no matter what." Cleo said from behind me. I jumped at her voice. She was looking over my shoulder reading text messages.

"But-"

"No buts! I already paid for your costume and ticket."

I almost corrected her that my father was the one paying for everything, but avoided the argument.

"I'll be alone-"

"I was hoping she'd ditch you anyway." My stepmother said. "She's a bad influence and will just drag you down in life." That made me glare at her. Sure Kasay might've been bad sometimes, but she didn't really drag me down… at least I didn't notice if she did… "And don't forget, if a boy wants to dance with you, you must be at least one foot away from him."

"Yes mother." Only in my head was I brave enough to roll my eyes at her.

"You ready?" she grabbed the car keys.

"No."

"Good, let's get you out of here," she said icily.

~*~

"Cleo-"

"Rosaline, if you don't get out of this car now, you're grounded for a year," she threatened.

"You can't do that!"

"Yes I can, I am your legal guardian and your mother."

"You're not my mother…" I whispered, only loud enough for myself to hear.

She sighed impatiently before turning to me. "Get out now."

I finally gave in and got out of the car. "You're not my mother, and never will be." I said before slamming the door. The cool air whipped around me as I rushed to the entrance. She stayed parked there, watching me like a hawk.

I clutched onto my phone, not having anywhere to put it. I walked to the front door and handed a teacher at the front desk the ticket. "Have fun," the old hag grumbled when I walked passed her.

"I won't," I mumbled to myself more than anyone. I walked into the gym area where all the dances were held. I felt a nagging sensation in my stomach; this was not going to be good. I walked into the room slowly. The sound of thumping music blasted my eardrums when I stepped in.

Everyone I walked passed people seemed to turn to me and stare. I pulled my dress and slid the phone in the spandex I was wearing. Hopefully, it'd stay in. Once the song ended, 'Beauty and A Beat' started playing. Most people cheered and started grinding to the music.

The commons was almost completely dark. Surprisingly, there were no teachers in there. Only chaperones who looked like college students. The place was filled with people grinding against each other, while the side of the room was filled with couples making out, and the stairs down to the commons held all the lonely people who no one would dance with.

I immediately knew I belonged there. Maybe if I could just sit there until my stepmother could pick me up... I made my way over there quickly and took a seat on one of the steps. I watched the people dancing having the time of their lives. A few moments later, someone in front of me cleared his throat.

I looked up to find a very attractive Justin or Dustin standing before me. The twin was dressed in a shirt that read 'Drunk 2' and jeans. He offered a hand to help me up, but I just stared up at him with one eyebrow raised. He looked down at his own hand before meeting my eyes again. "Want to dance?" he asked.

"Do I have a choice?" I chuckled nervously.

"Of course, you can choose whether you want to dance with me or not," he smiled.

I accepted his hand, letting him pull me to my feet. "Then yes, I'll dance with you." I smiled back. He seemed like a nice person.

We moved to the middle of the dance floor. He kept his hands on my waist and I had my hands on his shoulders. I swayed to the music nervously. "Do you go to this school?" he questioned.

I shook my head in reply.

"I should've known." He said with a cute smile on his face. "But you look awfully familiar." He commented. I noticed he had a left dimple. I crossed my toes, hoping he wouldn't suspect me of being anyone he knew.

"Which one are you, Dustin or Justin?" The questioned slipped out of my mouth before I could stop it.

I could never tell them apart since they were kids. Both of them had blonde hair and bright blue eyes. They were the exact same height and had the exact same facial features, making it impossible to tell them apart.

"You can't tell can you?" he asked with a smile on his face.

I shook my head in reply.

"No one can tell," he grinned. "I'm the better one, Dustin."

So he was the nice one… "Hi Dustin," I greeted. "So how do I tell you two apart?"

"That's pushing your luck a bit, isn't it?" he raised his eyebrows. "It's a miracle I told you who I was." He pointed out. "Plus, you still haven't introduced yourself to me."

"I'll make you a deal." I said with a small smirk on my face. "I'll tell you my name if you tell me how to tell you two apart."

"But no one knows how to tell us apart." He frowned at me. "Our parents can barely tell us apart already."

"You wouldn't want to tell your friends you were dancing with a stranger all night, would you?"

"If you put it that way…" He removed a hand from my waist to scratch the back of his neck.

"I won't tell a single soul," I promised.

"Take a random guess." He told me, placing his hand back on my waist.

I bit my lip, thinking about it. "Is the difference exposed?"

He smiled, showing off his left dimple again. "It is."

I couldn't take my eyes off that dimple no matter. "I'm just going to take a wild guess." I looked back up to his eyes. "Your smile?"

"Close, very close." He grinned.

"Your dimple," I blurted out.

His mouth fell open in shock. "H-How…"

"I'm a very observant person." I grinned at him.

"Nobody has ever noticed…" he trailed off.

"I'm not a nobody," I replied simply. "But really, why'd you decide to tell me out of everyone?"

"Because I just felt like it." He shrugged with a small smile playing at his lips. "Your end of the deal."

"I'm Rose." I blurted out. Technically I wasn't lying since Rose was short for Rosaline. It was just that no one ever called me Rose. Everyone at school besides Jaxon and Kasay called me Rosaline.

"Wait- I know where I've seen you!" Dustin's eyes widened as he said that. My heart stopped. Oh no, if he knew I was Rosaline- "Weren't you the girl running across the back yard half naked?"

I sighed in relief, making him cock an eyebrow at me. "Yes, I was." I grinned sheepishly. He was going to say something else, but was interrupted.

"Bro!" someone called. Both our heads snapped in Justin's direction. He was wearing a shirt that said 'Drunk 1'. Justin smirked at me before sending me a wink. He slapped his twin on the back. "You got lucky bro."

I didn't know how to handle the situation. I was being complimented and flirted with very openly. I seemed to freeze up. Matt came up behind the twins wearing his football jersey and put them both in head locks before letting them go. He eyed me up like a fresh piece of meat. "Who's this pretty little thing?"

"She's-"

"I didn't ask you," he interrupted Dustin rudely.

Well, what a friend he was.

Matt smiled sweetly and put on his charm. "So what's your name babe?"

"I-I'm R-Rose," I stuttered nervously.

"Rose," he repeated before grinning. "That's my favorite name."

"Thanks," I mumbled in reply. I remembered weeks before he was insulting my name and calling it old and haggy.

Dustin snorted while Justin snickered, making Matt glare at both of them. "If you guys don't mind, I would like to dance with Rose."

Dustin had a disappointed look on his face when he nodded along with his brother. I mouthed a 'sorry' to him and he nodded understanding. The twins disappeared into the crowd, leaving me and Matt in the middle of the dance floor surrounded my strangers.

Matt pulled me to him and placed a hand on my waist. His cologne was so strong, I felt like puking at the smell of it. I had a feeling he took a bath in cologne. He stroked played with my hair using his other hand.

I felt a tap on my shoulder before I spun around. Standing before me was a very pissed off Layla. She was dressed in a tight black mini skirt and a tight tank top that made her boobs pop out. She had cat clipped to her head with a tail clipped to her behind.

"Rosaline?" Layla hissed rudely. I felt my heart stop at that moment. She knew who I really was.

"No! How could you compare her to that bitch?!" Matt gasped. "This is Rose."

Suddenly her eyes softened and a smile formed on her lips. Her sudden change in emotions scared me. "I'm so sorry," she apologized. "I thought you were someone else from behind." She sounded sickly sweet. She didn't give me a chance to reply. "You don't go here, do you?" she asked.

I nodded in reply, not trusting my voice to speak.

She frowned at me. "So do you go here or not?"

"I don't," I replied in a confident voice. I was shaking inside, afraid of what she'd do if she found out I was Rosaline.

"You look so familiar." She commented, staring straight into my eyes. She was intimidating. "But then again, I know too many people." She laughed it off. Layla placed a hand on Matt's shoulder. "Don't hurt this girl, or I'll kill ya'."

"I won't," he grinned. "Unless she asks me to." He added, making her laugh. What was that supposed to mean? Matt grabbed my hand and gaze me a reassuring squeeze which hurt. Layla disappeared back into the crowd. He turned back to me, noticing the difference in me.

"Don't worry; she's just my best friend. Nothing more than that, I promise." That sounded like the typical fuck-boy line.

I nodded, thinking about the way she reacted. When she thought it was me, she looked incredibly pissed off. But when she found out I wasn't who she thought I was she warmed up immediately.

"I have a question," he said, "actually, I have two."

I nodded for him to continue.

"The first question is: what are you supposed to be?"

I looked down at my costume. "I'm a dark angel," I replied.

"Huh, I've never seen one before. Is there supposed to be another meaning to that?" he wiggled his eyebrows suggestively.

I furrowed my eyebrows together. "What's that supposed to mean?"

He just ignored my question. "My second question is: are you still a virgin?" he asked bluntly.

My eyes widened. Did I hear him right? "W-W-What?"

"Are. You. A. Virgin?" He repeated slowly this time.

My mouth fell open in shock.

He sighed while running his hand through his hair. "Look, let's go somewhere private and talk about this."

I shook my head quickly. There was no way I was going to a private place to talk to the pervert. I backed away from him slowly.

"Come on Rose, don't be that way." He gave me a flat look. "You're dressed like that for a reason, right?"

I shook my head again before rushing away from him. Of course since he was the football quarterback, he caught up with me. He placed a hand on my shoulder. I spun around and glared at him. "Just one more thing." He looked impatient. "What's your number again?"

"I never said it," I replied simply before slipping away from him quickly.

I slipped to one of the dark corners of the room and saw Matt desperately looking for me. I decided to find a quiet peaceful place to hide out in until my stepmother came to pick me up. I tried the girl's bathroom, but there were too many gossip girls in there.

I tried the classrooms, but they were all locked. The commons hall was filled with teachers having their own little gathering, so I couldn't hide out in there either. The library was locked too. I almost gave up on hope, but I remembered a place barely anyone knew about.

When I was proctor in my sophomore year, and one of the office ladies made me go get something in the ISS room. (In School Suspension Room) There was a door behind the teacher's desk which led to a balcony looking down onto a valley. Since my school was built on a hill, the view from the balcony was stunning.

The balcony was built for science purposes, but no one seemed to know about it. The reason I discovered it was because no one was in the room when I got there, so I decided to peek through the door. I stood in front of the ISS room, just staring at the door. I felt something odd inside...

I tried opening the door, and luckily, it was unlocked. It was completely dark besides the moonlight seeping through the tiny window. There were no windows in there, besides the one on the door leading to the balcony.

I walked behind the teacher's desk and slowly opened the door to the balcony, but someone was already there.

~*~

Chapter 10 A NIGHT TO REMEMBER [PART 2]

Standing before me was Axel with his back faced to me. Time seemed to stop. His blonde hair looked gelled, but was however slightly messy. Almost as if he messed it up on purpose, because he couldn't stand looking formal.

I could see his muscular body under the dress shirt he was wearing. He had on a vest over his dress shirt and a pair of faded jeans. The cool air had absolutely no effect on me, in fact, I even felt hot. I blamed the hormones.

He turned around slowly and met my eyes. My eyes widened when I saw his perfect grass green eyes up close. They were hypnotizing me the way Sleeping Beauty was hypnotized to the spindle. That ended badly of course and I hoped differently for this situation.

I was too mesmerized to do anything. All I did was stand there and stare, the same thing he was doing to me. After a few moments, I decided to speak. "Hi," I said in a surprisingly confident voice. I mentally slapped myself after that. Out of all the things I was dying to say to him, all I said was 'hi'. Where was my brain when I needed it-?

"Hi," he said back, still gazing into my eyes.

I was in shock that he had replied. My heart seemed to race with the wind. Inside I was jumping up and down squealing happily like a little girl. I felt as if sunlight had just entered my world for the first time, as if it had started to rain the middle of my drought, as if a light had been lit in my darkness.

The feeling I got from talking to my crush to my crush for the first time was absolutely amazing. All I felt was pure happiness, even though we had only said one word to each other. "Do you mind if I join you?" The question slipped out of my mouth before I could stop it.

He smirked at me. "What are you, a vampire?" I just stood there as still as stone not knowing how to react. "I'm just messing around." He chuckled, before awkwardly asking. "But did you get that joke?"

I furrowed my eyebrows together. He was telling me a joke...? It took me a few seconds to process it before I started laughing. "I get it now; vampires have to be invited in."

"Are you a blonde like me?"

I just chuckled nervously, "I am, I mean- I should be. My hair's brown right now, because uh... I kinda' dyed it. My biological mom naturally had dark hair though, so I don't really know how I got naturally blonde hair... but if you're talking figuratively, then sometimes I'm quite a blonde-"

I stopped rambling when he started laughing.

I shut myself up, and before I knew it, my feet carried me over to him without me controlling them. The wind blew the door shut which made me jump. He seemed to calm like it was second nature to him. When I caught him stealing a glance at me, I leaned on the railing of the balcony and looked out into the distance.

I looked at the pleasant view of hills and grasslands before me. A few barns decorated the landscape here and there. I felt his eyes on me which made me feel self conscious. We were both silent at that moment. All I could hear was the sound of the wind blowing. His eyes wouldn't leave my face so I turned to him.

"Is there something on my face?" I asked as I felt my face for any sigh of something alien.

"No, no, no," he rushed out.

"Then why are you staring me?" I furrowed my eyebrows together.

He turned away from me with his cheeks tinted red. I stared at his cheeks harder. How could it be possible? Axel Storm Spencer- the school's bad boy was blushing from something I said. It was either that or he was cold... but I liked to think it was because of me.

A smile crept upon my lips as I watched him turn away with flushed cheeks. "So how did you find this place?" He questioned, obviously trying to change the subject. "The last time I checked, no one knew about this place except for a few staff."

I just shrugged, "intuition?"

"I know you from somewhere," he suddenly said. "You go to this school?"

"Maybe," I shrugged.

"You obviously do since you know about this place." He furrowed his eyebrows together and reminded me of an adorable confused puppy.

"Maybe I do, maybe I don't." I replied simply with a small smirk on my lips.

He narrowed his eyes at me. I froze up in fear. Did I just piss off my crush? All of high school I was looking forward to this moment and I ruined it because of being too confident. I was so stupid- A smile crept up on his lips. So he wasn't pissed... "So what brought you here?" he questioned.

"I don't really do dances." I admitted. "My stepmother made me come because she wanted me to be 'social'." I quoted with my fingers.

"Really?" he looked surprised.

I nodded.

"I would imagine a girl like you going to every social event." He smirked a little.

I raised an eyebrow at him. "What do you mean 'a girl like me'?" I quoted.

"You know, the popular girl-"

"Stereotypical," I scoffed. "Never judge a book by its cover."

He looked at me oddly, "you mean you don't go to parties?"

"I hate them," I replied. "I hate all kinds of social gatherings."

"Why?"

"They make me feel uncomfortable."

His gaze stayed on me a little longer before he nodded, "me too." He admitted as he rubbed his hands to keep them warm. I didn't know how cold it was until I noticed his breath in the air. He looked even far more handsome in person.

Once I thought hard on his reply, I furrowed my eyebrows together. I didn't understand what he meant by 'me too'.

"I hate social gatherings and shit like that," he explained. My eyes slightly widened in surprise. Was Axel not the one throwing the biggest parties of year?!

"If you hate social gatherings, then why do you throw all those parties?"

"You seem to know a thing or two about me," his joke almost made my heart stop in fear of him finding out how much of a stalker I was, but he continued, "I never said I go to parties I throw," he smirked.

"If you don't go to your own parties, then why do you even throw them?"

"For the fame," he laughed, "so people won't bug the shit out of me."

He was the most complicated person I had ever met.

I looked out at the wonderful view from the balcony as the moon crept up higher in the sky. The clouds unfolded slowly, uncovering the moon little by little. I stood there watching the clouds until the moon was full and glowing bright in the sky.

"Incredible," I whispered as I watched the bright moon above us.

"I know," he said, looking straight at me.

The moon glowing in the sky looked so blue. I was hypnotized by the blue moon. Blue had always been my favorite color since I was a child. I didn't know why, but I just loved it. Maybe it reminded me of how blue the sky used to be when everything was perfect when I was a child...

"I love blue," I suddenly blurted out. My cheeks got hot when he turned to me.

A smile crept up on his lips. "That's my favorite color."

"It's mine too!" I beamed.

We both had the same favorite color; I knew we were meant to be. I mentally slapped myself. Someone's favorite color didn't determine who they were meant to be with. His emerald green eyes melted into mine searching for something. We stood still, staring into our eyes for a moment, before he cleared his throat and looked away.

"So what are you going to be after we get out of this hell hole?" he asked casually. It had to be impossible for someone to be that good looking. The wind blew his blonde hair, making it a little messier. I smiled and folded my arms across my chest.

"I use to want to be an artist," I admitted shyly. I was never comfortable with sharing my dreams. Because all most people did was try to ruin them.

"An artist?" he parroted. "You draw?" he smiled. I wasn't expecting that reaction from him. I was expecting something more in the terms of 'That's impossible' or 'just give up now'.

I tried to play it cool and shrugged in reply. "No one has seen it before so I don't know."

"You should show me sometime." He nudged my arm playfully. At the spot he touched, I felt tingles shoot up my arm from that little gesture. We both froze after the little touch. Was it possible he felt it too?

"No one actually knows about me doing art..." I trailed off.

"Why not?" he frowned.

"They'll laugh..."

"How do you know?"

I shook my head.

76

"You should."

"They'll make fun of it."

"How do you know?"

I shrugged.

"You don't know for sure until you show them."

I shook my head again.

"You could show me, I promise I won't laugh."

I shook my head quickly. I would never show anyone my artwork. What if he hated it? What if he thought I was untalented and suddenly disliked me for it?!

"So what do you want to be when you grow up? Well okay- I'll rephrase that since we're technically adults- or almost adults, uhm, what career do you want to go into?" I asked changing the subject.

"Even if I told you, you'd never believe me."

"Really?"

"Really."

"Try me," I challenged.

"I want to be a vet," he replied watching my face very closely.

My eyes widened. Once again, I was in shock. A vet? I must admit, I did not see that coming. I should've known he wanted to be a vet, since his super old photos on social media showed him with different type of animals, mostly farm animals though.

I recalled the photos I saved of him from back then. He was always wearing his favorite blue baseball cap. He had an adorable smile in every picture with animals in it. One of the pictures I looked at showed him standing behind a bunch of cows proudly.

I respected the fact that he wasn't embarrassed to show pictures of him like that on social media. I really admired that about him. He didn't give a shit of what other people thought about him. Well, he was hot anyway so that wouldn't matter with girls.

He chuckled. "Don't judge a book by its cover."

"You're using my own words against me!"

"I'm one to do that," he winked.

He was cocky like any other jock or jock-wannabe at times, but he had his own style. He wasn't completely bad like other people thought he was. He seemed so soft, so fragile on the inside.

"So... what made you come to this dance?" I asked.

"A dumb ass psychiatrist my dad hired made me come."

His words smacked me in the face.

Psychiatrist.

Spencer.

Cleo.

I panicked.

I could not let him know it was my step mom who made him come. If he knew he would never end up marrying me, let alone talk to me because of my stepmother.

"That really... sucks," I said sounding as if I were constipated.

"Yeah," he agreed. "So what made you come?"

"My-" I hesitated, but decided to tell him the truth, "step mom." I secretly hoped he wouldn't make the connection.

"Don't you hate step-parents?" He forced out a laugh.

"Well, I guess mine's not the worst, but she can be annoying as hell sometimes."

He sighed running his hand through his hair.

"Well, I hate mine," He said more to himself than to anyone else, "step-dad," he added, because he didn't know I already knew details about his family... Yep, I was definitely a creep.

"Why?"

Me and my big mouth! I shouldn't have asked him that! That was so rude of me! How stupid of me-

"He's a rich bastard. Used to beat me with his belt every day after school because I wanted to go live in California with my real dad. My mom of course, didn't believe me when I told her about the beatings. She thought I was lying to her, so that she would send me back to California." He shook his head. "But thankfully, the beatings stopped. He's always taking my mom on vacations to different countries. They're never home, but at least they leave me with money."

I wasn't expecting him to tell me that much...

His eyes shined with sadness that made me want to go embrace him immediately. I wanted his smile to reappear. I felt pain when I saw the broken look on his face. I was speechless and I didn't know what to say.

"My real mom left when I was 7," I took a deep breath to hold back emotions, "she was an alcoholic and a drug addict. Abusive to me... and finally left.

My dad got me.

He runs a business though, so he's never home. I'm left with his new wife... I mean, she's never beaten me or anything, just a few slaps here and there... I guess it's better than nothing."

He stared at me... the emotion in his eye wasn't pity... but it seemed almost like admiration...? We both shared very valuable information about our lives to each other.

"Is that why you always act bad?" I broke the silence.

"Huh?"

"Is your stepdad the reason you're failing and getting in trouble? Is it a way to persuade your mom to come home and divorce him?"

His eyes widened, he was speechless.

The look on his face was clear that I had hit the bull's eye.

"I'll take that as a yes."

"You're intelligent beyond your years... you know that right?"

I shook my head, "I'm just observant."

"Plenty of people are observant, yet they still can't conclude that."

I shrugged, "call it a talent."

"You know, you're not like the other girls I met before."

I didn't know how to react. Was that a compliment? Or was that an insult? I didn't know what to say, I was speechless. No reaction from me. Whenever I would get in a socially awkward situation, I would freeze up.

"That's a compliment," he quickly said.

"I don't know what to say," I admitted.

"You aren't like other girls. You don't drool over me, you don't rudely gawk at me, you don't act stupid or change your personality to try to get me to notice you, and throw yourself at me."

That was a lie, and I knew that by heart. I drooled over him, I gawked at him, and I tried to get him to notice me by acting stupid and if I had the chance I'd throw myself into his arms and beg for him to sweep me off my feet. I was a whole different person behind this mask I was wearing.

I felt bad and I felt like a liar.

You know that nagging sensation in your stomach when you lie? Well, that was exactly what I was feeling.

"You don't judge people… and I love that."

At least that part was true. I smiled awkwardly and thanked him.

Suddenly, I heard a soft song with a nice beat. I started tapping to it as he stared at me smiling.

"You dance?"

I turned to him and shook my head, "no."

"You should."

"Why?" I asked.

"You've got a nice f-form."

I stood there confused, "Form?"

"Uh," he scratched the back of his head, "body."

I didn't know what to say again. I was hoping he couldn't see the blush rising up on my cheeks through the dark. He offered his hand to me.

I looked at his hand then looked up to meet his magnificent green eyes again.

"What?"

"May I have this dance?"

~*~

Chapter 11 REALITY

Waking up from a wonderful dream is hard, but waking up to a bad reality is harder.

The night of the dance was probably the best night of my life. The first time of my life being noticed by... *him*.

The first night talking to him- heck even being able to have a deep conversation with him. Just the thought of it made me smile and blush crazily. I would've given anything to go back in time and replay that moment over and over again.

I wish that moment never ended.

But of course, like a fully bloomed flower... it lasted but a minute of my tragic hour.

Just like every other good or happy moment, it had to end.

Going our separate ways.

Snuggling into my pillow deeper, I tried to remember the minty breath he had when our lips were an inch apart. How his wonderful green eyes glowed in the moonlight.

I never wanted to wake up. I wanted to lie like that forever and replay the wonderful moment in my head again and again. My heart pounded against my chest crazily every time I thought of him, every time I replayed the moment.

I was so out of touch with reality. Still in my costume, I dreamt of the future I wished we could have.

I wanted him so bad last night.

Thinking of how his wonderful blond hair was being blown by the light wind. Of how the sexy golden/red mask covered half of his face making him look mysterious and beyond hot. How his perfect full lips looked so... yummy.

I probably sounded like a pervert, but if anyone were in my situation, they'd be thinking the same thing. I was in love with him since I started middle school, and I was graduating this year. I spent those six years stalking him, figuring how he acted, why he did what he did, and pinning up photos of him when no one was home.

He was a puzzle I desperately tried to solve.

Yep, I was a crazy stalker madly in love with the school's badass, someone I had absolutely no chance with.

One thing I didn't get was why Layla nice to me. I expected her to be a total bitch to me for dancing with her 'best friend'. A mystery deemed to be solved.

I felt so lucky I was able to even talk Axel, for getting to know him better. I thanked the skies above for the opportunity to be alone with him.

He was troubled.

Misunderstood.

Left out.

Judged by others.

He had trust issues.

I coped with my heartbreak by obsessing over him.

He coped with his by shutting everyone else out.

I grew to understand how he wasn't able to have any best friends or maintain relations with any females.

The one time he tried getting involved with a girl who was three years older than him, but she cheated on him at a party with the entire football team... He didn't seem too upset though, his ego was just hurt. She even blamed him for not 'giving her anything', so she had to get it from other guys.

From my perspective, she was just an experiment to him.

An experiment which proved to him that he truly couldn't put his trust is anyone, no matter how genuine they seem.

I felt like I understood him far more than anyone else could.

"Rosaline Arlene Winnefred! Get out of bed right now!" My stepmother yelled from downstairs.

I buried my face deeper into my pillow. The last thing I wanted to do right now was to get out of bed and face my step mother downstairs. I snuggled the pillow feeling comfortable as I could be, replaying the night over and over again.

Oh, how his grass green eyes shined. How his arms were wrapped around my waist protectively while we danced. How my head rested on my chest comfortably-

"I'm not joking young lady!" Cleo yelled.

I just ignored her drifting off into happy lala land. I heard some loud footsteps up the stairs and I heard my door slam open. I squeezed my eyes shut tighter so I didn't have to face the footsteps that were coming closer and closer.

"Rosaline Arlene Winnefred! What the hell is going on here?!" My stepmother shrieked.

I covered my ears and groaned. "What the hell?!"

"Don't disrespect me! You didn't pick up your phone!" She yelled so loud, I could've sworn it damaged my eardrums.

"Where's your phone?!"

My eyes widened. I frantically felt the pockets of the shorts under my costume but there was nothing there. My eyes widened and the world froze. Shit. It was somewhere at the dance... I couldn't even remember when I last had it.

There was a very slim 0.9% chance of it being found, since I wondered around the whole school trying to find a hiding spot. I tried to think of the last place I had it but I just couldn't.

Judging by how many reports there were of things getting stolen in school, someone had probably already taken it.

I realized I had a lock on my phone. I set it based purely off of Axel. During freshman year, I sat directly behind Axel during an Algebra class. The teacher had demonstrated a very simple example that reminded me of the shape of a heart, so I put it as my phone's password... I was beyond cheesy... a bit borderline creepy...

"I lost it..."

She shook her head. "I can't believe you're this irresponsible!"

"I'm sorry..." I was prepared for her to yell at me, but she didn't.

She shook her head, "Irresponsible! Your father will get you a new one."

I nodded numbly.

"Where were you last night?"

"At the dance."

"Don't lie to me," she warned. She glared daggers at me, and took in a deep breath. She somehow managed to stop herself from strangling me, "The dance was on Friday."

"Yesterday was Friday," I replied in a 'duh' tone.

That was when it seemed to hit her. She was no longer angry, but confused and slightly amused. "If yesterday was Friday, how come today's Sunday?"

~*~

"You were out for two days?! No way!" Kasay was in disbelief.

"I don't even know what happened... guess I was exhausted."

I took a sip of the strawberry milkshake she ordered me and looked up at her waiting for a reaction. She looked at me like I was crazy for a moment before her emotions suddenly changed.

"How was it though?"

I was a bit droopy, so I didn't respond until she asked me again.

She snapped her fingers, "wake up Sleeping Beauty! I asked you how the dance was!"

I shrugged, downplaying it.

"Details girl! Details! Did you meet your prince charming?!"

I raised an eyebrow at her, "prince charming?"

She nodded eagerly, "Prince charming, your prince charming. Every girl has their prince charming somewhere. Like for example, me. I found my prince charming with Rix-"

"That's not even his name-"

85

She completely ignored my comment. "Your prince charming is the guy who you'll end up falling for and marrying! The guy who calls you beautiful even when obviously you look like a worthless piece of shit. The guy who treats you right and will always be there for you. The guy who's meant for you! The guy who-"

I interrupted her, "that's ridiculous-"

"No it's not! Every girl has her prince or princess charming! Unless she's asexual, then she has charming fingers-"

I faked a cough to get her to stop talking. The girl was real irritating sometimes… talking nonsense about 'prince charmings'. She was just temporarily glad she found her thirty first one of the year. I realized I was starting to sound jealous of how she found someone... I mentally slapped myself. How could I be jealous of one of my best friends?!

If prince charmings were real, I didn't have one. Axel liked me for who I wasn't.

He liked the 'me' that wasn't fully me...

He probably didn't even know I existed.

Axel definitely wasn't my prince charming.

He was too good for me. I was just a nerd, bullied by most of the school population. He obviously wasn't made for me. I was just a lonely girl with no 'prince' to help her; a hopeless romantic who would somehow make herself happy someday.

The thought of being without Axel made me sad and hopeless, but I had to face the truth.

"Nope, not for me. I'm meant to be alone," I pursed my lips together.

"Shut up! Your prince charming is out there somewhere!"

I shook my head, "he either met someone else and ended up with her along the way, died, or was never born in the first place."

She sighed, "that's not true! He's out there somewhere! Who knows where he is-"

"He probably doesn't even know I exist. Heck, he's probably in some chick's bedroom."

She nodded, "in his sister's bedroom, getting' information about you."

I rolled my eyes, "he's in Vegas-"

"Getting gifts for you," she grinned.

I shook my head.

"He's going to show up sooner or later. Don't worry, he will."

She could be incredibly immature sometimes.

"I promise!"

"Don't make a promise you can't keep."

She took a sip of her coffee and shook her head. She wiped her mouth on the back of her hand before looking up at me. Her face was serious this time.

"There is someone out there for you, a prince charming-"

"Cut it out with the stupid fairytales!" I cut her off. "There's no prince charming and there never will be. Stop being childish and grow up!" I snapped. "I've accepted the fact that there is no one for me. I will always fall for someone who doesn't love me back."

She was taken back at first. "First of all, you're never too old for fairy-tales. And secondly, there is a prince charming for every girl in this universe. Heck! There are probably prince charmings for bacteria and aliens in the universe! So quit denying!"

I rolled my eyes. I needed to stop rolling my eyes or my eyes might roll back all the way in the back of my head. I knew I was denying the part I met someone at the dance, but I would never plan on telling her about Axel.

"What'd you do at the dance? Did you at least have a good time?" She asked.

I decided to lie, and tell her the exact opposite, "Worst day of my life..."

It came out more like a question than an answer. She didn't believe me.

"I know you. In fact, I know you really well."

I pulled my innocent card. "What do you mean?"

"I know when you're lying or hiding something from me. There's always this sparkle in your eye."

We drowned down the rest of our drinks and left the cafe. I had my dark brown hair in a bun and tucked under a baseball cap so people wouldn't notice my change.

I was wearing a grey tank top and grey sweat pants. We walked down to the general store. I had to get my natural hair color back before tomorrow. I dreaded Monday. I would be the nerdy Rosaline again and no one would like me.

I actually liked it how once in my life I got to be someone that people liked. Someone that people wanted to befriend and talk to. And mostly, someone that Axel favored. Someone he felt comfortable with, and someone he wanted to hold-

"Why are you blushing?" She questioned with a smirk.

"I made a friend," the words slipped out of my mouth.

She gasped.

"I met someone I enjoy being around more than the rest of the school population...."

Her eyes widened in excitement and she grinned. She clapped her hands together and squealed. She started jumping up and down then she grabbed my arm and started dragging me down to the general store.

"TELL ME EVERYTHING!"

She knew it wasn't just a new friend.

Why couldn't I control my mouth?

~*~

Chapter 12 WORST MONDAY EVER

"Details girl! I need details!" Kasay bugged me as I put my books in my locker.

I groaned. After we went to the general store, I told her I'd tell her, but I didn't. I realized the risk of spilling out my feelings, so I kept changing subjects and avoiding the topic until I made it home without giving away any information.

"You have to tell me!"

"Actually, I don't."

"Tell me now!" She demanded, pouting like a puppy-except she wasn't cute.

"Why should I? You have the biggest mouth."

"I'm your best friend though!"

"So is Jaxon."

"But I've never had a massive crush on you."

I rolled my eyes, "he's never liked me like that."

She ignored my statement, and continued pestering me, "Spill! You can't just leave me hanging!"

Before she could say anything, a loud gasp was heard. "AXEL?! He would never show up to a school dance!" It was Layla's voice.

"I swear, I saw him! No guy in this town has a butt that firm-"

Layla interrupted the girl she was with, "Trust me when I say it wasn't Axel! There are plenty of other guys."

"True... but he's the hottest," the girl giggled.

I felt angry hearing that. I wanted him to be mine. She didn't even know him.

Neither do you.

I kicked myself.

"Anyways, who was the redhead you were with?" The girl asked Layla.

Another girl joined in. "I wouldn't say he was hot, but he was pretty cute."

Kasay and I exchanged looks as the cheerleaders came around the corner in their little group. Layla of course, being the ringleader of their little clique, walked in the middle with the other girls surrounding her.

Her brown eyes found mine and something inside of her changed. It was like a switch was pulled, and her face hardened. Her cheerful smile was replaced with a bitter scowl. Her friends whispered something into her ears when they saw me. She started giggling.

It was about me.

My insecurities hit me once again.

She gave them high fives before turning back to me smirking evilly. It was not a good sign... Kasay glared, threatening the cheerleaders.

"Can we leave?" I asked Kasay in a whisper.

She shook her head, and kept glaring. "Someone's gotta' each them a lesson."

The look in her eyes truly scared me. I quickly grabbed my stuff from my locker.

"The nerd removed her braces!" Layla laughed aloud in such a condescending manner I wanted the floor to swallow me up.

"What do you want from her?" Kasay snapped.

Layla and her friends snickered.

"Shouldn't you be cutting yourself, little emo?" She gave Kasay a sickly sweet smile, "defend yourself before you can defend your friend."

Kasay's nose flared and her hands balled into fists. "Leave my best friend alone and fuck off."

Layla and her friends laughed as Kasay turned red in anger.

"Give me a good reason why I should," Layla stepped forward, challenging Kasay, "You have no idea how much trouble your 'best friend' has caused me." She snapped her fingers and pointed straight at my female best friend, "So watch your mouth, before a little birdie tells on you."

Tells on her? For what?

Kasay didn't reply, but kept her glare on the cheer captain.

"Oh, and I didn't know devil worshippers could have best friends, yet alone friends at all."

I kept my head down and stared at the floor. Kasay should've let it go. We were obviously outnumbered. Layla's insults were quite limited anyway, like her vocabulary.

Though Kasay was glaring at her, I felt Layla's glare on me...

Why me?

What did I ever do to her?

From what I remembered, I had never done anything before. It was obvious I wasn't her competition; I was geeky, nerdy, and guys never paid attention to me.

Yet... why did she choose to be nice to me at the dance?

Why did she hate the nerdy Rosaline Arlene Winnefred, but was alright with Rose. It didn't make any sense to me.

Layla took another step closer. I kept my eyes glued to the ground, and prayed she'd disappear. I saw Kasay tense her fists from the corner of my eye. She was a predator ready to strike.

"You know what?" Kasay spoke up.

"What?" Layla dared to ask.

"Frowning uses more muscles than punching you straight in the face."

A few moments of utter silence passed by... I was contemplating in my own world, then...

Layla fell to the ground in front of me. Her nose was bleeding, and she was starting to cry hysterically. Though she seemed upset... she didn't seem afraid. There was a glint of entertainment in her eyes which scared me.

Tears poured out of her eyes as she scurried away from Kasay. Kasay looked utterly confused and shocked. Ms.

Puessy, my chess teacher, yep... that was her name, scurried over to her and helped sobbing Layla up.

She started screaming. Layla started screaming too... accusing Kasay of things I had never heard before.

Drug dealing?

Blowing guys for drug money?

I had never witnessed any of it, yet alone heard of Kasay doing those things.

"I DIDN'T HIT HER!" Kasay yelled, "She hit herself! She's lying! I've never done anything-"

"DID SHE DO IT?!" The teacher asked me as she shook my shoulders.

I was still in shock...

I didn't witness what had just happened. I was staring at the ground...

I couldn't answer. I was unable to speak.

"She was staring at the ground the entire time! She didn't see!" one of the cheerleaders said.

"Is that true?" The teacher stared me straight in the eyes.

I didn't have to think, so I told her the truth and shook my head.

~*~

According to Layla and her friends, I was spacing out at that moment so I didn't know what happened. According to the geeks, I saw the whole thing but I was kissing Layla's ass so I wasn't saying a word about it.

And according to Jaxon, I knew what was happening, but the cheerleaders were being bitches and lying about it. My best friend helped me through it. He swung his arm around me as he helped carry my gym clothes to gym.

"They'll be all over you when you go in there." Jaxon said as I approached the girl's locker room entrance.

"I know..."

"Aren't you going to stand up to them?" he asked as he handed me my stuff.

I frantically shook my head. "Kasay-"

"She has a violent temper, you kill em' with kindess."

"But what if she didn't even hit them-"

"Layla wouldn't go that low to lie about something like that, trust me."

I looked him straight in the face with disgust, "You can say that about the girl who's ruined my life?"

He cupped my cheek, realizing what he did, "I'm sorry, I didn't mean it like that. I just meant to say Kasay has a violent temper, so it's easier for her to get in trouble. You on the other hand- they wouldn't dare to anything to you... just trust me on that."

I smacked his hand away, "They would. They hurt Kasay, and they're going to get you next. And once they cut everyone who cares for me out of my life, they'll be able to destroy me without even touching me-"

"You're over thinking, Rosie."

"We're not like Kasay. Teachers love us-"

"There are exceptions-"

"Still," he nudged my arm. "They trust you, they know you're a good student, and they know you couldn't hurt a fly."

I didn't know whether to take that as an insult or a compliment.

"We all have different weaknesses, Rosie. Kasay's is violence, and substances which happen to be illegal-"

"Kasay doesn't do drugs."

He pursed his lips together, "That's a conversation for another time... As I was saying, we all have our weaknesses. Just don't let them discover yours."

Axel...

I took in a deep breath and nodded.

No one was going to take Axel away from me.

~*~

Axel was on my mind through the entire class. What if Layla did find out I was in love with Axel? What if she

93

managed to convince him to hate me too? What if she was able to convince him to hurt me?

But I would die for just another touch from him...

I would still yearn for his touch, even if his hands were around my neck...

Nope, too morbid.

"OPEN YOUR EYES!" someone on my volleyball team screamed.

I looked up at the volleyball flying straight towards me and panicked. Right before it could smack my face, I tried to slap it away with my hand. I flinched when it smacked hard into my palm and left a red mark there.

The other girls on my team groaned in frustration and glared at me. I flinched and looked down. I sucked at sports and everyone knew it. I sighed and walked further away from my team. My P.E teacher, Mrs. Trint, stuck me on their team for no reason.

"Can't she at least pretend to try?" A squeaky red head on my team whined.

Another girl put her hand on her hip. "Yeah! She's not even trying."

"She does nothing for our team! She just stands there and does nothing!" someone complained.

There was a chorus of 'yea's and 'yup's. We were playing against Layla's undefeated team.

"Shut up and play already!" Layla whined from across the court.

Layla smoothed out her t-shirt and twirled the hair in her ponytail with her finger. My team gloomily got to their spots before Layla grabbed the volleyball. All eyes were on her as she threw it up in the air and smacked it hard with her hand.

The ball flew over the net and fell in the red head's direction. The red head then smacked the ball with her forearm. It flew across the net again. The blonde from the hallway earlier hit the ball back to our side.

Another girl from my team passed it back to the other side of the court. With my head down, I stood there staring at the floor. They didn't need me, no one did. I sighed and thought. Why did everyone have to hate me?

Why couldn't I do anything right for once? Am I not good enough? Am I not pretty enough? Are my boobs a size too small? Is my ass not as big as it should be? Am I too skinny? Too many questions were flooding my head.

Suddenly, something hard smacked the side of my head, knocking me off balance. I tried to keep my balance, but instead I slipped and my foot hit the wall real hard as I fell to the ground. All I could feel was a throbbing pain on the side of my head and in my ankle.

I heard some laughs around me before the world started going black. Shit! No! Not another black out! I hate those. Wake up Rosie wake up! But it was too late; darkness welcomed me. At least it got me out of that class.

~*~

"It was an accident!" Layla's annoying voice broke into my peaceful sleep.

"It was! We saw it happen!" An annoying voice squeaked.

"I saw it too!" Another high pitched voice agreed.

"All right then! Thank god she's ok, and it was an accident, or her mom would've pressed charges." What sounded like Mrs. Trint said.

That was something my step mom would do. She let people push me around to a certain limit, but if it interfered with her work she would phone up her lawyer. Happened in elementary school once.

This girl kept pushing me around and thankfully Jaxon was there. He protected me from her but I got a scratch on my face. My step mom phoned up her lawyer and got really pissed because we were having our family photos that week. She went too far at that time. The girl moved to another state and we never heard from her again.

I tried opening my eyes to see what was up but my eyelids felt too heavy. I heard the door slam closed.

Something really cold and wet pressed against the side of my head. My eyes shot opened immediately. I felt the throbbing pain in the side of my head and groaned.

"You'll be okay honey," an elderly lady who was the school nurse said pressing the icepack to the side of my head.

She then took another ice pack and put it on my ankle. My ankle throbbed painfully too. It looked all swollen and purple. I flinched at the touch of the ice pack, but once it was on it felt a lot better. I thanked her.

"You're very welcome. Thank goodness your ankle's not broken."

I nodded numbly. What the hell was going on? What happened? I didn't notice I asked that out loud until the nurse answered my question.

"I heard that cheerleader smacked the ball and it hit the side of your head. They also told me you tried balancing yourself, but tripped and somehow hit your foot against the wall. I still don't understand how you managed to do that," she shook her head.

I chuckled awkwardly as she walked to her desk. She mumbled something about stupid paperwork and got to it right away. The office door slammed open as Axel walked in looking hot as usual. He was wearing his red cap, a red hoodie, and matching shoes. How fashionable of him…

His jeans weren't that loose and weren't that tight. His blonde hair fell just above those gorgeous emerald green eyes. There was another guy beside him and an annoyed looking Mrs. Meisty behind them with her arms crossed across her chest.

Axel adjusted his baseball cap and looked right at me. I gulped as my heart pounded against my chest crazily. This was the very first time he's ever noticed me as Rosaline. My hands started to shake a little as I wiped them against my shirt to get the sweat off.

All the little hairs on my neck were standing and I felt goose bumps form on every single inch of my body. My eyes were glued to his and I couldn't get them off his gorgeous face. He had such an innocent face; however the things he's done were far from innocent.

Axel nudged the guy standing beside him and pointed at me. The guy looked at me. The guy standing beside him was no other than Dustin. He smiled and his left dimple showed. He was cute but nothing compared to Axel.

"I just want to knock that kid up." Axel said using his thumb to point at me.

My mouth fell to the floor. What did he just say?! He wanted to... My crush who I've been stalking for a fair amount of time just said something perverted about me. And sadly, I didn't walk straight up to him and slap him.

Realization seemed to hit him, and he looked slightly shocked too, however he recovered quickly.

I just stood there with my mouth wide opened not knowing what to say. The nurse looked at him in shock and disapproval.

"Axel!" She scolded.

"What?! It's true- I mean I shouldn't have said it, but it's true!" He defended himself putting his arms up in the air.

Mrs. Meisty slapped him upside the head with her Geography textbook. I giggled as he adjusted his cap and gave her a dirty look.

"Spencer, quit being a pain and try to act decent for just once."

Axel rolled his eyes, "crabby old bitch," he mumbled.

"I heard that!"

He ignored her and walked over to my bed and sat on the edge of the bed I was lying down on. He looked up at the nurse.

"I need my record," he said to her.

"And?" She questioned without looking up at him.

"Can I have it?"

"No," she replied simply.

"The fuck?!"

Dustin and Mrs. Meisty shook their heads at the same time.

"But she said-"

She cut him off before he finished, "You didn't say the magic word."

"Fuck the magic word!"

She gave him a flat look, "Repeat that to my face."

"I'm not fucking five. You all treat me like I'm retarded."

She continued to ignore him.

"This place is a fucking joke."

She sighed, then grabbed some paper work from her drawer and handed it to him. He looked at me for a moment then looked back at the nurse.

"What's wrong with her?"

"Got hit in the head and sprained her ankle real bad.," she said shaking her head.

He looked at me, "you okay?"

My heart stopped. I was shaking inside.

I nodded quickly as he got up. I couldn't read the emotions in his eyes.

"Take... care." His hand brushed my leg, I couldn't tell whether it was intentional or not, "and uh," He lowered his voice down to a whisper, "sorry for being... fucked up." With that, he left with Mrs. Meisty.

I didn't even know what he meant by that.

Dustin stood at the doorway with his arms folded across his chest. The nurse looked up at him and smiled sweetly. "I've got some stuff to do, you can take over." With that, she left us two alone.

"We meet again, Rose."

Chapter 13 DUSTIN

My eyes widened in shock, and I almost choked on my own saliva.

He knew.

Dustin knew it was me all along.

He smiled and walked over to me. He bent down so our faces were at the same level. Our noses were inches apart. My heart pounded against my chest crazily as he inched closer. Not the way it would beat for Axel, but it was beating with anxiety.

"Have anything to say?" he asked.

His hot breath tickled my lips as I shook my head. He pulled back and crossed his arms across his chest. He then laughed and shook his head.

"Actually, I don't know what you're talking about?" My reply came out as a question. Why couldn't I lie?

I knew exactly what he was talking about.

He caught me.

Who was I trying to kid? He knew it was me. It was obvious I wasn't going to be able to convince him otherwise.

He pinched the bridge of his nose and sat down on the bed making it dip down.

"I might not have sixth sense, but I know you're lying."

I decided to give in, "H-How?"

"You forgot this at the dance," he pulled out something from his pocket and waved it in my face.

MY PHONE. It was in the same condition as before but it had fingerprints all over it…which meant that someone was trying to figure out the password. I snatched the phone from his hands quickly and tried unlocking it, but it was switched off.

Weird... I never remembered turning it off when I was at the dance. I pressed the power button to turn it on. There was still battery, which meant it didn't die. That's odd...

Dustin peeked over my shoulder and watched me closely.

"Did you mess with it?"

"No... well, I kinda' tried, but your pattern password is damn hard," he admitted.

"There's this thing called privacy," I muttered.

"Well, I didn't know who it belonged to at first, so I had to at least try! Mrs. Puessy said it was probably yours."

I was too nice, "Thanks for keeping it for me."

"You are very welcome my dear lady!" He was such a cheerful soul.

I turned the phone away from him and unlocked it. My mouth dropped to the floor when I saw the number of missed calls on there. Seventy four missed calls from Cleo, from Kasay and of course, from my very best friend Jaxon.

"You're popular."

"With three people."

I tossed my phone aside and crossed my arms over chest. The ice pack was still on my ankle and it was so cold, it was burning my skin. I closed my eyes for a moment wishing the pain could go away.

"So," he started, "what's the whole Cinderella thing you're trying to pull?"

My eyes were still closed, I just wanted time to think, "I'm not trying to pull anything."

"Then explain."

I sighed, "It's a long story."

"I have time."

Did he have to be as annoying as Kasay? I opened my eyes to him grinning on my phone.

"DUSTIN!" I tried snatching the phone from him, but he just leaped away.

He looked up with an evil sparkle in his eyes. He stood up slowly, pacing around me like a tiger circling its prey. His grin was so playful... After tapping on it a few times, he showed me the screen.

"I didn't know you were a stalker!"

On full display was a photo of Axel in his swimming trunks.

"GIVE ME BACK MY PHONE!" I tried getting up, but it was so painful I fell to the ground. "FRICK!" I hissed.

He placed the phone on a shelf far away from me, and helped me back up on the bed, "I didn't know you had a crush on Axel Storm Spencer! Interesting choice by the way, I wouldn't have guessed that was your type."

"I don't have a crush on him!" I protested.

"Looks like it's more than a crush now," he grabbed my phone and started scrolling through it again.

"Please... give me my phone," I begged, "My life sucks enough!"

"Why don't you just go up to him and tell him you're obsessed with him?" He kept scrolling through my phone, "If anyone was this crazy about me, I'd be damn flattered."

"Please-"

"WOAH! You even have photos of him as a kid!"

I hid my face with my hands.

"You stalker!" he teased.

"I swear I'm not!"

"Then explain why you have hundreds of photos of him on your phone."

I felt my face flare up even more than before. I glared at him as he smiled at me showing his dimple on his left cheek. It was so hard not to smile when he was looking that adorable. It truly wasn't fair on my behalf.

"Is that why you pretended to be the Rose at the dance?"

I stayed quiet.

"You pretended to be someone else, so he could notice you?" He questioned, serious this time.

"It's not only that-"

"I won't tell anyone, I promise."

"But-"

"Come on," he practically begged me. "You're not the only one needing to get something off your chest."

I didn't know what to say, so I just gave him a questioning look.

He sighed and sat down on the edge of the bed. He ran a hand through his hair and shook his head. "Look, do you know how it feels to have a secret you can't tell any of your friends about? You know they'd laugh and judge you for it?"

His genuine ocean blue eyes stared into mine. They looked so peaceful, so calm, so innocent... I got lost in them for a moment, before I nodding my head slowly.

"We've got the same problem."

"What do you mean?"

"Same issues with our love lives."

I didn't believe him, "I don't think so."

"I'm serious-"

"I highly doubt that."

"Then tell me. Tell me what your situation is; tell me how you truly feel." He pleaded.

He seemed like a trusting person, but I didn't know him that well. I had a few classes with him through the years, but never had a full conversation with him before. I saw him so often I felt like I knew him really well for some reason. Or maybe it was just the way he was.

He must've felt the same way from the way he was talking to me. He conversed with me the way long lasting friends talked. I smiled at the thought of having him as a friend. I really needed more of them. At least someone besides Jaxon and Kasay wanted to get to know me in my nerdy Rosaline form.

I felt like I could trust the guy with my life. I blamed it on his eyes; I had a thing for beautiful eyes, and his were just too warm and too trusting.

"I'll tell you my situation if you tell me yours," I finally said.

He snatched my right hand and shook it right away, "deal!"

~*~

"Wow!" He said at the end of my story.

Yep... I just trusted someone I wasn't even close to with my entire life...

I told him the whole situation about Axel and I.

I spilt feelings I wouldn't dare tell Jaxon or Kasay.

Thankfully, no one had bothered us while we were in the nurse's office, so we had privacy. The nurse was busy outdoors arguing with some school secretary about a paycheck.

Dustin had a sympathetic look on his face. He forced a smile as he reached over and tucked a loose strand of hair behind my ear then he looked down. He was staring down onto the floor. It looked like he was lost in his own thoughts.

"So... how bad is my situation?" I asked.

I was obviously afraid of the answer, but I was willing to hear it. I needed to know what he thought of me. An outsider's opinion on the entire situation would give me a clearer picture of how messed up it may have been. Hell- I just wanted to know if Axel had noticed me at all. If he even acknowledged my existence!

Dustin slowly looked up and gave me a smile, "You call yours bad?! All I hear is assumptions from you. You assume he's never noticed you, or he's never acknowledged your presence!"

"Well I assume because I know the truth! He's never looked in my direction!"

"You've never considered maybe every time he looks at you, you look away?

I stopped to register what he just said, "do you know something I don't know?"

He avoided my eye contact, "Please just know that your situation is not as bad as you make it out to be."

"You *do* know something I don't know."

"I don't know any facts," he said. "Like I said, your situation is nowhere near bad. You're just oblivious to things around you.

"How am I oblivious?!"

He ignored my question, "Just know that mine's way worse."

Worse my ass. Any girl would've fallen for Dustin. Messy hair, ocean blue eyes, caramel skin, and a cute dimple.

But then again, he did have an identical twin brother, and no one could tell them apart if they weren't speaking. They did have quite different personalities. One was tough and mean while one was always playful and nice.

But some girls probably wouldn't have liked the nice and playful one and would go for the tough and mean one. Aggressive trouble makers were hot... at least to me they were...

Talking about aggressive...

I saw a few of Axel's fights before. He looked so cold every time he threw punches at his opponents. It scared me, but I was so attracted to it. I hate to admit it, but he looked damn sexy after he fought. He would sometimes have a bruise on his cheekbone or a busted lip.

Somehow, I found that extremely irresistible.

"How could your situation be any harder than mine?"

"It just is," he replied simply.

"I'm all ears."

"It's a long story."

"I've got time," I smirked, using his own words against him.

He groaned and buried his face in his hands. "You wouldn't believe me if I told you."

"Try me."

His eyes met mine, "I think I'm in love with your best friend."

I froze. My best friend.

"JAXON?!"

"Uh, no."

It took me a few moments to process in my head who he meant by my best friend.

"You're in love with... Kasay?"

He nodded slowly.

I was shocked. Dustin having a crush on Jaxon would've been less surprising than him liking Kasay. The more I thought of it, the worse I felt about the situation. Did she even notice him? Did she even know who he was?

She had never liked the jocks or cheerleaders, but she did occasionally exchange bodily fluids with a few of the football and basketball players. I doubt she knew who Dustin even was...

Maybe his situation was just as hard as mine.

What shocked me most was Dustin falling for someone like Kasay. The perfect jock, falling for the tough pessimistic gal' who usually viewed the world as her enemy.

Well... I guess I fell for the opposite too.

I was the nerd who always followed orders, who almost never spoke against anything... and I fell for the guy who rebelled against everyone and anything.

I felt really bad for Dustin.

I mean, Kasay was one of my best friends- one of my only friends, but she was the type of girl just looking for a quick high, not something serious.

I understood the feeling of having a crush on someone who didn't acknowledge your presence. Yet, you noticed every single detail about them; from their smile, their eyes, their face, and how they chose to dress, how they acted during certain situations-

"You've been silent…" He looked worried, "so, what do you think?"

I looked up at him and tried my best to give him a reassuring smile.

"Does she even notice me?"

His ocean blue eyes held a sliver of hope. Did I tell the truth about her hating jocks and not wanting to settle, or did I tell him a sweet lie on how she did notice him?

Being the coward I was, I avoided doing either.

"I don't really talk to her about her love life, she's quite a closed person," I told him part of the truth, "I'll find out for you."

"Thanks Rose! You're great!"

I nodded.

"Still think your situation is worse?"

I nodded again, "I've liked him way longer."

"When did you fall?"

"Middle school…"

He was in shock, "d-didn't you go out with Ricky though?"

"I did, but-"

"You were pressured. To be honest, I could tell you didn't really like him."

"I mean, I guess there was a point I genuinely did… but it faded pretty fast."

"I get it," he ran a hand through his hair, "but since middle school? That's damn long!"

"Concludes why my situation is worse."

"At least he's never told you to 'fuck off'."

My eyes widened, "she told you to?"

He nodded sadly. His trace of playfulness was completely gone. I knew straight away he couldn't be bluffing, because that truly something Kasay would do."

I couldn't stand seeing him sad, "She probably thought you were Justin."

That visibly cheered him up, "never thought of that," he took it into consideration.

"And at least she noticed you! Unlike with me-"

He shook his head, "you've talked to him. You know him, he knows you. I saw you both leaving the ISS room side by side."

"That was Rose, not me- Rosaline-"

"Let me repeat that, he knows you. Kasay told me to fuck off the first time I tried talking to her."

"He may know I exist in Rose form, but he doesn't know ME! Rosaline Arlene Winnefred!"

"What if he does know-"

"He doesn't. If he did, he would've came straight up to me and talked to me about that night. But he hasn't. He doesn't know Rose is me."

"That's true..." he frowned, "but my situation is still worse. You still have a chance if you tell him the truth! Reveal that you're Cinderella-"

"No! You could still go to Kasay and explain how your twin brother is the jerk, and you're the nice one. Plus, I have an influence on who she likes, so you've got a better chance than I do. I'll introduce you two, and bam, you'll take her to prom at the end of the year!"

"Easier said than done."

"Just talk to her! She doesn't like shy guys-"

"I am shy. It's who I am."

"Just DO IT! For her, for your future!"

"I'll consider it-"

The door suddenly flew open, Jaxon rushed in panting crazily. "ROSIE! Everything's going downhill," he breathed out as he clutched his chest, still panting. The kid really needed to exercise more... said the girl who couldn't even hit a single volleyball.

His red hair was messy, and he was sweating up a storm. He wiped away his sweat and looked surprised by the fact that

Dustin was in the same room at me, but ignored it. He sat down on the edge of my bed while whispering to himself.

"What's wrong?" I asked, "Jaxon?"

"Kasay…" he turned to me with wide eyes. Uh oh… "got expelled."

"WHAT?!" Dustin and I yelled at the same time in horror.

~*~

Chapter 14 POWERLESS

I was frozen, and so was Dustin. Jaxon nodded as he wiped the rest of his sweat away from his forehead.

"We have to do something!" I yelled.

"There's nothing we can do about it. She's already expelled, thanks to the help of Layla's dad."

My blood boiled underneath my skin. I clenched my teeth and balled up my fists. Dustin put a hand on my shoulder trying to calm me down. I was surprised he wasn't the one freaking out.

I turned to face Dustin.

"You alright?" I asked.

He gave me a sad smile and nodded. We stood there a while before Jaxon cleared his throat.

"Am I missing something here?" He asked glaring at Dustin.

Dustin and I exchanged looks before we turned back to my best friend. Jaxon gestured over to Dustin. "What's he doing here?" Jaxon asked quite rudely.

I hesitated for a moment before I replied, "he's a friend."

"Just checking up on her since she got injured during P.E."

Jaxon completely ignored the friendly guy, "friend?"

Both of us nodded in confirmation.

"Since when?" Jaxon asked looking confused. "Wasn't he the jerk twin who showed up at my door with those other dickheads?"

"Jaxon!" I scolded, "this is the good twin!"

Before I could say anything else, Dustin extended out a hand to Jaxon with a friendly smile. Jaxon looked down at the hand then looked up again.

"I'm Dustin."

Jaxon looked down his hand again before he took it and shook it.

"Jaxon."

"Wait, aren't you playing the lead in this year's play?"
Jaxon nodded proudly.
"Oh my god, dude! That's so cool," Dustin praised.
Ass kisser. He was trying to get on Jaxon's good side and he
knew exactly how to. If anyone praised Jaxon's skills or
anything related to drama he melted immediately. Dustin and
Jaxon were definitely going to get along. Dustin was far more
clever than I had originally thought.

The two started discussing Shakespeare's works, while I sat
there with my arms folded across my chest bored. The two
started giving one another those guy hand shake thingies, then
they created a new one from one of Shakespeare's plays.

I must admit, it looked pretty feminine. At least it was a new
hope, that Jaxon would stop discussing boring plays with
Dustin instead. I sighed and grabbed my phone. I went onto
my social media account and checked Axel's page.

Dustin was right, I was a stalker. I scrolled down his news
feed and found nothing but comments of girls flirting with
him.

"Ugh you're so hot;)"
"Text me;)"
"Pweasee replyyyy"
*"What's your #? Mine's 785-***-**** call me xoxo"*
*"Heard you're into blondes! I'm 17! ☺ <3 Hmu sometime
tho!"*

I scrunched up my face in disgust. Didn't they have any
dignity at all? They seemed so desperate for his attention. I
shook my head in disapproval. I mean, I wanted his attention
too, but I wanted only his undivided attention, no one else's.

As I scrolled through all the crap posted on his timeline, I
came across one status that made my heart stop.

'Whoever you are, I will find you. It may not be tomorrow,
but someday, I know I will.'

Excitement bubbled in through me. It must've been about
me. It had to have been! I clicked on the status to check the

date. The morning after the dance. My heart fluttered crazily. I scrolled through the comments.

"IT'S ME!!!"

"OMG who is this about?!"

"You've already found you babe ☉ I've been in your dm's for weeks."

I found comfort in the fact he never replied to anyone who responded on his statuses. I scrolled further down to see if he had any more recent posts about me.

'This place sucks. I want to move back to Cali.'

My emotions of happiness vanished. I felt like crying. I looked at the date, it was posted weeks ago... so it really couldn't mean anything, right? He could've changed his mind by now... I mentally slapped myself.

Like I even had a chance with him...

I took in a deep breath and tried to calm myself down. Of course, I know I was over reacting but I couldn't help it.

I fell for him. Hard. I was waiting for him to just notice me.

I may have not been any different from the desperate girls, but I felt I had talked to him before, so I had more of a chance. Boy, did I sound pathetic. Stupid me.

A little voice screamed in the back of my mind that I did have a chance. Rose had a chance.

But till then, I had to do something about Kasay.

~*~

All my emotions were crashing on me like tsunami waves. I letting my anger out in a single argument.

"Miss Winnefred, please do not interfere with this situation-"

I refused to listen, and interrupted my principal rudely, "they're all on her side! They're her best friends for Christ's sake!"

"You cannot do anything to make this situation better-"

"NO! I refuse to believe that! I allow people to treat me like shit, but not my friends!"

"Watch your language Miss Winnefred-"

"I don't have to watch my fucking language!" I screamed, "Do you realize how those people treat me?! Do you realize how almost every single person treats me?!" I slammed my fists on the desk, "Kasay was one of the only people who's tried helping me! One of the only friends I have-"

"But she's been a terrible influence-"

"She's helped changed me, she's made me more confident-"

"Miss Winnefred, true friends don't change you. They support you and help you gain your confidence-"

I was too emotional to listen to what my principal had to say, "She has made me more confident than I have ever been in my entire life!"

"If confidence is you swearing in my office, then she is a terrible influence. She has also been involved in numerous illegal activities in and outside of school-"

"She's not guilty! She's been framed! She'd never do anything like that-"

"Look, Rosaline, I know you thought you were close to her. But you don't know her as well as you may think. We'll let the courts decide whether or not she's guilty-"

"I'm tired of people judging each other based off of their appearance or what they choose to show people!" It wasn't even about Kasay anymore, "FUCK THIS PLACE!" I was on the verge of tears.

"That's it," my principal had had enough of me, "I'm afraid you've just earned yourself your first Discipline Referral."

"WHAT?!" I gasped.

Why was I even shocked? What took over me?

My first ever discipline referral. This couldn't be true. I have had a clean record since kindergarten! Kindergarten! I had never gotten in trouble even once! Not even in P.E. when I couldn't do a single thing!

"I'm sorry, I didn't want to, but I had no choice. You were using very explicit language in school-"

112

"But..."

My perfectly clean record... ruined... on my last year of high school...

"I hope this is the last time you get one-"

The door flew open revealing a very pissed off Mrs. Meisty. She stomped straight in and threw a pack of condoms right in his face. Luckily, he closed his mouth before it could fly straight in. He picked it up and examined it.

With her arms folded across her chest, she glared down at the principal. He looked up at her, obviously confused. She smiled bitterly.

"You must be curious to why I brought these in for you today." She rested both her hands on his desk and glared down at him, "Axel thought it'd be funny if he took magic markers and wrote down inappropriate things on them. He stuffed them in my drawers, and threw ones filled with water at passing teachers and students." Her face was redder than any tomato.

Her tone of voice frightened the hell out of me. I looked at her curly blondish-white hair and saw a condom stuck in it. I tried reading what was on it, but she noticed and snatched it out and threw it onto his desk. The principal picked it up and attempted to read it, "I bl-blow in public rooms on the week-"

She snatched it out of his hand and threw it into the trashcan.

He stood up and gave her a small smile, "I don't think we should be having this discussion about another student in front of any other student. Please, let's take this-"

"We're not taking this anywhere! Not until I get some things cleared here! I don't want him stepping foot in my classroom ever again. I told you I didn't want to teach him, yet you still stuck him on my god damn schedule!"

"Someone has to teach him-"

"He's set off firecrackers in my class, he's set textbook pages on fire, he ain't stupid, I tell ya'! He's smart in a

113

disrupting way, and I can't take it! He's a pain in my god damn ass!"

The principal cleared this throat and hissed at her, "there's a student in here!"

"I don't care! He's causing trouble in my classroom and I want him out. Hell, I want him out of this school! I don't want to see him here again-"

"You know we can't do that." The principal interrupted her.

"Why? This is a public school! His dad being a rich bastard shouldn't-"

"There is a student in here!" The principal snapped. "And no student will be hearing teachers using inappropriate language!"

With my right leg crossed over my left, I looked up at the two adults staring down at me expecting me to say something.

"What?" I asked innocently.

The principal sighed and whispered something into her ear. She rolled her eyes and mumbled something like 'ass kissing prick' or something along the lines of that. The principal turned back to me.

"And you young lady, will not say a word about that." He said putting the boxes of condoms in his drawer.

"When is my punishment?" I asked with a hint of bitterness in my voice.

"Tomorrow, just so you know it's an all day thing." He stood up and gestured his hand to the door, "you may leave."

I deeply desired to go tell him to please himself until he ejaculates, but held my tongue. I wished I were like Axel.

~*~

"He gave you a fucking D.R. for that?!" Jaxon asked in disbelief.

I nodded and groaned out loud. "Quit bugging me about it."

"I still don't believe you said the f word. But congratulations girl! You finally got in trouble!" Kasay said nudging me playfully.

"But he expelled you!" I half screamed. "You have to go battle in court soon too! How can you be so calm?!"

"Don't worry about it," Kasay seemed way to chill. "I'm supposed to be on house arrest, but I can still go out and have fun!"

"Isn't that illegal?" I asked.

She just shrugged.

"Little princess is finally getting used to bad words," Jaxon joked.

I smacked him playfully upside the head. He grabbed my wrists pushed me against the wall. He had both my wrists secure above my head as me grinned down at me.

"You can't get away with slapping me like that Rosie. You have to pay!" He laughed evilly.

I made a shock face expression. "Oh my god! I'm so scared. Someone! Save me!" I mocked sarcastically.

He smirked down at me. "Yes Princess Rosie, your prince charming is nowhere in sight!" Then he laughed evilly again.

His hazel eyes were so cute under his flaming red hair. Looking into his eyes made me think back about the time I saw him come out of the shower. And he was in only a towel wrapped around his waist. I had to admit, he looked pretty damn good.

I scolded myself. Checking out my best friend, seriously? The ball must've hit my head too hard. I felt the heat radiating from his body before he let go and looked down at my foot in a cast.

I didn't know the exact terms the doctors were using, but dislocated was one of them, and damaged tendons was the other. I was daydreaming too much about Axel...

"Guys, seriously. Go get a room," Kasay shooed.

Jaxon grinned mischievously. "So is it cool if we use your mom's room since she's not home?"

I slapped him playfully. "Pervert!"

"You love it when I act like one," he winked.

I imagined Axel saying it to me instead.

"I hate you."

"You're lying. You love me." He kissed my cheek and plopped down onto Kasay's bed.

"So what school are you going to go to now?" I asked.

She looked up with me with horrified eyes. "If I don't have to go to jail, my mom's sending me to a Catholic school."

"What?!" me and Jaxon yelled at the same time.

"Plan my funeral. They'll turn me into a fucking nun there!" We were all horrified. "I hope I end up in jail."

~*~

Chapter 15 DISCIPLINE REFERRAL [DAY 1]

"You need to explain to me right now how you got your Discipline Referral."

I was shaking. Cleo was beyond intimidating, "I-I was talking back-"

"Tell me exactly what you said."

"I-I can't e-exactly remember ma'am.."

"You can't remember?" She asked sarcastically, "You lose your phone, and you get in trouble?"

"I found my phone-"

She completely ignored me, "you're grounded."

I was expecting that.

"For two weeks."

That was expected too.

"I'm sending the doctor's note to your principal."

"What doctor note-?"

"You're taking the remainder of the week off of school to recover from your sprain."

"But it's only a sprain-"

"I need you well for my studies," she said before waving her hand dismissively, indicating that I go away. The moment I was out of her study, I stomped upstairs to my room, slammed the door, and locked it. I skipped doing my homework for the first time, and just collapsed down onto my bed.

Ignoring my responsibilities felt odd, yet satisfying. It was like a heavy weight lifted off my shoulders. It was a change.

"Two weeks," I stared up at the ceiling.

I grabbed one of my cheesy romance novels and started reading right away.

I dreamt that one day the story of Axel and I would end up on someone's shelf, and our love would forever stay engrained into the pages of a love story.

~*~

"Uh, hi…" I said to the old secretary who was currently doing work in the school's office.

She ignored me and kept typing using only her index finger.

I cleared my throat, trying once again to get her attention. "Excuse me…"

She still ignored me.

"Ma'am…?"

Maybe I was invisible, because she didn't notice my presence at all. I tried clearing my throat again to get her attention, but unfortunately she still stayed as blind as a bat. I pretended to knock her container of pens over, "oops! Sorry about that!" I picked up one of the pens and put it in the container, leaving the rest scattered across her desk.

She finally looked up, but she was glaring at me. "What do you want?" she asked in a cranky voice, obviously pissed off she was disrupted.

"I'm here to serve my sentence," I said.

She stared at me blankly.

"My punishment," I tried again.

Her face remained the same.

"I got a DR last week-"

"Good for you," she looked back at the screen and continued with her work.

I tried being nice, "So um, do I go straight to the ISS room?"

No reply.

"Ma'am?"

Still no reply.

"Sorry to bother you, but do I go straight there?"

She still continued to ignore me.

I wasn't going to respect elders who had no respect for me.

Beyond frustrated with her, I slammed my DR slip onto her desk. She jumped at the sudden movement and stared at me in shock as if I had just stabbed someone in front of her. I was

118

shocked myself that I had the nerve to do that, but I composed myself quickly.

"Do I or do I not go straight to the ISS room?"

"That's rude of you to do, don't you think? Could've gotten my attention politely," she grumbled. I had to put invisible restraints on my wrists to stop myself from throwing something at her face. "If you do that again, it'll be an out of school suspension." She went back to her work.

She still didn't answer my question. I grabbed my slip and before I left the office, I leaned next to her ear, "have you considered retiring a few years early?" I didn't get to see her reaction, but it felt damn good getting back at someone who was rude to me, even if it was just small revenge.

I went up to the ISS room and knocked on the door, but there was no reply. I waited a little longer, and even tried knocking again, but no one came to the door. I pushed the heavy door open and made my way in.

The moment the door behind me clicked shut, my eyes quickly scanned the room.

I froze.

Air was caught in my lungs.

I swear, my entire body went numb.

All I could feel was my heart violently beating against my ribcage.

Axel Storm Spencer was currently in the room.

His feet were on the desk in front of him, and his baseball cap was pulled down enough it barely covered his eyelids.

He had headphones on and was sleeping like a baby. He was right in the back corner of the room. I looked over the teacher's desk and saw a teacher in his late 40's sound asleep with headphones plugged in both ears.

Justin was in the other corner of the room throwing paper balls at Ricky, who was sitting in the front row and giving him the finger. The door slammed shut and all eyes of those who were awake were on me.

"Holy shit," Justin blurted out. "Look who showed up with a slip."

Ricky was shocked too. The teacher and Axel were still asleep. I put the slip on the teacher's desk and tried to find a seat. I took a seat in the middle of all the desks there and put my head on the desk.

Ricky and Justin moved closer to me and started whispering. Justin stood in front of me with a smirk on his face.

"So what brings you here, nerd?"

"Dude, I think I might consider her again. If she quits being a prude and fucks me," Ricky laughed.

I lifted my head up and flipped them off. They both started laughing hysterically. What was so funny about me flipping them off?

"Oh Rosie, you've changed," Ricky chuckled.

"For the better," Justin added.

"Changed since I left you," I mumbled.

"She bites back!" Justin exclaimed.

I didn't feel like taking any of their shit, "can you two piss off?"

They stared at me.

"Go jack each other off or some shit. Just leave me alone."

"You are quite a girl Rosie, you are," Ricky said as he wiped a fake tear away from the corner of his eye.

I just gave him a flat look. I wasn't planning on being nice or friendly to him anytime soon, considering all the shit he made me go through.

"Now, quit playing hard to get and get on your knees. I'll shut you up with these nuts!"

"Fuck off Ricky."

"Or what, what could you even do?"

I felt conscious of a pair of eyes on me. It wasn't Ricky or Justin… someone else was watching in the room. I glanced at the teacher, and he was still fast asleep. Good. I smirked and got up.

"You really want to know what I'll do?"

Ricky raised his eyebrows. "Of course, the most you could do is attempt to discipline me." He wasn't taking me seriously at all.

I smirked at Ricky, "if you want to see what I'm capable of doing, try me."

I got up from my seat as Ricky came closer grinning evilly at me.

"You're playing with fire babe," he warned.

I laughed, "you're an open flame under a rain cloud."

"Since when did you become so... challenging?"

His manner was so aggressive; I desperately wanted to leave the room. I just shrugged in reply.

"Was it when I dumped your sorry little ass because I realized how worthless you were?" He inched closer, "remember? You thought you were irreplaceable... always wanted to do things your way," he spat out, "selfish!"

His words first hurt me, but I couldn't let him break me down. I was in the same room as Axel, if he suddenly woke up and saw me crying, he'd probably see me as weak. I glared hard at Ricky. I wasn't the selfish one, he was.

"You're projecting," my voice sounded far tougher than how I felt inside.

He looked a bit taken back by my tone, but obviously didn't understand the meaning of what said.

"Some people are insecure deep down inside, and realize how shitty they really are... so instead of trying to accept it, they accuse other people of being that way." I gave him a small smile, "and just for the record, I dumped you after I found out you cheated."

He knocked my desk onto the floor and grabbed me by my shirt collar. I winced at the pain and tried prying his hands off, but he kept an iron grip on my collar and shook me painfully, "You piece of shit-"

I cut him off by kneeing him in the crotch as hard as I could. The old Rosie would've said 'violence doesn't solve anything', but I knew it would in this case. He cried in pain and fell to the ground.

A stream of curse words flew out of Ricky's mouth as he clutched his balls. Justin just stared blankly, not knowing what to do.

"Do something!" Ricky hissed at Justin as he held onto his crotch like his life depended on it. Well... maybe his life did depend on it.

I picked up the desk he had knocked over and sat back down in my seat. Justin looked at me, before looking back at Ricky who was still on the ground.

"Don't mess with me, or you'll end up like him." I didn't even realize I was capable of threatening people.

I smiled at him as he backed away. Ricky tried getting up, only to fall to his knees again.

Someone chuckled behind me.

I turned around.

Axel was watching amusingly. His feet were on his desk, and he was staring straight at me.

I didn't know how to react. I felt my cheeks grow hot.

"Good job, Rose..." My heart dropped, "...aline."

I almost sighed in relief, "thanks...?"

"He deserved everything he got, and more." Axel placed his feet on the ground.

Ricky and Justin were watching us closely, but they didn't dare say a single word. No one messed with Axel.

"How'd you get in here anyway? I thought you were..."

"A nerd?" I finished for him. "Stereotype," I snorted, "don't judge a book by its cover."

Déjà vu.

122

He stared at me oddly for a moment. I held my breath, hoping he wouldn't make any connection.

"I've heard that one before, Little Rosie."

I completely ignored his statement, but focused on the nickname he gave me, "Rosie?"

He smiled knowingly.

"Don't call me that." Why was I being so defiant?

"Then I'll call you nerd." He was starting to sound like Layla.

"I don't like it."

"But I do."

"Please don't be a prick," I turned away from him and avoided looking in his direction. Did I just blow one of the first times talking to him? God, I didn't know what to say when I was with him. "You can call me Rosie."

"Rosie," his voice was so faint, so innocent. I avoided turning back to him, in fear that I'd faint if I saw my name actually come out of his mouth.

I grabbed a piece of stray paper lying on the next desk to me, and pulled a pen out of my pocket. I saw the door to the balcony behind the sleeping teacher, so I sketched it. But I sketched how it looked that night; the night I met Axel.

How his emerald eyes shined so bright, how he genuinely seemed interested in getting to know me, how he opened up to me, and how I felt like I had a chance. How my sliver of hope grew to the size of two slivers. Once I was done, I crumpled the piece of paper and tossed it onto the floor.

I needed to stop daydreaming.

Ricky was glaring at me from across the room while whispering things in Justin's ear. The teacher was still fast asleep, and glancing back I saw Axel looked like he was asleep too. His earphones were tucked into his ears, and he looked so innocent. I shook my head. I tried to avoid staring at Axel, but it was an impossible task for me.

He was so peaceful with his eyes closed. It was hard to believe, such a young face could cause so much trouble. His boyish features flared of the innocence his soul seemed to lack.

I smiled as I watched his chest rise up and down. I pretended to drop my pen on the floor, so I could get closer to Axel. I took my sweet time while I was on the ground to study his face up close without being noticed.

His jawline was so sharp, it could've given me a paper cut. His lips looked so soft, so kissable. His hair was long enough to cover his eyes. I felt like extending my hand out and brushing it out of his face.

My heart was still pounding against my chest crazily, yet at the same time, I felt calm. When I was talking with him this time, I felt like I was really myself with him. I didn't have to pretend to be anyone I wasn't. I said what I wanted to. Heck, I was even a bit rude, and he still said my name afterwards.

He was rough around the edges, and I could see passed that.

I kept my eyes glued on him, even as I moved back to my seat.

Faded jeans, a tight black tee, and worn out sneakers. I wish I could've taken a photo. It was a moment I knew I'd always remember.

"Isn't that considered weird, Rosaline?" Ricky spoke up, "staring at someone while they're sleeping?"

"Maybe little nerdy Rosaline has a crush on Axel!" Justin grinned.

"No one will ever want you," Ricky made sure to add, "So why not save everyone some trouble and slit your little wrists now?"

That was my snapping point. I was a calm person, but that was it. Too far. I was far too patient with him before. I got up and glared at him.

"What are you gonna' do? Knee me in the balls again?"

I smirked at him and shook my head. Without thinking, I grabbed a Math textbook and threw it at them. Of course, I sucked at sports and my aim was way off. I closed my eyes and begged it to hit one of their heads.

I heard a loud thump and slowly opened my eyes. Oh, it hit someone's head alright.

~*~

"I didn't mean to hit his head! It was an accident!" I gushed, trying to convince the principal that I wasn't guilty.

"You have changed Rosaline! What has gotten into you?" My principal was stressed out, "First you swear at me, then you throw a textbook at a teacher's head!"

"It was an accident! I didn't mean to hit his head! I meant to hit Ricky!"

Boy was I stupid. The principal looked at me with in disappointment and sighed. He sat down and pulled out some papers. He started writing on them.

"I'm afraid to say this, but you've gotten yourself another discipline referral."

My eyes widened, "What?!"

"Actually, no- I'm sorry."

I sighed in relief, but not for long.

"You've gotten yourself two more."

My eyes widened again, this time far wider than they were the first time.

He nodded and smiled at me.

"You're kidding! Please tell me you're joking," I begged.

"Next time, don't go around causing trouble. One Axel is already too much for us to handle." He then waved his hand dismissively and handed me the two slips.

I felt like tearing up at that moment. I was so dead. My perfectly clean record was ruined by a bunch of fucking morons! I grabbed the slips and left immediately.

Once school was over, I walked over to Jaxon's locker. As he saw me coming closer, he grinned.

"How was it?" he asked, putting his books in his locker.

"I damaged Ricky's testicles," I mumbled, looking down.

Jaxon was quiet for a moment, before he started laughing hysterically.

"I'm so proud of you!" He laughed, "Finally got the balls to! Get it?! My pun!" He started laughing even harder. He closed his locker and locked it, and then he swung his arm around my shoulder.

"And," I started.

"There's an 'and' too?"

"I was throwing a textbook and it accidentally hit someone else's head."

"What do you mean 'someone else's head'?"

"I was aiming it at Ricky or Justin, but it ended up hitting someone else."

"Who else was in the room?" he asked.

"A teacher and Axel."

He stopped walking. I stopped too and turned to him.

"And who did you hit?" he asked worriedly.

His hazel eyes were filled with paranoia and worry. I sucked in a deep breath.

~*~

Chapter 16 SUSPICIOUS

"Nice throw, Rosie."

I'd recognize that voice anywhere.

Axel brushed past us and gave me a wink. His wink felt like a bullet to my chest, it made my blood rush to my cheeks and boy, I felt like dying. A good feeling of course... I didn't even know what I was rambling about in my head, I was too distracted by the fact that Axel- my love- had just winked at me.

His arm touched mine. I almost died.

"See you tomorrow, nerd!" He called out as he exited the building.

He didn't say 'nerd' like the others though, it sounded almost like a compliment, and he also smiled when he said it, so it must've meant something!

"I'm guessing the book didn't hit him," Jaxon said, but I was too busy staring at the door Axel had left through.

I just nodded, still dreaming about Axel.

Jaxon cleared his throat, "What did he mean by 'see you tomorrow'?" He was clearly bitter about it.

I bit my lip, but finally decided to tell him, "I got another DR..."

His mouth fell to the floor.

"Just kidding," I laughed.

He patted his chest, pretending to have recovered from shock, "got me scared for a moment!"

"I actually got two more DR's."

This time, he was truly in shock.

"Yep," I said, popping the 'p'.

"How are you not freaking out about this?!" His voice was as high as Mariah Carey's.

The true reason I was so comfortable was because it was just another excuse to be in the same room as Axel, and to possibly talk to him again too. I just shrugged in reply.

"THE NERD GOT IN TROUBLE!" Layla's voice rang through the hall.

I closed my eyes and took in a deep breath. I didn't feel like dealing with her, especially today. Today was not my day. I was ticked off enough.

Layla stood there with her arms folded across her chest in her cheerleader uniform. Her sidekicks were right behind her, ready to back her up. It was such a stereotypical scene. Her dark chocolate brown eyes were cold, with a hint of something else I couldn't pin point. She smiled cruelly at me, before her eyes moved to Jaxon who was next to me.

Something stirred within her.

One of the twins appeared behind us. The gentle look on his face made me recognize it was Dustin. He looked between Jaxon and Layla.

"Rosaline, let me take you home," he grabbed my wrist and tugged me along with him. His tone told me not to refuse. He was the perfect excuse to get out of there.

"I need to talk to you," I heard Jaxon say to Layla coldly, "privately."

"Dustin, what's going on?" I asked in him a hushed tone.

He pursed his lips, "not my story to tell."

Once we reached the exit, I tried pulling my wrist away, "my house is really close, I can walk."

"Do you walk when you're with Jaxon?"

I nodded, "we always walk home together."

He nodded, "well I guess I'll see you tomorrow then." He gave me a smile and a small wave before walking in the opposite direction as me.

I suddenly realized Cleo was waiting for me at home.

Since she was so involved in my school life, she had probably already found out about the other two DR's I had received. I was already grounded anyway, which made matters worse.

"WAIT!" I tried sprinting towards Dustin, but ended up tripping on my shoelaces and falling. I got up quickly and sprang towards him, "WAIT! DUSTIN!"

He stopped before he got into his car, "what's up?"

"I don't want to go home, can you take me with you?" I pleaded.

He didn't ask any further questions, "hop in!"

~*~

--- *Jaxon's P.O.V.*---

I ushered Layla into an empty classroom and locked the door. She turned to me, glaring at me with her chocolate brown eyes. She placed both her hands on my chest and pushed me into the desks.

I stumbled a bit, but didn't feel any pain. I stalked towards her until her back hit the wall. She was so... fragile. Yet, when she was angry she scared the daylights out of my poor soul. How could such a beautiful woman torment another innocent being?

"You always defend her!" Her jaw was clenched, she wanted to rip my heart out, "you don't know what pain she's caused me!"

"I don't know what pain she's caused you, because she's never caused you any pain." You had to be tough to get your way with her, or to get something into her thick skull. The girl was feisty.

"Is that so?" She turned cold once again, "you have no idea what she's done to me."

"She couldn't hurt a fly, even if she wanted to."

"You pretend you know her best," she pushed me away from her.

I knew my best friend inside and out, like the back of my hand. She was an ocean, and I believed I had explored all her depths.

"I don't get you. You're supposed to be on my side."

"Not if you're being immature like this," I leaned against one of the tables.

She took slow steps towards me. With every step she took forward, I took one back. Her sharp features still looked stunning in the dark. From her high cheekbones, her prominent nose, to her red lips.

When my back hit the wall, I spun us around, so she was against the wall instead. She gripped my hair on the back of my head and pulled my face down so we were eye to eye. Her cherry scent was suffocating, yet satisfying.

"I'm only this way because of what she's done to me, Jax."

I did not have a single clue to what she was going on about. Last time I checked, Rosie had n ever done anything to Layla. I knew Rosie my entire life, and she had always been the sweetest soul ever.

With our bodies pressed up against each other, I felt the strong urge to press my lips against hers, but I held my pride. I hid it through my superb acting skills. Her gaze moved from my eyes, down to my lips. She stared at them for a few moments, before looking into my eyes again.

I could've sworn her brown eyes were a shade darker than they were before. She crushed her lips against mine. They weren't as soft as they looked, but it was still damn satisfying to be kissing a girl desired by many.

She moaned against my mouth as I bit her lower lip.

It was clear she had lots of experience.

"I've wanted you so bad Jaxon. I've wanted you since the dance," she breathed.

"I've been dying to feel you since sixth grade."

~*~

--- *Rosie's P.O.V*---

"Seriously?"

I nodded in reply.

We were parked in front of Kasay's house, which by the

way was the ugliest house I had ever seen. It was a two story pink house with a green roof. The lawn looked like a never-ending yard sale, from pink flamingoes, to Jesus statues scattered across the yard with piles of dog shit here and there. Her mom was a severe Catholic, and her main hobby was damning anyone she didn't like to hell. She carried around holy water in a little flask, and often used it as a weapon. She tried bargaining with a clerk from Walmart, and ended up in court for attacking the poor lady. Her mom also enjoyed balancing the bible translated in different languages on her head... she was a peculiar one.

Within the house was a scene from a horror movie. The floorboards creaked, candles lined the walls, and the furniture was from the 1940's- not to mention, bug infested. The mother at least allowed Kasay to express herself by decorating her bedroom...

Kasay's room was completely black. From the walls to the carpet, from the ceiling to the furniture. Hell, she even spray painted her toilet seat black.... unless she was lying and it was just really old stool.

"Are you sure she'll like me? I mean- I'm a strange guy randomly talking to her- what if she thinks I'm a weirdo?!"

"She has no right to call you a weirdo, especially with the way she acts."

"But what if-"

"Cut it out and grow a pair! Just come!" I got out of the car. My annoying ankle was still bandaged, though it no longer hurt, even when I fell. I walked up confidently to the front door and knocked on it.

Dustin stayed in the car, still too afraid to come out. He truly wanted to impress her.

The door swung open, revealing Kasay's mother. She was a middle aged woman dressed in a nun robe... as in- a bath robe with the word 'nun' written on it...

"Hi!" I chirped cheerfully. It was best to get on her good side.

"What do you want?" She asked crankily.

"I'm here to see Kasay-"

"Request denied," she slammed the door in my face.

I knocked on the door again, "Hi ma'am, I'm here take Kasay to bible study class." I was getting good at lying.

"She's being punished right now, come another day." Once again, she slammed the door in my face.

I knocked once again, this time she was holding a bible in her hand, "listen here, Kasay has her own private bible study classes in here," she jabbed a finger on her bible. When she looked back up, she observed my face. She recognized me, "YOU!" She gasped. "YOU GOT KASAY EXPELLED!"

"WHAT?! NO!"

"SATAN!" she started shrieking, "SATAN'S CHILD!" She hissed like a cat.

With that, she slammed the door in my face, and I heard a series of locks behind the door. What the hell just happened? I stared at the door, still registering what just happened. A bathroom sink was thrown out of the second floor shattered window, and landed close to me. Luckily, I jumped out of the way in time. The sink broke and landed on a statue of the virgin Mary.

Kasay's crazy mother started screaming from the second floor, "YOU DEVIL WORSHIPPER! YOU TRIED KILLING MARY!"

I scurried away quickly before she was able to kill me, I whispered a quick, "I'm so sorry," to the broken statue of Mary as respect.

"Did I just really witness that?" Dustin was visibly shaken by the drama he had witnessed.

"She's kinda' insane."

"So… Kasay's stuck in there?"

I nodded, and thought about what she said. Did I really get her expelled? If I hadn't been friends with her, Layla probably never would've noticed her, and she wouldn't have gotten in so much trouble to the point she got expelled.

"Did I really cause it?" I whispered to myself more than anything.

"Cause what?" Dustin asked, visibly worried.

"Her to get expelled-"

I didn't even get to finish my sentence, he interrupted me first, "NO! Of course not!"

I covered my face with my hands and let a few tears fall, " she said it was..." Maybe Ricky was right... I should've just saved everyone the trouble and slit my wrists.

He reached over to my face and tucked a strand piece of hair behind my ear gently, "it wasn't your fault, Rosie..."

"How do you know?"

"I just do."

~*~

"Rosaline Arlene Winnefred," my stepmother greeted coldly the moment I stepped into the house. She was waiting for me.

"Where were you? The school's security cameras said you left at approximately 3:48 PM sharp-"

I couldn't take it. I truly couldn't take it anymore. I couldn't take being pushed around by her. "YOU'RE NOT MY MOM, GET OUT OF MY LIFE!" She tried grabbing my wrist with her sharp nails, but I pulled it away, not caring if her nails dug into my skin or not. I didn't realize I had started crying until the tears blurred my vision. "STOP PRETENDING YOU CARE, BECAUSE YOU DON'T!"I screamed, running upstairs.

Once I got inside, I locked the door behind me. I ran to the shower, stripped all my clothes off and turned on the scalding hot water. What the hell was wrong with me? I groaned and banged my head against the wall tiles in my bathroom.

I calmed myself to the thought that if Axel could get through the hurdles his stepfather threw at him... then I could too.

~*~

I went extreme extents to avoid facing my stepmother. I got out of bed at 4:30AM, and got ready by 5. Before leaving, I grabbed a couple of pop tarts from the kitchen. I had missed dinner the night before, so I was starving. I managed to get a hold of her purse which was filled with cash, so I snatched a few hundred dollars from it.

I didn't count it as stealing; it belonged to my father anyway. If I didn't spend it, she'd spend it on her ridiculously expensive brand named purses and manicure.

Luckily, Jaxon's parents were out of town, so I managed to sneak in. To my surprise, he was already awake.

"From my guess young lady, you are here because you are avoiding Cleo," he faked a British accent. I stuck two pop tarts in his toaster.

"You are right, sir. What are you doing up so early?"

"Gotta' wake up early to practice my acting."

Jaxon was dressed in a pair of dark jeans and a bright orange t-shirt. His hair was of course, styled with gel... I sniffed the air and gave him a funny look. "Why do you smell like..." I couldn't pin point the smell.

He sniffed himself, "like what?"

"A bit like... fruit punch?"

"Oh, it's my new fruit punch cologne!" He said, overly enthusiastic.

I gasped jokingly, "you didn't tell me you were gay!"

"I'm not!"

"Who's the girl? Or guy for that matter?" I winked.

He started blushing. HO HO HO!

"Start spilling young man!" I put my hot pop tarts into a plate.

His cheerful expression turned into a pained one.

"Uh, Jaxon?" I called out, but he didn't even look up at me, "what's wrong?"

He hadn't acted this way since he was a kid, right before he admitted to his mom that he used her toothbrush to scrub a stray dog's mouth.

"It's nothing, really."

I decided not to push him any further. I knew the best thing to do at the moment was to shut up. He did something he wasn't proud of, and I didn't want to stress him further.

I had my own shit to figure out.

~*~

Chapter 17 DISCIPLINE REFERRAL [Day 2]

I walked to the school's office, since the principal had notified me that I had to sign in before I went to I.S.S. I walked up to a random teacher in the office.

"Excuse me, but where do I sigh in before I go to I.S.S?" I asked politely.

The teacher scowled at me and pointed at the old secretary. I mentally rolled my eyes, not her again. I stomped up to her desk. She was doing work and writing again, totally unaware of me standing in front of her.

I cleared my throat, but of course she totally ignored me. I tapped my foot impatiently and tapped her desk impatiently. I cleared my throat again.

"Excuse me," I said trying to sound patient.

She ignored me again. I felt like groaning in frustration, but I knew I couldn't. I stood there tapping on her desk with my fingernails. She sighed and finally looked up to me looking bored out of her mind.

"Um, excuse me. I got a Discipline Referral-"

"Good for you," she interrupted sarcastically and went back to her work.

I should've known she was going to say that.

"Excuse me, but where do I sign in? I mean, before I go to I.S.S?" I asked politely.

"Where do you think?" She replied rudely without looking up to look at me.

I groaned aloud in frustration. Not again.

"Ma'am, please! I really need to know." I was as polite as I could've been.

She looked up and gave me a flat look, before going back to her work. Heartless bitch. I noticed a whiteboard marker on her desk, so being the nice nerd I was, I took it and helped her sign me in. I pushed her aside, and wrote 'ROSALINE SIGNING IN' on her computer screen. With that, I tossed the marker on her lap as she stared at me in shock, and I walked straight out of the office.

I couldn't care less if I got in more trouble.

I walked straight to the I.S.S room. As I walked in, I was greeted with a paper ball flying straight at my head.

Luckily, I ducked right in time. If only I could duck like that in P.E…

The paper ball flew out the door and hit a random person outside. I quickly shut the door behind me and scanned the room. Ricky was throwing paper balls all over the place while Justin was grinning at his phone like an idiot.

Axel was nowhere to be seen and the teacher who was supposed to be watching us was sleeping on his desk just like yesterday with his earphones plugged into his ears. No wonder these guys didn't mind in school suspension at all.

I walked to the desk I sat at yesterday and slumped into my seat. There were no other windows in the room besides from the small one on the balcony door, and I was bored out of my mind. There were only stupid posters around the room about discipline and crap like that.

There was absolutely nothing to do, so I decided to take a little nap. I laid my head down on the desk and covered my head with my arms.

Smack!

Smack!

Smack!

My eyes shot open immediately. I lifted my head up to see what it was. Ricky was aiming the paper balls at me. When he saw me looking at him, he gave me a sheepish smile and started aiming them at Justin who gave him the finger.

Ricky then sighed and walked over to me. I tried to ignore him but he sat on my desk and leveled his face inches away from mine.

"Watcha' doing?" he asked.

I just ignored him and avoided eye contact.

"You're ignoring me."

I ignored him again and looked around the room. Why did they allow to let students get this bored?

"Why are you ignoring me?" he pouted.

I didn't bother to reply.

"Rosaline."

I kept ignoring him. I still remembered every word he said to me.

"Rosie?"

Don't give in.

He made a puppy face that every girl would fall for, one that even I fell for once. But never again would I be that stupid and ignorant to fall for a stupid player like him.

I thought it was my fault at first.

I thought that I didn't please him enough.

I thought about going back and begging for him, even after I dumped him, but thankfully Jaxon talked some sense into me. Jaxon was always there for me. Through my ups and downs.

He was kind of like the brother I never had. But I was attracted to him. He was undeniably cute and adorable, but I had a thing for bad boys... specifically Axel.

But he did have a reason for being bad. He just wanted his mom to leave the step dad, and wanted to go live with his dad, that's all. Back to California. I frowned at the thought. He couldn't go back...

He was mine, yet he wasn't.

I shook my head to clear my thoughts. No he couldn't move back. His mom was keeping him here and there was no way he was going back. A pair of fingers snapped in front of my face, pulling me out of my thoughts.

I shook my head and looked up. Ricky was looking down at me with a guilty expression on his face. He gave me a sad smile and gave me a questioning look. I cocked an eyebrow at him.

"So, what do you think?" he asked hesitantly.

"Think about what?"

"What I just said," he replied in a 'duh' tone.

"Uh, I-I-"

"You weren't listening…"

Why was I so afraid of admitting that? "You knew," I laughed nervously. Why couldn't I just tell him up front I didn't give a damn about what he had to say?

"Rosaline… I know you like I know the back of my hand."

I backed away and shook my head, "you assume you do, but you don't. You don't know a damn thing about me."

"Your favorite color is blue, your best friend is Jaxon-"

"Anyone could guess that, Ricky. That's not going to get you in my pants- nothing will."

"Let me finish what I have to say," he snapped. "You hate your stepmom, your real mom left when you were small, you're rich as hell because your dad works all the time, and you're becoming a rebel because of how strict your stepmom is."

Did my ex boyfriend just try to summarize who I was in one short paragraph?

"You only have two friends, you like reading cringey romance novels, you're too afraid to talk to guys, and you're closed as fuck- it's quite annoying actually."

"You've only scratched the surface."

Before Ricky could say another word, Axel appeared out of nowhere. He was wearing a pair of dark jeans and a white tee which clung tightly onto his perfectly sculpted body.

He gave me a small smile and sat down in his usual seat. His eyes looked at me with… sympathy? Did he feel sorry for me? How much did he actually hear? Comparing both our lives, I'm not sure whose life was sadder. I looked back at Ricky.

His grayish-bluish eyes were pleading into mine. Why did he want another chance all of a sudden? I fell for them many times, and I promised myself never again. I forced myself to brushed off the fact that he knew and remembered a few facts about me and smirked cruelly at him.

"And I know a thing or two about you too. You don't care about anyone. You're observant, you pretend you care, but you don't. You don't care about anything unless it benefits you in some way. You use girls for sex, and you use guys for popularity and to hook you up. You're a pathetic excuse for a guy. You're a fuckboy."

His mouth was in an 'O' shape, and his eyes flashed with nothing but anger and hatred. He narrowed his eyes at me and moved closer to me, but someone stopped him.

"Get any closer to the girl and you won't be able to fuck another chick for the rest of your life."

The voice gave me butterflies and made my heart pound against my chest crazily. I turned around to look at Axel. His intensely green eyes were narrowed at Ricky and his body was in a striking position. He was ready to bounce right off his seat and beat the living shit out of Ricky.

"What are you going to do? Knee me in the balls like she did?" He laughed.

Axel kept his eyes narrowed at Ricky and smirked.

"I thought you didn't have any."

Ricky's jaw dropped to the floor. A small giggle escaped my lips before I contained it. Axel's lip perked up a bit, before returning to its serious position. Ricky kept his glare on Axel.

He then shut his mouth and balled up his fists to his sides. Axel lounged in his seat and folded his arms behind his head. He swung his feet onto the desk then sighed while looking up at Ricky.

"Thinking of a comeback pretty boy? I can just hear the gears grinding up inside your little head of yours."

140

Ricky eyes held nothing but hatred now. His face was red as a tomato and his fists were balled up on his sides.

"Say another word and you're going down, pussy." He hissed through his teeth.

Axel yawned lazily and stretched a little.

"How long did it take you to come up with that? A day? Two days? A week-"

Ricky cut him off, "shut the fuck up! I don't want to have a problem with you; I'm just here to talk to the nerd."

"You pick on her; you have a problem with me. Leave her alone," his tone was so threatening.

Ricky glared at Axel, "What the fuck is your problem? Why is she so important to you?"

"She isn't," Axel replied simply.

My heart shattered. My stomach twisted painfully. No, I couldn't cry in front of them.

"Then why are you helping her?" Ricky asked raising an eyebrow.

Axel got onto his feet, "because I feel like it."

"You're just trying to get some."

"I'm not like you. I don't fuck anyone."

Ricky laughed, "pussy!"

"Quit reminding us, we get it. You have one."

Ricky looked like he was about to attack Axel. Even though Ricky was a bit taller than Axel, Axel was more toned, far more experienced, and overall just stronger. I glanced at Justin from the corner of my eye.

Justin was sitting on a desk watching them both amusingly. I backed away from both of them slowly. A low growl escaped Ricky's mouth as he lunged for Axel. Axel slipped out of his seat and missed Ricky's lunge.

Ricky fell into the desks and groaned in pain. Axel shook his head chuckling at how pathetic Ricky was. A low chuckle escaped Justin's lips, before Ricky shot Justin a glare to shut him up.

"Come at me, big boy," Axel's tone was menacing.

Ricky's face turned redder than it was at first from anger, as he lunged for Axel the second time. Axel just simply stepped out of the way and let Ricky hit the floor in full force. Ricky winced again as Axel chuckled at his stupidity.

A small giggle escaped my mouth as Axel turned around and smiled proudly. He slung an arm around my shoulder and gestured his hand towards all the desks that were knocked down by Ricky. My breath got caught in my lungs.

"And that is why you don't fuck with me if you don't have brain cells," Axel laughed.

His arm around my shoulder made my heart pound against my chest crazily. The thought of his arm slung around my shoulder made my cheeks heat up furiously. Suddenly, someone crashed into Axel from behind.

Axel lost balance and pulled me down with him. In most of the cheesy romance novels I've read, the girl's supposed to land on top of the guy or the guy lands on top of the boy and they stare at each other. But of course, my life was no love story.

Instead of landing on top of Axel, or Axel landing on top of me, Ricky landed right on top of me. His muscular chest was right in my face. I tried to move but I couldn't, he was too heavy. My still bandaged foot wasn't helping either.

The pressure of Ricky on top of my ankle, made me wince. The amount of pain it made me feel almost made me scream. Axel pulled Ricky off me in a swift move. Axel had a bloody lip making him look completely badass. His hair was messed up and his shirt was stained with drops of blood from his mouth. Axel positioned himself on top of Ricky as Ricky struggled to get loose.

Axel wasted no time as he griped Ricky's shirt collar and threw his first punch at Ricky's face. A loud crack was heard, and Ricky's nose started bleeding almost immediately. Axel kept throwing punches at Ricky until Ricky was knocked out cold. I screamed for him to stop but he wouldn't.

Justin was in a corner watching in horror as Axel beat the living shit out of Ricky. I screamed for him to stop over and over again but he just wouldn't. I forced myself up even though my ankle was still aching painfully. I rushed over to Axel and started pulling him away from Ricky, but Axel wouldn't budge.

His emerald green eyes no longer were hypnotizing. His green eyes were hard showing no emotion as a cruel smirk was on his lips as he kept throwing punches at Ricky. I brought both my hands to his face and cupped his cheeks.

His grass green eyes softened as he met my eyes. He let go of Ricky's shirt collar and got up slowly. His cruel smirk was gone, but replaced with a frown. He looked down at my foot.

"You alright?" He asked, seemingly worried.

I let go of his face, nodded and gave him a small smile.

"You sure?"

I nodded frantically, "I'm sure." I reassured him.

Justin watched both of us. His ocean blue eyes were filled with horror.

Axel turned to Justin and pointed at him. "And you, my friend will say nothing about this or else," Axel threatened. Justin nodded frantically.

Justin looked so scared, he looked like he was about to crap his pants. Axel wiped the blood on his fists off on his jeans. His white shirt already had drops of blood on it; it would be pretty hard to wash off.

Focus, Rosie.

Life isn't always about washing clothes. I mentally slapped myself as Axel smiled at me. I sighed and ran my hand through my tangled blonde hair. I felt Axel's stare and blushed under it.

My heart still wouldn't calm down. I was happy of him accepting me as the nerdy Rosaline. I wonder if he really meant something by all this. A frown fell upon my face when I remember he said I wasn't important to him.

But it couldn't have been entirely true, right? Since he did help me in this situation... Axel frowned and poked my cheek. I slapped his hand away before he chuckled and shook his head.

"You're cute when you smile."

And that, ladies and gentlemen, made my heart stop.

~*~

Chapter 18 DRAMATIC

---*Jaxon's P.O.V*---

"Axel got in a fight with Ricky!" Trent screamed as he ran across the stage. The kid was an obnoxious messenger owl.

A chorus of questions were asked. He didn't answer any of them; instead he searched the crowd and stopped when his eyes met mine. He rushed over to me, obviously excited about the drama happening. He was interrupting our rehearsal.

"Dude, did you hear-?"

I interrupted the annoying guy, "the biggest asshole in school gets in another fight- woohoo- such shocking news! What do you want from me?"

"Dude," he gave me a shove, "quit being a dickhead, I'm tryna' help you here-"

I shoved him back.

"What the hell?!" he growled, "I'm only tryna' fucking help because Rosaline's involved."

At the mention of her name, my whole body tensed up. I took no time to register anything. Rosie was in trouble, and the only thing I had to do at that moment was, help her.

"Where is she?!" I asked.

I didn't notice I was yelling until some of the cast members came up to me and tried calming me down. Trent backed away from me before answering.

~*~

"Calm down and-"

I cut Justin off, "what the hell happened to Rosie?!"

"Chill! She's okay-"

"Cut the crap twin!" I growled.

Just then, the other twin rushed into the office sweating and panting crazily. He was clearly worried for my best friend; I could tell he felt the same way I did. God! I shouldn't have told Rosie about Kasay so soon and let her freak out like that.

145

If I didn't tell her in the nurse's office, she wouldn't have started freaking out and swearing at the principal like that. This meant she wouldn't have gotten the DR and got caught up in this situation…

If anything happened to her, it would be my fault. I couldn't let her get hurt. I wouldn't be able to live with myself if anything bad happened to her. I ran my hand through my hair which was currently styled with gel; fashion always mattered.

"Does anyone here know what the fuck happened to Rosie?!"

One of the twins shook his head frantically. "You don't know?"

I shook my head and buried my face into my palms. I had no idea what happened to her, but it was all my fucking fault! Her ankle was still bandaged, which worried me more. We were all gathered in the principal's office.

There were four of us here, the twins, Trent, and myself. The nicer twin was trying to calm me down as I shook with anger. The other twin was sitting in a chair playing with his hands nervously while Trent was texting on his phone.

He was probably spreading gossip about the fight. That was something Trent would definitely do. I tried getting to know the guys once, but it didn't work out. We were too different. I preferred expressing myself on the stage, and they preferred chasing a ball around outside.

I preferred being with Rosie anyway.

Rosie.

I could never quite figure her out.

I loved her dearly, but she always seemed a bit distracted.

I had tried talking to her about how I felt towards her before, but she still stayed completely oblivious. I was far too afraid to bluntly state that I liked her; I didn't want to lose her. I couldn't bear the thought of rejection or destroying our friendship.

She was my everything.

146

Over the years I had showed her how much I cared, but still, she stayed clueless. She never realized the little ginger who built sandcastles with her during recess was head over heels for her. Even after ditching everyone for her, she was still too innocent to get it.

The chase was fun, I admit... but it grew tiring.

Asking her to prom, taking her on dates, being there for her whenever she needed someone... just to get friendzoned.

Hints, clues, compliments, kind words, yet her eyes still gazed into the distance searching for someone else.

I got tired of waiting.

Since she went out with Ricky, bitterness grew inside of me. She gave that dickhead a chance, but not me?

That's when my liking for Layla grew stronger.

Layla was the prettiest and most popular girl in our school-heck in our entire town ever since she moved here. I had no chance. Girls always went for the dickheads.

Layla went straight for Axel, but he kept his eyes elsewhere.

I never understood why Axel paid no interest in such a perfect girl. Instead, he lingered a bit little too long around *my* best friend. She never noticed of course, but they would conveniently end up in the same rooms or same hallways regularly.

Axel was the biggest asshole on Earth. There was no question it. He was a player who many girls have *claimed* to have slept with, he beat up other people just because he felt like it, and he hosted the biggest parties of the year which encouraged underage drinking and drugs.

He hated me and I hated him.

I tapped my foot impatiently waiting for someone to inform us on what had happened to my Rosaline. Dustin was wiping sweat of his forehead repeatedly. I was starting to question whether or not he was interested in Rosie.

Thinking about someone else being with Rosie made my stomach churn, but thinking of someone else being with Layla made me clench my fists. I was supposed to be over Rosie, but here I was thinking about her.

She was my best friend after all.

Dustin still looked very concerned about her, too concerned.

I forced myself to calm down; it wasn't his fault if he liked her. Any guy close enough to her falls for her eventually. You could say she was Cinderella.

She was shy, cute, smart, kind and caring. She was beyond calm, and stood for things she shouldn't have. When she was younger, she had severe anger issues. I had promised not to tell anyone about this, and I had kept the promise so far.

I didn't plan on telling anyone about it, but I had to at least warn Layla. Because, if Layla kept pushing Rosie's temper, she was going to snap... and it wasn't going to be pretty.

The principal came into his office grumpily, swearing to himself. He completely ignored us as he behind his desk and pulled out a sheet of paper. He kept talking to himself as he scribbled on the piece of paper.

All of us standing in his room just stared at him, waiting for him to realize he wasn't alone. It was completely silent in there, except for the breathing and Trent's tapping on his phone. I swear to god I heard Dustin's heartbeat increase rapidly.

"Where's Rosaline?" Dustin and I asked at the same time.

We both looked at each other before turning back to the principal. The principal looked up from the paper he was scribbling down on and clicked his pen.

"How is she?" I asked.

"She's fine," he replied simply.

"Where is she?" Dustin asked eagerly. I stopped myself from glaring at him.

I needed to see her as soon as possible and apologize for getting her into this mess. My inner self told me to stop blaming myself, but I blocked it out. I needed to listen to myself, not my weird inner voice.

"In the nurse's office," he looked at me suspiciously and narrowed his eyes at me, "why?"

"I'm her best friend."

"And?"

"And I need to check on her and see if she's alright or not," I don't know why I even bothered explaining myself.

Dustin stood next to me rubbing his hands against his jeans. Just then, Axel walked into the office with drops of dried blood on his white shirt. My eyes widened, that couldn't have been hers... could it? I felt my heartbeat increase.

Describing my own heartbeat... yes, I was overly dramatic sometimes.

Axel took his time to walk over to the principal's desk and took a seat on the principal's desk. Justin was staring at him in fear, while Trent stared at him admiringly.

I had to admit, the hardest person to read was Axel. One moment, he gives you a friendly handshake, and the next moment, he knocks both your front teeth out. He was a dick and no one liked him, well all the girls certainly found him attractive.

He was lucky and was born with features that girls seemed to love. He was shorter than some of us, but he was well built. You could tell he worked out- God! I sounded beyond feminine. I swear I wasn't checking him out.

"So are we allowed to visit her sir?" Dustin asked politely.

The principal nodded and waved his hand dismissively, telling us to scram. We rushed out and started walking down the hall. I didn't notice we were actually running until Mrs. Meisty yelled at us and told us to slow down or she would write us all up.

Justin and Trent were just tagging along, probably to see and gossip of what condition she was in. Every step I took closer to the nurse's office, the harder my blood pumped through my veins. I wondered if she would get mad at me and kick me out.

I wondered if she would hate me because I technically got her caught up in this situation. I mentally punched myself; boy, I was stupid stupid. Rosie was a very forgiving person. She would never do that to me.

She needed me and loved me, and I knew it.

Maybe that was why I didn't like the idea of her having a boyfriend. Maybe it was because I didn't want her to depend on someone else that wasn't me. Maybe I liked how I was her only male friend.

Maybe, I was glad Kasay got expelled.

Because that meant I had Rosie all to myself.

~*~

---Rosie's P.O.V---

The first day of middle school...

It felt so real, just like yesterday. Jaxon and I were walking side by side. He walked me to my locker which was at the end of the hall, right by one of the smaller exits. Once I reached it, he left to go search for his own locker.

Down the call, someone caught my eye.

A boy, merely inches taller than me, standing as his locker gloomily. He was so sad; a cute frown was plastered on his face. He kept trying to open his locker, but it wouldn't open. He was starting to get aggravated. I wanted to go up to him and help him, but I was far too afraid. I kept my distance and looked at him from behind my locker door.

Then, Matt came.

He was at least 6 foot; puberty had hit him fast. The guy walked straight up to Axel and shoved him straight in his locker. Axel fell to the ground. His lip started bleeding. I witnessed the entire thing.

The blonde boy wiped his mouth with the back of his hand and stared at it. Blood was smeared all over his hand. From a distance, his face hardened. His jaw clenched. You didn't have to be close to see how his features changed in an instant.

It was like he was switching personas. I could tell how dangerous he really was when he got up from the floor and took a swing at Matt's face. Matt fell straight to the ground, and Axel took the opportunity to climb on top of him and beat the hell out of his face. Though I had never liked violence, my eyes stayed glued to the scene.

Axel stood up for himself. He refused to be pushed around. I admired him from afar.

He dared to do things I would never dare to do to the people who had hurt me; physically and mentally. He was fearless, and drop dead gorgeous.

After seeing him beat someone merciless, I should've been repulsed... but that turned me on.

My head was throbbing painfully and my ankle was aching. My eyelids felt heavy; overall I just felt unpleasant.

"She's not awake yet," the nurse said. I heard some groaning in the background.

"Please! I need to see if she's okay or not!" Jaxon's voice rang through my ears.

I heard some shuffling around and the door shutting.

"Please," it must've been Dustin, "I can promise we won't wake her up."

I heard her sigh, "fine, but if you wake her up, I'll make sure to kick all of your little buts out."

I heard some chuckling before footsteps approaching. Then I heard someone's voice I definitely didn't recognize.

"Dude, she looks dead."

Then I felt a poke on my cheek. I flinched at the warm finger.

"Dude!" Dustin hissed.

"Touch her again and you'll die," Jaxon growled.

"It's alive!" The unknown voice exclaimed in a dramatic tone.

I lifted my heavy eyelids up slowly looking at the sight before me. I was staring up at a white ceiling, before four heads blocked my view. Their faces looked blurry to me at first, but then my eyes adjusted.

Jaxon's flaming red hair stuck out first, making me notice him immediately. The next thing that came into focus was a pair of ocean blue eyes. I didn't even have to think about whom those eyes belonged to, they were definitely Dustin's.

But then, another pair of ocean blue eyes came into focus. Wait, two pairs of ocean blue eyes. Who could the other one be? I blinked twice as my eyesight adjusted again, and I saw everything clearly. Jaxon, Justin, Dustin and surprisingly, Trent were all looking down at me.

Trent was one of the last people I expected to be present. I mean- he was the 'gossip king' of the school, but I would never expect him to care enough to check up on me. Dustin and Justin were both looking worriedly at me.

Since they both had a look of slight concern on their faces, I truly couldn't tell which one was which. They were identical, from their eyes, to their noses, from their cheeks, to their lips... how did their parents tell them apart?

I slowly got up so that I was sitting on the bed. They all moved back and gave me some space as they stared at me.

Jaxon pulled me into a bone crushing hug.

He cupped my cheek and he kissed my forehead. I felt awkward because so many people were present.

"I'm so sorry," he mumbled as his thumb rubbed my cheek.

I just stared at him, utterly confused. For what? He sighed, pulling away from me. Everyone else was just watching us closely.

"I'm sorry for getting you into this situation." He mumbled quietly, but just loud enough to hear.

"You didn't get me into this situation, I got myself into this." I said studying his facial features as he ran his hand through his hair. I still didn't understand what he meant..

152

"No you didn't, I did. I shouldn't have told you about Kasay getting expelled-"

I interrupted him, "don't apologize, you didn't do anything! Never apologize for telling someone the truth."

"But-"

"No buts. If you keep blaming yourself, I'll kick you out." He looked so guilty. He brushed some of his red hair out of his eyes so he could look at me.

He looked up meeting my eyes as a small sad smile appeared on his lips. He brushed his flaming red hair out of his eyes. His hazel eyes held nothing but guilt. I avoided him and turned to the twins.

"You two look cuter when you smile," I said as an excuse.

Sure enough, one of them smiled. His left dimple told me exactly who he was.

"Dustin," I greeted, "nice of you to drop by."

Everyone besides us two were shocked.

"What the hell?" Justin asked, "what kind of witchcraft are you using?!"

"Observation," I replied.

"Heard you were in the middle of a fight," Trent started. There it was, the line which should be the shovel he could use to dig out the drama. He got up on my bed and started jumping on it like a kid.

I raised my eyebrows at him.

"So what happened to you?" He wasn't bothered by the fact he was bouncing on my bed at all.

I thought of an answer, but I couldn't. The last thing I remembered was Axel complimenting my smile... My face heat up immediately. I fainted because of a single compliment. I felt beyond embarrassed about it, so I avoided telling them about it.

"I can't exactly remember..."

Jaxon was clearly pissed about my answer. He stormed out of the room. The twins started talking amongst themselves,

153

and Trent being the childish person he was, was still bouncing up and down on the bed.

"What's up with Jaxon?" I asked the hyper boy.

Trent shrugged like it was nothing serious, "he's just going to fight Axel."

I almost stopped breathing, "WHAT?!"

He nodded, "on his way right now!"

~*~

Chapter 19 SUSPICIOUS

My blood ran cold, and my breath caught in my lungs. I felt all the blood drain from my face. Jaxon fighting Axel?! I knew they already had a problem before all this, but Jaxon was about to make the biggest mistake in his life.

What was wrong with him?!

Axel was going to kill him, LITERALLY! I had to stop them. I crawled off the bed carefully and slid both of my feet on the floor. My ankle was still aching, but I bit into my cheeks and suppressed the pain.

I had to save Jaxon before he got the living shit beat out of him. Trent grabbed my forearm quickly, stopping me from getting up.

"Woah woah woah, what's the rush?"

"I have to go stop him!"

"Why?"

Why did I have to explain? "Why do you think?!" I tried peeling his hand off of my forearm, but he refused to let go. "Let me go!" I growled, but he refused. I never like playing the sympathy card, but I had to, "Ow! Please let go, it hurts!"

Trent let go of my arm immediately. I pushed him onto the bed as hard as I could, and ran out of the office. It hurt like hell, but I kept going. Dustin rushed to my side, "how do you even know where they are?"

I held onto his arm for support and speed walked instead of run, because my ankle just couldn't take it, "B-Hall, Axel's locker."

I could hear Trent yell from a distance.

"We need to go faster!" I complained.

He stopped, and lowered himself, "get on my back."

I was caught by surprise, "really?"

"Quickly!"

155

I hopped onto his back and hooked my arms around his neck. I secured my legs around his waist as he held onto my legs and stood up. I almost fell off.

Dustin wasted no time; he started going as fast as he could carrying me on his back. The wind whipped around my head, making my hair fly all over the place. I had to tuck my head behind his neck to stop hair from getting in my eyes.

As we entered B-Hall, I heard people chanting 'fight' over and over again.

There were people formed in a big circle blocking our view from seeing what was in the center. My hands started to get sweaty as we neared the crowd. I felt a drop of sweat roll down my back, and Dustin's body heat radiating onto mine wasn't helping either.

I patted Dustin's back telling him to stop. He put me down gently allowing me to rush over to the crowd. I pushed people out of the way trying to get through.

"Look, I don't want to hurt you." Axel said.

"FUCK YOU!" Jaxon yelled.

After a minute of apologizing to people who I pushed and shoved, I ended up in the circle. People probably thought I was a crazy nerd just sticking my nose in other people's business.

I was shocked to see there were four people in the circle. Axel was being attacked by Jaxon and his two friends. My mouth fell open in horror, there was blood splattered all over the floor.

A random girl nudged me, "it was four against one, but Axel already took one down." Why was she so excited about Axel getting attacked?!

Jaxon's flaming red hair was wet from sweat and his face was smeared in blood. The smell made my stomach churn. Jaxon had a large bruise forming on his jawline and a black eye forming while Axel had a small cut on his lip.

One of Jaxon's friends lunged for Axel, but Axel grabbed him and twisted his arm until there was a crack. The guy cried out in pain. Just then, Jaxon and the other guy knocked Axel down while he was distracted. Jaxon positioned himself on top of Axel as I screamed for them to stop. The other guy grabbed the broken-armed one and helped him out of the circle.

As Jaxon was about to throw a punch at Axel's face, Axel somehow knocked Jaxon off of him and switched places. Axel was now positioned on top of Jaxon preparing to throw another punch at Jaxon. The guy came back into the circle and yanked Axel's hair, catching him off guard. Axel fell backwards, banging his head against the tiles of the floor.

"STOP!" I screamed, but the chants were too loud.

Jaxon got on top of him and started throwing punches at him. As Jaxon was about to hit Axel again, Axel grabbed his fist in mid air before it could hit him. He squeezed it and twisted it making Jaxon groaned in pain.

I kept screaming for them to stop, but they completely ignored me and kept fighting. I couldn't stand seeing the two guys I loved most hurting each other. I tried pulling Jaxon off of Axel, but he wouldn't budge.

Axel's emerald eyes met mine.

That's when the tables turned.

Axel spun him around and got on top of Jaxon. With one hand on Jax's throat, he knocked the other guy out with the other hand. He beat Jaxon over and over again, even when Jaxon was knocked out cold. Jaxon's face was bloodied, almost lifeless.

The bad boy's eyes were cold and held no emotion. A cruel smirk tugged at his lips as I backed away from him. The person in front of me was not the Axel I had met the other night. This Axel in front of me was cold blooded with no conscience.

His face scared me. I didn't want to go anywhere near him. He threw punch after punch at Jaxon's face, until Jaxon was knocked out cold. I don't know what got into me, but a burst of confident flooded me. I had to stop him from killing my best friend.

I yanked Axel's arm, but he didn't even flinch. It stayed in its position as he continued to beat the life out of Jaxon. My fingers felt hot against his skin, I was touching him. But I was too freaked out to enjoy it. I kept yanking on him, but he didn't even turn to look at me. I screamed until my voice ran out.

I couldn't stand it anymore, I couldn't stand seeing my childhood best friend unconscious and covered in blood. I jumped onto Jaxon and sheltered his body with mine. I half expected to get hit, but I didn't. I looked back up at Axel.

His hard eyes met mine.

Everyone had stopped cheering, it was almost completely silent.

He placed a hand on my waist, and tried gently moving me out of the way, but I refused to budge.

"NO!" I screamed at him.

But he still tried to move me.

I did the unthinkable.

I brought my hand up and slapped him across the face.

Some people in the crowd gasped.

Axel glared down at me for a solid moment. He was... hurt? Disappointed?

Realization struck me like a bullet in the chest.

I had slapped the guy I had admired from afar since day one.

I wanted to apologize and beg him for forgiveness. He had defended himself after all... but he should've stopped when Jaxon was out, yet he still continued. He was outnumbered, but brutally beat them.

I felt like I had ruined my entire life.

I could've called the teacher to pull them apart- well they probably wouldn't be capable of doing so, but they'd at least call security. Instead, I had to get myself involved and ruin my chances with Axel by hitting him.

But if I didn't hit him, who would've stopped him from killing Jaxon?

Jaxon was lying there in a small pool of blood on the floor, his chest moving up and down slowly. Axel's eyes drifted to Jaxon's body before he looked down refusing to meet mine. The crowd around us stayed completely silent.

Axel looked up again, but this time his emerald green eyes were filled with anger and misery. He got up off the ground and glared at me.

"Thanks for enlightening my fucking day," he spat out sarcastically before walking away. The crowd parted for him as he left.

I felt my heart break into a million pieces. What did I just do?

~*~

"Are you sure you're alright?" the nurse asked for the thousandth time.

I sighed and smiled at her sweetly. She was such a kind woman, but she was a little too worrying sometimes.

"I really am, thank you for checking." I replied politely.

She nodded and gave me a small smile before walking back over to her desk. I watched Jaxon in awe. He was utterly adorable. His features looked so calm when he was asleep.His flaming red hair was dried off and his face was wiped clean.

All the blood from earlier was completely gone. He had a black eye and a bruise on his jawline. His pale lips were formed in a straight line.

I might've sounded creepy describing how adorable my best friend looked when he was knocked out cold, but if you were in my situation, you would too.

My eyes drifted over to his chest before I mentally slapped myself. Day dreaming about my best friend was a no-no! I sighed as I started thinking about Axel again.

Axel.

The only name that could make my heart flutter and give me butterflies.

The only name that could make my face heat up. There was no one who could make my heart beat faster than him.

Axel Storm Spencer.

The guy who beat up my ex boyfriend and my best friend in the same week. I don't know whether I should be the one apologizing to him, or he should be the one apologizing to me.

My life was so messed up. I was supposed to be in I.S.S, but ended up in the nurse's office because I fainted when I received a compliment. Then my best friend got in a fight with the guy I was head over heels for. At the end of the day, I ended up in the nurse's office again, watching over my best friend who was knocked out cold by my crush.

I buried my face into my palms and tried to calm myself. Could life get any worse?!

I couldn't stop thinking about Axel.

I desperately wanted to talk to him.

Suddenly, the nurse's office door flew open revealing none other than Layla. Oh shit, karma proved me wrong.

Life could get worse.

Layla rushed into the office and started talking to the nurse. The nurse nodded in our direction, before Layla rushed over to us. I looked up at her expecting her to say something rude to me, but surprisingly, she didn't.

She put her palm on Jaxon's forehead before behind down and pressing her ear against his chest.

What the hell?

Was I missing something?

I was completely baffled.

Why was she touching him like that?

Did he know?

Did he give her consent?

Why wasn't she bullying me?

How the hell were they connected in any way?

Layla looked at me with a blank expression on her face.

"I'm not here to make your life a living hell," she stated, "I'm here to check on him, so if you excuse us," she looked gestured over to the door- asking me to leave.

My mouth fell open.

I scurried out of the nurse's office.

Why wasn't she mean to me?

I was honestly expecting at least a rude remark from her, but I got... nothing?

I left school rethinking everything.

Was she finally growing a heart inside that empty rib cage of hers?

~*~

"But what if she doesn't like me?!"

"Dustin! You do not have to worry about a thing! She'll love you!" I exclaimed throwing both my hands up into the air.

"What if-"

"Cut it with the what if's! She will love you! I've known her since sixth grade." I sounded like I was trying to reassure myself rather than him.

"But-"

I interrupted him once again, "no buts! She will love you." I got out of his car and slammed the door shut.

Kasay had agreed to sneak out so that we could talk about everything that happened. And I thought it would be a great chance for Dustin to get to know Kasay too! I was playing Cupid here. I went up to her front door and texted her.

I'm here. –Rosie

My phone beeped in reply almost immediately.

Ugh! Finally!!!xXxX ~KasayxP

I jumped when the front door opened. Kasay got out and shut the door quickly and quietly. She held her index finger up to her lips motioning for me to be quiet. I nodded as we both walked over to Dustin's car.

"Whose car is this?" Kasay asked as I opened the back door and slid in.

"It's one of the twin's car. I'm sitting in the back, so you should sit in the front."

She nodded and slipped into the front seat. She turned to meet him before she let out a small shriek and backed away from him.

"What's wrong?!" I asked.

He looked completely shocked from her sudden outburst. He backed away until his head hit the car's ceiling. Kasay started hitting the car's windows trying to get out. I grabbed her by the shoulders making her stop.

"It's thing number one.." she said quietly.

I laughed to myself before shaking my head at how she was acting.

"Firstly his name is Dustin," I started. "As you already know, he's one of two twins. The one you might be thinking about is the asshole, this is the nice one." I explained.

She stayed completely silent.

"He's very sweet, very kind, and caring. You'll like him, trust me."

I nodded, giving Dustin the green light.

Dustin extended his hand out to her for her to shake. She looked down at it, unsure whether to take it or not. Finally, after staring at it for a solid minute, she grabbed it and shook it. I could tell she was squeezing hard on his hand, because his face was clearly in pain.

She was enjoying every minute of it. She grinned as she squeezed harder onto his hand making him wince aloud. I slapped her shoulder and gave her a don't-you-dare look before she let go and laughed.

"So," Kasay started grinning at him, "nice to finally meet you, Rosaline's crush!"

~*~

Chapter 20 KASAY'S WAY

Dustin looked utterly confused.

"No!" I exclaimed to prevent any further misunderstandings.

An evil little smile tugged at her lips.

"Sure," she said in a disbelieving tone.

I gave her a flat look.

"What?" she played innocent.

"He's not my crush-"

She gasped, "he's your boyfriend?! CONGRATS!"

"NO!" Dustin and I exclaimed at the same time.

Dustin played with the collar of his shirt uncomfortably.

"Sure," she smirked.

"I'm serious, we're not dating."

She kept smirking, "uh huh."

"You don't believe us?"

"Us?" she winked.

I groaned in frustration.

Kasay just loved teasing me about boys or getting information about who I liked, but she' always failed to find out. I knew exactly what's going on in her head right now.

"Cut the crap Kasay," I snapped.

She jerked back and hit her head against the car ceiling.

"Damn! You on your period or something? No need to be so harsh."

I sighed and leaned against the back seat.

"And if it's not true, why so aggressive?" she smiled.

I sighed again and buried my face into my palms.

"Sorry for being a total bitch."

She smiled and nodded, accepting my apology.

"How was your day?"

"Peachy," I replied.

I almost forgot Dustin was there until he cleared his throat.

"Ladies, where are we going?" Dustin asked politely.

"The mall," Kasay answered.

He glanced over at me to make sure I agreed, "wherever she says."

~*~

"I don't get it, so what is it are you depressed about in this thingy?" Kasay asked again for the hundredth time.

I groaned in frustration. I told Kasay about how I got suspended again for 'accidentally' throwing a book at someone's head, then I told her about Ricky, and how Jaxon got the living shit beat out of him... but I didn't have the guts to tell her who did it.

"Rosie, you've got to tell her the whole story if you want to get if off your chest," Dustin said, looking at me straight in the eyes.

His ocean blue eyes found a way to break a barrier I was holding up down. He was right, but he was the only soul who knew about how much I liked Axel, apart from me.

"Rosie, what are you hiding from me in that little head of yours?" Kasay questioned putting a finger on her chin pretending to think.

I rolled my eyes and took a sip of my latte which was sitting on the table. Dustin ran a hand through his hair before he looked up at me.

"Can I please excuse myself to give Rosie a little prep talk?" he asked Kasay politely.

She had a weird look on her face from the language he chose to use with her, and then nodded. Dustin had been acting really odd with Kasay. It was like he was becoming someone he wasn't just for her. He was acting like a guy from the 1950's... it was just peculiar.

If I were her, I'd find it pretty creepy to have a teenage guy talk to you like he's an old professor. I would even think he

165

was possessed by an evil demon of some sort. Dustin got up from his seat and motioned for me to follow him.

After exchanging weird looks with Kasay, I got up from my comfy seat and followed Dustin outside of the coffee shop. When we were a few shops away, he turned around to face me.

"Rosie, if you want her to help you with your problems, you've got to tell her everything."

"You don't get it, I can't!"

He shook his head, "you can, you're just choosing not to."

"It's not that simple! She'll think..." I trailed off.

"What are you afraid of? That she'll see you differently? She's your friend, Rose. There's nothing to be afraid of."

"But-"

"No buts," he interrupted me. "What is there to be afraid of? She seems really trust worthy and I'm sure she won't tell anyone about how you're in love with-"

"Shut up!" I hissed. "We're in public."

"Sorry," he lowered his voice. "But I mean, what is there to be afraid of? The only person who knows about your whole situation and how you're in love with Axel is me. No one else. It wouldn't hurt for you to tell her instead of keeping her in the dark. Secrets make friends, right?"

"She's already my friend."

"Doesn't she tell you everything about her life?"

"Well I'm starting to doubt she does."

"That's beside the point. I just think she's been your close friend long enough she deserves to know."

I sighed giving up.

"Fine, I'll tell her."

The edges of his lips curved upwards forming a smile showing off his left dimple.

"Then, I guess we should head back!" he grinned, getting a heads start back to the shop.

"Wait."

He stopped walking.

"Why do you act that way when you're with Kasay?" I asked.

He looked confused, "act like what?"

"You talk like a guy straight out of the 50's."

He furrowed his eyebrows.

"Your choice of language is just odd. You talk like an old man, and a creepy one too" I tried explaining.

"I do?"

I nodded.

"I thought Kasay would like a gentleman."

I shook my head. "You couldn't be more wrong, but even if she did, she wouldn't understand what you're talking about. She doesn't even understand basic vocabulary. Do you really think she'd understand half of the words you've said today?

"Then what kind of guys does she like?" he asked.

I took a moment to think. What kind of guys did she really like?

I had never seen her with the same guy longer than a month. Wait, no.

I had never seen her with the same guy longer than two weeks.

From what I had gathered, she had never taken a relationship seriously. I guess she liked easy going guys that didn't complain, and guys who were older than her. She seems to like guys who were free and allowed her the freedom she wanted. The kind of guys who didn't want commitment.

She liked guys who slept around, guys with experience. Guys who couldn't stay with one girl too long, guys who wanted a no strings attached kind of thing.

A light bulb lit in my head, "she likes assholes."

Dustin's smile vanished off of his face.

"Assholes?"

I nodded in confirmation.

"So... she'll like me if I act like an asshole?"

167

"Well, you have to be a specific kind of asshole- not just any random asshole like your brother."

"Assholes," he repeated again, "not being cocky, but I'm probably the nicest guy I know."

"You're one of the nicest guys I know too."

"Do I have any 'asshole' qualities in me?" He seemed a bit hopeful.

"Definitely not," the answer slipped out of my mouth before I could stop it. "But, there have been exceptions…" I thought back to the orthodontist dude who temporarily ruined my teeth. He wasn't that bad to her. "Just be yourself. If she likes you, she likes you. If she doesn't, she doesn't. Rather her like you for who you are, than like you for who you're not."

He smiled. We shared a moment of peaceful silence, before he excused himself to the bathroom.

I made my way back to Kasay.

"It's about time you came back," she huffed.

I took a deep breath, "I have something to tell you."

"You kissed him didn't you."

What?

"I KNEW IT! I KNEW YOU TWO HAD A THING!" she fist pumped the air, "MY INSTINCTS ARE ALWAYS RIGHT-"

"Kasay-"

"MIXED BABIES ARE SO ADORABLE! I SWEAR I'LL BABYSIT IF I'M NOT IN JAIL-"

"Kasay-"

"I'M SO PROUD OF YOU, HE'S NOT UGLY EITHER-"

"KASAY!"

She stopped talking and blinked at me twice.

"I don't like him!"

"What?"

I sighed, "I have something to tell you. Please don't interrupt this time."

She made a zipping motion over her mouth, and nodded.

"Remember how I said I didn't like anyone? Well... lied."
She started squealing aloud, causing some nearby people to turn and glare at us. She placed both hands on my shoulders and shook my fragile body.

"Who is it?! Who's the lucky bastard?!"
I grabbed both of her hands and pulled them off of my shoulders.

"Calm down."
She was far too excited, and I was far too nervous.

"I can't! I mean- this is so exciting! I really need to know who it is!" She bounced up and down excitedly. It reminded me a tad bit of Trent. "Now TELL ME ALREADY! Who's the bitch?!"

Getting the name out of my mouth was a lot harder than I had anticipated. I had to practically pry myself open to get a single word out. So I just didn't.

"It's the same person who beat up Jaxon..."
Her excited grin turned upside down, literally. She kept her eyes glued to me. I decided to keep talking even though she was completely silent.

"The first time I talked to him was at the dance.... but I was someone else. The first time talking to him as Rosaline," I gestured down to my nerdy self, "was in I.S.S, he didn't know I was the girl he met at the dance..."

Her lips were slightly parted as an unknown emotion shone in her eyes. I kept going on with the story anyway.

"I passed out after he beat the living shit out of Ricky and ended up at the nurse's office. Jaxon then misunderstood and thought he had caused it by hurting me, so Jax gathered a few people to try to jump him. But he was stronger and beat the living shit out of Jaxon too..." I trailed off.

"Rosie, I have a question," she lifted her index finger up.
I nodded for her to continue.

"This guy you're talking about."
I nodded for her to continue again.

169

"Is he hot?"

I blushed a little and nodded.

"He's a blonde… right?"

I nodded again. This time, she sucked in a deep breath and looking very concerned..

"Is this guy… Axel Storm Spencer?"

Silence.

After a few moments of silence, she broke the silence.

All her excitement was gone, "I'll take that as a yes," she said, placing both hands on her lap and avoiding eye contact. Her reaction wasn't a positive one.

"So, what do you think?"

Another moment of silence passed between us.

"Honestly?" she questioned.

I nodded frantically.

"I never expected you to like someone like him. I mean, he's your polar opposite; he fights, you're too scared to do anything, he's violent, you're obviously not, and he's just brutal. Sure he's hot, but he's trouble. He doesn't seem to care for anyone but himself."

"But you don't know him-"

"Neither do you," she interrupted me. "It's just a crush, it'll fade eventually."

I wanted to speak up about liking him for years, but I knew she'd probably shit on me for not telling her. "I talked to him Kasay… alone. He's not how you described-"

"One conversation doesn't change who he is."

"But maybe who he truly is isn't what he chooses to let other people see-"

She interrupted me once again, "you're defending someone you barely know. Don't let it bite you in the ass."

I wanted to tell her I knew him. I knew him quite well, probably far better than anyone else. The fact he opened up to me gave me hope. I had always seen vulnerability within those green eyes.

"You're inexperienced," she stated the obvious, "look what happened last time. I'm sorry, I just don't see it working-"

"Kasay, he defended me."

That seemed to hit her.

"He told Ricky 'if you mess with her, you mess with me too'."

She stared at me blankly.

"To be completely honest, Axel doesn't deserve you."

I felt disappointed. I was expecting her to help me with this, or at least try to support it. But instead, she was against it. She was like the others in a way; judging him based off of his past actions. I was expecting her to be more open minded. I thought she'd be the one screaming, 'YOUR BABIES WOULD BE SO ADORABLE!!!'

She sighed, "honestly, I'm torn. I don't know what to do."

I bit my lip.

"Even though he's a complete asshole, I'm your friend. If you're confident in your judgment, then I will try to help you."

A grin spread across my face. That was the Kasay I knew. I hugged her tightly, "thank you Kasay, thank you! You won't regret it!" I pulled away excitedly, "I'll prove you wrong about him. I know he's a good guy."

"I hope you're right," she patted my head like I was her puppy, "I'll help you in whatever way I can."

Suddenly, she smirked, "you know if he were to knock you up, your kids would be adorable as fuck!"

My mouth was hung open in shock as she laughed hysterically. Why was I even surprised? After a few minutes of her laughing and rolling around the floor with the cashier in the coffee shop looking at her like she was nuts, Dustin came back.

"What'd I miss?" Dustin questioned, watching Kasay roll around the floor like a mental patient.

"A lot," I replied, still staring at the girl.

"Oh by the way, guess who I ran into," he wiggled his eyebrows.

I stared at him with wide eyes, he smirked and nodded.

"And I know exactly where he's going tonight."

"I thought the stalking was my job," I lowered my voice to make the joke which Kasay wouldn't understand.

He chuckled, "he's going to a party tonight. I ran into him in the guy's bathroom."

"Who's party?"

"Not sure, he just told me he was gonna' get wasted."

"I GOT AN INVITE!" Kasay squealed, getting off of the ground. The girl had amazing hearing. "I GOT AN INVITE FROM SOME COLLEGE GUYS WHO ARE GOING!"

Dustin looked slightly concerned and the mention of college guys.

"You're going!" she grabbed me by the shoulders and shook me.

"As much as I want to see him, I can' t go, I'm grounded."

Kasay snorted out loud. "Grounded my ass. That didn't stop you from coming to the mall with us! Oh, and I have this red dress that will fit you perfectly! It's tiny, I wore it when I was like nine, but it'll fit you! It was for my uncle's wedding- I was kicked out for arousing the old men-"

"We didn't need to know that…" I trailed off.

She continued, completely ignoring me, "I also have some of that dark brown hair coloring left-"

"Kasay, I'm not going!" I interrupted her.

"Yes you are!" Kasay snapped her fingers at me. "You wanted me to help you, so I'm going to fix you up!"

~*~

Chapter 21 CINDERELLA WORE RED

"So, how do I look?" I spun around so Kasay and Dustin could get a good view of me in the dress.

"Oh my god! You look fucking stunning! I feel like I dumbass for wanting to throw it out!" Kasay squealed as she grabbed me by my shoulders and shook me.

Dustin just sat on the bed staring at me. I couldn't describe the emotion in his eyes, but it was one I've never seen before.

"Dustin," I called for him.

He shook his head clearing his thoughts and looked up at me, "what?"

"What do you think?" I asked as I spun around for me to get a view of my whole body.

His eyes scanned my body, taking in every detail carefully. I noticed a bead of sweat trickle down from his forehead to his neck. He was probably nervous about Kasay being there.

"Um, you l-look really ni-nice."

I smiled and thanked him before I sat down on the bed. Kasay grinned as she walked out of my bedroom. I groaned in frustration before burying my face in my hands.

"When's your step-mom coming home?" Dustin asked sounding worried.

I shrugged, "I'm guessing around six?"

"Where is she? I thought she worked at home."

"Well she writes her articles from home. I don't really know where she disappears to."

He nodded, acknowledging what I had said. "So we have to be out of here by five forty five, in case she comes back earlier than we expect."

"Who's using the math now?" I teased.

He flashed me a cute smile showing off his left dimple, before he shook his head and leaned against my headboard.

"I still don't know how to face him," I admitted.

"You could try to convince him to forgive you- the Rosaline you are everyday."

The corner of my lips lifted up into a small smile.

"How though? Wouldn't he be suspicious about me knowing what's going on in his life?"

"Say you're Rosaline's cousin?"

"Oh god, that'll spark up suspicion.

Dustin bit his bottom lip. "You could just hint at it, just hint at forgiving someone he's mad at. Or try telling a story about someone in a similar situation and how not forgiving someone doesn't help at all."

"I might try that," I considered.

Kasay came in holding a large pink box. It must've weighed at least ten pounds by the struggle on her face.

"What is that?"

"Your step mom's makeup kit," Kasay grinned.

"WHAT?! DO YOU HAVE A DEATH WISH?!"

It was obvious she couldn't care less. She walked over to where I was sitting and placed the makeup box beside me.

"I'm still glad I had some of that hair coloring left." Kasay beamed at me.

I touched my hair which was still a little damp. Kasay dyed my hair earlier with the hair dye left from last time. But we? We could never make it? What does she mean by that?

"Um, Kasay?"

"You're coming this time, right?"

"Of course!"

"Wouldn't people at the party know you usually hang out with me? The 'nerdy Rosaline'?"

Kasay visibly tensed up- she hadn't thought of that.

"You could have a makeover too!" Dustin suggested.

Kasay's eyes widened, "fuck no."

~*~

Stood before me was… uh… a thing with a long blonde wig which reached her waist. She wore a pink party dress which looked unfashionably tacky, (that's what I found in Cleo's closet), and her makeup was done terribly… Sure I could draw- but I couldn't do makeup. It took me a while to explain to Dustin that sketching and doing makeup were two different things.

"She looks like a drag queen…" Dustin looked horrified.

"Isn't that the point of it? We were supposed to just make her look unrecognizable?"

"She sticks out too much."

"Which means it's the perfect disguise. The more she sticks out, the less obvious it'll seem she's trying to hide her identity!"

I had confused them both.

He felt the wig, "it feels like… a broom. Why does your stepmom even own a collection of wigs?"

"Good question," I couldn't answer him.

Kasay groaned and put her hands up to her face, "I hate myself!"

"It's not you though! You can't hate it yet, you haven't seen it."

"I don't want to see; knowing you can't do makeup for shit!"

Under all the thick gothic makeup, Kasay was simply a pretty girl.

I rushed her to my bathroom so she could go look in the mirror. I stood her in front of the mirror at grinned at her. Her mouth fell open as she observed the girl in the mirror carefully.

"I'm…" she trailed off.

"Come on; if you really want to make me go we better go right now. We're gonna' be late," I rushed her.

She nodded numbly before following me out.

~*~

"And turn right! I heard it's the big cream mansion to the left," Kasay told Dustin the directions.

I sat in the back seat, leaning forward staring at where we were going. I was incredibly nervous... an odd feeling in my chest told me a lot was about to happen.

As we got closer, we could hear music pumping from blocks away. When he tried entering the street Axel lived on- he couldn't. The street was filled with cars of all types. Mostly fancy ones I might add. At the end of the dead end block stood a large cream mansion... it was far bigger than any house I had seen before.

"So it's not to the right, its right in the center," Kasay mumbled to herself.

The mansion was three stories tall with vines climbing up the sides of it. There was a large fountain in front of it which people were splashing around in.The view was breathtaking. The mansion's gates were open, allowing strangers to flood in. There was a short driveway before we could reach the mansion. The traffic was horrible, cars were lining up to drop people off or park.

Dustin gulped as he turned to us with worried eyes. Kasay was just grinning at the house as I admired it from a distance.

"Oh my god..." Dustin trailed off, looking up at the house.

"It's big isn't it?" Kasay stared up at it.

Dustin turned to both of us. "Do you realize whose house it is?"

Both of us shook our heads.

Dustin looked straight at me, "its Axel's."

I screamed, "WHAT?!" After years of stalking him, I still didn't know what his house had looked like!

"Well, that'll just make it easier! You'll be able to find him for sure!" Kasay said.

My face grew pale. Axel's house. I was attending a party at Axel's house. They had a reputation for being the wildest, the most dangerous, and the most memorable. People from around the district came. There was a rumor that a couple of guys from the NBA even showed up once...

"I can't go in there," I stated.

"You have no choice, you asked me to help."

I couldn't take her seriously with that makeup.

"I can't lie to him in his own house."

Kasay shook her head, "technically you've barely lied!"

I thought about it. I told him my name was Rose, which wasn't a lie- because it's short for Rosaline. But I did change my appearance.

"I'm still tricking him though-"

"Shut up," she rolled her eyes at the traffic, "we'll walk," she said to Dustin, before dragging me out of the car with her.

~*~

Katy Perry wasn't joking about pink flamingos in someone's yard at a party. There were pink flamingos laid out across the lawn with curse words spray painted on them. Oak trees which lined up by the driveway, were filled with toilet paper and the water in the fountain was completely red – I prayed it was food dye.

I could already tell some clever teens were at this party, (note my sarcasm). The heels were starting to hurt my ankles as we reached the front door. The front door was open letting people come and go as they please.

There were couples making out on the front steps of the mansion. I gulped as I walked through the front door. The music was pumping so loud, I felt like my eardrums were about to explode.

"Hi there, mystery girl."

I jumped immediately. Too close for my liking was a very wasted Matt. His breath smelt like at least five bottles of whiskey.

"Fuck off," Kasay growled beside me.

Matt scrunched up his face in disgust, "Jesus Christ, what are you?"

Kasay balled up her fists but kept them by her sides.

"I'm going to tell you nicely only one more time. Fuck off, asshole."

Suddenly, Layla appeared behind him. She was wearing a tight red dress which showed off her curves with matching heels. Her 'dress' was strapless and only hung to where her underwear lining was. Her bright red underwear was visible. It was too short if you asked me...

Her chocolate brown hair was wavy and reached to about her back. She had bright red lipstick on, matching her outfit.

"What's the problem here?" Layla asked as she looked between me and Matt.

I heard Kasay growl beside me.

"I'm sorry, but is my friend bugging you?" Layla asked politely.

My mouth fell open. She was acting too nice. I had to mentally remind myself, I wasn't the nerdy Rosaline, I was the Rosaline she saw at the party. The pretty one who wasn't me.

"Yes," Kasay answered for me.

"I have to apologize for him, he's a bit tipsy," Layla smiled.

Layla turned to me; her brown eyes recognized me.

"Rose, right?" she questioned.

I nodded. She flashed me a bright smile.

"Nice to see you again!" Layla beamed at me. "Look, we're almost matching!" I could sense a bit of hostility in her voice. "Usually people aren't brave enough to wear red," she laughed, "we're the only two hot enough to pull it off!" Was she tipsy?

I nodded and tried smiling, "thanks..."

She gripped Matt's arm and pulled him away from me.

"I'll see you around!" she said before pulling Matt away from us.

Kasay turned to me, completely shocked by what just happened. "I don't get it. Why is she so nice to you when you look like this, but she fucking hates you when you're Rosaline?"

I had already asked myself all those questions, so I just shrugged.

We both walked into the living room, which had literally, no furniture. All the furniture was pushed out of the way leaving a big dance floor for people to grind up against each other. Kasay grabbed me by the shoulders.

"Find Axel!" she mouthed.

I couldn't hear what she was saying because the music was so loud. They were playing Right Round by Flo-rida. There was a girl on a large speaker screaming the lyrics as she started to strip live. I quickly looked away and covered my mouth so that I wouldn't puke.

---Flashback---

I closed my eyes and let the music get into me. I heard nothing but the music. The only thing I could feel was the beat getting to me. I started to sway my hips from left to right. And before I knew it, my body was moving to the beat of the song.

"Can you put on a little show for me?" Ricky whispered huskily in my ear.

I immediately shook my head, but he placed his hands on my waist.

Everything felt like it was moving in slow motion. Ricky started to slide his hands up my shirt slowly. No, no, no, this isn't happening.

His hands crawled up my stomach slowly as he nibbled on my earlobe softly. He placed his lips on my neck and started to kiss his way up to my jaw. Everything felt so... blurry... and just plain wrong... I wonder what he put in my sprite earlier.

He suddenly lifted my shirt off. I was hit with a wave of cool wind on my stomach. I felt cold without my shirt on, but my arms felt too heavy grab it back.

I looked around us. It was a pool party after all... so it wasn't that embarrassing.

Ricky pressed his lips against mine roughly and smirked against my lips.

He parted my lips with his tongue quickly and took over the kiss. His tongue which tasted of alcohol and cigarettes invaded my mouth, exploring every inch of it. I felt like puking. I was feeling too tipsy to do anything, even though I didn't drink alcohol.

He tried going under my swim suit, but I groaned in protest.

His body seemed too big for me, like it was built for someone else, but I accepted it for the moment. I searched for someone to take away the pain of my current life... why wasn't he enough for me?

He said he loved me, it couldn't have been wrong...

Why would he want to hurt me?

The party was his choice for a date... how could I say no?

Ricky tried going under my swimsuit again, but was suddenly pulled away from me.

"Please, just let her go home." Jaxon said.

"Fuck you! Why are you here?!" Ricky growled, shoving Jaxon into the crowd.

Jaxon wrapped a towel around my body. "Her stepmom's looking for her."

"That's her problem, not yours."

"I'm sorry for interrupting you guys man," Jaxon held onto me, "I'm just tryna' help. I don't want her to get grounded from going out again."

"Fucking take her then!"

---End of Flashback---

Jaxon never fully defended me… he never stopped Ricky from doing half the things he did like Axel did. Axel beat Ricky for even stepping near me. Yet, Jaxon still respected the poor excuse of guy.

"Rose! You're spacing out!" Kasay pulled me out of my thoughts.

"Sorry, sorry," I shook my head, coming back to reality.

She pulled me into the kitchen and got me a drink. I instantly shook my head. I didn't drink. She pushed the ice cold beer for me to take once again, but I still refused.

"I don't drink."

She rolled her eyes, "just take it."

I sighed and grabbed it from her. The beer can froze my hand almost immediately. I looked down at the beer can.

"Hey Rose, I think I'm gonna' give that twin a chance. I'll go dancing with him and see where we'll end up. You go looking for your guy, okay?"

I nodded numbly as Kasay disappeared out of the kitchen. I sighed as I opened the beer can. I never planned on drinking, but I just needed something in my system to get me confident enough to face Axel.

I lifted the beer can up to my lips and let the bitter liquid flow through my throat. I started coughing immediately; to me, it tasted terrible. How were people able to consume so much of it? After finishing my first can, I grabbed a small bottle from one of the refrigerators. It looked like water, but the bottle said 'VODKA'.

I almost died.

It burned my throat, and gave me chest pain. I got a few odd looks from the few alcoholics that stuck around in the kitchen, but I recovered. I squeezed my nose shut and forced the liquid down my throat.

My eyes scanned the place for Axel, but still, no luck. Every time I went looking for him and didn't see him, I went straight back to the kitchen to get myself a new drink. I tried almost everything there.

It made me feel kind of funny after a while.

I decided to mix the whiskey with Mountain Dew. It tasted really odd, but satisfying to me. I drank it, and tried throwing the glass into the sink. With my terrible aim, I hit the only person left in the kitchen with me; someone wearing a hoodie. It hit the back of his head and shattered against his hoodie.

The guy groaned in pain.

"I'm so, so, so, so sorry!" I apologized.

The guy didn't reply.

I pulled off his hoodie, and put my hand on his head, "is it bleeding?! I'm so sorry- I should've known my aim was terrible! I always miss everything anyway-"

I stopped midsentence when I saw his face.

Holy mother of unicorn shits!

His blonde hair was slightly messed up. He looked tired and worn out. His lip was busted from earlier today, still giving him that badass look.

He pulled his hoodie back up, "don't let anyone know I'm here. I just came down to get a bottle."

I was speechless.

His voice came out soft this time. It sounded so sweet, like it was laced with honey. His amazing emerald green eyes shone with happiness and another emotion I couldn't tell.

"A-Axel-"

"Your aim sucks, please don't ever play beer pong. You'll die of alcohol poisoning," he joked.

I felt like we were the only two in the world in that moment. It was probably the alcohol kicking in. He flashed me a breathtaking smile showing off his dimples. My heart stopped at that moment. There was no one but him in the world.

He smirked, "I didn't know Cinderella wore red.

I don't know why I found that statement so funny. I started laughing nonstop. I didn't notice he was standing in front of the refrigerator until he closed the refrigerator door with his foot. He had a bottle of vodka in his hand. All the alcohol was definitely kicking in.

He looked at me oddly before tilting his head to the right. It looked like an action a curious little puppy would do.

"Are you drunk?" he laughed.

I shook my head furiously before I hiccupped.

"Nope!" I answered popping the 'p'.

He laughed and shook his head. His Wizard of Oz emerald city green eyes shown with amusement as a smirk played at his perfect lips.

"You are."

"No I'm not," I denied with a hiccup.

He laughed and shook his head. He walked over to me and grabbed my hand. At his touch, my whole hand felt tingly. My heart raced at this little action. With a bottle of vodka in one hand, and my hand in the other, he led me out of the kitchen and up a large marble staircase.

"Axel?!" someone gasped, "Oh my god, you're here! Where are you going?" an annoying blonde who was wearing a bikini asked.

Who wears a bikini in late October?! I heard Axel curse under his breath. Oh, she must've been bad if he doesn't like her. Not today, bitch.

"Fuck off!" I told her, giving her the finger.

The blonde's mouth dropped. I recognized her with that facial expression! She was a cheerleader at our school, one of Layla's sidekicks. I heard Axel chuckle behind me.

"Did you hear what she just said to me?!" the annoying blonde cheerleader asked in her incredibly high pitched voice as we tried getting away from her.

"Yes, so please fuck off, Mindy." Axel said pulling me up the staircase.

The blonde who he called Mindy stomped her foot childishly and rushed off. We went up a flight of stairs and after a few moments of me stumbling up stares with heels, I couldn't do it anymore. My legs gave up and I sat on one of the steps.

We were on one of the upper floors and there was no one up here.

"Why aren't people here?"

"All the doors are locked."

"Why?"

He was so patient with answering my questions, "so things don't get destroyed."

"Why?" I took off my heels.

"When things get destroyed, they have to get replaced. So I make sure stuff on the second and third floor doesn't get destroyed, so moving guys don't have to bother me."

Woah, complicated.

"Where are we going?" I asked him in a whiny voice.

"Just a few more flights to go."

"Where are we going?" I repeated myself.

He sighed, seeming embarrassed, "my room."

~*~

Chapter 22 BAD, BUT A GENTLEMAN

"Your room?" I parroted.

He nodded. His room, why was he taking me to his room? Maybe he wanted to show me his dollies. Yay! Dolls! But I've always hated dolls though. I frowned.

"But I don't like dolls," I whined.

"Uh…" he looked utterly confused.

"But I do like remote control cars though," I said with a hiccup. "Cleo never let me play with any since she moved in. She said those are for boys!"

"How much had you have to drink?" he questioned, grabbing my waist to support me.

How much did I have to drink? The beer, the bottle, the second bottle, the third bottle.... uh… I gave up.

"I hate math!' I yelled.

Axel chuckled. I looked up at his face. He was so hot.

"For real, I actually hate math! It's so annoying, I prefer drawing."

"You are really drunk."

"No! No I am not!" I protested as he lifted me off the ground, so that I was standing on my two feet.

Aye, why do we have two feet anyway? I mean, we could all have one foot and hop around like kangaroos. But kangaroos have two feet too, why don't they just have one? And why do dogs have four feet… except they're not feet- they're paws. Why though?

Why don't dogs just have two feet and piss like normal people do? And why don't dogs wear shoes so their paws don't get dirty?

Why are humans so complicated? Why can't we just sniff each other's butts to show the other person we want to make babies with them? Why are emotions so complicated?

185

I didn't realize I had said everything out loud until Axel started laughing. "Come on, let's go," Axel said lifting me up off my feet.

Wow, he was acting nice to me today. My heart fluttered as he carried me up the stairs bridal style. My love, carrying me bridal style up to his bedroom- my dreams were coming true! All the stalking was finally paying off.

Except, why was he taking me to his bedroom? Did he want to frickle frackle with a girl like me? A small giggle escaped my mouth. One could only dream... oh naughty Rosie! I would like it if he threw me onto his bed and-

"Shut up!" I said to myself, "no, no! No one would approve of such a thing!"

I definitely wanted him to do naughty things to me.

---*Unknown P.O.V*---

Hiding in his walk-in closet wasn't the brightest idea, but I just had to see her. I saw him talking to her in the kitchen, and I knew immediately that he wouldn't be able to resist bringing her up to his bedroom. It was the perfect opportunity.

Axel was so down from getting hit by the nerd, that he even left the key in the bedroom door. It would be a waste if I didn't come inside. I heard some giggling from outside of the room, and I knew who it was immediately.

The girl had me wrapped around her finger the first time I saw her. She was so stunningly beautiful; I couldn't get her out of her head! I met her only once. I remembered her dark angel costume, her bright blue eyes, and her body...

She had me obsessed with her from that moment on. I couldn't concentrate on any of my studies (I never did anyway), and I couldn't even concentrate of having sex with any other girl. She wasn't my usual type.

But I wanted her, bad.

I usually liked big boobs, nice ass and the experienced type. But I could tell that Rose wasn't experienced at all. She was pure innocence, ready to be corrupted. She was shy, yet confident at the same time.

It was a combination I had never seen in someone before. No girl had rejected me like that and get away with it. But with her, it was special. She had a special charm to her. Something else no other girl had. She could get away with setting my car on fire.

The only other girl who's ever blown me off was Rosaline Winnefred. That bitch had caused Layla so much pain. I still didn't understand why Layla didn't give me the green light to gather a few guys to get our way with her. A quick gang bang couldn't have been too traumatizing, especially if we let Ricky spike her drink again.

I felt so... gay... hiding in a guy's closet.

Axel kicked his bedroom door open revealing him and Rose. He was carrying her in his arms as if she was his bride. Through the little crack in the closet door, I couldn't see very well. He closed the door with his foot behind him.

She giggled as he carried her over to his bed. Before he could drop her on his bed, she hooked her arms around his neck and brought him down with her. She hiccupped and giggled like it was the funniest thing ever. Why was she even like a guy like him?

I was far better in every way.

She was either incredibly drunk, or someone put something in her drink. You could just tell by the way she was acting, she was wasted. Axel landed right on top of her. She pressed her small boobs against his chest while giggling.

He grabbed her waist and pulled her off him. She fell onto the bed giggling, and still hiccupping. She smoothed down her red strapless dress and pulled her bra up. Axel looked incredibly nervous.

I had always suspected he was a virgin.

He stared at her for a moment.

Just staring at her like a fresh piece of meat ready to be put on the grill.

Lucky bastard.

I wasn't expecting what he decided to do next; he turned around and headed for the door.

"Axel!" Rose called out.

He turned around and walked over to her. She stared up at him, her blue eyes turned into puppy eyes. He raised an eyebrow at her.

"Where are you going?" she asked in a whiny but cute voice.

He sighed, "I'm going to go get you some pills so you won't have that bad of a hangover."

"No! Stay here with me!" she reached out and grabbed his arm.

He tried peeling her arm off, "I'll be right back."

She shook her head furiously and gripped tighter. They stared at each other for a few seconds, until she made a move. A move that I would never want to see her do to anyone, but me. She crashed her lips against his with everything she had.

My hands started to shake. Fuck! This wasn't supposed to happen!

He was supposed to try to get into her pants, and she wouldn't want to do it! Then I would come out and be her superman and save her.

---*Rosie's P.O.V*---

The alcohol I had earlier was definitely kicking in. I sucked on his bottom lip, begging to feel his tongue. Once his lips parted, I savored his taste. I wasted no time exploring him at all.

My stomach was filled with flying unicorns, my heart was pounding against my chest crazily and I felt incredibly hot like I was on fire. I was afraid he wasn't going to respond to the kiss, but he did. I couldn't believe what I was doing.

His lips tasted minty and sweet at the same time. The perfect combination. My body ached for him, every part of me was screaming to him. I needed him so bad, but I guess the logical side of me forced me not to tear his clothes off right at the spot.

Everything felt perfect.

One of his hands was resting against my lower back, and his other hand was pressing my mouth into his. It felt like a dream. I didn't want to stop. I wanted the moment to go on forever and ever.

I wanted to be in his firm, tight grip. I wanted to feel his heated hot lips on mine. I wanted his minty sweet tongue exploring my mouth like I did to his. I wanted him so bad! I moaned against his mouth, wanting more of him.

His hands moved from my lower back and my head, to my shoulders. He pulled me off him and looked at me straight in the eyes. His intoxicating green eyes burned into mine.

"I can't do this," he panted.

I felt as if someone had just hit me straight across the face, with a baseball bat, with needles sticking out of it. My throat started to wobble, as my eyes started to cloud up with tears. He was rejecting me, right after he had kissed me.

"No! Not like that!" he quickly said. He didn't know how to handle a crying girl.

A tear escaped down my cheek. He quickly wiped it away with his thumb before it could fall onto my chest. His emerald green eyes were filled with hurt and regret. He took in a deep breath.

"I can't take advantage of you while you're wasted like this."

I sniffed some tears away, "but you're not taking advantage of me!"

"Yes I am. You're drunk and when you wake up tomorrow, you'll probably hate me for kissing you."

"But I won't-"

"I don't want you to regret anything about me."

I stayed quiet, "I won't, I promise-"

He sighed, running a hand through his hair, "let me get you some pills, then we'll talk."

And with that, he left the room. I stared at the closed door blankly. So he wasn't rejecting me because I was ugly or weird, but he rejected me because he was afraid of taking advantage of me. My vision was pretty clear, but a little blurry.

His bedroom walls were light grey, and his comforters were grey and black. His floor was a white marble. All the rest of his furniture was either black, grey or white. His room was gigantic. The biggest bedroom I had ever seen.

It was probably the size of Kasay's house, or larger. After exploring the bedroom with my eyes, I threw myself onto the bed and waited for Axel. I felt weird and tipsy. I felt nauseous.

Suddenly, a hand clamped my mouth and someone got on top of me. The face that I had been avoiding for a while came into view.

He pinned both my hands up over my head with one hand, while his other hand was clamped over my mouth. I tried screaming, but it was muffled by his palm.

He pressed his body against mine as he leaned in so that his mouth was beside my ear.

"You left me unsatisfied," he whispered harshly in my ear.

I gulped. His body was too large and caged me down. I could feel something hard poking at my thigh. I squirmed, trying to break free, but he gripped onto my tighter. His skin was painful against my skin.

190

He looked down at me. He looked like a lion, eyeing up its prey. I tried to squirm out of his steel tight grip, but he held on tighter.

He buried his face into the crook of my neck and started sucking on the skin on that area. I squirmed harder, but he bit down. I screamed. He painfully pressed down onto my mouth. I couldn't even open my mouth with his palm against my lips. "That's what you get for being such a fucking tease."

He started licking from the crook of my neck all the way up to my earlobe. He moved down so his face rested where my breasts were. He gripped both my wrists with one of his hands, and with the other tried pulling my dress down.

I screamed as loudly as I could, and kept squirming until he had to cover my mouth. "Be quiet!" he hissed. I tried to knee him in the balls, but my knee went nowhere. "Feisty one, aren't you."

His brown eyes were sadistic and cruel, teasing mine. I always avoided his eyes because of that reason; he got to you when he looked into yours.

To stop me from screaming he pressed his hard lips against mine and shoved his nasty long tongue down my throat. It tasted of cigarettes and lots of alcohol. I tried to scream, but I choked. His hand crawled up my thigh slowly.

I tried thrashing around, but he held me tight in place. He pulled his hand from out of under the dress. He moved it to the zipper on the dress behind the dress. He slowly unzipped my dress as his tongue was shoved down my throat.

I tried to push him off, but he was too heavy. No matter how much I tried squirming, kicking or pushing him off, he stayed in place and kept his tongue shoved down my throat. I brought myself to a conclusion.

I bit down onto his tongue hard. So hard I tasted lots of blood that wasn't my own flowing into my mouth. He quickly pulled back, let go of me and grabbed onto his tongue.

"Da faq?!" He yelled at me.

It sounded like that because he was holding onto his tongue. I backed away and wiped my face. After wiping my face, I looked at my hand. Shit! Mascara was running all over my face. I probably look like shit right now.

Wow! Drunk Rosie! Worse time to think about how pretty you have to be! I got up and sprinted for the door. But I broke one nerd rule. Never make the school's quarterback angry. He grabbed my waist roughly and threw me over his shoulder.

He threw me onto the bed roughly and got on top of me. He tore my dress off this time. What was I gonna' wear?!

Suddenly, the door flew open revealing a very pissed off Axel. He was holding a small medical bag filled with medicine his hand. His eyes widened as he saw Matt on top of me and me squirming beneath him.

Axel wasted no time standing there. He ran towards Matt and tackled him to the ground. Even though Matt was taller and bigger than him, but Axel still fought him like there was no tomorrow. They rolled around the floor throwing punches at each other.

Matt got on top of Axel and started throwing punches at him nonstop. Axel kneed Matt in the gut and spun them around, so that he was on top. Axel three punches at Matt's face nonstop. He held on to Matt's shirt collar with one hand, while with the other hand, he threw punches at Matt.

This time, I didn't stop Axel. I let him beat Matt.

What he did to me was processing in my head. He tried to rape me…

I quickly pulled Axel's covers so that they were covering my exposed body parts. They rolled over so that they were fighting near the nightstand. Matt got on top this time, and started throwing punches at Axel's pretty face.

Without even having to think, I grabbed a glass lamp and smashed it against Matt's head. He fell face first onto Axel. A small high pitched giggle escaped my lips. Okay, so this was the worst time to laugh. Axel wiped a small amount of blood from his nose away before he looked down at me.

He quickly got up and sat beside me on the bed. He stroked my cheek with his thumb softly.

"He tried to rape you, didn't he?" Axel was scary, but he was so sweet to me. "I'll fucking kill him," he was about to punch Matt, but I grabbed him.

"Don't cut yourself!" I pointed to the shattered glass.

He nodded, getting up and kicking Matt straight in the face. I flinched when I heard something crack. He kept kicking his face over and over, until I couldn't stand to see anymore. Murder was wrong.

I gently touched his arm.

He stopped almost immediately.

"I'm okay now, let's dump his body."

Axel still glared at Matt who was passed out on the round, "he touched you."

He was so dangerous, it turned me on.

I grabbed his collar, and slowly pressed my lips against his soft ones.

Other people were addicted to drugs.

I guess we all have our addictions.

Because he was mine.

I shut my eyes and enjoyed it. So inviting...

He pulled away and stared at me.

"I won't take advantage of you."

Not again. I wanted him so bad. A small smirk appeared on his lips.

"But that doesn't mean I won't let you take advantage of me."

~*~

Chapter 23 SOBER THOUGHTS

I tried pulling him to me again, but he stopped me, "let me get rid of the cunt first." He pulled Matt's body out of the room. Once he was back in, he made sure to lock the door. He headed to his bathroom.

I followed him in, my feet felt cold against the tiles. I had his comforter wrapped around me to cover my body.

He was washing the blood off of his hands.

"I shouldn't have left you alone, I'm sorry."

I could see his face from the mirror.

"It wasn't your fault, you didn't know." I said quietly.

"So many people want to hurt me," he balled up his fists under the running water and leaned over the sink, "it's not fair to get someone else involved."

"But if someone truly wants to be a part of your life, they've gotta' deal with it." I leaned against the door frame. "Love is *always* worth the risk."

"What would *you* know about love?" He shot at me.

His words felt like bullets, but I took them. "I know more than you do."

"Have you ever been in love?" He asked, staring at me through the reflection.

I tilted my head to the side, "have *you*?"

"The real question is: what *is* love?"

"Why not find out for yourself?"

He washed his face before turning off the faucet. "I take punches, cuts, kicks- hell- I even have a few knife wounds," he took off his shirt and tossed it on the floor, "but internal wounds aren't something I want to experiment with."

He looked so… broken.

Pained.

Hurt.

Fragile.

This was Axel.

He was internally conflicted. He was bad for a quick high, a quick distraction from his past scars. His habits for dealing with pain weren't ones that would take him far...

"Axel, why do you hurt yourself?"

He spun around, "hurt myself?"

"Sometimes," I pursed my lips, "you're acting bad to get back at your stepdad, to pressure your mom to divorce him-"

"That's not the only reason-"

"I know, but please hear me out." I interrupted him. I sounded completely sober, maybe I was. He listened patiently, "its like someone tripped you, and you fell over and got cut. Now, instead of putting medicine on it, trying to ignore it and move on, you choose to focus on the cut. You jab it over and over again, until the wound expands. You drag the bully who tripped you, and force him to stare at your cut. Of course, that only satisfies him- but you hope it'll change his mind and upset him. You won't let the cut dry into a scar, instead you pick at the scab until it bleeds again."

He took my words into serious consideration. "That's a... very interesting way of viewing things." He seemed genuine. "But, what if your bully won't move on, and he won't leave you alone? Let's assume this bully is a very powerful man," he was clearly talking about his stepfather. "Now, this bully has power over someone you care for. He forces them to turn against you. You're alone; no one gives a fuck. You're ignored. You're unhappy. Obviously, you'll do something about it. Instead of doing what they want, you do the complete opposite to make them feel even a quarter of the pain you're feeling. You get high, throw parties, try to distract yourself from the loneliness. You want to anger them to the point they cannot spend a happy or calm moment."

I pursed my lips, "you're not alone."

"I was..."

"But you're not anymore."

We stared at each other for a few moments. "Why do you care so much?"

Because I've been in love with you for about seven years to be exact, and I can't stand seeing you in pain. I want to change your life; I want to make you happy.

"I have my reasons."

He observed me very closely, "well, you shouldn't care."

Ouch.

"You'll just get hurt."

Why did he want to destroy me?

"I'll let you use the bathroom if you want," he brushed past me.

I wanted to cry.

Did he just reject me?

I let my comforter drop to the ground before stomping into the bathroom and locking the door. I was regaining my consciousness, and I didn't like it.

His bathroom was massive.

I looked around the bathroom and something caught my eye. It looked like a clear bag with two piece of candy in it. Something sweet would help distract me through my shower.

I tossed the two in my mouth. They tasted... odd....

I shrugged it off and continued my shower.

Everything around me was... warping. The bathroom started changing colors in front of my eyes... pink... orange... stripes... the showerhead grew into a green lizard that smiled at me... A giant bee flew past me.

That wasn't candy.

I grinned, what pretty creatures.

I grabbed a towel, but it turned into cotton candy. It still felt like a towel. I bit into the cotton candy, but it tasted like cloth! I wiped my body with it, and threw it onto the floor. I grabbed my undergarments from the floor- at least they looked normal. The ground turned into yellow sand, but still felt like the tiles.

"What!"I gasped. The mirror had a face!

Axel knocked on the door, "is everything okay in there?"

The mirror's lips moved to Axel's voice... "THE MIRROR TALKS!" I screamed with joy.

The entire bathroom was transforming and moving in front of me.

"ROSE!" Axel banged the door again. "Let me in!"

"CANDY!" I squealed at the toilet that turned into a chocolate bar.

He swore from the other side of the door, "Please tell me you didn't eat anything in there."

A few moments later, the chocolate fountain flew open. Why was it solid?

Axel!

His face didn't change at all.

He had a floating crown around his head.

He grabbed me and pulled me out of there.

The bedroom looked like a colorful jungle.

"THE FLOOR IS LAVA!" I screamed, jumping onto the prince. "KISS ME!" I crushed my lips against his. Tasted better than any candy I had ever tasted.

He didn't push me away, instead he held me close. His minty sweet scent was intoxicating. YUM! We made out for a long time, until my lips hurt. I stared into his eyes, wow he was beautiful.

I ran my hands over his abs... damn. He buried his head in the crook of my neck and started kissing and sucking...

I breathed heavily and let all the sounds flow out of my mouth. I felt so... energetic! So hyper! I wanted more, more, and more!

We were now on the bed, and I was on top of him; straddling him.

The candy creatures had faded, but I still felt lightheaded, bubbly, and excited. I wanted to jump on the bed and do splits mid air!

The moonlight was the only thing that lit the room.

I bent down to kiss him. He grinded against me, "Rosaline."

Both of us froze immediately. We stared at each other with wide eyes. What. The-

"Please tell me I didn't just say that..." he breathed out, obviously in shock himself.

I didn't even know how to react.

He said my name.

My *real* name.

The *real* me.

I truly didn't know what to say, or what to do, so I let my body decide.

I wasn't sober enough to react sensibly anyway.

So I kissed him.

~*~

Chapter 24 HANGOVER

Soft breathing fanned my back, as my eyes fluttered open. The first things that I felt, was a headache. Then I felt soreness between my legs. Ouch! What the hell happened last night? I looked around and observed my surroundings.

I was in what looked like a very modern bedroom. I tried to get up, but an arm was draped over my waist. My eyes widened in fear. What kind of shit did I get myself into when I was drunk? I took a deep breath and slowly turned around.

I found myself facing none other than Axel Storm Spencer. It was my ultimate dream come true.

I thought I was going to have a heart attack.

He looked so peaceful and innocent. His lashes, his face, his lips, his nose, his structure, and last but not least, his sandy blonde hair falling above his closed eyelids. I felt like reaching over and brushing his hair, but I wasn't brave enough to.

I inhaled his scent and enjoyed being in his arms. It felt so right. I even sniffed the breath coming out of his mouth, he still smelt like mint and candy. How was it possible to be so perfect?

I thought about last night.

What could've led up to us falling asleep on his bed with each other.

I looked at the position we were in.

Did something happen between…. us?

My eyes widened.

No…

The thought gave me butterflies, but also had me sweating.

No, no, no, we couldn't have- I cleared all my thoughts when I saw a small box lying on the floor. In bold letters the box said 'TROJANS'.

My palms started to get sweaty.

Oh no, I couldn't have- I mean, how?
Then it hit me, how wasted was I last night? I didn't even
remember what I forgot. I tried to piece the puzzles together. I
remembered being in the kitchen, I remembered drinking,
meeting Axel.
Matt...
My skin crawled just thinking of his name. I couldn't
remember everything exactly...
I looked under the comforter to see if I had anything on. I
sighed; at least I had undergarments on.
At least the box of condoms on the floor did indicate that if
we did... 'do it', we did it the safe way and used protection. I
let out a breath I didn't realize I was holding. At least I didn't
have to worry about being pregnant. Softly, I picked up his
heavy arm and lifted it off of me. I felt so empty and
vulnerable without it around my small body.Quickly and
quietly, I lifted his arm off me and got out of his bed.
I found the red dress I was wearing last night. It was
torn...from the top all the way to the mid section.
Damn, I really liked that dress.
I quickly slipped it on, but it kept sliding off. I couldn't
remember anything after I drowned down those drinks last
night. I couldn't just go out with a dress ripped and sliding off
my body. I looked around the room and saw a wire from a
broken lamp lying on the floor.
Aha! I tiptoed over to the broken lamp and got a small piece
of wire from it. I then used the wire to tie the dress together. I
didn't have a needle, so I used my nail and dug into the
material creating a hole.
I looped the wire through the whole then made another
whole in on the other side of the dress. I put the wire through
that too, and I knotted the wire. I tied it together somehow.
I'm not even sure how I managed to do that.

The dress held up. You could still see the tear and the wire, but it didn't slide off. Yes, you saved yourself Rosie. I guess that was one good thing about being a quick thinker.

"Shoes," I whispered to myself.

I looked around for my heels, but I only found one. I grabbed it and left his room, leaving the sleeping angel sleeping soundly. I made a dash for it down the stairs; I couldn't afford getting caught sneaking out of his bedroom.

After running down three flights of stairs, I finally reached the first floor. A bunch of teens were passed out on the floor, lying on top of each other in creepy angles. Ew. I looked around for Kasay, but I found one of the twins.

"Smile," I greeted.

"It's Dustin."

I believed him.

"Hey," he said gloomily.

His eyes were blood shot, his face was paler than he usually was, and his blonde hair was messy in a cute boyish way. He looked tired and worn out though. His voice was raspy like he was yelling a lot.

"Where's Kasay?"

I had hoped Kasay and Dustin would get together. Judging by how he looked… either nothing happened, or something terrible happened.

"She's in one of the bathrooms… with my brother."

I froze and blinked twice.

Kasay, disappearing into a bathroom with Justin?!

Kasay had always had a problem with remembering names. Like that dude Rex, she always called him Rix… but I really didn't think…

Oh who was I trying to kid.

Justin and Dustin were identical in every way, and I had never told her how to tell them apart. Oh god… Just then, I heard a door on the second floor shut loudly. Kasay, with the blonde wig put on sideways, walked down the stairs proudly. The pink dress she was wearing was all wrinkled up.

Her makeup was smeared across her face. She looked like she had a pretty rough night, if you know what I'm talking about.

"Just the person I was looking for," she beamed at me.

I just stared at her. Dustin walked the other direction.

"What's his problem?" She huffed about Dustin.

I grabbed her arm and dragged her out of the house. Once we were far away from any passed out bystanders, I stopped. "What the hell happened last night?"

She looked proud, "I had sex with the nice twin you hooked me up with."

"Nice twin? You sure?" I pursed my lips together, "what's the nice twin's name."

She rolled her eyes, "as if I'd forget! His name was Justin of course!" She said in a 'duh, I know' tone.

I massaged my temples, "I set you up with Dustin, not Justin."

Her eyes widened, before her face grew paler.

"You were supposed to get with Dustin! The guy who's had a crush on you for a long ass time! Not his twin brother who sleeps around with everyone!"

"Well I guess Justin and I have more in common..." she trailed off, "Why didn't you tell me I was with the wrong twin!"

"You left me in the kitchen! And it just goes kinda' blurry from there..."

She was shocked, "you mean- you don't remember what you did last night?"

I nodded slowly. She put a hand on her hip, thinking.

"Where'd you wake up?"

I froze.

I knew she'd freak out if I told her.

But she'd be even more freaked if I lied.

I gulped and waved for her to come closer. She put her ear out so I could whisper in it.

"In someone's arms-"

Before I could finish whispering, she screamed out.

"What?!" she screamed. "WHO?!"

I didn't answer the question, and avoided looking at her face. She was far excited to care whose arms I slept in.

"Did you have sex?"

"NO!" I mean- I didn't think so, so I just didn't say anything.

"What happened to your dress anyway?!" She cut me off.

"Sorry... I accidentally tore it."

"Bullshit, you had sex."

Someone cleared their throat from behind us. "Excuse me if I interrupt, ladies?"

We both turned around to see who it is. I almost choked when I saw who it was. Justin was standing there with low hanging jeans showing of his V line torso, and showing off his abs. He had no shirt on and his hair was messy.

Just telling by his attitude and how he was showing off, you could tell he was definitely not his twin brother.

"Babe, you still haven't told me your name," when Kasay turned in his direction he practically screamed. "YOU LOOKED LIKE A TEN LAST NIGHT! WHAT THE HELL!" With that, he ran away from us.

We just laughed.

With one heel on, I stumbled to Dustin and clung onto him for support. He helped walk me to his car and got in. No one uttered a word in the car. It was incredibly awkward between Dustin and Kasay. Dustin dropped me Kasay out at her house first.

Right after Kasay stepped out of the car, Dustin let out a long sigh in relief. I got into the front seat and buckled my seat belt, before turning to Dustin. I spoke first, before he had the chance to.

"You know, Kasay had no idea who she was sleeping with, right?"

He shrugged.

"Kasay has always had a problem with names. And you and Justin look exactly alike, so she got you two mixed up."

He sighed, "She didn't even remember my name."

"She was drunk…"

"Not when I told her."

"Well people forget things when they're drunk, and everyone was dead wasted last night-"

He interrupted me, "I wasn't."

"Well, you were probably the only one sober there. But everyone else was wasted. Hell! I don't even remember what I did last night!"

"Axel clearly wasn't either."

"How do you know?"

"He was pretty sober the entire night."

"How do you know?" I repeated my question once again.

"You went up there for hours, and then you came stumbling down the stairs screaming some crazy shit. Everyone was passed out by then, but I was chillin' on the couch with some chick that almost puked on my crotch. Well, I saw everything. You turned on some Spongebob and started dancing on his pool table like a baboon."

"What time was this?"

"Can't remember exactly- about 3AM? You looked like you were on something. When I tried to get close, he told me he had his eyes on you and told me not to intrude. He was very protective of you."

I listened in awe, "he was?"

He nodded, "gotta' give him points for patience. You were screaming some pretty sexual things, I'm guessing you lost your virginity last night?"

"What exactly did I scream? And I don't remember…"

"Nothing I'd like to repeat," He chuckled, "you passed out and he carried up to his room."

I turned to him with wide eyes, "he did?"

Dustin nodded, "I've never seen him that way with *anyone*."

A small smile crept up on my lips. "What else did I miss?"

"Well, Layla left right after you and Kasay arrived, Matt got the living shit beat out of him, Justin banged Kasay, Ricky got his head stuck in a fish tank downstairs because he was trying to French kiss a clown fish, some of the drinks were spiked-"

I cut him off, "the drinks were drugged?!"

"Happens at every party, you just gotta' be careful."

"Do you think the reason I don't remember anything was because..."

Dustin nodded again, "it's a possibility, or it could just be you. How many drinks did you even have?"

"A few," I lied, but then felt guilty. "Maybe a ser few..." I thought again, "actually, I didn't keep count."

He just rolled his eyes, "you're lucky you have someone like Axel to take care of you."

"Was Matt the one who tore your dress?"

"How'd you-"

"Judging by how beat up he was, it was probably Axel's doing. I just put the pieces together."

"You're too clever for your own good."

"I wish I wasn't."

I furrowed my eyebrows, "what? Why not?"

"I wish I were more like Justin."

"Why? I mean- you guys look exactly alike... so you're already like him-"

"I'm not like him. He gets all the girls I could never get."

"How? You're identical-"

"His personality attracts girls more than mine," he was telling me how he felt far more in a few days than Jaxon had through our entire friendship, "I try Rose, I really do. I try to be polite, respect the girl, and take it slow... but Justin always snatches them before I even have a chance to get to know them." He sighed, "I'm sorry. I really shouldn't be letting my anger out on you."

"You don't have jack to apologize for. You're a nice guy Dustin, and nice guys finish last."

"But all girls go for the bad ones-"

"Not all. Maybe in high school most of them do, but in college I'm sure many stop going for the fuckboys."

He smiled at what I said. "I hope so, I sure hope so."

We spent the rest of the ride singing along to random songs on the radio. When he finally pulled up to my place, I froze. The ride went by so quickly.

"We're here," he announced.

I sighed. I wasn't ready to face my stepmother yet. I knew the moment I stepped in, she'd start screaming and ground me for another two months. I mean, I was already grounded- but she was going to make it worse.

We sat in silence for a few moments.

"Dustin."

"Yeah?" he turned to me, looking slightly confused why I wasn't out of the car yet.

"I can't go home."

"Why not?"

"She'll murder me."

His mouth formed an 'O'. He nodded, "so where do you want to go?"

I didn't have to think twice, "Could you just pull up to the house a few houses down. That one over there," I pointed over to Jaxon's.

"Sure," like the rule follower he was, he pulled into my driveway instead of making a u-turn in the middle of the road. He slowly drove over to Jaxon's place. A pink mustang was parked in the driveway. I recognized that car; I'd seen it around school before.

"Do you know whose car it is?" I asked Dustin, pointing to the pink mustang.

He nodded. "It's Layla's car."

"Layla's car?" I parroted.

He nodded in confirmation.

I really wasn't in the mood with dealing with Layla right now. I turned to Dustin with the sweetest smile I could plaster on my face.

Why was she even with him?

My massive hangover was already killing me, so I didn't feel like dealing with that issue yet. I wanted to live in the thought that I was Axel's one and only.

"Mind if I crash at your place for the meantime?"

~*~

Chapter 25 SKIPPING SCHOOL [PART 1]

"Um.."

"Please," I fluttered my eyelashes at him sweetly. I really had nowhere to go.

Please give in, please give in.

He bit his lip, "I'm not sure-"

"Pretty please," I made a puppy face.

He pulled at the collar of his shirt, like he was getting hot."I really-"

"Pretty please with whip cream and a cherry on top?"

I was practically begging him by now.

He sighed in defeat, "fine."

I gave him the best smile I could, since he just saved my life. Then, I realized something.

"What day is it?" I asked.

"I think it's the 26th or 27th?"

I stiffened, "what day of the week is it?" I asked slowly.

"Friday, why-"

"OH MY GOD!" I screamed.

Dustin flinched and covered his ears. I pulled my knees up onto the seat and hugged them to my chest. Oh no, this couldn't be. I started sobbing quietly, as Dustin stared at me in confusion. He probably didn't know what to do with a sobbing girl in the car.

"What's wrong?" he asked, putting a hand on my shoulder.

I jerked away from his touch and kept crying. No, I couldn't believe this. Why me? Why me?!

"Rose, what's wrong?" he asked gently.

His voice sounded so soft and heartwarming. Wait, did I just think that? I sniffed some tears away. I had just ruined my life! My twelve years of hard work!

"Rose, I'm really worried."

Tears kept rolling down my cheeks. No, no, no. This couldn't be happening. My whole future was ruined by me being careless!

"Rose, please tell me what's wrong," he pleaded.

I shook my head and kept sobbing. I heard him sigh, before grabbing his phone and stepping out of the car. Tears were rolling down my cheeks nonstop. How could I be so stupid?! This was one of the biggest events in my life.

---*Axel's P.O.V*---

I groaned as I stretched out my sore muscles.

Last night was eventful.

I shook my head and got up to an empty bed. I was a little shocked. I honestly wasn't expecting this bed to be empty when I woke up. I looked around my room. She was nowhere to be seen. I got up and checked the bathroom. Not a single trace of her.

The roles were truly reversed.

I broke my other lamp. Why the hell would she leave?

I got into bed again, trust to relive last night. For the first time, I didn't feel lonely. Someone gave a fuck. I inhaled the scent she left behind. Damn, I was starting to act like a little bitch.

Something started vibrating.

I rubbed my eyes and grabbed my phone, before looking at the screen. I was surprised the name that flashed on the screen.

' Thing 2 '

Yeah, real mature of me. But hey, I get their names mixed up all the time so I just called them by that.

If it were me on any other occasion, I would've tossed my phone aside. I tried ignoring it and walking over to my bathroom, but something inside of me made me go back and pick it up. I had seen him talking to *her*.

I threw my head back and groaned. I really wanted to know what he had to say to me- and if anything was about her. Like they say, curiosity killed the cat.

"What do you want?" I answered.

The guy sounded stressed. He sounded like he really needed a joint, "You've got to help me. Please it's urgent- you've got to come right now- I have no idea what's wrong or what happened-"

Even he was overwhelming me, "Chill, what's up?"

"Rosaline-"

That was the thing I needed to hear to get my ass out of my house.

~*~

---*Rosaline's P.O.V*---

Dustin brought me back to his place and gave me a bottle of a magical solution Kasay gave me to remove the coloring. He seemed pretty freaked out after my balling fit. I was still upset over how I ruined my life, but at least now I was in Dustin's shower.

All the brown hair dye came off my hair pretty easily. I scrubbed myself clean with the soap and shampoo. After I finished showering, I felt the towel rack for a towel.

"Shit," I hissed. "Not again."

I forgot a towel! I peeked out from behind the shower curtain to make sure there was no one around. And I sighed in relief when there wasn't. I banged on the bathroom door.

"Hey! Can someone please grab me a towel out there?"

No reply.

I cleared my throat loudly. "Excuse me! Could someone please get me a towel?"

No reply.

"Hello? Is anyone out there?"

No reply.

"Seriously, please! I really need a towel," I pleaded.

No reply.

"Someone out there! Please! Please grab me a towel!"

No reply.

I sighed in defeat. I couldn't go out there, or someone would see me. Obviously, no one heard me. Wait! What if they forgot about me?

What if they were to forget about me being in here forever and forever. I'd end up starving to death. Oh god. I was too young to die! Too many places I haven't gone, too many things I haven't done- I face palmed myself.

Cut it out!

I shook my head at how dumb that was. How could someone possibly forget me in this bathroom forever? Someone would eventually show up. People lived here for Christ's sake!

I planned on waiting until someone came up.

But then my stomach growled aloud.

I hadn't even eaten breakfast yet!

Yep... I was going to have to sneak out. My stomach was delicate. Cleo once told me if I didn't eat for a day I'd die, but then Science class taught me otherwise.

I banged on the door once more. "Hey! Can someone out there please get me a towel! I really want to get out of here and I'm really hungry!" I yelled.

My stomach growled again.

If no one heard my calls, it must've meant no one was around... which meant it was safe to go out. I took in a deep breath.

I placed my hand on the door knob and took another deep breath.

If anyone sees you, it'll be the death of you.

I told the voice in my head to shut up. I twisted the door knob slowly, and pushed open the door. I should've learnt my lesson from last time.

I looked around the bathroom trying to find something to cover myself with. Well, there was the shower certain, but I would have to somehow climb up and unhook it from a bar it was hanging on, there was a roll of toilet paper, and there was a bathroom mat.

I quickly picked up the bathroom mat and put it in front of my body. Hey, at least it covered up the front part of my body. I put my hand on the door knob again, but this time, I opened it all the way out. I tiptoed out of the room, hoping no one would see me.

I searched the room trying to find a towel, before my eyes landed on the bed. Bingo! A blue towel was folded neatly on Dustin's bed. I let out a sigh in relief and tiptoed my way over to the towel. As I were about to grab it, another hand beat me to it and grabbed the towel.

I froze.

The hand belonged to someone who was stood behind me.

Someone had the perfect view of my naked behind.

I spun around, keeping the mat to my chest. My eyes slowly travelled up the body of the guy, before my eyes landed on the face. My heart skipped a beat as I stared at the male angel before me. The angel who had a full view of my ass and possibly some side boobage.

I didn't know what I was doing. I just stared at his face in utter shock. The matt was barely covering my front side too. He was smirking down at me. I let out a high pitched scream before I tried grabbing the towel from him.

I missed and it dropped to the floor. Oh no. He looked down at me, amusement glowing in his green eyes. I gulped and looked down at the towel lying on the floor.

If I bent down and picked that towel up, he would get a full show of my boobs in 4D- but he'd realize how small my boobs were. I gulped.

"Aren't you going to pick that up?" he asked, his smirk playing on his lips.

My face heated up even more. He was definitely enjoying my humiliation. I wanted to do two things to that smirk. One of them was slap it off his handsome face; the other was kiss it off his face. I shook my head to clear the thoughts.

"Can you pick it up for me?" I asked, trying to flash a polite smile even though my face was a tomato.

He smirked and shook his head. "I think I'd prefer it if you did."

I shook my head. "But you'll get a clear view of my boobs," I blurted out.

He grinned evilly at me, "exactly."

"I'm serious, can you please pick that towel up for me?"

"I'm serious too," he took a step forward so we were even closer than before, "can you please pick that towel up yourself?"

"Why are you here?" I asked, trying to change the subject.

I had hope he'd forget, or maybe leave so I could pick up the towel. Or maybe even better, he would pick up the towel for me and gladly hand it over to me nicely.

He shrugged, "nice attempt to change the subject."

"Just hand me the towel, please!" I begged.

"No, I'm not letting an opportunity like this slip through my bare hands."

"The opportunity to see my boobs?"

"Bingo."

He was enjoying this too much. It was time to get rougher, "cut the crap and please pick up the fucking towel!"

"Did Ms. Goody Two Shoe just swear?" he gasped in fake shock.

I gave him a blank stare, "just pick up the towel."

He smirked, "no."

"Please."

"No."

"I swear to god-"

He shook his head.

It was time to change tactics, "I'm begging you-"

He just laughed at my attempt.

"I'll do you a favor."

"Nah."

"I'll do your homework for a week."

"I don't do my homework."

"I'll help you piss people off."

"I manage on my own."

I was on the verge of selling my soul to the devil to get that towel off the ground and around my body.

"I'll help clean your locker out-"

"I don't need it clean," he cut me off.

"Then what do you want?!" I groaned in frustration.

He pleased smile formed on his face, "I was waiting for you to ask that."

He stepped closer to me, closing in all the distance between us. I felt the heat radiating off his skin. I gulped from the closeness. My heart raced with the wind- wait there wasn't any wind. Okay, my heart pounded against my chest violently as I took in his minty smell.

Oh my god, he smelt so good. And the only thing separating us was the mat covering the front of my body and the layer of his t-shirt. His emerald green eyes didn't leave mine. He moved his mouth so it was right by my ear before he whispered.

"You want to know what I really want"" he whispered in my ear.

Goosebumps broke out across my skin. I nodded frantically.

"I want-"

He was cut off by the door slamming open. Justin was standing in the doorway with a chimpanzee mask on and boxers.

"Am I interrupting something?" He asked, as he backed away from the doorway slowly.

I felt the tension in the air. Axel looked visibly pissed off. I took a step backwards.

"Hey Justin, do you mind picking up the towel on the floor and handing that over to me?" I asked, smiling at him hoping he would do what I said.

He nodded and quickly grabbed the towel off the floor and handed it to me.

"As long as you don't knee me in the balls," he handed me the towel.

Still looking straight at Axel, I thanked Justin.

"No problem."

And with that, he left us two alone again. I smirked at him before wrapping the towel around my body. I dropped the mat to the ground. I wasn't quite sure whether I wanted to hear what Axel wanted or not.

"Don't think I'll let you off so easy," Axel said, smirking at me.

Oh no, not again.

"Because I have something you might want," he held up a pile of girl's clothes that looked about my size.

How could the day get any worse...

~*~

Chapter 26 SKIPPING SCHOOL [PART 2]

I took in a deep breath to try to calm myself down. Come on Rosie, you can deal with this patiently. I forced a smile onto my face.

"Can you please hand me the clothes?" I asked him nicely.

"No," he smirked.

He was really testing my patience right now.

"Please hand me the clothes," I pleaded through gritted teeth.

He still had that stupid, handsome smirk on his face. "Nah, I think I'll keep em'."

"I'm being nice," I growled.

"I'm being nice too."

It was just so tempting to knee him in the balls and get the clothes. Even though he was incredibly hot, and had been my crush since middle school I still felt incredibly annoyed by his actions. His grass green eyes travelled down my body, not trying to hide the fact he was checking me out.

A part of me felt incredibly happy that he was checking me out without a care in the world, but the other one wanted clothes.

"Enjoying the view?" I teased, with my own smirk plastered on my face.

I had never felt this confident before, even with my clothes on.

"Actually, I am. Thanks for asking."

I was honestly not expecting that as a reply. He blew out a low whistle.

"You should wear this outfit to school more often."

His comment confused me, "I've never worn it to school though, and it's a towel." I stated.

"Exactly."

"Just please hand me the clothes!" I practically begged.

He tapped his chin pretending to be thinking.

"What will I get out of it?" he asked, cocking an eyebrow at me.

"Anything."

Oops! I shouldn't have said anything.

"I want-"

"Not sex though," I quickly cut in.

"Do you think of me that lowly?" He asked, taken back by my comment.

You're just saying it because if he asked for it, you would be willing to give it to him.

No! Even though I was in love with him, I wouldn't just put myself out like that.

Liar.

Am not!

Are too!

Wait, why was I arguing with myself? I mentally slapped myself.

Shut up!

"What?" Axel asked, looking at me warily.

I cocked my eyebrow at him, "what?"

"You just said shut up."

Oh, so I just said that out loud.

"Yes you did," Axel replied.

Okay, now I said something out loud again.

"Yeah, you did… again."

"Can you just stop listening to my inner self speaking. She's a little unstable and she randomly blurts things out and stuff," I tried explaining. "It hasn't happened in a long time- but could you please give me my clothes?"

"Your inner self?"

I nodded.

He looked at me like I was crazy. "So does your inner self tells you to do things?"

"Sometimes."

"So let me get this straight. She tells you who to love or murder?"

Oh, so this is what he was getting at.

"I'm not crazy!" I snapped at him.

He put his hands up in defense. "I never said you were."

"You were heavily implying it."

He ignored my comment, "Does your inner self tell you how hot I am?"

YES! YES! YES! SHE DOES! SHE WANTS TO TAKE YOUR CLOTHES OFF AND PULL YOU TO HER AND-

"Of course she wouldn't! PFT! Why would she say that?" I wouldn't have believed that if I were him. I was a terrible liar.

"Just checking, because a little birdie told me you have a crush on me."

All the blood drained from my face before I stiffened. Oh no. Where did he hear that? Only three people know my dirty little secret, including me. Kasay and Dustin, but neither of them would tell him. Both were honest...

"Hey, are you okay? You look a little pale."

I nodded numbly. My dirty little secret was now out to the whole world. Oh no, I can't go to school anymore! I'll have to home school since every single girl will probably sending me daggers, and all the guys will laugh and make fun of me. I'll have to get Jaxon to get all my food supplies. I'll lock myself in my room for about 15 years, and maybe I can come out to face the outside world. I've got to let them forget about me and how I have a crush on Mr. Bad Boy!

"Um, actually no I'm not."

He looked at me before bursting out laughing. I stood there confused, staring at his angelic face and how perfectly his face was when he laughed. He looked adorable and incredibly sexy at the same time.

His laugh was like music to my ears. I have never heard anything more pleasant. His amazing laugh drew a smile onto

my face. I couldn't keep the smile off my face, no matter how hard I tried. I should be mad at him, but yet, I was watching him laugh in complete 'awe'.

I know it sounds super creepy, but I just couldn't help it. He was the bad boy every good girl was waiting to change. But I didn't want to change anything about him. He was plain perfect. Except when he's in fight mode.

This stone cold eyes brought me goosebumps. His eyes had no emotion when he was throwing punches at Jaxon. He was heartless and blocked out every single emotion he had. His cold face still looked like a Greek god's face, but it was emotionless.

It frightened me in a way. I felt like I knew him in and out from everything I heard and knew about him, but when I saw him fight up close, I realized I was completely wrong. I realized I barely knew him at all, even if I felt like knew him. He wasn't an easy person to read. I knew some of problems, but I didn't know them all. Yes, I was kind of a stalker when it came to him, but I wasn't that creepy about it. I never followed him home or anything, but I might've followed him halfway home...once or twice...

"I was just fucking with you," he laughed, snapping me back to reality.

"What?"

"About the crush thing, that was complete bullshit. I didn't think you would actually take it to consideration or think I really meant it." he explained, still laughing hysterically.

Oh, so it was all a joke. I mentally kicked myself for even considering hiding my face from the whole world because of people hearing about it. I relaxed and let out a breath I didn't realize I wasn't holding. He looked down at my body, before looking up at my face again.

He had his sighature smirk plastered on his face. Cocky much? I looked down and realized I had a towel wrapped around my body. How did I manage to stay calm while in a towel? My face heated up immediately.

"So what do you want?" I asked, changing the subject. "I really want to put some clothes on."

"Since sex is out of the question, I don't really know," he scratched his chin, pretending to think.

Pervert!

"Quick, just name it so I can put the clothes on. I'm freezing!"

"Nice try, the heater's on."

"Just because the heater is on doesn't mean I can't feel cold!"

"But your face is hot, so how could your body be freezing?"

My cheeks heated up more.

"Just please give me my clothes!" I begged. "What do you want from me?!"

"I want two things actually," he stated, walking around me like he was the predator and I was his prey.

He was eyeing me up from head to toe. And I had too much skin exposed to my liking. I gulped.

"W-what do you want?" I stuttered.

"You're nervous."

"Why were you freaking out earlier?"

I bit my lip and avoided eye contact. I really didn't feel like telling him..

"Let it out."

Maybe he was right, maybe I just had to tell him and get over it. I took a deep breath before talking.

"IwasballingearlierbecauseIskippedschoolforthefirsttimeever.
"

He just stared at me.

"Say that again, ten times slower."

I drew in a deep breath, "I was crying and stuff... because I skipped school for the first time... ever." I felt embarrassed and ashamed.

He just stared at me blankly, like he was taking in the information.

Suddenly, he started laughing.

He was laughing like earlier, but this time, he was laughing a lot harder. How did he find this situation funny? I had just ruined my record that I was trying to keep clean my entire life… and he was laughing at my pain?!

"You find humor in this?!" I snapped.

He wiped a tear away from his eye. "S-so let me get this straight," he managed to spit out between laughs. "Y-you were b-balling earlier just because o-of that?!"

"You have no idea how hard I've worked for this record! I've never missed a day since pre-school without being ill! Hell! I've never missed a day since kindergarten!" I yelled. "I've left school when I don't have classes, and I've taken time off when I'm very ill or the doctor tells me so- but I've never missed A SINGLE PERIOD OF CLASS!"

He kept laughing. Even though his laugh was incredibly sexy, and his face was the most adorable thing I have ever seen at that moment, I was still pissed at him. Laughing at the fact I ruined my future! What kind of guy would do that anyway?

Oh right, the guy I loved most.

"Rosie, you shouldn't freak out over just that!" he laughed.

He had kept his nickname for me.

"Just that?! You have no idea what you're talking about." I turned away from him and scowled at the wall.

"Don't tell me you're mad at me now."

"I am!" I huffed.

"I just don't like seeing you frown; your smile is fucking adorable."

He could turn my day upside down with one statement.

My heart skipped a beat.

Why did he have to be so frustrating, yet romantic?

I just couldn't hide the blush off my face after what he just said. My heart was pounding against my rib cage crazily.

"Are you still mad at me?" he asked, sounding a bit too cocky for my liking like he already knew I was going to forgive him after what he said.

I didn't reply to him, but I guess that was a good sign for him.

"I'll take that as a no."

"Give me back my clothes or I will be," I threatened in a weak voice.

My voice was so soft and venerable after what he just said to me. It was like my voice box melted after his compliment. He laughed before holding the clothes up high in the air, just high enough for me to reach.

"You're as threatening as a toothless puppy," he laughed.

I glared at him, "I'm stronger than you think."

He grinned, "mhmm."

"Shut up."

He had an adorable playful smirk on his face as he stared down at me.

"Just give me my clothes," I groaned.

"I haven't told you what I want yet-"

"I already told you why I was crying-"

"That didn't count."

"What?!"

He just ignored my response, "firstly, I want you to stop taking shit off of people."

I just stared at him silently.

"Especially Layla, seeing her push you around pisses me off."

I blinked again. He… noticed? He noticed I exist?

"The soup thing… I wanted to punch her *for* you."

I was still processing everything in my head.

He noticed me.

"Secondly, I want you to tutor me."

What.

"WHAT?"

"I've decided I want to try to do better in school. I have to at least pass."

"That's great!" I grinned.

He shrugged and looked away, "but don't tell a single soul, or else..." His threat made me a bit hesitant.

"So what makes you want to get better grades?" I asked.

I really wanted to know, but then I regretted asking the question.

"It's none of your business actually, but I'll answer anyway. A girl," he admitted... quite confidently actually.

My heart literally broke in half.

I felt as if someone tore my heart out of my chest, cut it in half with a chainsaw and stomped on it over and over again.

A girl who obviously wasn't me. Disappointment, hurt, heartbroken, all the emotions that flooded me were depressing.

"Who's the girl?" My tone was cold and harsher than I had hoped it to be.

He stared at me, grinning happily before answering. "You'll find eventually."

Of course, he had no idea what he was doing to me.

He had just slit my throat and was waving the bloody blade in my face.

Right after he admitted he wanted to impress some girl, he told me that I'll find out who she is 'eventually' whilst grinning ear to ear. Of course he had no idea I've had a huge crush on him since the day I saw him.

It was all my fault.

I blamed myself.

It was because I had never told him how I felt for him, that's why he ended up falling for someone else. It was because I was too shy, too quiet, and too afraid of getting rejected so I didn't tell him.

Not telling him made it worse, it made him fall for someone else.

I blamed myself for him liking someone else. If I told him in the first place, he might've even looked my way. If I even dared enough to spoke to him, maybe he wouldn't have met whoever he had his eyes on. But of course, I was just the random school nerd to him, why would he care about me anyway?

I wasn't as pretty as other girls, I wasn't as outgoing- I was shy, I was awkward, inexperienced, and the list went on and on. That was why he didn't even look my way. It was because I was nothing compared to all the other girls.

I forced a smile onto my face. It hurt me even looking at him, "now can I have my clothes back?"

He smirked before holding out the clothes for me. When I was about to grab them, he dropped them to the floor.

"Oops," his smirk stayed plastered on his face.

Asshole.

That's what he was after all.

Axel Storm Spencer.

The guy's whose initials spelt 'ass'.

"Aren't you going to pick them up?" he asked, with an innocent sweet smile on his face.

I glared at him, but it was just so hard! He looked like an adorable puppy, wanting to play around. But I was in no mood to play.

"Pick. It. Up," I growled.

He put his hands up in surrender before picking the clothes up for me. I quickly snatched the clothes out of his hands before he had the chance to do anything to it and rushed over to the bathroom.

I slammed the bathroom door shut and locked it, before pressing my back against it, breathing heavily. I put a hand on my heart to try to slow it down. It was pounding so hard against my chest, I felt as if it were about to fly out of my chest.

I couldn't keep crushing on him like this anymore.

I just couldn't.

It wasn't even a crush anymore.

I had fallen.

For someone who liked someone else. Just mentioning her made him grin- she must've made him so happy. I wanted to be her. I wanted to have him wrapped around my finger. I had no idea who she was, but I was going to find out.

But who could it have been... if it wasn't me. He kissed me. He took care of me. He risked himself for me. He opened up to me.

He's a bad boy- he'd do it with any girl if he had the chance.

But he didn't-

I removed the thought from my head.

It could never be me. I was beyond imperfect- why would he even consider going for someone like me.

I wanted him to crush on me the way I crushed on him.

But once again, it was just a dream that could never come true.

The more we talked, the more I got to know him, the more I fell.

Everything about him was just intoxicating. His smirk, his amazing green eyes, his lips, his expressions, his switch of emotions in seconds, his vulnerability, his teasing manner, his protectiveness, the fact he defended me multiple times in one day, how selfless he was- hell, he got himself beat up for me. Multiple fights in one day... just for a girl... like me.

Everything- everything- everything about him was perfect.

He was perfect.

At least to me he was.

I shook the thoughts out of my head. If he had feelings for someone else, I needed to stop my feelings for him. The more

I fell for him, the more it was going to hurt. I needed to stop daydreaming about it. Stop it all. I couldn't afford having a crush on him after someone else was with him. I shook my head. I had to get over him real quick before I ended up doing something stupid.

"You have to get over him Rosaline. You have to get over him." I whispered to myself.

You know you can't.

Chapter 27 SKIPPING SCHOOL [PART 3]

"Are you done in there yet?" Axel banged on the bathroom door.

I quickly slipped on the clothes given to me.

"Almost!"

I quickly opened the bathroom door, coming face to face with my heartbreaker.

"Took you long enough, Flower," he walked over to Dustin's bed and sat down.

I raised my eyebrows at him, "Flower?"

"Your new nickname. Rosaline's too long to say, and I heard other people calling you Rosie. I wanted something more," he paused, "personal."

I had no idea in what way he meant by 'personal'. "Out of every name, why choose Flower?"

He shrugged, "Rose is short for Rosaline, right?"

I prayed he wouldn't be able to make the connection, and nodded.

"But you see, no one calls you Rose, and some of us may or may not already know someone named Rose. Do you?"

Was he toying with me?

"So since a Rose is a flower, I'm calling you Flower. Plus, you really remind me of a flower, I don't even know why, but now you're *my* little flower," he finished.

His little flower?

His.

He claimed me as his…

I stood there, slightly confused. Did he mean it in that way?

Suddenly, his eyes widened. I guess he finally realized what he said. "Oh no! Not like that! I mean, you're like a little flower, that's how I came up with the nickname- I didn't mean to imply I own you or anything- I was just tryna' say the nickname is mine- fuck- mine as in ownership of the nickname, not you. Oh god, this is getting confusing. What I mean is-" he took a moment to think, "how the hell do I explain myself now?"

He was beyond cute flustered. He looked like a frustrated puppy trying to figure out something. He was so innocent- a word that no one else would use to describe him. "It's okay," I laughed. "I get it."

"You do?" he was surprised.

I nodded in reply.

I couldn't stop the smile that tugged at my lips. Just seeing him frustrated was freaking adorable. My heart fluttered while watching the confused expression on his face as he stared at me.

"Why are you smiling?" he asked, staring at me with wide eyes.

A small giggle escaped my lips before I could contain it.

"What's so funny?" He started fidgeting, almost as if he was insecure.

I couldn't stop myself from laughing at his question. He was just so cute in every way. He could be sexy, cute, hot, amazing, adorable and handsome at the same time.

"Flower," he said my name, but I still couldn't stop laughing. "Answer my question.

Turns out the school's bad boy looked like a lost puppy when he's frustrated.

"It's nothing!" I tried containing my laughter.

"You're lying," he stated.

"What are you, a psychic?"

"Possibly."

"You're definitely not," I said with a small smile playing at my lips.

"What are you hiding from me in that little head of yours?"

I smirked at him, "a lot of shit."

"I can see," he attempted to sound posh, but failed miserably.

I laughed, "You have no idea what you do to me, bad boy." There was a tremendous amount of truth in my 'joke'.

I was glad he didn't take it seriously; he only took it as a joke. He grabbed my hand by surprise and placed a soft gentle kiss on the back of my hand. My whole body froze as I felt a tingly sensation on the back of my hand. It was like... that cured my banging headache. He distracted me from the pain I was feeling.

Shivers ran down my back and I started getting goose bumps on every inch of my body. My heart pounded against my ribcage violently. He held eye contact as he kissed my hand. It was something out of a fairytale. I was stuck in the moment. Everything seemed to move so slowly, and I felt like we were the only people in the world.

All that mattered to me was him. It was a moment that meant so much to me, even though he was just playing around.

It showed that he wasn't disgusted of me. He didn't think I had germs on the back of my hand, and clearly didn't think I wiped snot on my hands. But then, like every other great moment it had to end. He pulled away smirking at me.

"What's taking you two so long-" Justin stopped at his tracks when he saw us both and the odd position we were in.

Axel had his mouth inches from my hand and he was bowed down so he could reach my small hand. He was staring at me through his lashes with a smirk on his face while I was blushing like crazy. Justin backed away from the door slowly.

"Am I interrupting something again?" he asked nervously.

"N-no not at all," I answered.

"I always knew you had a thing for each other." He looked at us in awe.

If my face could get any hotter, it did. My face was on flames as I looked away from both of them. Axel looked a little red too himself, I assumed it was because he was pissed off.

I don't know how Axel managed to keep his cool, "we don't." He sounded as cold as stone.

Ouch.

What was I expecting? Him to admit he liked me too?

Unlike Axel, I couldn't deny Justin though. I couldn't deny what was true.

Axel glanced at me and our eyes met for a short moment.

"Sure," Justin said in a disbelieving tone.

Axel sent him a death glare. "What do you want anyway?"

"Just making sure you don't have sex on his bed," Justin replied, folding both his arms over his chest.

I couldn't believe how much Justin and Dustin looked alike. They were identical twins and you really couldn't tell which one was which unless you saw their dimples. But if you were with them enough, their personalities were different.

"Come on Flower, let's go," Axel said grabbing my hand.

Tingles shot up my whole hand and arm from his touch. His skin was incredibly soft and warm. He pulled me along until we were out of the room. With my hand still in his, we went down a flight of stairs until we were in the kitchen.

"Thanks for the call," Axel gave Dustin a quick handshake.

"No problem, good luck." Dustin smiled at him.

"I'll need it," Axel mumbled under his breath, before pulling me out of the kitchen and out the door.

What was that about? Luck? I would imagine that someone like Axel wouldn't need any luck with his strength and good looks.

"Where are we going?" I asked as we walked out the door.

He turned to me with a poker face, "since you're now my new tutor, we should get to know each other a little."

"So where are you taking me?"

"Anywhere, where do you want to go?" His grass green eyes twinkled mischievously.

I tapped my chin while thinking. Nowhere romantic… I couldn't fall for him even more. "Anywhere that's not awkward?"

"Sure, I know a place," he pulled me along.

We stopped in front of a slick black motorcycle. I wasn't very fond of them. And to be honest, I had never ridden one before. I didn't plan on riding one anytime soon. Axel hopped on the motorcycle and put his keys, starting up the engine.

The engine roared to life, making me jump ten feet back. There was no way I was getting anywhere near that beast! Axel motioned for me to get on, but I shook my head refusing his offer.

"Get on," Axel had to yell over the rumbling of the engine.

"No thank you!"

If I had to get on that thing, I was seriously going to crap my pants.

"Come on Flower, it's not that bad!"

"I'm not getting on that motorcycle!" I yelled over the engine.

He turned the engine off, "it's not a motorcycle."

If he was thinking of tricking me and telling me that wasn't a motorcycle so I would get on it then he was another level of stupid. Even though he was my one and only love offering me a ride on a motorcycle, I wasn't going to take the offer.

"If it's not a motorcycle, then what is it?"

"She's a Ecosse Titanium Series FE Ti XX, powered by a 2,409cc billet engine with Ecosse's highest ever horsepower figure-"

"Hold it there! She?" I parroted in disbelief.

He smiled down at his bike like it was the most beautiful thing in the whole world. His face was filled with adoration.

"Yes, Elisa."

"Who's Elisa?" I asked with a pang of jealousy.

"This baby," he replied, running his fingers along the slick surface of the motorbike.

"You named your motorcycle?!" I asked in disbelief. This boy was something else.

"She's not a motorcycle; she's Ecosse Titanium-"

"I get it," I stared at him in disbelief. The guy named his motorcycle... "But I'm still not getting on."

"Why not?"

"Because, she-" I couldn't believe I was using a vehicle's preferred pronoun, "IT looks scary and I don't know the number of girls that have ridden that thing." I scrunched up my nose in disgust.

"Actually, you're the only girl I've asked to ride with me on my baby."

That warmed my heart knowing that I was the only girl he's invited to ride with him on that motorbike.

I huffed, "still doesn't pursuade me."

"You'll get to hold onto me if you ride with me."

He *must've* known I had a thing or two for him. Either that, or he was beyond conceited. His offer was great, but my inner self was stubborn, so I decided to decline it. I shook my head at him.

"You get to be real close to me."

Even though I wanted to scream 'yes!' at him, I turned it down. "I don't care whether or not I get to touch you!" I lied. My voice always came out high when I was lying, and I was confident he saw right through.

"Aw, come on Flower. It's not scary at all!"

"You have no say in that. You're not someone who's never ridden a motorcycle before!"

"You'll be wearing a helmet! Nothing's going to happen!" He groaned.

I rolled my eyes. "Something could happen if I fell off!"

"You won't fall off unless you let go of me."

"No, I'm still not getting on."

"Come on, Rosie."

"I'd rather walk."

"Flower, you do realize that you *will* get on." It sounded like a threat to me.

I rolled my eyes and turned away from him.

"Whatever." I grumbled before walking the opposite way. I gave him a small wave as I sauntered away from him. I did feel bad in a way, but I wasn't going to get on that beast! As I was walking further down away from him, I heard his engine roar to life.

"I'm not letting you walk there!" he yelled from behind me. "You don't even know where we're going!"

I did something I never imagined myself doing to him. I flipped him the bird. I heard him laugh and make a comment about me being a bad-ass-goody-two-shoe before the sound of the engine came closer. I kept walking away as fast as I could.

Don't look back Rosie, don't you dare look back!

"Hey Cinderella, I'm coming after you!" Axel sounded much closer now.

Cinderella?

What was up with all the nicknames?!

Don't respond! Pretend he's not there!

He slowed down next to me on his motorcycle. We were just a few feet apart. I was on the sidewalk while he was on the road.

"Get on," he ordered.

Ignore him Rosie! You're not getting on that running death machine no matter what!

"Please?"

Don't fall for his angelic voice no matter what! His voice might be dripping honey but he's no good!

"Flower."

Keep walking! He'll get bored of you ignoring him and leave you alone.

"You know I'm not going to leave you alone until you get on, right?"

Don't listen! Block out your ears, you're now deaf to everything he says to you!

"Are you ignoring me?" he asked.

Don't reply, keep walking.

"Please get on."

Distract yourself!

"Flower?"

He was driving right next to me now. It was getting incredibly hard to ignore him.

"Please stop ignoring me." He pleaded.

Distraction, I need a distraction!

"Rosaline Arlene Winnefred!"

Why did he have such an effect on my heart?

I didn't know he even knew my full name...

"Come on! Just please ride with me, it's not that bad, I promise."

Twinkle, twinkle little star, how I wonder what you are. Up above the world so high like a diamond in the sky-

"If you don't do this the easy way, we'll have to do this the hard way." He warned.

Uh oh.

Twinkle, twinkle little star, how I wonder what you are-

"Hard way it is." He huffed, turning off the engine.

I kept walking while forcing myself not to turn around. I heard footsteps coming closer and closer to me, but I chose to ignore them. A bead of sweat rolled down my back. I had no idea what he was planning in mind, but I had a feeling I wasn't going to like it.

I couldn't hold it longer. I couldn't stand ignoring him and I was dying to know what he was planning to do to get me ride with him. I turned around to face him quickly. I bumped right into his rock hard chest. Ouch! My poor little nose! He looked a little shocked to see me not ignoring him anymore.

"What evil master plan do you have in mind?" I asked him suspiciously.

He had both his hands shoved into his jean pockets. Oddly, nothing looked suspicious about him. He looked like a normal hot guy taking a walk. I narrowed my eyes at him as he looked around him with confusion.

"What?" he asked.

"What are you doing?"

"Walking." He answered in a 'duh' tone.

"Where's your bike then?"

"Parked in the middle of the street."

"What?!" I screamed at him, looking at the street behind him.

Sure enough, his motorcycle was parked right in the middle of the road without any care in the world. Thank god there were no cars around, or a car would've run it over.

"You can't just park it in the middle of the road like that!" I shrieked at him.

"Why not?"

"The cops would tow it, or a car might run it over!"

He shrugged. "Whatever, my stepdad's rich, he'll pay for it."

I just stared at him in shock. He had no care in the world.

"Besides, I can get a new one anyway." He just shrugged like it was nothing. "I'll name the new one 'Rosie caused this'."

Even though my dad was rich, he was nothing compared to Axel's step dad. And even if I were that rich, I wouldn't be that careless or carefree as him.

"Please! Go re-park it."

"No, I'm not moving it unless you ride with me."

So this was his way of getting me to ride with him.

Don't give in! Don't give in!

"Fine!" I huffed.

How could you just give in like that?!

I felt like slapping myself, but I didn't after seeing the cute boyish grin on Axel's face. He ran back to his motorcycle and started the engine before driving it over to me. He handed me a helmet before grabbing me by the waist and helping me get on.

Boy, this was going to be a long ride.

~*~

Chapter 28 SKIPPING SCHOOL [PART 4]

"I hate you," I grumbled as the engine roared to life below me.

"No you don't."

I could imagine him smirking while saying that.

"Whatever helps you sleep at night, Mr. Bad Boy."

"Mr. Bad Boy?" he parroted sounding slightly amused.

"Yeah, your pet name," I smirked.

He laughed and shook his head before slipping on his helmet quickly.

"You might want to hold on tight, princess."

"Princess?"

"You remind me a bit of Cinderella."

I prayed he hadn't made any links yet. I followed his advice and put both hands on his shoulders. He shook his head though.

"Hold onto my waist, it's more secure."

I nodded quickly and hooked my arms around his waist. My heart was pounding against my chest crazily from the closeness of our bodies. I guess my life was a little cliché. The good girl gets on the motorcycle with the bad boy, gets scared and holds on tightly to the bad boy.

Once we were ready, we took off at a high speed, I was expecting myself to fall off die, but I didn't. The wind whipped around us violently as we sped down the road. As we went along, it didn't seem so scary after all.

I felt free.

Like I was capable of controlling my own destiny.

Something inside of me that I had never felt before struck me.

Something inside me came to life. It felt like my heart suddenly lit on fire. And then I felt it, I really didn't give a damn about my safety on the motorcycle.

What was there to lose?

My dad was never home, my stepmother was being horrible, my childhood best friend was acting suspicious, and my crush saw me practically naked in my friend's house, what was there to lose?

I did something I thought I would never do my whole life. Maybe there was a little trace of alcohol in my system? I slowly let go of his waste as we were speeding down some empty roads. We were heading out of town, and there weren't many people in that area.

First, I unhooked one arm around his waist before pulling one leg up to my chest.

"What the hell?!" His voice was muffled.

Then, I unhooked my other arm that was around his waist and brought my leg up to my chest. I heard him try to say more stuff to me, but I couldn't hear him over the wind and with the helmet on.

I slowly slipped off my helmet and put it between my feet before getting up slowly. The wind whipped around me, but I held my balance. My legs were pressed against his back and my feet were on the seat. I was surprised I didn't slip right off though.

I slowly extended both my arms out like Rose in titanic.

My slightly damp hair was loose and flying in all directions, also slapping my face in the progress. I felt Axel's back vibrate as he tried to yell at me, but I just decided to ignore him since I couldn't hear him over the wind anyway.

One of his hands grabbed my leg, preventing me from falling off. He was driving with one hand.

Every part of my body was screaming excitement. I really couldn't care less about my well being, all I cared at the moment was how great it felt as the wind whipped around me. I started laughing for no reason.

I guess it was probably because I was doing something that my usual self would disapprove of. I started laughing a lot louder. Someone definitely slipped something in my drinks last night, and it was affecting me right now.

The motorcycle had to slow down for some distance before it came to a stop in the middle of the road. We were now out in the country, and luckily there were no cars passing by. I slipped my feet off the seat quickly and got off before I would lose my balance.

I walked to the front of the motorcycle and folded my arms across my chest. "Why'd you stop the motorcycle for?" I asked in a whiny voice. Did he really have to stop the motorcycle when I was having so much fun?

He took his helmet off and wiped some sweat of his forehead. Damn! He looked incredibly sexy. Well, wasn't he always? His hair was a little damp from his sweat, making his hair stick to his forehead. He was incredibly pissed off.

"What the hell was that?!" he yelled at me.

I was not expecting that.

"Huh?"

"That stunt you pulled!" he motioned to the motorcycle seat angrily.

Oh, that.

"You could've gotten hurt! Hell, fucking killed!" He stomped towards me.

"I-"

"First you're too afraid to even get on a motorcycle, then you pull a stunt like that?!" he yelled right in my face.

"But-"

"I can't believe you did that! You even took off your fucking helmet- what if you fell off?!" He grabbed my shoulders.

"I-"

"What the hell were you thinking?!" He gripped my shoulders. "How fucking careless can you be? I'm fucking shocked," he laughed without a single trace of humor.

"Shut the hell up and let me finish!" I yelled at him.

He shut up immediately. I sighed and ran a hand through my tangled hair. "I was just trying to have fun-"

"There are plenty of other ways to have fun without trying to fucking kill yourself!"

"What is there to lose?!" I yelled.

You.

I pushed all the hopeless romantic thoughts out of my head for the moment and concentrated on the situation. He stayed quiet and stared at me. I couldn't see through his emotions.

His eyebrows furrowed, making him look like a sad little puppy for a moment. "I understand the feeling," he said in a soft voice. We just stared at each other for a moment.

The only movement was the wind blowing passed us. On either side of the road were grasslands. That's what you get for living nearly the center of America. The very few trees around us were shedding their leaves.

His eyes reminded me of the blades of grass in the summer. They were such a special color. I don't think I've ever seen them before. I took time to just study his amazing facial features. His full lips were in a frown, his perfect nose bridge, his jaw, his cheeks looked so pinch-able...

How did I get so lucky to spend time with this guy?

The guy I had been drooling on since middle school, the guy who got in trouble 24/7, but managed to not get held back. The mysterious guy who bottled up everything.

The guy who was rough around the edges, sarcastic, mean, cruel, but soft and caring in the inside. How did someone like me, the school's nerd, get so lucky to spend time like a guy like this? I broke eye contact first and cleared my throat.

"Let's move before a car comes," I said.

"When it comes to this stuff you care about safety," he huffed.

"I care about your safety, and the people driving."

He remained quiet and hopped onto the motorcycle. I did the same. We put our helmets on, before taking off he said in a low voice, "you shouldn't care about mine."

I didn't know what to say.

~*~

"Seriously?"I asked in disbelief.

"Well, you said somewhere not awkward...." he trailed off.

He had a point.

And he brought me some place 'not awkward'...

... for 3 year olds!

We were standing in front of a colorful ice cream shop decorated with a bunch of fairytale princesses. The place was crowded with loads of hyper little kids who were bouncing up and down with ice cream smeared all over their little faces.

"You're not embarrassed to be caught walking into a place like this?" I asked.

"Nope, not as long as I'm with you."

I don't know how he did it, but one way or another, he got my heart racing. Just little gestures here and there, little replies like that just made weak. I wonder if I was the only girl he's said it to...

What was I thinking?

He had girls pooling at his feet. Why would someone as incredible as him pay attention to only a nerd like me?

We walked into the crowded shop and went to the counter to order some ice cream. On the way there, I tripped on an ice cream cone some kid had dropped.

Right as I was about to fall on my face, Axel caught my arm in time. My face was merely inches away from the floor. Luckily, no attention was directed towards us. All the parents and excited children were too busy checking out the princesses.

Axel pulled me up and grabbed my hand. He leaned in close and whispered in my ear, "you owe me." I rolled my eyes before trying to pull my hand out of his warm one, but it was no use. He had a soft, iron grip on my hand- it was an oxymoron in itself- it was like he was delicately holding onto me… tightly. I couldn't find the right words to describe it.

"Let go," I tried pulling my hand out of his tight iron grip.

"Why should I?"

"You'll cut of my hand circulation!"

"I'm not holding on that tight, Cinderella."

I rolled my eyes at the nickname he gave me. "Why do I remind you of Cinderella so much?"

"I think you know why."

I froze and looked at him in the eye. He had an evil smirk plastered on his lips. I felt something odd in the pit of my stomach. Something was telling me to get the hell out of there, but I didn't. I just stared at him, lost in his eyes.

I shook my head, "but I don't know why."

He smirked and draped an arm around my waist before dragging me into his hard rock chest. "I think you do, Princess…" he said with his nose buried in my hair. It surprised me a little how I could hear him over the Justin Bieber they were blasting.

I felt a tug at my free hand. "Excuse me," a little voice called out from below. I looked down and saw an adorable little girl with midnight black hair and large round grey eyes stare up at me. I just couldn't help myself when a huge smile spread across my face.

"Hi there!" I said in the friendliest voice I could.

"Get lost kid," Axel glared at the little girl.

I nudged him in the ribs. "Be nice," I scolded.

"Why?"

"Because, she's so little and adorable." I grinned at the little girl in adoration. "I just wanna' take her home and pinch her cheeks all day long!"

242

"That doesn't sound wrong at all."

The little girl tugged at my hand again reminding me she was still there. I wiggled out of Axel's iron grip and knelt down so that I was at the little girl's level.

"Can you please help me," she asked.

I just couldn't say no to something so adorable, "of course! What do you need help with?"

I could feel Axel cringing from behind me.

"Can you please help me draw a picture of Cinderella?" the little girl looked at me up through her lashes.

I froze at her request. I had never drawn for someone, in fear of getting insulted. It was my little ounce of freedom from time to time.

"I can't draw," I laughed nervously.

"Yes you can," the little girl beamed at me.

"I really can't, I'm sorry," I scratched the back of my neck and got up slowly.

"She's lying, she can." Axel had to say. "I've seen her draw."

What? Since when?

The girl's eyes started to water. "I asked my mommy and she said the exact same thing, I just want someone to draw Cinderella for me."

"Um, little girl, please don't cry," I said awkwardly.

Tears started to pour of out the little girl's eyes.

"Shit," I muttered under my breath.

"Great job, now you've made her cry." Axel watched with amusement.

I just didn't know what to do with an adorable little girl crying in front of me. I mean I would've drawn her a picture, but I was too afraid of Axel teasing me or calling me untalented and telling me to give up.

"Princess, you better fix this I think her mom is nearby." Axel said gesturing to an older version of the little girl who was standing at the counter while ordering ice cream.

I really didn't want to do it, but I had no choice. I knelt down to the little girl and patted her on the shoulder. "I'll help you draw Cinderella," I offered.

She sniffed away her tears. "Really?"

I nodded. "Sure, it can't be that hard, right?"

I heard Axel snort behind me. The little girl beamed at me before grabbing my hand and dragging me along the shop. She pulled me up to a table and pointed to a piece of paper and a pink crayon on the table.

"So you want me to draw with a crayon?" I asked.

She nodded in reply while grinning at me. I laughed nervously. I had never drawn with crayon before.

"Hey Princess, you owe me more," Axel laughed while tossing a pen to me.

I tried catching it, but of course it fell to the ground. I fumbled to pick it up, "thanks."

He just laughed at the fact I couldn't catch.

I started to draw what I thought was the real version of Cinderella. She was in a large puffy dress and her hair was up in a high bun. It was just a special sketch, nothing special. I heard a gasp from behind me and turned around.

"Oh my gosh!" the girl's mother squealed at me, both her eyes were fixed on the paper on the table. "That's amazing!"

I tried to hide my blush but probably failed epically, "thank you."

The little girl looked at the picture and squealed before hugging my waist tightly. "I LOVE IT!"

I laughed before hugging her little frame. "I'm glad you do!"

Axel grabbed my waist from behind. "Now draw me."

Did he have a habit of touching me or something? Because he was really making me nervous.

"I really can't-"

"I've seen you with your little notebook or occasional scrap piece of paper sketching away."

I was shocked- he noticed?! "W-When?"

"Doesn't matter, you can draw. Don't put yourself down."

The little girl and her mother left, taking the picture with them. I smiled at myself. Finally, I could be proud at myself for something.

Axel bought us both an ice cream cone, he bought me vanilla, which was my favorite by the way, I had no idea how he knew and bought himself strawberry. Wouldn't really imagine a bad boy eating a strawberry ice cream...

"Axel?" a low pitched woman's voice called out from behind us.

What the-

"Axel! Oh my gosh it's you!" the voice called out again.

He grabbed waist faster than I could say 'shit'.

I heard him groan before he turned us both around. The action brought me flying unicorns to my stomach, but I concentrated on the Barbie before us.

She had dyed blonde hair, you could tell from the roots of her hair that she wasn't a natural blonde, her lips were far too large to be natural- they were so puffy you could tell she had lip injections, boobs the size of watermelons, a butt the size of the lid of my washing machine and a few pounds of makeup on her face.

She looked so fake.

"Axel! What are you doing here?" she asked Axel while attempting to bat her heavy eyelashes at him.

"None of your business," he growled at her.

Woah! What was that? His arm tightened around my waist and pressed me harder against his body. I looked up at his face to see him glaring intensely at her. She put her hand over her heart like he had hurt her feelings.

"Ouch!" she faked a gasp. "Don't tell me you're still mad about what happened."

He didn't reply, but he just kept his intense glare on her.

"Aw, come on babe you know you still want me," she winked at him seductively.

I really needed a bucket. I felt like throwing up. She was flirting with him knowing that he had his arm draped around another girl's waist. The other girl was going to do something about it!

"He doesn't want to talk to you so I think you better leave him alone." I told her bitterly.

She sent me a death glare. "Stay out of this bitch. You're just a little slut he's playing around with-"

"Debbie, shut your whorish mouth and fuck out of here." He had said it so loud, kids were watching, and parents had their mouths hanging open in shock.

The kid who dropped the ice cream earlier grabbed Debbie's hand, "Mommy, what does whorish mean?"

Mommy?!

"It's nothing Damie." Debbie glared at Axel before grabbing the little kid's hand.

Axel crouched down so that he was at the same level as her kid. "You want to know what that word means?" The little girl nodded eagerly waiting to hear his answer. "It means your mom," he replied with a smirk plastered on his face.

We heard the whole crowd gasp before angry parents started to yell at us.

~*~

"I can't believe we ran into her," Axel groaned throwing his head back.

I played dumb, "Who is she anyway?"

Axel hesitated before replying, "my ex."

I had to block out my jealousy. "Why did you guys break up?" I already knew the reason via stalking though.

"She fucked the football team, and then got knocked up by our rivalry team coach."

I didn't know she got pregnant!!

"What a-"

"Slut, whore, slot machine? Yeah," he laughed. "Thank god that's over with."

"You really hate her," I concluded.

"Of course I hate her," he scoffed. "She made all the footballers laugh and spit in my face by letting them all bang her. She cheated on me in the worst way possible. I mean, I didn't give a flying fuck at first, but I was lonely. I wanted something like in the movies, a partner in crime, Bonnie and Clyde type of shit, you get the picture?"

I nodded. I wanted that too, except a Cinderella and Prince Charming version.

"After getting beat senseless by my stepdad, I'd go to her. I trusted her with my problems. All I was asking for was someone to be there for me, and vice versa. She was always pushing for sex, but I wasn't ready- I mean, my life was way too fucked up to think about stuff like that."

I almost sighed in relief. At least he didn't sleep with her.

"She was the first person I decided to trust. She told her about her issues, how she felt insecure and she was jealous of the other girls on the cheer team. I trusted her, I really did. I guess that's the part that fucks me up the most. I chose one person to trust, and she stabbed me in the back."

"Not everyone's like that..."

"Almost every single person I met is no different." He was on the edge talking about this sensitive topic, "I never wanted to move here. I wanted to go live with my dad in California, but my mom won me over so I only got to see my dad in the summer."

I knew that from stalking him. Summer was the time of year I felt love sick, and pained. I only wanted to go to school to catch a glimpse of him.

"Mom remarried an asshole who took all his anger out on me. He beat me till a couple years back. I was finally big enough to beat him. He was rushed to the hospital." His jaw was clenched; I desperately wanted to hold him.

He ran a hand through his hair. "That day I finally snapped. What's pathetic is my mom has always been on his side. She always says that I'm the one to start all the fights and arguments because I'm immature. She even hired a new psychiatrist not long ago for me."

"Psychiatrist?"

"Some bitch named Cleo."

Yep, definitely my stepmother.

"My mom's tried everything. Everything to bring me back to the 'person I was before'. She always reminisces about the times I was innocent and sweet," he laughed without a trace of humor, "the little boy who'd smile and crack jokes all the time. But she was manipulated by my step dad. She chose him over her own son."

"D-do you still want to go back to California?" I asked him quietly.

"I did," I felt a pain in my chest, "until about... two weeks ago."

"What made you change your mind?"

He shrugged, "guess I found something worth staying for."

"Which is...?"

A small smile appeared on his face, before shrugging.

"Come on, tell me." I nudged his shoulder playfully.

"Pissing teachers off?"

I was kind of hoping for a different answer, but the least I could do was appreciate his answer because he didn't mention anything about another girl. We both laughed along from his answer.

"I still don't get how we managed to get ourselves kicked out of a freaking ice cream shop," I laughed.

"We got kicked out cause we're both too bad ass."

"Yeah, like I could pass for anything bad," I rolled my eyes. "What you're looking at here is all goody two shoe material." I gestured towards my body.

He checked me out from head to toe, "not really."

Surprised by his answer, I raised both eyebrows.

"Would a goody two shoe risk her well being and stand up on a motorcycle when Mr. Bad Ass himself wouldn't dare do that?"

"Not really," I grinned sheepishly.

"Yeah, so you're nothing close to good. I think you're pure bad ass, to be honest."

"How?" I scoffed.

"You're patient on a badass level."

"Patience isn't badass at all."

"I find self control to be."

I laughed, "whatever, Mr. Bad Boy."

He looked at me, "I can be anything you want me to be."

Be mine.

"So," he started another topic, "heard you have a stepmom."

I nodded.

"Is she my psychiatrist by any chance?"

"Yes…" I admitted, unsure of his reaction.

"Thought so."

"She's terrible."

"I know exactly how you feel."

"You do know I'm supposed to be grounded right now."

"Really?" He grinned, "Like I said, you're nothing close to good."

"I've been avoiding her. If she sees my face, she'll murder me. I know for a fact she'll ground me for a year."

"Want me to help you?" he offered. "I mean, for the convenience of you being able to help me."

"How could you possibly help me?"

"Trust me."

~*~

Chapter 29 MR. BAD BOY'S HELP

"So what's the plan?" I asked Axel as we walked out of the electronics store.

I slept over at Dustin's in order to avoid my stepmother. I snuck in at 4AM to pack my clothes in a suitcase. The twins had helped me; when Justin was on h is own, he was far nicer than I had expected. I was surprised Cleo hadn't called the police up and report me missing yet. I'm sure she must've been planning something big.

Since it was Saturday, I didn't have to worry about missing any school.

Axel had told the clerk that we wanted a high quality camera that was unnoticeable to make a porno. Creative much? When I got mad at him his excuse was 'So they won't get suspicious'.

"Be patient, Princess." Axel replied walking over to his motorcycle. "Hold this?" he passed me the bag with the video camera. I grabbed the bag from him.

"Can't you at least give me a hint of what we're about to do?"

He shook his head, "you'll find out soon enough."
~*~

We sped into the gigantic driveway of his mansion before he slowed down and stopped. He didn't bother parking his 'baby' in his garage. He snatched the bag with the camera from me and motioned for me to follow him.

I got up from the motorcycle quickly and followed him into his mansion like a lost puppy. Surprisingly the whole mansion was clean, considering there was a huge party Thursday night. "How'd you get it so clean?" I asked.

"This magical thing called maids."

I ignored his sarcasm. "But there weren't any maids here on Thursday night from what I remember."I scratched the back of my head.

He spun around quickly, making me walk right into him. My nose hit his hard rock chest. I looked up to meet his amazing emerald green eyes.

"What happened to little miss goodie two shoes?"

"I mean, I heard about the party and how big it was-"

He smirked down at me before cocking his head to the side. I felt like a deer caught in headlights. "There's no point in lying, Princess."

"I'm not lying," I lied again.

"And I'm not as stupid as you think I am."

"I don't think you're stupid."

"Obviously you think I am," he narrowed his eyes at me in a playful way.

"Fine, I was here Thursday night," I confessed avoiding his eye contact, "happy?"

He nodded, before turning around and going up the staircase.

"Who throws a party Thursday night anyway," I followed him up the stairs, "it's a school night."

"Who hits someone who was defending themselves because they got jumped and were outnumbered?" He shot back.

That shut me up.

After climbing up a bunch of stairs, Axel finally stopped in front of a dark door with a sigh that read 'Do Not Disturb'. He put his hand on door handle before twisting it opening the door. He stepped aside and gestured for me to go in first.

I observed the room as I walked in slowly. Dark brown wallpaper decorated the room and all the furniture in the room was hard wood. There was a large office desk beside some shelves and two chairs in front of the desk.

I stood there awkwardly just staring at different pieces of furniture in the room as Axel walked to one of the bookshelves and started setting up the camera we got earlier. He turned to me and handed me a cord.

"Charge my laptop," he said before walking out of the room.

He gave me the easiest job.

Once I was done with the simple task, I walked over to the large desk and looked at some of the picture frames on the desk. Most pictures were of an older balding man with a large beard with an older female version of Axel.

"You done?" Axel asked walking into the room.

I turned around so that I was facing him then nodded. He set his shiny black laptop on his step dad's desk before plugging another cable into the camera and hooking it to his laptop. He started installing something on his laptop. It was the camera's program.

Since the camera was wireless, he had to hook it up to his computer to install the software, so all the footage would be automatically saved to his laptop.

5% downloading...

We both stared at the screen with our fingers crossed behind our backs. If this didn't work, I would be grounded for a year. I kind of had an idea of what he was planning to do, but I was still not completely sure.

Both our heads snapped up when we heard voices from the other side of the door. We both turned and stared at each other with worried expressions.

"Okay, here's the plan. I'll distract him from here as long as I can, you just make sure it completes the loading process and when it's done meet me by my bike," he said frantically.

"I thought you said she wasn't a bike," I teased.

He smirked before shaking his head. "You never fail to make me-"

He got interrupted from the door knob twisting. "Shit!" he muttered before he got up and sprinted for the door. Axel left to room to confront his step dad. I grabbed the laptop from the table and set it carefully on the carpeted floor before looking back at the screen.

15% downloading...

I glared at the laptop screen. Couldn't it load any faster? And it was seriously getting hot in here. A bead of sweat rolled down my forehead.

"Axel Storm Spencer! Step away from my office door right this instance!" a deep voice yelled from the other side of the door.

---Axel's P.O.V---

"Axel Storm Spencer! Step away from my office door right this instance!" my asshole step dad in front of me yelled at me.

"Eager?" I raised an eyebrow at him.

For some reason I just loved getting on his nerves. I liked to see him on the edge and I would push him as far as I could to see if he would ever attempt to throw a punch at me again. Because if he did dare raise his fist, he was getting sent to the ER again.

"What do you want?" my step dad glared at me. "Money? I just transferred $50,000 in your account yesterday."

I shook my head before laughing humorously. "You know what I want."

He kept his glare on me. "I'm not sure what you want this time, Axel."

I decided to use the argument I used countless times, "I want you to leave my mom the fuck alone."

"Well, that's one thing I can't give you," Satan smirked at me. "Open your eyes and see child, your mother is in love with me and you can do nothing about it."

I growled at him while clenching my fists to my sides.

"I wouldn't attempt to hit me again if I were you. You don't want me calling the cops on you again, would you?" he laughed.

He's just trying to get under your skin.

"Motherfucker!" I yelled angrily.

"Now, now, that isn't how you show respect to your father."

"You are not my father," I glared at him.

His face was going to be my new favorite punching bag if he didn't shut up.

"Oh, but I am. Accept that kid."

I laughed, humorlessly, "What does mom even see in you?"

"Obviously everything she didn't see in your biological father."

"Like pussy."

"Get out of my way, I'm in no mood."

I laughed.

"I'll cut off all your credit cards, see if you'll be laughing then-"

"Not so fast, old man," I held up an index finger. "You wouldn't want to do that," I sang.

"Why not," he narrowed his eyes at me.

I checked my nails. Wow, my middle finger had a bit of dried blood under there. Was it from Ricky, Jaxon, Jaxon's buddies, or Matt? I looked up at the bastard.

"Because you can't risk me spilling."

~*~

---*Rosie's P.O.V*---

How do programs take to install?! I pushed the laptop so I was hiding under the desk. I wiped some more sweat off my forehead before glancing back at the screen.

63% downloading...

The yelling from outside was suddenly replaced by angry footsteps and the door slamming open.

"You should be grateful I actually gave your mother a second glance!" his step father yelled.

"You have no right to say that!" Axel yelled back.

"No man would ever take your mother seriously! Your mother did have quite a reputation-"

Axel's father was interrupted from finishing his sentence. I heard a loud crack before everything went silent. My eyes widened in fear. I really didn't want to peek from behind this desk and found out what that was.

"Y-y-you!" he was panicking, "I'm calling the cops!" The old man announced.

I squeezed my eyes shut and covered my ears with my hands. I hated violence, I just couldn't stand it! I couldn't stand seeing blood, bruises or anything or anything of that sort. I could just imagine Axel's stone cold emerald green eyes glaring down at his step father.

The image gave me shivers to the bone. Emotionless Axel scared me at times. He didn't care about anything and didn't give a damn about the whole world, all he wanted to do was hurt or kill.

After what seemed like an hour but probably was about 5 minutes, I slowly opened my eyes and uncovered my ears. The first thing I saw was the computer screen.

92% downloading...

I took in a deep breath and peeked from behind the desk. Axel's step dad got up from the floor slowly while wiping the blood off his nose with the back of his hand. He limped over to the table I was hiding under.

I bit my lip and crossed my fingers hoping that he wouldn't see me. He snatched his phone off his desk and dialed a number. It rang once before the person on the other line answered.

"Hello?" an annoying perky voice answered.

My eyes widened when realization hit me. Cleo?

"Darling, are you free?"

Darling?!

"Not at the moment, but I will be tomorrow." She replied in such a seductive tone, I almost puked.

"It's urgent; I need to see you as soon as possible."

"I will come tomorrow at..." she paused, "precisely 10AM."

"Thank you."

"See you, my love."

LOVE?

The call left me feeling confused and betrayed. Why were they talking to each other like that? It was obvious that they had a little affair going on, but my step mother with Axel's step dad?! That was just a no-no.

Axel's step father placed his cell phone back on his desk and slowly made his way to sit at his desk where I was hiding. Oh god, this was not going to be pretty!

~*~

Chapter 30 MR. BAD BOY'S ACHILLES' ANKLE

--Axel's P.O.V---

What was taking her so long? I bought her enough time to download the whole disk, stop by the bathroom on the way and come out here. But still, she wasn't here yet. I leaned against my baby. Maybe I should've bought her a little more time.

That girl has never failed to surprise me. I sighed and picked up a rock from the ground and aimed at my step dad's office window. Of course with my great aim, I missed it by a foot or two. Rosaline didn't know we had that in common, terrible aim. I huffed and grabbed another rock on the ground before aiming it for the window.

Karma was on my side this time, the rock crashed through the window and landed on something or someone with a thud. Oops. A few minutes later Rosaline came running like an insane person out of the house.

"You asshole!" she yelled at me running towards me with my laptop in one hand and a cable in the other.

I put both my hands up in the air in surrender and backed away from her.

"Did you throw the rock into that window?!" she asked, her eyes narrowed in slits.

"Did you set the camera on the shelf with a clear view?"

"Yes," she hissed, "I don't know how but I did!"

I sighed in relief.

"Did you throw the rock at the window?" she repeated her question.

Even though she was short, she sure knew how to intimidate people. I nodded slowly with both my eyebrows raised up. She set the laptop on the ground slowly before taking in a deep breath.

"You threw a rock!" she yelled angrily.

"So?"

"Look at that poor window!"

I glanced at the broken window, then looked back at her and shrugged.

"Do you have no conscience?!"

I flinched at her tone.

"What's wrong with throwing a rock at a window?" I asked.

"You could've hurt someone!"

"But I didn't."

"Actually, you did."

"Who?"

"The window."

I thought I had issues...

"The window isn't a living thing."

"It still has feelings!"

"How do you know?" I cocked an eyebrow at her. She was acting very odd.

"Because I've talked to it."

"You've talked to a window?"

"No, a wall," she replied sarcastically. "Windows have feelings, they get mad when people throw rocks at them and can get revenge sometimes."

She was really acting strange it was almost like she was on some kind of drug or something...

"Are you ok?" I asked worriedly.

She shook her head before wiping some sweat away from her forehead. "I'm perfectly fine, Prince Charming."

"Prince Charming?"

"Sometimes you act like a total jerk while other times you act like you care when you probably don't!" she said bitterly.

My eyes widened a little from her sudden outburst.

"I'm sorry, whatever I did, I'm sorry!" I apologized.

Why was I even apologizing?

I had no idea why. But she looked really cute when she was angry... She huffed and covered her eyes with her hands.

"Why do you have to be so cute? I can't stay mad when you're looking that cute!" she whined.

Did the seriously say I look cute?

I've been called hot and sexy before, but I've never been called cute. A bead of sweat rolled down her forehead. It wasn't even that warm out here, how could she be sweating?

I slowly reached over and felt her forehead. Her forehead was burning hot like a pavement on a hot summer day.

"You've got a fever," I told her gently.

"No I don't."

"You've got to get some rest."

"I already slept last night."

"Obviously not enough."

No wonder she wasn't thinking too straight, she had a fever. It explained her change in behavior.

"What's this funny business with your stepdad and my stepmom?!"

I ignored her, "where are your clothes?"

"Kasays, why-"

I stored the laptop in my baby's compartment. Everything was set, the program was installed, the camera was in the room, but....

"Did my step dad call your step mother up here?"

"She's coming tomorrow 10AM."

"Good. I'm taking you home."

"Cleo's there."

I cursed, "Hop on." I handed her a helmet.

"We're not going to my house right?"

I shook my head.

With her arms around my waist, we sped into the distance. She gave me the directions to her female best friend's house. It was tacky as hell. Possibly the ugliest house I had ever seen.

The lawn decorations were beyond tacky. The house itself looked unstable- the government seriously needed to put a sign up telling people how dangerous that shit was.

When her friend saw me, she freaked out.

Rambling shit to Rosaline, as Rosie stood there, obviously half unconscious- it was going in one ear and right out the other. I kept my eye on Rosie, she really wasn't feeling well. We enough clothes for two nights in a backpack, and sped off.

I wasn't in the mood to deal with my stepdad, nor her stepmom, nor anyone else... so I took us to a motel on the outskirts of town. I stopped at a pharmacy along the way to pick up a couple of things for her.

She didn't protest, in fact, she barely talked.

I bribed a nurse at the pharmacy to write a doctor's note saying Rosie was too sick to go to school, just so she wouldn't freak out if she couldn't make it into school on Monday.

Even though we got the biggest room in the motel, it was still pretty small. I had gotten separate twin beds for us, since she probably wanted to sleep alone. She was the walking dead- literally. The girl barely had any energy left.

I had to help her into the bathroom. I noticed she kept the door unlocked the entire time she was in there, but I had respect, though it was hard to resist, I didn't take any sneak peeks at all.

Of course, she screamed out from the bathroom, "I forgot a towel!" with the energy she had left. I rushed over to her and handed her one.

The poor girl was only able to put on her underwear and shorts, before she fell against the sink. I heard the fall, and rushed into help her up. She was passed out from exhausted. I lifted her up with the towel around her chest and carried her to the bed.

I couldn't let her sleep with merely a towel covering her chest, so I helped her put on her shirt. I sat behind her, and kept her sitting up. Slowly, I put her head through the hole, and each arm through the arm holes following that.

Her skin was like Egyptian silk. I found satisfaction in helping her. Helping her made me feel like I finally had a purpose.

While helping her put on her shirt, my hand brushed her breast. It took every ounce of my strength to hold myself back from holding her close.

What was wrong with me?

I put a damp towel on her head to soak the heat. I remembered my mom helping me as a kid the same way.

I ran my thumb over her cheek. She was truly something else.

I had to stop myself from further touching her by showering and distracting myself.

She had become my soft spot; my Achilles' ankle. She could break or make a man. I let the hot water run over me. I thought about life.

I thought I had no purpose.

But simple actions.
Standing up for her, and standing by her side.
Gave her strength.
And I really loved seeing her fight back.
I liked seeing her with the power she possessed.
She was a queen, earning her crown.
Everyone was trying to prevent her from doing so.
Jaxon.
Layla.
Matt.
Even Kasay.

I felt they all needed her for selfish reasons.
So do you.

261

I wanted to make her happy. I didn't mind being lonely, as long as it made her happy. I wasn't selfish with her. I wanted her to gain her strength, her freedom...

I thought about her being with someone else, and almost broke the bathroom tiles with my fists.

I needed her to breathe me.

I needed to be all she desired.

I needed her to gain her freedom, but *choose* to come back to me.

~*~

Chapter 31 FEVER DREAMS

I woke up before Rosie did. My stomach was painfully growling. We had skipped dinner last night because I fell asleep from the moment I put my head on the pillow. I got a quick shower and changed into some spare clothes I always kept in my baby's compartment. That place could fit wanders.

It was actually pretty chilly in the morning. I locked Rosie inside to make sure she was safe, and took a short walk outside. I walked to a little diner down the road. I could've taken my bike, but I just needed more time to think about things. Damn, I should've brought a jacket.

The road was completely empty. We were outside of town anyways.

I pushed through the doors and was hit in the face with the smell of bacon and cheese. Thankfully, it was warm inside.

"Mr. Spencer," the old cook greeted.

"Jeff," I greeted back. He used to work at the house, but my dad fired him because the food was 'too greasy'. I liked my food cooked that way. Greasy and fried. "Got anything for a sick girl to eat here?"

"We have some cream mushroom soup, today's special."

"I'll take one of that then."

I looked up at the menu. Would Rosie get full with just a container of soup?

"You got a girl?"

She wouldn't be coming to this diner anyway, so I might as well… "Well I don't have her, but she's the best one yet," I smiled.

"Hope she's no trouble maker."

"Oh no, no," I shook my head, "she's… a good gal'. Straight A's, calm, kind, patient, and looks at the world positively most of the time."

263

Jeff's lip tugged upwards as he flipped a patty, "you should hear yourself. Ain't love a pretty thing?"

"Oh no, no, I'm not in love-"

"You can't deny that smile on yer' face boy."

I didn't want him getting the wrong idea... well, I gave him the idea in the first place. So I was to blame.

"Why don't you make her yours?"

I was taken aback by his question.

"If she makes ya' that happy, why don't you marry the girl?"

"Marrying is a bit too far-"

"Make her yours boy! Before someone else sweeps her off her feet."

The guy had a point.

"What else would a girl like on your menu?"

"Most girls are picky. Take one of everything, and then see what she likes." He joked.

I did exactly what he said.

~*~

Walking back with two paper bags full of food earned me weird stares from the maids at the motel. I was used to em'. They must've thought I was feeding an entire family in the room. I unlocked the door, and slipped in quickly to stop the cold from getting in.

I was so tempted to say, 'Rosie I'm home!', but I stopped myself. That'd be a bit weird for her. It felt so nice going back to place where someone who cared was waiting for you.

"Rosie," I called out.

She still lay asleep. Somehow, she still managed to look adorable with bed hair.

"Rosie," I called out again.

She still didn't wake up. I unpacked one of the boxes that contained a dish with bacon in it. I opened it and waved it in front of her nose. Her eyes flew open immediately.

"HUNGRY!"

I was so startled, I almost dropped the box.

She lifted herself up and sniffed the air, "you have food?"

I nodded quickly, holding up the box, "I got you some food."

She looked behind me, "what's that?" she pointed at the paper bags I had carried in.

"Drugs," I joked.

She screamed.

Wrong move Axel, bad timing.

"Just kidding, I'm only playing," I quickly put the box down in front of her and went to open the paper bags to prove it was just food.

She calmed down.

"Sorry, I don't feel too well," she said, seeming aware.

"Well, I got you breakfast." I brought over the containers of food and placed them on her bed. She got off of her bed to make room for the food.

"Thank you," her voice was so sweet. It was satisfying to hear her approval, "How much did you get?"

"I didn't know what you wanted," I got picked up the last container of food and placed it on the bed, "so I got one of everything."

She seemed to be slipping in and out of self awareness. She started laughing; "really?" her voice was high like a little girl's voice.

I frowned, "is that bad?"

She suddenly seemed aware again, "no, no, will we finish it though?"

"How hungry are you?" I asked.

Her stomach growling was an answer for me.

"We'll manage." I opened the container of soup and handed it to her with a spoon, "Since you're not feeling too well."

She finished the soup in less than a minute.

It was good I had brought more food.

I chose what she didn't seem to want to eat. I gave her the first picks. There was something comforting in seeing her being treat with respect and seeing her being put first for once. No one else seemed to realize they didn't treat her too well.... Except Dustin.

The guy was *too* nice to everyone.

I made sure to keep a close eye on how close he and Rosie were. He seemed like the type of guy she'd end up falling for.

"Eat more," she tossed me a breakfast burrito. Even with her terrible aim, I still managed to catch it.

I noticed her slowly shift towards me on the bed we were sitting on. I don't know whether she was doing it consciously, but I'd like to think she was.

Surprisingly, we only had a breakfast burger left. We were so hungry, we managed to finish everything else.

"I feel gross, I haven't brushed my teeth."

She was slipping back into her unaware self. I felt her forehead with the back of my hand; the fever was still there. She needed to sleep it off.

"Do you want to go home?"

She shook her head, "step mom."

"She's going to my step dad's at 10." I glanced at my watch, it was 9:23. "We can head there now and just go in when she leaves."

She seemed aware once again, "we can't risk it. What if she's gone for only a short time?"

"She's usually there for hours at the least-"

"What if she decides to turn around and come home?"

"We can lock the door."

"What if she breaks the door down?"

She was getting a bit silly again.

"What if she doesn't?"

"But I'm saying what if she does?"

"And I'm saying what if she doesn't?"

She groaned in annoyance, "you're impossible."

"Impossibly sexy?"

"Sometimes," she mumbled.

Yep, definitely not fully conscious.

"What was that?" I smirked at her.

"Nothing..."

"Whatever you say Princess, but I'm taking you home, and there's no way you can talk me out of it."

"But-"

I put my index finger on her lips to stop her from talking, "Don't even waste your breath, Flower."

She rolled her eyes at me, "Whatever Mr. Bad Boy."

~*~

---Rosie's P.O.V---

On the way to my house, I felt myself get a little hotter every second, but I was too tired to complain. Axel didn't mind me wearing his helmet while I had a fever. He also didn't mind the fact that I was clinging onto his waist like a baby monkey clinging onto a branch.

I leaned my head against his back and sighed as we sped down some streets. Even though I was wearing a helmet, I could still smell his rich scent. His scent was intoxicating and addicting. I just couldn't get enough of his smell.

I wondered what cologne he used. Maybe I should've asked him. I felt a bead of sweat roll down my forehead. Axel said it wasn't even hot out here. It was almost November; it shouldn't have felt like mid-summer. Especially in the state we lived in.

"You okay?" Axel asked.

I nodded against his back. I didn't want to get it him worried over my stupid fever.

"You sure?" he asked again.

I nodded again, "stop worrying."

I thought I heard a faint, "I can't," but I ignored it. It must've been my imagination. Axel wouldn't say that to nerdy Rosaline.

"Where are we?"

"Almost there," his voice soothed me.

I yawned.

A few moments later, we pulled to a stop in front of my house.

---*Axel's P.O.V*---

"How do you know where I live?"

I scratched the back of my head. How was I supposed to answer that question without creeping her out? She sounded out of it and not sober. She probably wasn't thinking straight with her fever.

"Well, aren't you going to tell me?" she asked.

I decided not to reply at all.

"I'll just assume you stalk me then."

I could never expect what she was going to do or say next. "I don't stalk you."

"Sure you don't," she said in a disbelieving tone.

"But I don't!"

I was obviously guilty.

"Then how do you know where I live?" she challenged me.

"A little birdy told me," I lied smoothly and crossed my fingers behind my back hoping she wasn't thinking straight enough to catch the horrible lie.

"What birdy?" she asked suspiciously.

Relief washed over me as I realized she wasn't thinking straight at all. "Tweety," I replied lamely. I was even shocked at how dumb I sounded.

I heard her curse under her breath. "Damn it! I should've known he was a spy all along."

I stared at her, amused. She was actually upset with herself. Fantasy and reality were getting mixed up in her head.

I quickly got onto the bike and motioned for her to follow. I drove a couple houses down to watch Rosie's stepmom leave her house. She drove a pretty new convertible. She treated herself well with the money Rosie's dad gave to them, yet didn't save any for Rosie. It made my blood boil.

Once the car had left, I drove us back to her house, purposefully parking my baby right in the driveway so she wouldn't be able to park in the garage.

"Let's go inside," I motioned for her to follow me. She quickly followed me. "Do you have a key with you?" She stared blankly at me.

"Key," I made a hand action of unlocking the door.

She stared at me, before looking at the ground. She started talking to herself. "No, I can't let that happen," she whispered.

"Let what happened?" I asked, snapping her out of her daze.

"Nothing," she replied a little too quickly- indicating she was lying.

I didn't push her on the subject; she was half asleep anyway. "Okay then, we'll just have to find another way in then." I looked up and observed the medium sized house. She lived in two story cream house with a brown roof.

There was a window opened on the second floor, but it'd be quite a climb to get up there. I could've broken the door down and hoped her stepmom wouldn't mind. Oh, hell with her evil stepmother. She had been sleeping around with my stepdad for nearly three years.

I felt so stupid for knowing it all along and saying nothing to Rosie. She could've used it to her advantage. I had always been afraid to talk to her, since middle school. Sometimes in the hall I would catch her staring at me, but pretend not to notice and look away.

Most people stared at me because I was 'different'. They couldn't seem to grasp my concept of life. The schools' in school suspension room had been my classroom since 7th grade. I moved to this sad town at the end of 6th grade.

My mom divorced my dad because she thought he was a 'loser', and she could do better. Dad worked in a garage and fixed cars. We weren't the richest family, but at least we had enough to get by. But mom wanted more. She went for one of the richest business men in the country.

I didn't really know what was going on back then. She'd disappear for days, telling me 'I'm finding you a better future'. She cheated on my dad with my current step dad. She wasn't the nicest person, but she was my mom.

The most ironic thing about this whole situation was that she had the exact same thing happen to her, (except for the money part). Karma got her back. But it was unfair; I didn't deserve the wrath she brought on. I guess that's why I didn't feel the need to break it to her until it benefitted me.

Moving back to California wasn't a priority anyways.

So a couple hundred thousand dollars shut me up temporarily.

I avoided em' both.

Mom wanted nothing to do with me.

Rose suddenly spoke up, "Did you know that what is called a 'French kiss' in the English speaking world is known as an 'English kiss' in France?"

I turned to her and studied her carefully. Her bright blue eyes, as bright as the summer sky were staring at me with expectation. I had no clue what she was talking about, "no?"

"Well, you should've known that," she crossed her arms over her chest and narrowed her eyes at me.

"No need for the attitude, Princess."

"You should know that, because you've probably done it with plenty of girls," she said bitterly.

"Where'd you get that idea from?" I cocked my eyebrow at her.

She huffed, "everyone thinks you're a player, and it's probably true."

"Then everyone's a fucking retard," I growled.

For some reason I hated her saying that to me. I hated her accusing me of being a player. I usually didn't care when other people judged me, but for some reason I hated it when she judged me.

Especially judging me for something that wasn't true. Her disliking something about me made me feel like the worst thing alive. She made me actually feel ashamed of myself for doing the shit I did. Since I had started talking to her, I hadn't touched any kind of drug. She was the only girl who could actually make me feel bad.

No other girl had that effect on me.

Rosaline was different.

Something in her made her stand out in an ocean of faces.

She seemed vulnerable, yet strong. A person of such contrasts. She was quiet for the most part, yet had an air of authority around her. It was the other people around her who tried to stop her from becoming who she was meant to be.

She was confident, yet shy at the same time. A combination I had never seen before. Not to mention she was drop dead gorgeous. Her long beach blonde hair reached down to her upper back, she had amazing blue eyes and a petite face and body.

I walked around the house searching for an open window or somewhere easier to break in. I could easily break the front door down, but I didn't want the cops being called on us. It was easy to get caught in a town like this.

Luckily, the kitchen window was open. It wasn't too high off the ground; it was just about half a story off the ground. It looked pretty simple to climb through, but it was harder than I had expected. I had broken into a couple places before- not to steal, just to break some shit and cause trouble.

I tried climbing into her window with my bare hands, but I slipped right down. Damn, I wish I was taller. The cold biting into my skin wasn't helping either. I stepped about 10 feet away and took in a deep breath. I prayed I wouldn't break any teeth.

I stepped away about 10 feet and took in a deep breath. "Don't be a pussy, you can do it." I encouraged myself and took another deep breathe. "Axel Storm Spencer, don't be a fucking wimp."

I sprinted as fast I could towards the house. When I came about two feet within reaching the house, I jumped up as high as I could. Thank god the window was opened wide enough, otherwise I would've broken a limb flying through the window.

I flew right through the window and crashed straight into the kitchen wall inside. Thankfully my side hit the wall and not my head, or I would've had to switch plans and take care of myself instead of her. I got up and brushed off a little dust that got on me.

I smiled to myself. That wasn't half bad. I managed to fly through the kitchen window without getting injured. This was the first time in years that the odds were in my favor. I started taking steps out of the kitchen but I stopped.

I turned and looked at the wall I crashed into. There was a large crack in the wall. I was pretty sure Rosaline wouldn't mind. I shrugged, walking out of the kitchen. I walked carelessly through the hallway headed to the front door.

Her house was tiny compared to mine, but it also held a sense of coldness.... not the homey vibe I was expecting. The floor was hard wood with carpeting here and there, the walls were painted grey few picture frames on the walls. Before I let her in, I looked at a few of the photos.

Surprisingly, none were of Rosie at all.

All of them were of her father and her stepmom. It was like they didn't even want her under the same roof. The house was something glittering vampires would live in. I cringed at my own thought. I was listening to drunken girls rambling on too much.

I shouldn't have said the odds were in my favor this time.

Before I could reach the door, I tripped on something and

fell right into the doorknob. With my shitty luck, my left eye smashed into the doorknob. The impact caused me to hiss out in pain and fall to the ground. My hand immediately flew up to my face to cover my left eye. I cursed under my breath as I cradled my eye carefully.

I was about to open the door, but then I realized something. Rosaline couldn't see me injured like this! She'd think I was a loser and would never give me a second glance. She conclude I was some clumsy crack head, which I was weeks ago. I ran back to her kitchen, franticly searching for something to cover my eye with.

There was absolutely nothing. Not even a single kitchen towel... did the woman ever cook? I ran up the staircase in search of at least a small handkerchief to cover my eye with, but I found something else.

I went into the first room I came to. I knew it was Rosaline's room from the moment I stepped in it. Unlike the other rooms in the house, her rooms was colorful. It was the most girly rooms I had ever seen in my life, ever.

It wasn't what I was expecting; I was expecting a room full of books with cobwebs, but this was My Little Pony heaven. I felt like gagging at all the stuffed animals. It was cute, but a bit too much. Her curtains were white with pink polka dots. I felt like shaking my head at her style, but I was more concentrated on finding something to cover my eye with. I went straight to her drawers and started going through them.

I felt creepy going through her drawers to find a handkerchief. I couldn't find any in her top drawer; all I found were school papers. With my hand still covering my left eye, I searched the other drawers.

I opened the second drawer and quickly shut it when I saw what was inside. Now I felt like a real pervert opening her underwear drawer. Wait, maybe there were some handkerchiefs in her underwear drawer...

I took a deep breath and opened it again slowly. It wasn't like I had never seen girl's underwear before; I had seen plenty of girls' underwear. But this was different, this was *her* underwear. I felt my cheeks warm up, but I bit my cheek to stop myself. No, don't blush. Bad-asses don't blush.

Who'd ever imagine the big bad boy blushing over girl's underwear?

The more I thought about it, the hotter my cheeks grew. I had never blushed before. It scared me. What the hell was this girl doing to me?

Secretly, I had always had a little thing for her. Thank god no one ever caught me glancing at her. It started out as fascination. Why was she so patient with everyone who picked on her? Why was she so closed? Why would she hide her head in a book whenever she was alone? After math class, I'd watch her put her books away sometimes.

She was so gentle with everything she did. Layla would sometimes bump into her on purpose and make her drop her books. Of course, I was too afraid to go over and help her or at least talk to her. Whenever she would feel my stare burning into her, she'd look up but I would always be looking in another direction.

I noticed her only dimple on her right cheek, I noticed how when she was nervous she would either bite on her lip, run her hand through her hair or furrow her eyebrows. She was so kind... even when Layla humiliated her, she still didn't want to slit the girl's throat. If I were her, Layla would be long dead.

I've had suspicions of why she picked on Rosaline, but I was never sure.

I've always assumed it had something to do with her messed up family, but I never really paid much attention to it.

I knew Rosie was upset about her emo friend getting expelled, and blamed Layla for it. But if you asked me, the emo had been doing lots of shit behind Rosie's back. She was just oblivious to everything; the violence, the drugs, and the reputation she had.

Layla had reasons for doing things, obviously her reasons for torturing Rosie could never justify her actions, but Layla didn't torment everyone just for fun. I saw the way she was with different people. A bitch to some, sweet to some... and an absolute monster to Rosie.

The true monster was Matt. Layla's sidekick who had a thing for Rosaline, so he tormented the fuck out of her, because he knew she'd never get with him. He was a sick minded cunt, who took advantages of girls at parties. He tried to rape...

I didn't notice I was gripping one of Rosaline's undergarments until I looked down.

My good eye widened before I quickly let go of it. I quickly went through her drawer. I explored the drawer with her undergarments with my hand. My hand felt something hard under all that stuff. I pulled out a little pink diary.

I never knew this nerd had a diary. Then again, I really didn't know her that well. I may have felt like I knew her really well, but I probably didn't. I was about to open the diary and read it, but then I decided to put it down and went back to finding a handkerchief.

After digging through her undergarments, I finally found a little white handkerchief. I quickly tied it around my eye, making it look like a pirate's eye patch, and then quickly ran downstairs to open the door for Rosaline.

Even though I ran down the stairs, I managed not to trip on anything this time. Before I reached the door, I made sure to make extra cautious steps to the front door. I got a tight grip on the doorknob that hurt my eye and opened it.

Rosaline was bent over picking reaching into a flower pot. She didn't realize I was watching her yet. She pulled out a key from the flower pot and looked at it dreamily. I sure hoped that was not a certain key I thought that was...

She looked up at me light a deer caught in headlights. She gave me a sheepish smile while holding the key tightly. I leaned on the door frame and cocked an eyebrow at her. "What door does that key open?" I asked, hoping the answer she was going to give me was going to be different from the one I was currently thinking of.

She chuckled nervously. "Cinderella's attic door?"

I narrowed my eyes at her, "I'm serious."

She scratched the back of her head nervously.

I went through all that trouble just to open the front door for her, and the key was in the flower pot right next to the door all along... I injured myself just to open the god damn door for her.

"You made me go through all that trouble and you had the key all along?!" I raised my voice.

She flinched at my yelling. She looked like a puppy cowering from its nasty owner. I felt horrible after that. She started tearing up, "I-I'm s-sorry Axel."

I felt like a complete asshole, "Sorry, I didn't mean to yell at you." I almost forgot she wasn't thinking straight.

"No, it's okay." She sniffed away some tears. But when she looked up at me again, a giant grin was spread across her face. "So are we playing dress up?"

"Dress up?"

She nodded excitedly. "Yup!" she replied popping the 'p'. "Aren't you dressed like a modern pirate?" she cocked her head to the side.

I felt the handkerchief on my left eye. "Yes!" I laughed nervously, hoping she wouldn't get suspicious of what was under there.

"Fail though," she snickered.

"Fail what?"

"Failed dress up, silly!" she brushed passed me into the house. "I always win dress up with Jaxon."

Hearing his name was like hearing an elephant fart, or someone's nails against a chalkboard. I shut the door behind her and locked it.

"Why are you even friends with him?"

"Because he's my best friend, he's never left my side, and he loves me!"

"You think so?" Boy was she clueless.

"I know so," she replied confident.

I didn't want to rain on her parade, "how do you know he hasn't changed?"

Though she was half awake, I hoped I could still talk a bit of sense into her.

"Because we hang out all the time," she replied.

"You've barely hung out the past weeks-"

"He's been busy with stuff, duh." She liked him so much, she made excuses for him.

"Specify, what kind of stuff has he been doing?"

Leaning Layla over the tables and claiming her and his.

"Like…" she tried to play it off as if she knew, "stuff."

"What kind of stuff?"

"Why are you even asking me this?" she snapped, glaring at me.

"I just want to make sure he's good enough to be your best friend."

"You care? Never thought you did."

"Why do you think I never cared?"

She started talking in third person, "Because the first time you actually talked to Rosaline, was when she was in the nurse's office because of an 'accident' in P.E… and you said something really inappropriate." She said the last part quietly.

I frowned at the first part, but then I smiled that she remembered… even though it was something perverted. "I'm glad you remembered that day."

She huffed. "Why wouldn't I remember that day? One of my best friends got expelled that day."

"Oh yeah..." I was pretty disappointed, "sorry."

She shrugged it off. "I'm tired again, I want to go to bed," she said, climbing up the stairs. She made it a few steps before she tripped and almost tumbled down, but luckily I caught her by the waist in time.

"I'll help you up there." I offered, bending down so she could get on my back.

"Um, what are you doing?" she asked, sounding slightly confused.

"Get on."

"Piggy back ride?"

I nodded in reply.

"Jaxon used to give me those."

"Quit talking about Jaxon."

"Why?"

"Because it pisses me off."

"Why?"

"Just does."

"But... why?"

"Get on my back, Flower."

"Answer me first."

"Flower-"

"Don't 'Flower' me, answer me!"

I sighed, "I just don't like him."

"Why? There must be a reason."

"He's doing something behind your back."

"Like planning a surprise?"

"You could say so."

She clapped her hands, "I love surprises."

"It's a bad one."

She gasped, "what is it?!"

"I think you should hear it from him rather than from me."

Thankfully, she didn't push further, "alright..."

She got on my back and hooked her legs around my back. I easily lifted her up and carried her up the stairs. Damn, how much did this girl weigh? 60 pounds?

She giggled, "Dustin let me ride on his back too."

Jesus, how many guys did I have to compete with?

I carried her up to her bedroom and laid her down on her bed gently.

"How did you know which room is my bedroom?" she asked.

Another awkward question I didn't know how to answer. "A little birdy told me," I used to lie from before.

"Tweety again?" She yawned. "I'll have to get him later." Her eyes started to close and she curled up into a ball on her bed. "Hey, can you please grab me and extra blanket? It's cold in here."

I did what she asked, except I placed the blanket on her. I handed the blanket to her and noticed she was shivering. I put my hand to her forehead and flinched from the heat.

She was hot, both ways. "You have a fever."

"I do?"

"Yeah, let me go get a towel and an aspirin for you." I went out of the room and into the bathroom. I soaked a towel in water and came back and put it to her forehead. She stayed there silently, not complaining at all.

After that I found her an aspirin from the nearly-empty kitchen and gave it to her. I held a cup of water to her lips and helped her through the process of her swallowing the aspirin. "I've always had trouble swallowing stuff." She said right after she swallowed the aspirin.

I laughed at her silliness and shook my head. She was acting like she was high. When I turned around to put the cup away, she grabbed my hand. Was it just me or were there electric currents flowing from her hand to my arm?

"Don't go," she pleaded.

"Don't worry. I'm just going to put the cup down," I reassured.

She sighed in relief. "Can you please tell me a bed time story?"

I hesitated.

"Please?" she pleaded, pulling puppy eyes on me.

Of course with her adorable face I had to give in. "Fine." She scooted over so I had space to sit on her bed. "So do you want me to read a specific story?" I looked at her shelf filled with romance novels.

Was she the type who would be wooed with roses?

Because if that were the case, I was not the person for her.

She shook her head like a little kid, "tell me one you know."

I really didn't know what story to tell her, so I just took a deep breath. I wasn't creative, so I was going to have to improvise.

~*~

Chapter 32 THE TALE OF PRINCESS FLOWER & THE BAD ASS PRINCE

I was under pressure, but I was also enjoying every minute I spent with Rosaline. I took a deep breath and started improvising. "Once upon a time there was a princess named Flower. She was really hot but she didn't know it-"

I paused to look at Rosaline's wide crystal blue eyes. "Keep going!" she chirped excitedly.

"So like I said she was really hot but didn't know it. All the jerks in the high school- I mean in the kingdom would always stare at her ass swaying from left to right every time she walked down the hallway. Her father was never in town and from my opinion was an asshole. She lived with her evil step mom named… Hoe."

I was terrible at this.

"Her step mom was a real slut and slept around with almost every single guy in the town-I mean the kingdom. Flower's stepmother caused lots of people to hate Flower, and blame Flower for her mistakes.

Flower was clueless though, and blamed herself for everything. There was a masquerade ball in the shit hole called palace, and Flower decided to attend it. She didn't want anyone to recognize her, because she felt everyone hated her, so she put on a mask and fixed herself up to go to the ball. She assumed no one could see through her mask.

Everyone who was mean to her before then thought she was a complete stranger and treated her with respect because they didn't know who she was. Flower had a lot of fun at the dance and lots of guys wanted to dance with her. But then an evil guy- I mean ogre named mango tried to get Flower. He saw how innocent she was and wanted to destroy her in his sick ways. He made her squirm under his touch, and made her feel uncomfortable because he was a fucking pervert.

Flower wandered around, and dropped her phone- I mean shoe- no, I mean diary. Yeah, she dropped her diary when trying to escape Mango. Later that night, Prince Bad Ass found her diary and decided to go through it. He figured out the pattern used to open the lock of the diary, because he had recognized it from somewhere.

He saw some of the photos and drawings Princess Flower did. They were breathtakingly beautiful…." I had to calm my beating heart. I hoped I was doing a good job. "He went through her photos, and found that she was lonely… very lonely indeed. Some of the photos showed her backstabbing best companion holding her very close."

Princes Bad Ass knew about the secret that her best friend was keeping from her. Her companion was doing bad things that Flower did not know of behind her back. Her best friend also wanted to keep Flower under his control. He never wanted to tell her about how she was royalty, so he could keep her all to himself.

Anyways, back to the dance- fuck- ball. Princess Flower met Prince Bad Ass on a hidden balcony. They shared their feelings, and Prince Bad Ass was moved as fuck by her. He went back home and teared up like a little bitch thinking about how perfect she was. Let's not talk about that in detail.

After the ball a bunch of crap happened that I don't want to go into about girls slapping each other. Flower was really angry, but she was powerless and couldn't do anything about it. She got pissed off at the judge so the judge put her in prison, where Prince Bad Ass was kept. Prince Bad Ass pretended to be sleeping with his crown covering half his face and watched her interact with the other prisoners.

One prisoner went too far with her, so Prince Bad Ass kicked his ass for her. But Flower hated violence. She despised it so much that she couldn't stand to look at it. The look in her face when she saw violence was heartbreaking.

But of course, Prince Bad Ass didn't know how to act. His life was violent.

Princess Flower looked was like she was about to break down or melt down and cry. Prince Bad Ass liked violence sometimes, but hated the look on Flower's face whenever that happened. Prince Bad Ass then told Flower that she looked cute when she smiled, then Flower fainted. But he'd like to think it was from all the violence she witnessed so she fainted.

Her evil best friend thought it was all Prince Bad Ass's fault, which it probably was, and decided to go beat up Prince Bad Ass, but Prince Bad Ass was the best fighter in the whole kingdom and won the battle.

Near the end of the fight, Flower showed up to protect her evil best friend and slapped Prince Bad Ass across the face. Prince Bad Ass yelled at her but felt bad after. He felt as if he got stabbed in the chest with the sharpest blade ever.

But that night Flower came back to Prince Bad Ass. She attended a ball he threw and met a few people on the way. Then she drank too much wine and got dizzy and didn't know what she was doing.

Prince Bad Ass of course came to the rescue and carried Flower up to his bedroom to protect her. Flower was wasted and needed some medicine so Prince Bad Ass left Flower for a moment to go get some medicine for her.

But then Mango showed up and tried forcing himself upon Flower, but Prince Bad Ass showed up and beat the living shit out of Mango. Then Flower started acting all weird and started touching,"" I made quotations in the air with my fingers, "Prince Bad Ass inappropriately."

Talking about it made me really excited. I bit my lip and tried to hide it by crossing my legs but it kept poking out more. Rose rubbed her eyes sleepily. "Why'd you stop?" she asked.

"Um, I forgot how the story went," I lied lamely.

"How could you forget how the story went when you made it up yourself?"

"I didn't make it up."

"Yes you did, out of all the fairytales I've read, I've never come across this one before."

"Think harder, Princess. I need to use the bathroom," I excused myself, getting up slowly. "I... uh... need to pee."

"You can bee with a boner?"

I looked down and my eyes widened. I seriously fucked up. How could she be so observant with a high fever and meds to make her dizzy and not think straight? Well, she never failed to surprise me. "How'd you-"

"Just shut up and finish the story," she cut me off.

If she were someone else, I would've come up with a smart ass reply. But with her, I held my tongue. I sat back down, "where was I?"

"Where the prince got touched inappropriately," she replied.

"So after that some stuff happened... Prince Bad Ass wanted Flower to think he fell for her disguise like everyone else, so he played dumb. In the morning she snuck out of his room and left him lonely. He truly felt alive when he was with her. He had never felt that way with anyone before."

I was genius. I thought about being a children's author as a possible career choice. "Then the next day all the people who came to the ball in the kingdom had really bad hangovers and shit. Pretty sure a few got pregnant too. Flower didn't get to go to... uh... the library, and started freaking out that she had skipped the library for the first time and ruined her clean record. Then-" I stopped when I saw Rosie sleeping silently in her bed.

The only word I could process in my head was 'adorable'. I never described any other girl that way before. I smiled at her little self curled up in a ball on her bed.

I shook my head and got up from my chair. My little buddy was calm now and there was no need to go fix him up in the bathroom anymore so that left me free. As I was about to leave her room, she snored loudly making me jump.

I bit my lip to stop myself from laughing and slipped out of the room. I left her house and jogged over to my baby. I lifted up the compartment in my baby and grabbed my laptop.

"She's not the one to blame!" a guy's voice yelled.

"She's one of the people to blame!" a high pitched girl's voice yelled back.

Fuck. Two cunts in the same neighborhood...

"No she isn't!" he yelled.

"Don't you dare yell at me Jaxon Kent Smith!" Layla threatened.

I turned to where the voices were from and sure enough I saw them both standing there arguing with each other. I shook my head at them, what a couple. I just couldn't imagine what would happen if those two drama queens got married.

"Chill out drama queens!" I yelled at them.

Both their heads snapped in my direction.

"Mind your own fucking business Spencer!" Jaxon growled at me.

I smirked before flipping him off. "My middle finger salutes you too, Smith."

Layla rolled her eyes at the both of us. "Mind your own business if you value your testicles, ass."

"Just because my initials spell ass doesn't mean you have to call me that."

"You beat the living shit out of my boyfriend, don't make me do the same to you," she glared at me.

"Oh I'm terrified!" I said sarcastically.

"Motherfucker!" Jaxon growled.

"At least I don't masturbate to Shakespeare."

Jaxon balled up his fists. Oops! I guess I pissed him off. Layla stepped in front of him and put her hands on his chest as she whispered something in his ear to calm him down. Ha!

What a loser. Jaxon said something back quietly, but he didn't look happy.

"Just let me fight him," Jaxon groaned throwing his head back.

"Are you fucking kidding me? Look what he did to you last time! And you had multiple guys jumping him Jaxy!" Jaxy? I cringed.

"This is the first and last I'm going to tell you to listen to your girlfriend," I said sincerely.

Layla turned around and sent me a death glare before turning back to calm down her boyfriend. I had no idea they were official now though, guess I was slow on gossip.

"What are you doing at Rose's house?" Jaxon asked.

I didn't feel like telling that asshole anything so I just shrugged.

"What are you doing at my best friend's house?" Jaxon asked in a lower tone of voice.

"Why do you fucking care?" She snapped at her redhead boyfriend, before turning to me, "Why do you have a handkerchief wrapped around your eye?"

I shrugged in reply at both of their questions. I really didn't feel like talking to both of them. Those two drama queens were made for each other. To be honest, Layla wasn't that bad except for the fact she picked on Layla like her dinner plate.

Layla was rotten on the outside and Rose could see that, but with Jaxon it was different. Jaxon was rotten on the inside and was sweet to her on the outside. Even though those two just started having their flings not long ago, Jaxon wasn't that good of a friend to Rose.

Sure he might've cared for her and helped her with some stuff, but when people hurt her he really didn't do anything about it. He was a coward and was too afraid to help his own childhood best friend. I really wanted to show Rose how Jaxon really was, but she would've definitely picked him over me.

They were friends since in diapers, and I showed up merely two weeks ago. I had to gain her trust before making any blunt move.

"Now someone has lost his voice box," Layla teased.

"At least I didn't lose my virginity in the school's parking lot-" Before I could even finish my sentence, I was interrupted by a stick hitting my bad eye. "Shit!" I hissed while grabbing my eye I banged on the knob earlier.

Looking on the bright side, at least it didn't hit my other eye. One black eye was enough for me. And at least I wasn't as beat up as Jaxon. I was pretty proud of what I did to him; I glanced at his bruises and admired my work. If I were that flexible, I'd give myself a pat on the back.

"What are you looking at?" Jaxon glared at me.

"The damage I've done to you," I smiled proudly. I just loved getting on people's nerves for some reason; it was one of my favorite hobbies if you ask me. "And the damage I'm about to do." I referred to Rosaline, and he knew.

I didn't have anything else to say to them so I just turned around and headed back to Rosie's house. I heard Jaxon call for me but I just ignored him. I really didn't feel like getting to anymore drama. Once I was back inside I decided to go check my eye in the mirror to see how bad it really was.

I stood in front of the mirror awkwardly before setting my laptop down on the sink counter and pulling the handkerchief off of my eye. I flinched at the sight of my eye. Sure I've been in a bunch of fights before and I got pretty bruised up. Thankfully, this wasn't that bad.

It was a silly bruise to get. I was adapting to Rosaline's habits... I shook my head and smiled a little. Was it possible for a guy to get butterflies?

Man, that didn't sound like me. I went back upstairs to check on Rosie and sure enough, she was sleeping like the dead. She was even snoring a little. I felt like a stalker when I sat on the floor near her bed and just watched her sleep. I rested my back against the wall and drifted off to sleep...

Knock!

Knock!

Knock!

I rubbed my good eye and stretched before I walked extra carefully to the front door and opened the door. As soon as I saw who it was I quickly slammed the door on his face. I turned around made my way up the stairs.

Knock!

Knock!

Knock!

What the hell did that asshole want?!

I closed my eyes and took in a deep breath to calm myself down. I had to calm down before I did something I would regret. Rosie hated violence, and violence wasn't the answer to stop him from knocking.

I went back downstairs to face the asshole. I opened the door and glared at timid Jaxon on the front steps.

"Can I talk to Rose?" he asked.

"No," I answered before slamming the door in his face again.

Knock!

Knock!

Knock!

I opened the door again.

"Sorry that wasn't supposed to be a question."

"Do I look like I care?" I slammed the door in his face for the third time.

Knock!

Knock!

Knock!

Did this dude know when to give up? I opened the door again.

If he didn't stop knocking Rose was going to wake up. And if he did interrupt her sleep, I wouldn't be forgiving about it. "Quit fucking knocking!" I growled at him.

I saw him gulp before replying. "No, not until I get to talk to Rose-"

He didn't get to finish his sentence, because I slammed the door in his face once again. What did he not get by 'no'?

Knock!

Knock!

I pulled the door open with so much force; the door slammed into the wall and left an imprint of the doorknob in the wall. I was going to break everything in her house… and the only thing I wanted to break was her bed.

"What part of no don't you get?" I glared at him.

"I need to speak to-"

"No," I cut him off.

"I need to explain some things to Rose. I feel really guilty…"

Guilty my ass, Jaxon knew nothing about being guilty. "Explain what?"

"Just let me talk to her."

"Explain about you've been banging her worst enemy? How you're dating the girl who's been trying to ruin her life? The girl who's caused her so much pain and made every single day for her a living hell?"

"Is this true?" someone asked in a small voice behind me.

Both our heads snapped in the voice's direction. Rose stood there in an oversized t-shirt staring at us looking as fragile as a glass slipper. Her blonde hair was a little messy but it still looked incredible on her.

Her crystal blue eyes were still shining bright but were filled with an emotion I couldn't read. Her full pale pink lips were pulled in a straight line and her face was as beautiful as always. I felt my heartbeat increase as I studied her facial features.

I knew I sounded cheesy, but I couldn't care less, because my eyes were laid on one of the most beautiful things I have ever laid eyes on. And that was-

"So is it?" she raised her voice pulling me out of my thoughts. She stared straight at Jaxon this time. I had a feeling she was going to get so pissed. But I was secretly enjoying every moment of this, because I knew at this moment I would mean more to her than Jaxon would.

"Let me explain-"

"How long?" she interrupted him.

"How long what?" he asked.

Her tone was cold, "How long has this been going on?"

"Layla and I?"

She nodded.

"We were official after the dance..." he answered.

She stayed quiet for a moment, staring off in space deep in thought.

"How long?" Jaxon asked.

"How long what?"

He grew tense, "You and Spencer." Seemed like someone was ticked off.

"We're not going out-"

"You don't have to lie to me, everything's out."

I secretly hoped she would've said we were a thing... but sadly, she didn't.

"But we aren't-"

"Then what is he doing at your house?" Jaxon asked her while sending me a glare.

"He was helping me."

"With what?"

"She got sick after a party, take a fucking chill pill," I answered for her.

Jaxon looked horrified. "You went to a party?!"

"No, she went to church," I replied sarcastically.

"Mind your own," Jaxon growled.

"Don't talk to him that way," Rose snapped.

"Why? Why are you on his side?" Jaxon looked heartbroken while asking the question.

"Because he has never lied to me."

That was the candle on the cake. I felt beyond satisfied; floating on cloud nine. Jaxon better have some medicine to treat burned area. I felt like high fiving myself at that moment. I meant more to her than Jaxon did.

"But we've been together since forever. You can't suddenly ditch me for some asshole!" Jaxon raised his voice, "am I that disposable?!"

He had no right to be yelling at her. I wanted to slam my fist into his face again, but I held back. This was her battle.

"People change Jaxon, don't you get it?" she said, her crystal blue eyes were watery. "You chose the person who hurt me most. Out of every girl, you picked her... someone who you knew purposefully hurt me-"

"She didn't mean to hurt you-"

Rose cut Jaxon off.

"Oh, yeah, sure didn't mean to get one of my best friends expelled, she didn't mean to pick on me and make fun of me from junior high till my senior year, she didn't mean to dump her lunch on me, she didn't mean to humiliate me in front of the entire school, she didn't mean to get her whole gang to pick on me! She didn't mean to do a fucking thing to me?"

She started to make her way closer to Jaxon. With every step she took forward, he took a step back until he tripped down the stairs.

"You've hid stuff from me too;" he shot back, "partying? I never knew-"

"That's nothing compared to what you've done to me," a tear slid down her cheek. I stayed leaning against the doorway watching the entire thing play out in front of me. Rosaline was about to be my best friend.

"I got with Layla, you got with Spencer- we're even."

"Don't you even dare," her voice was like a knife slicing through his skin, "Axel hasn't done anything to you. The only time he hurt you was because you attacked him first."

"He took you Rosie. He's taken you away from me. That's far worse than anything Layla could do-"

"Don't," she put a hand up, indicating he stopped talking. "You know what?" she laughed coldly, "I don't want to see your fucking face again."

He had no chance with her now.

"I'm so sorry, I'll make it up to you, I promise-"

"No Jaxon, no..." she took deep breathes to calm herself down. "Goodbye Jaxon..." she said.

"Rose I didn't mean to-"

Before he could finish his sentence, she slammed the door in his face. Damn, I had never seen her that pissed before. She was pretty hot when she was pissed.

~*~

Chapter 33 REVENGE IS BEST SERVED SWEET [PART 1]

If only looks could kill...

She was glaring so hard at the door, I almost felt sorry for it. Oh god, I was really becoming soft. Caring for a door? I was adapting her manners and thoughts

She locked the door and slammed her fists into the door over and over again. Though she couldn't really punch, she beat the door until she slightly cracked the wood. I didn't want to interfere. She needed to let her anger out.

"Why her?!" she screamed at the door, but I knew it was directed at Jaxon.

"Out of ever filthy whore on the surface of the Earth, why her?!" she walked passed me and grabbed a lamp off of a stand next to me. She smashed it against the door with full force. Still, I wasn't planning on stopping her anytime soon.

Even if she decided to burn down the damn house, I wouldn't stop her. Well, that was a bit extreme... But sometimes people have to take all their anger out on something or someone to feel better. A little harmless violence wouldn't hurt.

"Why her?!" she grabbed a picture frame of her dad and slutty Cleo from the stand beside me and smashed it against to door, causing glass to shatter all over the place. "I've been hurt, manipulated, and trapped!" she screamed on the top of her lungs, "I'm sick of it!"

I thought that was the end of her tantrum, but that was just the beginning. Her ice blue eyes were filled with so much anger I thought they were going to explode. Her body was shaking uncontrollably and her face was red from anger.

"Her office," she whispered to herself before stomping away.

Instead of discouraging her, I wanted to give her a high five for finally doing something about her situation. She was treated like shit for so long, she was about to reach her snapping point. I quickly followed her into the kitchen and watched her grab stuff out of her fridge.

She grabbed a jar of pickles before popping the lid off and sniffing it. She made a disgusted face before closing the lid and pulling out five more jars of pickles out of the fridge.

Who the hell has six jars of pickles in their fridge?

She grabbed two boxes of whip cream out of the fridge while mumbling something about them being expired.

She left the fridge open and grabbed a bottle of ketchup and a bottle of mustard from the kitchen counter. She went back to the fridge and grabbed a pack of eggs before shutting the fridge. She got a few cans of tuna out of a cabinet before attempting to carry all that.

"Let me help," I offered.

"I can do it," she replied, trying to carry all that in one go. I admired her stubbornness and her capability to carry five jars of pickles at the same time, but she couldn't carry all that by herself. I had no idea what she had planned ahead, but I decided to help her anyway. I almost felt excited because of how unexpected she was.

I grabbed the other jar of pickles from the ground and scooped up all the other food in my arms. The smell of the food was really making me sick. All the food smelled like shit. "It's all expired."

Was she psychic or something? "Why the hell do you have six jars of pickles in our house?" I scrunched up my face in disgust.

"She loves pickles," her voice was laced with hatred.

"Obviously not only this kind," I joked.

I couldn't really see where I was going, but I followed her footsteps to what looked like an office door. She kicked the door open and set the jars of bad pickles down. I did the same and set the food down next to the jars of pickles.

The room looked like it was built in the 1800's. Looked like a vampire built it or some shit. There were bookshelves along the walls and the wallpaper was old fashioned. So this is what a coffin looked like... I was interrupted from my thoughts by Rose grunting as she tried pushing the desk over.

I helped her knock it over with one hand.

The drawers came flying out. Not that much stuff was ruined though. Damn, her stepmom was an organized psycho.

Rosie couldn't have cared less.

Huh, I liked this Rosie.

She pulled open one of the drawers from the desk and went through it. She grinned evilly as she pulled out a red folder. "What shall I do with you?" Her fingers frantically flipped through the pages contained within the file. Her evil grin widened, "I feel so... evil." She giggled to herself.

I just stood there staring at her, shamelessly I might add. My eyes traveled from her feet to her face. I couldn't care less at how nuts she sounded at the moment. She pulled out some papers from the folder and set them on the ground. Then she grabbed a jar of pickle juice and poured it onto the carpet around the papers before turning to me. Afterwards, she also grabbed a bottle of water and poured on top of the pickle juice. "Got a light?"

I pulled out a lighter and handed it to her.

"You smoke?"

"Used to," I shrugged while handing her the lighter.

"Good you stopped," she accepted the lighter from me.

"Why is good I stopped?"

"Smoking kills you," she stated. "And I hate the smell, and the taste."

"Why, you knew someone who smoked?"

"A few."

"Guessing you kissed Ricky?" I tried to ask coolly, but it came out aggressive.

She nodded, "and smelt it from my mom."

"Cleo?"

She swallowed like it was hard for her to say, "Biological mom."

I was quite surprised by her answer. To think about it, she didn't really talk about her mother. "Where's your mom now?" I immediately regretted the question after it came out of my mouth.

"She left," she replied in a tone as cold as ice. "Don't know where she is."

"I'm sorry-"

"Don't apologize for asking questions," she cut me off. She avoided eye contact with me and grabbed the papers from the ground. She smirked while lighting the papers on fire. She threw the burning papers to the ground where the pickle juice was.

I had to admit, she was a genius. She poured pickle juice and water on the carpet so that the fire wouldn't spread as the paper burned. Ha, I never would've thought about that. She grabbed the red folder and pulled out of the rest of the papers before folding them neatly.

"Stay here," she ordered me before rushing out to get something. I shrugged and obeyed her. I really didn't want her anymore pissed than she already was. She came back in wearing a tight white tank top and a pair of jean shorts.

She looked hot in the white tank top, but I wouldn't want her dressed like that outside. Too many guys would be staring at her boobs, and that was my job. I could tell she knew I was checking her out, but she just didn't care.

She grabbed a pickle jar and threw it against one of the bookshelves. The pickle jar smashed   against the shelf making small pieces of glass fly everywhere. I turned away so that the glass wouldn't hit my face, but Rose just stayed complete still.

She grabbed some photo frames off another bookshelf and threw one to me. I caught it before it hit my face and looked at the photo. It was a picture of my step dad, my mom, Cleo, and the guy I assumed was Rosie's dad. Huh, so they've all met before.

"Is that your dad?" I asked not bothering to look up from the picture.

"Don't really know anymore, he's never here and doesn't try to keep in contact," she replied in a cold tone. The tone obviously wasn't directed at me, but I still got chills from it. The four people were smiling at the camera.

"Do whatever you want to it," she gestured to the photo and smirked at me.

I smirked back at her, "I intend to." I threw the picture frame onto the floor and smashed my foot down onto it. I bent down and grabbed the picture out of the broken frame. A piece of glass cut me but I didn't flinch.

I was going to take all my anger out on this stupid picture. It was silly of me, but I felt like I needed it. We both needed it. "Hey, can I have the lighter?" I asked her. She tossed me the lighter to me without looking up from what she was doing. My aim was great, because her throwing still sucked.

I managed to catch it and lit the picture on fire immediately. I stared at the picture burning slowly. I watched the corners burn and curl up in the flames. I enjoyed every moment of watching their smiles disappear from the picture.

I let the picture fall to the floor and stomped on it over and over again. Those four deserved it. My mother deserved it for cheating on my dad and marrying an asshole. My step dad deserved it for having an affair with my mom while she was still married to my dad, and for beating me when I was younger.

Cleo deserved it for controlling and manipulating Rosie, making her life a living hell, and sleeping with my step dad while my mom was still married to him. Last but not least, Rosie's dad deserved it for never being there for her. He listened to everything Cleo had to say, but I could tell from her anger that he didn't care enough to talk to her. Instead, he chose to hear everything through his trophy wife.

A good parent should always be there for their kid, no matter how old their child is.

I was so concentrated on glaring at the photo that I didn't notice was Rosie had done to the room. When I looked up I was shocked. She had whip cream, mustard, and ketchup decorating the walls. She actually did the room a favor if you asked me.

"Like it?" she asked, admiring her own work.

"I love it," I grinned at her. I felt proud of myself for exposing her to the truth. I got her out of the dark and showed her what was going on behind her back. She grinned back at me.

"I haven't even started yet," she chuckled. "This is me warming up."

"Well, let's get started shall we?" I offered a hand to her. She accepted it and pulled me out of the room. Was it just me, or were there electric currents flowing through our hands that made me never want to let go? God, I was sounding cheesier and cheesier with every second passing by.

She pulled me into a king size bedroom and let go of my hand. I suddenly felt a little empty inside without her hand in mine. She rushed over to a closet and pulled out a suitcase flashy suitcase.

She zipped it open and started pulling out random women's clothes from the closet and dumping it in the suitcase. They seemed to be all brand named clothes. I saved a white dress that looked about Rosie's size from being terminated and placed it on Rosie's bed.

"Could you go grab some bad ham and expired milk for me please?" she asked politely. How could I say no to that? She poured everything into the suitcase. I smelt the expired milk from feet away. Gross. The milk was chunky and smelt sour. Rose's bright blue eyes glowed with an emotion I couldn't quite pinpoint as she watched the milk fall from the carton into the suitcase.

Once she was done, she threw the milk carton in there and went over to the bathroom in the bedroom. She came back out with soaps and shampoo bottles. "Wanna' help?" she raised her eyebrows at me.

"Hell yeah," I grabbed some shampoo bottles from her. We poured the shampoos into the suitcase and dumped the soaps into the suitcase as well. "I'm guessing this is your evil step mom's suitcase?"

"She's my ex step mom from now on," Rose replied.

"As soon as your dad sees the video, you won't see her again." I reassured her.

"I don't want my dad to be the only one to see it."

"What do you mean?"

She looked up at me. "I want the entire town to see it."

"Revenge porn is illegal."

She looked disappointed.

"But your wish is my command, princess."

~*~

"Did the file come through yet?"

"Still loading, it's in HD."

"Your laptop is impossible," she glared at my laptop before licking the whip cream off her milkshake. Yep, she dragged me to a café… to get a milkshake.

After destroying some more of Cleo's stuff, I couldn't get logged into the internet in her house because she forgot her wifi password so we decided to drive to cafe. I was still worried about the fever she had earlier, but she seemed okay now after taking some medicine.

"What time is it?" she asked.

I glanced at the corner of my laptop for the time, "about 8:30."

"We've been here for a long time," she huffed. "I've had two milkshakes and it's still not done loading."

"Again, it's in HD. Once I get the file, I'll have to scroll through and find when exactly they were doing their kinky stuff-"

"So you'll watch our stepparents having sex?" she scrunched up her face in disgust.

I almost puked even thinking of it, "I won't watch it, god no. I'll just find when the video starts and ends- that's it."

"You'll still have to see it."

"Unfortunately, unless you'd like to take the job-"

"No thank you!" She immediately declined, "your laptop is slower than two box turtles having sex."

"You know how long it takes two box turtles to have sex?"

"I-I-" she stuttered to say something but failed.

"You watch animal porn?!" I gasped loud enough for everyone to hear. Everything went quiet and I felt all eyes on us.

Her cheeks turned bright red. "N-no, o-o-of course not!"

"No need to lie to me."

She lowered her voice, "I Googled it in fourth grade out of curiosity. Out of curiosity only, I swear!"

By then everyone was back to their own business.

I gasped, "Naughty girl!"

"No! It was only for educational purposes-"

"Uh huh, still doesn't change the fact you watch animal porn."

"No!"

"You watch animal porn."

"I don't!" she hissed.

"You're transparent."

"What's that supposed to mean?"

I stared at her, "It means I can see straight through you."
She looked a little paranoid for a moment. "It means I can see
through your lies, or anything you're trying to cover up." She
visibly tensed up. Something was up, "It means I can tell you
watch animal porn."

She relaxed but still swatted my arm. Was it weird for me to
like it when she swatted me like that? "So like to watch turtle
porn?" I asked her and gained a swat on the arm again. "Box
turtle porn?" she swatted my arm again. God, I really was
enjoying her touch.

"I don't watch any porn," she said holding her head up high.
"Sure."
"I don't."
"I believe you," I held my laughter.
"No you don't."
"Damn."
"What?" she glared at me.
"Are you psychic babe?"
"Babe?"
Oops. I tried playing it off cool. "Don't you just love your
new nicknames?"
"Not really," she lied. She was so easy to read.
"You're like glass slipper, I can see right through you."
"Nice comparison."
"I'm serious."
"So am I," she looked me in the eye. I stared at her bright
blue eyes before looking at her milkshake.
"What are you looking at?" she asked sounding insecure. I
really don't know what she had to be insecure about.
Everything about her was perfect already; she had no reason
to be insecure.
"Your milkshake," I replied honestly.
An old lady walked passed us at that moment and gasped.
"You should be ashamed of yourself!" She swatted me with
her purse and left.

It left us both laughing.

"You deserved that," she teased.

"Meanie," I pouted.

"Seriously? Mr. Bad Boy actually called me a meanie?" she laughed.

"I like your nickname for me, it's very…. Creative."

"Why thank you, I thought you might prefer being called 'Prince Bad Ass'."

I froze up. Ah, fuck! Did she remember every single thing?

"What do you remember?"

"Hmm... let's see," she tapped her chin pretending to think.

I don't think my heart could've pounded any faster in my rib cage. I prayed that she didn't remember me getting a boner or me knowing all about her secret. Then suddenly, there was a little beeping sound from my laptop. I looked down and the video had finished downloading.

"It's done," I sighed in relief. "The video's downloaded."

"Finally! That was slower than two box turtles having sex-"

"Still, you read box turtle porn."

"Whatever Mr. Bad Boy," she rolled her eyes. "At least I didn't get a boner while telling someone a bedtime story."

Ah fuck, she was conscious…?

~*~

Chapter 34 REVENGE IS BEST SERVED SWEET [PART 2]

---*Still Axel's P.O.V*---

"What do you remember?" I narrowed my eyes at her.

"Good question," she smirked at me. I kept my eyes narrowed on her. She just kept smirking at me like she knew something I didn't, and she seemed too please about it.

"We've been here for hours, shouldn't we go somewhere else?" she asked with that smirk still plastered on her face.

"No, not until you tell me."

She challenged me, "Oh really?"

"What do you remember?"

She tapped her chin, pretending to think. "Hmm, I don't know…"

If it were someone else teasing me, I would've already snapped. But this was Rosie we were talking about. The Rose that I had caught staring at me in the hallways, the Rose that got picked on every single day at school, the Rose who was so confident, yet so shy at times.

Most people called me mysterious, but in all honesty she was ten times more mysterious than I was. She masked her emotions so well behind that pleasant smile, and she posed herself as a good girl so well I was shocked when she did something out of that character. Others classified her as a nerd, but she wasn't one.

I overheard my stepdad talking to Cleo about her cruel experiment on Rosie. She wanted Rosie to be the perfect daughter; to basically have no life and get great grades. She was forcing Rosie into someone else's shoes; forcing her to be someone she wasn't.

Deep down inside, Rose was tough. But she was too afraid to show that side of her sometimes.

When that emo chick who always hung out with her got expelled, that aggression and tough side of of hers deep down inside started to show. Just like me, she struggled with confidence, so she decided to become someone else. Through that persona, she was able to show who she truly was.

Truly a Cinderella story.

So basically she had a split personality. On, I wish I could hold down emotions or hide them deep down inside sometimes.

"What are you thinking about?" she asked, pulling me out of my thoughts.

"What are you thinking about?" I shot back.

"I'm thinking about what you're thinking about," she replied.

"So are you going to tell me what you remember?"

"Nope," she replied while popping the 'p'.

I leaned over the table and whispered in her ear. "You're lucky we're in a cafe and not alone or else..."

"O-or else what?" she stuttered, trying not to sound nervous.

"You don't even want to know, Princess." I whispered before pulling back and smirking at her flushed face.

"Yes I do, I want to know," she spoke back confidently.

"We could take this back to my room and I'll show you." I wiggled my eyebrows at her gaining a smack in the arm.

"Pervert!"

"I'm not the one who watches box turtle porn-"

"Oh don't even start with that Prince Bad Ass." Yep, she definitely remembered the story I told her. "Or should I call you Prince Boner?" she smirked evilly at me.

I was speechless.

No one *ever* left Axel speechless.

Some people sitting at tables near us turned to stare at us in shock.

"What are you looking at?" I called out the people staring.

That was all it took to get them to look away. Rose laughed

silently at me glaring at everyone. "What's so funny?" I huffed at her.

"Your face."

"I thought you like my face," I raised my eyebrows at her. She didn't reply. Instead, she stared at me with her corner of her lips slightly curved up. I truly couldn't read her emotions.

"It's done," I shut the laptop off, "Let's get out of here."

"Why, so you can force yourself upon me?" she asked while getting up.

"Don't tempt me, Rosie." I said in her ear before walking out of the shop.

I saw her gulp nervously through the corner of my eye before following me out of the shop. "You wouldn't."

"You're right I wouldn't," I replied. She visibly relaxed. "I wouldn't have to force myself upon you if you enjoyed it." I smirked at her. I took a moment to think about us. Her against my skin-

"Pervert!" she swatted my arm once again. "And don't even think of the box turtle porn comeback," she glared at me with bright red cheeks.

I walked over to my baby and slid my laptop into the compartment under the seat. "I wasn't thinking of that comeback."

She looked surprised. "You weren't?"

I shook my head.

"T-then what comeback were you thinking of?" I loved it when she stuttered.

"I wasn't thinking of a comeback," I replied simply while she looked at me suspiciously.

"Then what were you thinking of?"

I shrugged. "How amazing it would be to have you pressed up against a wall-"

She cut me off with a smack on my arm. When would she learn that she wasn't capable of physically injuring me? "I'm surprised you don't have a boner yet," she looked down at my pants.

"Hey, the real man is up here," I pointed at my face.

"Sorry, hard to tell the difference because you're both small."

My mouth hung open in shock. Out of all the insults she could've come up with, she had to use the one that hurt a man's pride most. "My little man is not small," I said in a strong voice.

She looked up at me. "How would I know?"

I could tell she was doing this to distract me from asking more questions about what she remembered.

"You're smart," I commented, "but not smart enough."

The smirk fell from her face. "What do you mean?"

"You're avoiding the subject. Tell me, what do you remember?"

"I don't have to answer that," she replied shortly before getting on my baby.

I leaned into her ear. "Don't forget Princess, we are alone now."

Her eyes scanned the parking lot with only a few cars parked here and there before looking up at me.

"Now tell me, or we'll have to do this the hard way."

"You wouldn't do anything to me," she sounded unsure.

---*Rose's POV*---

"You can't be so sure of that," he cocked his head to the side.

I was about to wet my pants and let him do whatever he wanted to me- because I desperately desired his touch, but the other part of me screamed for me to be confident, otherwise he'd think I was a wimp. "You wouldn't hurt a helpless girl in an empty parking lot."

He leaned into me until our noses were touching. "You don't know that."

306

I couldn't help it when his green eyes swallowed me in. There was a glint of something in there, but I couldn't tell what it was. All I know was I had never it in his eyes before. "Y-yes I do." I replied, trying to sound as confident as I could. He leaned in closer until our mouths were inches apart. "Princess, you barely know me," he whispered. I felt a stab in my chest from his words. I barely knew him? All the years I spent watching him, every move I observed, the amount of information I dug up about him... and he claimed I barely knew him?

I went to all the trouble... the stupid dance, pretending to be someone else to even catch his eye, hell- I did things for him I'd never do for anyone. I thought the deep conversations we had meant something.

It was hard being pissed at him when he was this close.

His hot breath was mixing with mine and heat was radiating from his body. My heart was beating harder than ever before. If I just leaned forward, our lips would touch. His lips looked so soft and inviting.

What if I leaned in and kissed him?

How would he react?

Did he just see me as a toy? Was he pissed off and going to get revenge because he knew I lied to him about being Rose? Well technically I didn't lie to him... I could barely concentrate on thinking with his lips so close to mine.

"But we should change that," he whispered.

He kissed me.

His lips were so soft and warm against mine. I was so shocked I didn't know how to react at first, but Axel didn't pull away. He just kept his lips pressed against mine. I came to my senses and brought my hands up to his hair and pulled him closer. He snaked his arms around my waist and pressed my body against his.

I felt his hard toned chest against mine. I felt different emotions explode inside me. Excitement, thrill, love... I felt like I hadn't really lived until now. Our lips waltz together. We were like two puzzle pieces that were finally put together. I had no idea where my confidence came from; I bit his lip playfully. Our tongues danced together in our mouths and that moment everything felt perfect. My life had never felt as perfect and complete before.

I was Rosaline.

The nerd who was too afraid to do anything.

He liked me...

Well I assumed he did, because most people don't kiss strangers unless they're fond of them.

Everything was buzzing inside of me; unknown sensations were taking over me. Was it just me or were there fireworks? My lips tingled with joy. The kiss was slow, yet so passionate. I don't know how long we were there, but when he pulled away I felt disappointed.

He leaned his forehead against mine and grinned at me. "I think we both know how we feel towards each other now, right?" I didn't trust my voice to speak, so I just nodded in reply.

"Rose, Rosie, Rosaline," he ran his thumb over my bottom lip. He was trying to figure something out. I shivered under his touch. "Let's get going," he pulled his hand away and got onto his 'baby'.

"Where are we going?" I asked, getting on his bike.

He shrugged, "My step dad is out to dinner with my mom so we can't pay them a visit yet. Want to invite your dad to their anniversary dinner?"

"Not in the mood yet," I replied coldly. He turned back. I felt bad for taking the anger I felt towards my father and stepmother on him out on him. He did nothing wrong, hell- he helped me! Yet I was being a complete bitch to him. "Hey, I'm sorry-"

"It's cool," he interrupted me. "I get it."

He didn't seem angry. Huh, what a sweet bad boy. Tough and threatening on the outside, but internally he was softer than jello- and I wasn't talking about his organs either. *I think we both know how we feel towards each other now, right?* I kept replaying that question in my head. I know how he feels? Did he kiss me because he pitied me and how I've been betrayed? Betrayed by my childhood best friend and my stepmother?

"You wanna' go anywhere in particular?" he asked.

I shook my head in reply.

His phone buzzed in his pocket so he pulled it out and checked it. He raised both his eyebrows before looking up at me. "The annoying kid's throwing a Halloween party, you interested?"

"Isn't Halloween on a weekday?"

He smirked, "Wednesday. I mean, if you don't want to then I get it-"

"Which annoying kid?"

"The one who's got a mouth louder than a megaphone."

"Trent?"

"That's his name?"

"I think so," I shrugged. "And sure, I've got nothing to lose now," I chuckled. If it were Rosaline from before, I would've declined the minute I knew it was on a school night. But I had missed out on so much on previous years. It was time to enjoy my Halloween this year.

I thought about it in my head. I wanted to party and get wasted like there was no tomorrow. I didn't have to care about my stepmother, or worry about maintaining a reputation- since I didn't have one to start with.

"I've got to show you something," he said, sliding his phone back into his pocket. "Hop on."

I got onto the motorbike and put on the helmet he gave me.

"Why do you have two helmets if you ride alone?"

"To confuse the fuck out of security at night."

He was far cleverer than others gave him credit for. He knew how to keep out of trouble when he wanted to.

"Hold on tight Princess, this will be a long ride."

The engine roared to life. I wrapped my arms around his waist and pressed my body against his warm back before we sped off. Everything flew passed us as we sped down different roads.

The wind was blowing crazily around us. The sky was dark and filled with stormy clouds. I really hated rain. I leaned my head against his back and just took the time to think. My life had changed so much in a couple weeks.

My conclusion?

Every mind held secrets. Some were just far more extreme than others. Some kept them because they were afraid, and others kept them to protect others. I held mine because of fear... fear of rejection, humiliation, and heartbreak.

But once I faced my fears, it wasn't bad. I was truly lucky Axel wasn't upset about it, because he knew I only did it because I was shy. He accepted it, and played along. I believed that was mainly for entertainment purposes, and to see how far I'd go to hide the fact it was me.

I don't know how long we were riding, but it didn't seem long enough with my head pressed against his back.

He took off his helmet. "We're here!" he announced.

I took off the helmet and looked up. We were facing a beat up metal gate that read:

DO NOT ENTER

"You're not going to hurt me... are you?" I chuckled nervously.

He turned to face me and stared intensely into my eyes. "Are you scared of me?" he asked seriously.

"N-no."

"Like I said, I can see right through you," his emerald green eyes bore into mine. "I'm going to ask you again. Are you scared of me?"

I quickly looked away from him, "no."

I lied.

Why was I scared of him?

He held my heart in his hand and I didn't know what he was going to do with it. I didn't know whether he was going to shatter it into a million pieces or treasure it.

"Rosie, look at me," he ordered.

"You can't make me," I said stubbornly.

He hooked his fingers underneath my chin and tilted my head up. "Oh really?" he cocked an eyebrow at me while smirking. "Answer my question," his face was back to serious again.

I couldn't.

"Why?" he let go of my chin. "Why are you scared of me?"

He had the ability to shatter me into a million pieces, he was violent, he had a terrible temper… though I was afraid of him, I was drawn to him at the same time.

"I guess I understand why you're scared," he tossed his helmet onto his seat.

I stayed quiet.

"I wouldn't hurt you."

A moment of silence passed between us.

"At least not intentionally," he added.

"Should I be scared of you?" I questioned.

He turned back to me. He looked so genuine… so vulnerable, "I think I have a better reason to be scared of you."

I walked towards him, "and what might that reason be?"

He smirked playfully, "kneeing me in the balls."

"Oh shut up," I rolled my eyes and chuckled. I started walking towards the gate.

"Where do you think you're going?"

"To see what's behind this old rusty gate," I yelled over my shoulder, not bothering to turn around. I heard his footsteps catch up with me until we were walking right next to each other.

"What's this place anyway?" I asked as we approached the beat up gate.

"A dumpster," he replied.

I stopped walking immediately and looked at him. "You brought me to a dumpster?!" I started panicking. Rosaline was back in action.

"Calm down-"

"Do you know how many hobos or thugs live in dumpsters?!"

"Rosie-"

"You're really going to murder me in a dumpster?" I backed away from him slowly. "At least kill me in a more hygienic place!" I was crushing on a killer?!

Lord, he had my heart, now he was going to get my body too.

"Rose-"

"Please don't kill me! I can't die without getting revenge-"

"Rosaline-"

"I haven't done so many things! I've missed out on so much in life-"

He sighed.

"I can't die yet! I can't die a virgin!"

"You're a virgin?" he sounded shocked.

Shit...time to panic about something else.

Whenever I went into Rosaline panic mode, I'd blurt out random shit that came to my head. The paranoia was triggered by Cleo to be honest, ever since I was a kid. Due to my big mouth, the bad boy now knew I was a virgin.

What if he preferred virgins?!

312

I quickly tried changing the subject, "that's a nice trash bag over there." I pointed at a random toilet seat. I mentally slapped myself.

Get it together, Rosaline.

"Are you alright?"

I nodded quickly.

He went back to the topic I dreaded, "you're really a virgin?" His eyebrows furrowed like he was thinking about something. That question hit me off guard. At Axel's party I woke up in Axel's bed with no clear memory of that night...

"Are you saying I'm not?!" I gasped. "Did something happen Thursday night?!" I threw my hands up in the air, cutting him off before he had the chance to speak. "At your party! Did you just tell me something didn't happen to prevent me from freaking out?!"

Everything felt jumbled up at the moment. I didn't know what to think or how to act. And there I stood in front of a junk yard with the badass I had been in love with for years.

"You really don't remember what happened that night?"

I shook my head in reply.

"What do you think happened?" he questioned warily.

"I don't know!" I yelled in reply. "That's why I'm asking you! I wouldn't ask you in the first place now would I?"

"Calm down-"

"So what happened? D-Did anything h-happen between u-us?" I asked while stuttering.

"Don't dwell on it. Nothing happened."

His answer was too short for my liking. "Nothing at all?"

He nodded.

The way he avoided my eye contact and the way his emerald green eyes looked deep in thought made me suspect he was hiding something from me, but I didn't push it further.

He'd tell me sooner or later... *right?*

"So why are we at a junk yard?"

"I need to show you something," he walked up to the gate and untangled the chains before pushing the gates open.

"Ladies first," he gestured me to go through first.

"Is that just a polite way of saying 'get in front of me while I check out your ass'?" I walked passed him.

"Pretty much," he shrugged with a small smile.

"Pervert!" I rasied a hand up to smack him, but he caught it in time.

"You love it though," he smirked making my cheeks heat up.

I looked around and all I saw were piles of junk everywhere. Thank god it wasn't completely dark though, or I would've thought he really wanted to murder me.

I mean, lights or no lights he could've kill me if he wanted to anyway. There were a few lights scattered about the place, but I didn't want to go anywhere near those lights because the bugs were swarming the lights like there was no tomorrow. I was surprised there were still many bugs due to how chilly it was.

I walked forward but tripped on a piece of scrap metal on the ground. Luckily, Axel caught my waist and hoisted me up so I was standing again. "Thanks," I said brushing the dust I couldn't see off my shirt.

He grabbed my hand and laced his fingers through mine. "Just so you don't fall," he said. My hand felt so small in his. His hand was so warm, and though his palm was rough, his fingertips were so soft.

What'd he use to moisturize his hands? I really needed the moisturizer he used for his fingertips... We walked through the junk yard and passed gigantic mounds of junk. No wonder there's global warming.

"Have you ever climbed a tree?" he suddenly asked.

I turned to him, slightly confused. "Is that a trick question?"

"No, it's a serious question. Have you ever climbed a tree?"

"Of course, but Jaxon helped me…" I trailed off. Thinking of Jaxon made my blood boil and my heart clench at the same time. I felt Axel's muscles tense at the mention of Jaxon.

"I'll help you this time."

"Woah! We're climbing?"

"Yeah," he said as we walked into a dark area with no lights.

"Uh, Axel… I can't see any trees…" my eyes traveled through the dark even though I couldn't see anything.

We stopped our tracks in front of the largest pile of junk I have ever seen up close in my life, "Rosie."

"Axel, there are no trees to climb here."

"No shit," he snickered.

"Then what the hell are we supposed to climb?"

"What do you see?"

"Nothing right now."

"What did you see when we got here?"

"Nothing, just piles of junk…" I trailed off. I froze when I realized what he was trying to tell me. Oh no hell no…

"Exactly," he replied smugly. Oh no we weren't! There was no way in hell I would ever climb up a pile of junk in a freaking junk yard! Not even if the hottest guy on Earth (which was Axel) was going to get me to go up there!

He squeezed my hand making it tingle even more. "It's not that bad."

Okay, maybe I was completely lying to myself about not going up there with the hottest guy on Earth. I was really whipped. Fu-

~*~

Chapter 35 TEQUILA & FIREFLIES

"Ladies first," Axel said while letting go of my hand and grabbing my waist.

"It's too dark to see my ass, you know?"

"Near the top it won't be as dark," he nudged me towards the large pile of junk. "Consider yourself lucky you aren't wearing a skirt."

"Leggings are just as bad," I grumbled before wiggling out of his iron grip.

It wasn't that steep of a climb to be honest, it was like climbing up a hill. I took careful blind steps up the pile of junk. Surprisingly it wasn't that bad. I heard the scraps of junk crunch beneath my feet. Stepping on the tires were the most stable. The hard rubber beneath my feet gave me comfort that I wouldn't fall through. Thank god I had sneakers on.

"Keep going," Axel said from somewhere below me. I bit my lip and concentrated on taking my steps. I took slow steady steps to make sure I wouldn't fall through the junk. I didn't want to fall on Axel.

My inner self giggled at the thought. Of course I wanted to fall on Axel. I wanted to feel his hard toned body pressed up against mine. I mentally slapped myself, now wasn't the right time to fantasize about him. "About that box turtle porn..." his voice was laced with amusement.

"Drop it, Axel."

"Aw, you're not calling me prince?" I could just imagine him pouting while saying that.

"Why, you want me to?" I retorted while climbing the pile of junk.

"Someone's grumpy."

"No thanks to you." I rolled my eyes, even though he couldn't see it. "Why are we even climbing this."

"I'm just tryna' get a good look at your ass."

I pursed my lips, trying to avoid any pieces of metal that I'd fall through.

"You're grumpy because I'm staring at your ass?" he asked, sounding amused. "Sorry, it's just so hard to keep my eyes off that beauty."

"No-yes-no-that's not the reason I'm grumpy," I snapped, "I'm just tryna' concentrate here."

"What do you need to concentrate for? I could climb this pile of shit with my eyes closed."

I rolled my eyes at him even though I knew he couldn't see it.

"Quit rolling your eyes."

Was he psychic?

Before I could even reply, he took the opportunity to say more.

"I know you a little better than you think I do," he chuckled. He did?

After taking a few more steps up I was on top of the pile of junk. There was a couch sitting on the top. How the hell did someone get a couch up here? It looked dangerous as hell.

"How'd you get this thing up here?" I asked, slightly shocked at the old couch in front of me.

"Magic," he said before pulling out his lighter. He grabbed an old jar from beside the couch with a candle in it and lit the candle up making the place glow a little brighter. I could see his face clearly above the candle light.

"There is no such thing as magic," I replied before taking a seat on the old couch. It looked really dirty, but my legs were killing me. I was too afraid to shift in the seat, was the thing even stable?

He gasped, "You just killed a fairy."

He was lucky he had his bad boy image, or everyone would assume he was a softy. Considering he quoted Peter Pan and fairies.

"The bad boy watched Peter Pan?"

"We were all kids once, oh- and be my guest, take a seat," he said sarcastically since I was already seated. He plopped down next to me, making the sofa dip. I almost had a heart attack. I didn't want the sofa to end up sliding off the hill of junk.

"How romantic," I said in a flat tone.

"That's a first," he smirked before looking away and staring at the view in front of us, "impressive, ain't it?"

I turned and looked at the view in front of us. The sky was dark but a million stars shone bright in the sky. Okay, I was exaggerating again. But the number of stars shining in the sky was just amazing. I had never seen so many stars in the sky before. Around us we were surrounded by nothing but fields. A few house lights shone here and there. We were really far out in the country.

Below us a few lights shone but disappeared quickly.

"Fireflies," he whispered in my ear.

I turned to look at him, but my nose brushed his nose making my face heat up. He bent over to the jar with the candle and put it behind the couch, letting the dark surround around us.

"Why'd you do that for? Now I can't-"

Suddenly, a small bright light shone in front of me making me shut up. A little firefly was flying passed us. I stared at it in awe, everything I was going to say about the dark before disappeared in my throat. "They fly up this high?" I whispered, staring at the firefly. I had never been high up in the sky outdoors before. It was definitely something new for me.

"You look so young when you're all fascinated," he chuckled while staring at me.

"Is that an insult or a compliment?" I stared into his emerald green eyes that shone bright in the dark. I was captivated by him. My heart was beating rapidly against my chest. I swear, I almost had a heart attack.

Thump.
Thump.
Thump.
"Compliment," he replied, still staring at me.
Suddenly he turned around, leaving me feeling empty inside. He got up and lifted up a pillow beneath him revealing a bottle of Tequila. He grabbed the bottle and sat back down. "First swing?" he popped the cap off and offered the bottle to me.

I was about to deny his offer, but everything about Cleo and Jaxon flooded back to me. I accepted the bottle from him and took a swing from it. The liquid burned my throat as it went down. It stung at first, but the feeling after was worth it. I coughed after drinking it before passing the bottle back to him.

"I'm a terrible influence," he said to himself.
"If it weren't for you, I'd probably be doing worse."
He covered up his guilt by taking a swing from the bottle.
"I'm corrupting an innocent princess."

Every time he called me princess, my heart fluttered crazily. Call me corny, but it was true. It was probably just a random nickname from the events that occurred, but I just couldn't help but to feel special.

I bit my lip while staring at his perfect form. Prince Charming drinking tequila, I've never heard that before. I giggled at the thought. Axel turned to me with raised eyebrows. "Are you giggling at me?"

I giggled even more, "maybe."

"Princess Flower dares to laugh at Prince Badass?" he joked.

"I am stronger than you think I am, Prince." I meant it as a joke, but he took it seriously.

His eyes suddenly softened, "I know." He looked away. "I'm sorry for all those times at school when I didn't help you.

I was just- I didn't know how to react or what to do around you. I usually keep to myself-"

I pressed my index finger against his soft lips. "It's okay, you didn't know me. You didn't notice me." I laughed, but he frowned.

"That's not true, I noticed you since the first day of school."

I rolled my eyes at him, "sure," I said in an unconvincing tone, "you wouldn't notice someone like me."

"But I did-"

I wasn't buying it, "prove it."

"How?"

"I don't know, but if you really did notice me... then prove it."

I was fully convinced he didn't notice I existed until this year. He had never glanced my way. He was just trying to make me feel better about myself.

"First day of school... middle school. I remember it pretty well. You were wearing a pair of shorts, an oversized white t-shirt that said 'Princess', and a pair of black high top converse. You had your hair up in a ponytail, and had blue bands in your braces.

You walked through the school doors with some kid who had a ginger afro- which I soon later learned his name was Jaxon. I saw you talk to Layla on the first day of school since she was new too. You told her your name and she disliked you immediately.

You met your emo friend in the school cafeteria while you were throwing your trash away. You two became friends right away because she was an outcast like you. You never got in trouble. You seemed to not mind being off the radar at school... self defense mechanism if you ask me.

Freshman year Layla threw a math text book in your direction and it hit your face. That gave you a black eye, and Matt tripped you, giving you a bruise right in the middle of your forehead. I'm not going to mention all the horrible things they did to you... this is just to prove that yes, I did notice you. And just about 3 weeks ago, or less than that, I witnessed you getting soup dumped on you when you were standing in line right behind me," he finished. "I had to get out of there to stop myself from punching the bitch right in the face."

My mouth hung open in shock.

He noticed me.

He noticed everything.

Even the slightest details I barely remembered...

He did.

From what I wore from the first day of middle school... to the things that happened during freshman year... till now...

He saw everything.

I was left speechless after his little speech. I didn't know what to think.

My head was a giant mess right now. I didn't know what to think, I didn't know what to say, I didn't know what to feel. A little part of me was angry at him for not stepping in to help me at all, but he had his own problems at home.

"I-I-" I stuttered, not knowing what to say.

He left me speechless. How come he had that effect on me when no one else did? I grabbed the bottle and took a swing from it. The liquid still burned down my throat, but it wasn't as bad as the first time. It actually made me think straight.

"Still speechless?" he smirked at me.

"You wish."

"Well then Princess, my wish came true."

"Whatever, ass," I chuckled, because his initials did spell ass. "Or should I say, Prince Boner."

"What'd you just call me?" he gasped.

"You heard me."

He grabbed both my hands and pushed me down on the couch before crawling on top of me. His legs rested on either sides of my hips and my hands were pinned above my head.

"Say it again. Say it to my face," he said in my ear, sending shivers up my spine.

"I-I don't have to." I tried to sound confident but failed.

He chuckled in my ear, "I can stay here like this all night."

I swallowed. Ah shit, what the hell was I supposed to do? A firefly landed in his blonde hair. "There's a firefly on your hair," I told him.

He gave me a flat look. "I'm not stupid."

"I'm not lying." I struggled to get out from under him, but I couldn't. A part inside of me didn't want to get out of the position, while the other part wanted to be straddling him instead, "get off."

"Push me off."

I tried, but failed. "Get. Off. Of. Me. Right. Now." I growled, attempting to be serious. Instead, I learned a laugh from him.

"You're so cute when you try to look angry."Even in situations like this he managed to make me blush. "Just say what you said to my face and I'll think about letting go."

"This isn't fair," I pouted.

"Life isn't fair sweetheart," he smiled sweetly down at me. I glared up at him. "Just let me go."

"Nah."

I stared at the firefly crawling onto his forehead. "The firefly is on your forehead now."

"You can't lie to me," he smirked.

"I'm serious, there's a firefly on your forehead." I said, still staring at the insect.

"You know, you're actually a pretty convincing liar," he chuckled.

"I'm not fucking lying," I groaned.

"Princesses aren't supposed to swear you know?"

I watched the firefly crawl from his forehead onto his nose.

"It's on your nose."

He scoffed at me. "You really think I'm that-" he shut up when he saw the firefly on his nose. His emerald green eyes widened at the bug. "Holy shit! Get it off!"

"How am I supposed to get it off you with my hands pinned to my head?" I asked annoyed.

"I don't know! I don't want to touch it!"

"You're afraid of fireflies yet you brought me here?"

"Well they've never landed on me before!" he sounded so funny when he was panicked.

"I don't want to hurt it! I'm not scared of fireflies, I just..." he trailed off while looking at the poor firefly on his nose in fear. He squirmed on top of me while shaking it.

"Get it off!" He squirmed on top of me. It almost felt like he was grinding against me. I personally didn't mind it.

"How?"

"Just blow it!"

"Blow it?"

"Yeah, do it quickly!" he said panting from his little fit.

"I don't know..." I trailed off with a smirk on my face. So the big scary bad boy was scared of fireflies landing on him. I took note of that for later.

"Please!" he said, he looked like a frightened little girl. I had to hold back my laughter.

"Fine, you owe me," I said before blowing the firefly off his nose. It flew away.

He sighed in relief, "thank god."

"What the hell is going on?!" a voice screamed from Axel's pocket.

Both our eyes widened at the voice.

What the hell?

"Shit!" Axel cursed while pulling his phone out of his pocket. "I must've accidently pressed a button when that thing was on me…" he trailed off with an apologetic look on his face.

I shook my head at him while biting my lip. He put the phone up to his ear. "Butt dial."

"Who is it?" I mouthed.

He either mouthed back Justin or Dustin, I couldn't tell.

"No," he said to the twin on the phone.

"What'd he say?" I mouthed to him, but Axel was looking in another direction.

"None of your business," he said to the person on the other end of the call.

I stayed quiet.

"No."

Moments passed of only the other party speaking.

"It's not what it sounded like-"

What sounded like?

"She's fucking fine!"

Axel was pissed off.

"Cut the crap, Dustin." Axel snapped.

Jeez, what did Dustin say?

"Don't tell me what to do, I do what I want."

Axel was getting angrier by the second.

"I don't owe you a fucking explanation."

If I were Dustin I would've shut up and listened to what Axel had to say.

"If you don't fuck off and leave us to our business, I swear I'll go over there right now and kick your ass."

"Axel, what's going on?" I asked.

"See? She's perfectly fine."

"I'm fine, what's going on?"

"No! How many times do I have to fucking tell you?! The answer is fucking no! Nothing happened! Even if something did, I don't have to fucking explain everything to you! You're not her fucking dad," he yelled into the phone.

What the hell did Dustin say to piss him off like that?

Axel ran a hand through his hair. "Find someone else to care about," his voice was stone cold.

I heard Dustin apologize on the other end, but Axel hung up on him shortly after without saying another word.

"What was that about?" I asked, hesitating whether or not to touch him arm.

He turned to me with slightly messy hair. "Do you really want to know?"

I nodded eagerly. Of course I would want to know what they were talking about. I was standing here for a while listening to their weird conversation over the phone.

"Dustin thought you were blowing me."

"But I was blowing you. I was blowing the firefly off of you-"

"Uh... by blowing I mean... giving me a blowjob," he told me honestly. "It's none of his business anyway, but he just heard me tell you to blow it and he assumed... because he thinks of me that lowly."

"D-Dustin seriously t-t-thought that?" I stuttered out. My cheeks felt hotter than a pavement on a summer's day.

He nodded, "he thinks I'm the kind of person who'd force myself on someone."

I started laughing for some reason. "You couldn't force myself on me, even if you wanted to."

He looked at me like I had grown a second head, "I wouldn't in the first place."

I just kept laughing, "because I'd let you take me," I tapped his foot with mine.

He just smiled oddly, "Rosaline, are you drunk already?"

I couldn't reply because I was laughing so hard. Why was it so funny? I had no idea, I just kept laughing. I laughed so hard I snorted.

Axel started laughing, "Did you just snort?"

My laughing no longer sounded normal, it sounded like I was having an asthma attack. By the time I stopped laughing there were tears running down my face. "Maybe," I giggled. I ended up snorting again.

Axel laughed.

He actually laughed.

It was the most genuine I had seen him laugh. It wasn't one of those snickers, smirks, or chuckles... it was a full laugh. I

"I'm impressed my princess knows how to snort," he laughed while throwing himself on the couch with me.

My princess...

At that moment I forgot about all my worries. I forgot about everything, I forgot my cheating step mother, I forgot about Jaxon and Layla, I forgot about the whole world.

The only thing I was concentrating on was Axel laughing on the couch right beside me. We both laughed until we couldn't breathe. Though we eventually stopped, we still grinned at each other like idiots.

He wrapped his arms around me before pulling me into his chest. I rested my head against his chest and listened to his heartbeats while staring up at the fireflies around us. He inhaled deeply before closing his eyes to rest.

I looked up at the clear sky, and how the stars seemed to shine just for us.

I had felt so lonely before. Like no one was truly there for me, I couldn't trust anyone with my heart. But with him, I felt like I could be myself. He was slowly setting me free. It was odd how he kept putting a bit of distance between us sometimes, almost to stop me from relying on him too much.

But right now, in his arms, I felt so free.

My heart was chained to him, but I felt so free to do what I wanted.

"I love you," I said in barely a whisper.

I had no idea if he heard me or not, but when I glanced at him through the corner of my eye he was already asleep with the cutest smile on his face.

Even if he didn't hear it, I felt like I got it off my chest.

~*~

Chapter 36 NO TEARS

---*Jaxon's P.O.V*---

My hands shook in front of me as I stood in front of an apartment building. Though the door was normal, I felt as if it was ten times my size. I felt so small and skinny. Well not everyone could build muscles as big as Axel or Matt. Just thinking of Axel made bile rise in my throat. He was the reason for all of this, if not for him maybe I would've gotten the chance to tell Rosie everything myself.

I lifted up my shaking finger slowly and pressed on a button which I thought was the doorbell. "Star's Residence how may I help you?" I guess it wasn't a doorbell...

"Uh, I'm here to see Layla."

"May I ask who this is?" the woman asked.

"Jaxon."

"Oh Mr. Smith! What a pleasant surprise! We'll let you right in."

"Thank you," I said pressing the button again shutting off the intercom. I had never been so nervous in my whole life. Even performing a Shakespeare play in front of college scholarship recruits wasn't as nerve-racking as this.

The door flew open revealing an old lady dressed, I assumed it must've been her housekeeper.

"This way Mr. Smith." she ushered me up a flight of carpeted red stairs. "Layla has told us so much about you," she gave me a kind smile. "I hope you don't mind of course, she tells me everything. I've never seen her this way before- well actually I have with four different other guys- but it doesn't matter she absolutely adores you! She can't go a sentence without mentioning your name!" the old made giggled like a school girl.

I gulped nervously.

Surely she had no clue at all why I was there for.

327

"All her hatred for that girl has turned her to bitter over the years," the maid shook her head sadly, "but her becoming captain of the cheer team and accomplishing a lot in school has helped her! You have too!"

My palms started to get sweaty as we walked up some more flight of stairs. What floor was her apartment on anyway? "I'm so glad you showed interest in her. It's good you have different interests! At first she was afraid that you'd reject her. Poor girl, she's had a rough life."

We walked through a hall filled with family portraits of the Star family. We stopped once we reached a white door. The maid knocked on the door softly. "Yes?" a voice replied from inside.

"Mr. Smith is here to see you."

The door flew open almost immediately. Layla was wearing a pair of black shorts with a pink tank top. Her chocolate brown hair was wet and looked as soft as Egyptian silk. Though she looked different without makeup, she still looked presentable.

When she saw me checking her out she smirked confidently and leaned against the doorframe. "I'll leave you two to your business," the maid bowed before scurrying off. That maid acted more like a slave than anything...

"Couldn't wait to see me?" she asked in a playful tone.

I wanted to smile at her like I always did when I saw her, but this time I kept my face neutral. "I need to talk to you," I said in a serious voice.

She frowned at me before pushing herself off the doorframe, "come in."

I stepped into her bedroom and looked around. The walls were light purple and covered with pictures of her at different ages with different people. I noticed most of the pictures were of her and Matt hugging and smiling.

He was the school's football quarterback. Why didn't she want him? Why did she want a guy who everyone thought was gay? Why would she want a guy who was in the drama club and loved being over dramatic about everything? The biggest question in my head was 'why would she be interested in a loser like me'?

I knew how much she hated Rose and how horrible she made my best friend's life, but I couldn't help but care for Layla. Under that cold mask she wore when she was around Rose, there was a beautiful young spirit beneath.

Sure she might've been annoying sometimes, but I knew inside she was a fairly good person. She wasn't the nicest at times, but she also wasn't the worst. I glanced at more of the photos on the wall. There were pictures of her and her dad, but none of her with her mom.

"Why aren't there any pictures of you and your mom?" the question slipped out of my mouth before I could stop it.

"Deadbeat," Layla shrugged like it was nothing. My eyebrows furrowed. Why did she hate Rose so much? The two had that in common.

"Why do you hate Rose?"

"I've told you a million times," she rolled her eyes at me. "She deserves to be hated."

"You've never told me the exact reason."

"I don't have to tell you." She crossed her arms across her chest.

"Why? Why do you refuse to tell me every time I ask you?"

"Because I don't have to," she shot back before throwing her head back and groaning. "We always get into an argument when we talk about her, so let's stop."

"No, I'm not letting it slip this time. Why do you hate her so much?"

"You came here to talk about her, didn't you?"

"No, actually I came here for another reason."

"Really?" she scoffed in disbelief, "what is it then?" she cocked an eyebrow at me. "Enlighten me."

"It's over."

She was shocked, "what?!" Her eyebrows furrowed and her chocolate brown eyes were clear with confusion.

"Us, we're over." I forced out.

I felt a painful tear in my chest, but I didn't back down. It was either Rose or her. I had to fix things with my childhood best friend. She had been there for me the entire time and I never really appreciated it that much until what we had was gone. I hurt her, I betrayed her... and I needed to make it up to her.

"It's because of that bitch, isn't it?" her chocolate brown eyes held so much anger, I wanted the ground to swallow me up.

"She's not a bitch! And no, it's not about her."

"Liar, it's about her. You want to fix things between you and her." Her voice was steady, which surprised me. Why wasn't she yelling or screaming? Was she expecting it?

"It's not about her," I lied. "You're a cheerleader, I'm a drama geek, you're popular, I'm not, you've got a pretty face, I don't, you're the life of the party, I'm a 'party pooper'... Layla... it was bound to end."

She shook her head at me. "That's probably the worst excuse I have ever heard. I know it's about that bitch, no need to lie." She was calm, *too* calm.

She knew the truth, and the more I lied, the worse it'd get. I admitted, "Fine. You win. I'm breaking up with you because of her." I felt tears on the corner of my eyes, "You happy?!" I yelled.

She didn't even flinch at my tone. Instead, she stood there observing me closely, making me feel uncomfortable. "You don't want to break up with me," she stated.

"If I didn't want to then why the hell am I doing this?"

"You're doing it because you want the bitch back."

I would say she was psychic, but I knew how smart and observant she was. "She's not a bitch," I went into defense mode, "But yes, that's one of the main reasons. I'm going to go fix things with her because she doesn't deserve any of this"

"Yes she does, she deserves all the cruelty in the world," Layla's once warm eyes were ice cold.

"What did she ever do to you?" I stepped closer to her. "No excuses to avoid the question this time. What did she ever do to you?"

Layla avoided my gaze. "Go ask her."

"Damn it Layla! She doesn't know anything! She doesn't know what she ever did to make you hate her. All she did was introduce herself to you, then from that moment on you hated her guts!"

"She took something away from me."

I was surprised at her answer. It was the first time she had given any detail or hint on why she hated my best friend.

I tried to dig deeper, "and what exactly did she take away from you? Because from what I've seen, she's never taken anything from you. In fact, you took away the smile she used to have on her face every day."

"Nice to know," she said sounding incredibly bored. "Are you done?" she looked up at me.

She couldn't have cared less about what I had said. Maybe she wasn't as good as I originally thought she was. I asked for more information, but she just shut me out. Just like she always did. I walked over to her door and opened it. "Do you even have a heart?" I asked. My voice filled with disappointment. I turned around to look at her one last time.

For a moment an unknown emotion passed through her chocolate brown eyes, but she quickly covered it up. She looked almost sad, "no, she took it away from me the day I turned four." And with that, she walked over to me and slammed the door in my face.

---*Rosie's P.O.V*---

Waking up on Monday morning after Sunday night with Axel was the hardest thing to do. I had to practically pry my eyes open. I had woken up bright at early, 5AM. I got out of my bed and rushed to get out of the house before Cleo woke up.

When I tiptoed past her room, I noticed that her door was open. I pushed it open and quietly stepped inside. The bed was empty, and the mess I had caused was the way it was when I left it there.

Huh... so she didn't come home last night.

So I took my time in the house.

I walked downstairs to the kitchen. It was so cold, so empty. I didn't like how quiet it was, but I was used to it. I got ready for school and made a cup of coffee as I sat down re-reading one of my romance novels.

One section in particular caught my attention.

'The scariest thing about distance is you don't know whether they'll miss you, or forget about you.'

– Nicholas Sparks

I sipped my coffee and thought hard. It made me feel scared. It was our last year of high school after all. I went up to my room and flipped through some files. University applications in particular...

Ivy League had always been my family's dream- well my father's and stepmothers. I just went along with it. But what did I truly want inside?

I opened up my laptop and scrolled through lists of schools. With grades like mine, any school would have to take me. But what about Axel?

After taking a hot shower and throwing on some 'Rosaline type' clothes, I grabbed my backpack and headed out to school. I left my house before the time Jaxon usually showed up. I didn't want to see him, I needed space to think.

Walking through the school doors was as awkward as always. I kept a low profile and made my way to the I.S.S.

room. This time I completely skipped going to the dumb secretary. She'd just make me snap again. There were a couple of other students there I had seen around school, but Axel was nowhere in sight.

Since the teacher supervising was sound asleep, I wrote a fake note about me being needed in the library to help organize books and left it on his desk. I fled the room and hid in the library for the rest of the day. I even skipped lunch, fearing I'd run into Layla. I really needed time to think, and I didn't need any distractions.

I thought about Axel all day.

Where was he?

Why didn't he come?

I checked all his social media accounts, but he didn't post anything.

I pushed down any negative feelings I had about the situation, and assumed he was tired from the previous night. Axel did skip school quite often.

I returned home and found Cleo's car parked in the driveway. Just then, my phone rang. It was my dad. I was so surprised I almost dropped my phone.

"Dad?!" I picked it up excitedly.

Unfortunately it was his assistant. "Hi Rosaline, your father said he'll be going back into town for a dinner with Mr. and Mrs...." I was rude to hang up before she even finished, but I didn't want to hear it. I felt like he didn't care about me.

---*Axel's P.O.V*---

With my arm around Rose's waist, I took another swing from the bottle of mysterious liquid in my hand. While I was sleeping, Dustin had to call me and wake me up from my peaceful sleep. I couldn't believe I slept for almost three days straight.

Dustin had to wake me up and tell me Rosie was in trouble.

I was beyond glad Rose decided to show up as her true self, not her Cinderella persona. She needed to grow confidence in her true image.

Rose started talking to a cheerleader not long ago. I was surprised at how that girl was actually friendly to her. She probably didn't know Rose was the one Layla hated so much, or Layla had sent her. The girl was obviously an innocent freshman or sophomore who had no idea about partying. She just came along with her friends, but then her friends ditched her for guys.

So now she was talking to *my* Rose.

Call me a selfish bastard, but I wanted Rose all for myself. I wanted her to pay attention to only me, no one else. Yeah, I was selfish. The girl had a high and squeaky voice that made my eardrums hurt, badly. But as long as she was being nice to Rose, I was ok with her being around.

"So are you two going out?" the girl asked. The question caught me slightly off guard. "Sorry I shouldn't have asked that," she quickly apologized. "It's obvious since he has his arm around your waist."

My arm around Rose's waist tightened.

"I'm so sorry if I offended you sir!" she gushed out. Sir? Was this chick high? "Please don't ban me from talking to your girlfriend!" she pleaded.

I opened my mouth to speak but she cut me off.

"I really enjoy talking to Rose and I really don't want to lose a new friend I just made."

This chick was seriously on something. Rose and I exchanged worried looks.

"I know I might not be new to this school or anything but I really need some new friends because all my friends care about are boys and cheer and nothing else. I want a friend who understands and won't ditch me at a party for some guy and a friend who'll stay by my side no matter what.

I want someone who knows everything about me and who will never lie to me. Please don't kill me after this because I'm too young to die, I'm just 15. I swear I'm not even lying you can go check my birth certificate! I might be a cheerleader but I'm not like the rest I cross my heart. I put it on all my nail polish that I'm not lying!

I don't really know you, but I've seen you around school and you're not that ugly in my opinion! You were so cool when you slapped your boyfriend for your best friend. I need that loyalty in my life!" She gushed out quickly.

I wanted a tornado to sweep her away. The chick was seriously on something strong.

"I-"

She interrupted Rose from saying whatever she wanted to say. "I know why Layla hates you so much, but you seem like such a nice person! Not like how she described you at all. Just give me a chance and I swear I'll prove myself worthy to you."

Rose narrowed her eyes at the girl. "You said earlier you didn't know why she hated me." The girl's eyes widened before she gulped and avoided eye contact with Rose. "Layla sent you, didn't she?" Rose was beyond intimidating.

"I-I-"

"Just do me a favor and get the fuck away from me," Rose growled.

"I'm so sorry! She forced me to-"

"I don't want to hear excuses," Rose interrupted the girl.

"Please hear me out-"

"No!" Rose yelled, attracting some attention to us. I couldn't care less about the people around us, but it seems the girl did.

"She said to choose between Matt and you, and Matt is really scary-"

"Didn't you hear her? Leave her the fuck alone!" I growled at the girl. She was ruining my night with Rose.

335

"Wait," Rose said, pulling away from me. "Why does she hate me?"

The girl started stuttering.

"Answer me!" Rose yelled. The girl flinched at her tone.

"I-I can't... L-L-Layla..."

"Layla will what? Take away your precious nail polish?" she laughed coldly.

"No, she said she would be sure I would never smile again," the girl said quietly.

Rose stepped closer to the girl. "Tell me now."

"I can't-"

"Bullshit!"

"I swear I can't-"

"Well, well, well, what do we have here?" I would recognize that annoying voice anywhere. The sarcasm in her tone made me want to throw her out of the house. My head whipped in the direction the voice was from. The music's volume lowered slightly so that we could hear her better.

There stood the brown haired cheerleader in a whorish cat costume that screamed 'I WANT ATTENTION!'

"Talk about the devil's bride," I mumbled.

"No comment needed from the lapdog." She raised her index finger in the air and looked at Rosie.

Of course being the badass I was, I couldn't keep my mouth shut. "You have no room to talk. You're banging the ginger drama queen-"

"Let your girlfriend fight her own fights, sweetie." She flashed me a sickly sweet smile. I glanced at Rose who gave me a nod telling me to back down. "Let's take this outside, shall we?" Layla raised her eyebrows expectantly at Rose. Rose furrowed her eyebrows at Layla confusingly. "Just to talk," Layla faked a smile.

"Sure," I rolled my eyes, "just to talk."

"I was talking to her," Layla looked at me, "ass."

"Fine, let's talk." Rose replied walking ahead of us. I followed her but Layla stopped both of us.

"Without your lapdog," Layla pointed straight at me.

"Call me lapdog one more time bitch-"

"Fine," Rose interrupted me before I could finish, "You go ahead, and I'll catch up."

Layla nodded before strutting away. Rose turned to me looking as amazing as always. "Please don't follow me out."

"What if she hurts you?"

"She said she just wanted to talk," Rose shrugged.

"You don't seriously believe her though, do you?"

She bit her lip before looking down. "She said just talk…"

"One way or another she's going to hurt you. If not physically, then emotionally." My words were like a slap in the face to her. "I'm not going to sugarcoat anything or keep you in the dark. You need to realize people are out to get you, people will hurt you."

"I have to fight my own fights Axel." Her bright blue eyes met mine. I don't know what it was, but I felt as if my stomach had just turned right into pink glitter.

"I think my stomach just turned into glitter," I blurted out.

She chuckled and looked down at my stomach. "It's called butterflies."

I scrunched up my face in disgust. "I don't get butterflies."

She just smiled up at me. Damn, how'd I get so lucky?

"Do you get butterflies when you're with me?" I dared to ask, and hoped for a 'yes'.

"No," she admitted. My smile turned upside down. She started laughing at me before putting both hands on my shoulders. "I get the whole zoo when I'm with you." And with that, she pressed her lips against my own.

~*~

337

Chapter 37 SNAPPING POINT

---Layla's P.O.V---

What the hell was taking her so long?

I peeked through a window and saw her slobbering Axel's face in the middle of the dance floor. They pulled away from each other after a few minutes and stared into each other's eyes lovingly.

I snorted out loud.

How fucking romantic.

Why did he ignore me for someone like that?

I just couldn't wait for the day he dumped her sorry goody-little two-shoes ass.

What was so perfect about her anyway?

Her high grades?

Her blonde hair?

Her blue eyes?

How she played the role of someone innocent so well?

Everyone wanted her and was willing to ditch me for her.

After a few major heartbreaks, I knew that no one would be there for me in the end. I was just a pretty obstacle along the way, and she was the real prize. I remembered seeing photos of her when I was just a little girl.

She was the perfect child that every mother wanted.

The little girl who would always listen to her mommy and daddy, the little girl who could melt hearts in a heartbeat... I grew up being the little girl who got made fun of at school because she liked to dance.

But that all changed when daddy decided to move us back here. Back to the boring old town where I was born. I had spaced out and not noticed that Rose was a few feet away from me. "I'm here, what do you want to talk about?" Rose asked, sounding as timid as always.

I put on the mask I always wore and turned around so that I was facing her. "You've got him back."

"Pardon me?" Ah, she always knew her wonderful manners. "Don't 'pardon me'." What a nerd. "You've got him back." "Who?" I kept my face neutral. Daddy always taught me how to hide emotions and never you're your enemies your fears or weak spots. They'll always use them against you. "Jaxon," I replied. "I don't want him."

"But he wants you."

"So you came here to talk about Jaxon?"

"No, he's just a little conversation starter. A conversation about him would be a wasted conversation, don't you think?" I cocked an eyebrow at her. *Ignore the pains in your chest, they'll fade.*

"Then why'd you come and talk to me?"

"Because I can," I smirked at her. She was twisting a piece of thread from her jean shorts around one of her fingers. It was almost too easy to get her nervous and intimidated like that... seeing her like that made me feel superior and stronger than her.

"I'm going back inside," she said turning around.

"You've got a cute little family there, Rosaline..." I commented, making her freeze. She turned around slowly.

"What do you mean?"

"You've got the perfect family."

"My family is far from perfect," she snapped. I was a little surprised from her tone. So she was being smart after ditching Jaxon to be with Axel? Pretty smart move if you asked me.

"Watch the tone, Rose." I almost laughed at her shocked face. Her mouth parted slightly and her eyes widened. Who did she think she could fool with that stupid disguise on at the Halloween dance? "Or do you prefer liar?"

"I'm not a liar," she said in a strong voice.

"You might've fooled Matt, but you can't fool me."

"Nice to know," she replied dryly.

339

Her new attitude pissed me off. "I'd hate for your boyfriend to find out-"

"He already knows," she dared to interrupt me. "He likes me for who I am, and you can't change that."

I licked my lips, she was right. I wasn't going to make him feel any different about her. I cocked my head to the side and raked my brain for a comeback. I didn't like how independent she was becoming. It was a threat.

I smirked; looked like it was time to break her down, "Tell me, does your mommy know about your new habits of partying?"

---*Axel's P.O.V*---

Hiding in the bushes wasn't the brightest idea, but it was the fastest thing I could think of. I stared at Rose and Layla and watched them to make sure Layla didn't lay a finger on Rose. I wouldn't hesitate to hit a girl if she touched a single hair on Rose's head.

"Tell me, does your mommy know about your new habits of going to parties?" Layla asked in her annoying high pitched voice.

"I don't have a mom," Rose replied, staring Layla straight in the eye.

"Sure you do," she flipped her brown hair over her shoulder. "What's your mom's name again?"

Rosie looked like she was about to punch the girl. I liked her new confidence, "I told you, I don't have a mom."

"Cleo, right?"

Rosie growled, "She's not my mom."

"Oh really? She spent every day when you were a little girl taking good care of you." Layla was so spiteful... I slowly pieced the puzzle pieces together...

"She's not my mom," Rose growled.

"Remember when you were about five she took you to the dentist on January 13th?"

340

Rose stared with wide eyes. "H-how'd you know…"

Layla had a cruel smile, but it seemed to be masking something. "From what I heard it was a pretty important appointment, was it not?"

"I didn't even remember that day until you reminded me…" Rose trailed off while playing with her fingers.

"Well guess what, I do." Layla took a step closer to Rose.

Rose's eyebrows furrowed before she looked up. "You didn't even know me back then. We met in middle school…" Rose sounded confused and frustrated. "Did Jaxon tell you all this?"

"I've known you long before we met," she cocked her head to the side. "And no, Jaxon would never open his pretty little mouth to tell me about you," she spat.

Rose looked hurt for a moment, but she covered it up quickly. Layla sighed and shook her head. "Want to hear a story?"

Rose hesitated, "what do you mean?"

Layla rolled her eyes. "I meant what I said," she looked straight at Rose. "Want to hear a story?"

I would've said no and told her to fuck off.

"Axel!" someone hissed from behind me. I jumped and bumped my head against a ledge. Ah fuck! I glared at one of the twins who was crouched down beside me.

"What the hell do you want?" I growled.

"Where's Rose?"

"With Layla."

"What?!" he yelled.

"SHH!" I put my index finger up to my lips before I pointed at Layla and Rose. He nodded and zipped his lips. From the way he was dressed, I would've guessed Justin on meth with some biker dudes, but I wasn't sure. "Which thing are you?" I asked in a whisper.

"What?" he whispered.

"Are you thing one or thing two?"

"Who's thing one?"

"I forgot."

"Who's thing two?"

"I forgot that too, retard. If I knew what thing one was, I would know who thing two was, wouldn't I?" I pointed out.

"Yeah, my bad," he shrugged, "take a guess."

"Dustin wouldn't be as cocky as this, so I say you're Justin."

"Maybe he would be," he shrugged.

"Just answer me, which thing are you?"

"I might be Justin, or I might be Dustin."

"If you're Dustin, you're on crack or some other hard drug."

"So if I'm stoned, I'm Dustin?"

I felt like breaking that annoying bitch's face right there.

"Just answer me!" I hissed.

He hushed me, "they'll hear us."

I grabbed his shirt collar roughly and pulled him closer to me. "Fucking tell me!"

"Jesus Christ!" he gasped. "It's me, Dustin."

I kept my eyes narrowed but let go of his shirt collar. "If I find out later that you're Justin, I'm kicking both of your asses."

"That's unfair for Justin."

"So you are Dustin." Dustin sure changed his image in a short time. He dressed in semi-fashionable clothes for once. The leather jacket was a bit much though.

"Yeah, I kind of changed my style," he looked down at his clothes.

"Why? I thought you had the 'take me home to meet your mom' look going on."

"Well I had to change that," he pursed his lips together. "My brother slept with the girl I like." The poor kid was genuinely upset. "And she likes bad boys like him."

"He's not even a bad boy," I scoffed. I was the real bad boy here.

"Well he's worse than me, and she prefers him over me."

"Sounds like a slut to me."

He just shrugged. "I was just wandering if you could give me some lessons of how to have that bad boy image."

I gave him a flat look. "I didn't choose the bad boy life; the bad boy life chose me."

"Well, then can you at least give me some pointers?" he pleaded.

"Maybe later, I'm busy," I replied, turning back to watching Rose and Layla.

"So your new habit is stalking your girlfriend while she's talking to people?"

I rolled my eyes at the clone. "Why are you here besides the fact that you want the bad boy image?"

"Can't I check on my two best friends to see how they're doing?"

"No, and I'm not your friend."

Dustin shrugged, "whatever you say, buddy."

"You're seriously getting on my nerves right now."

"And?" He was trying too hard to be someone he wasn't.

"If you don't shut up I'll do everyone a favor and break that pretty little face of yours so everyone can tell the difference between you and Justin."

---*Rose's P.O.V*---

I felt proud of myself for talking back for the first time. Layla has been walking over me for too long, it had to come to an end. "Cleo just married your dad because she wanted more money. And because she wanted a stupid little girl who wouldn't stick her little nose into people's business." Layla smirked, "you're dumb, and that's why she enjoys keeping you around."

My fists clenched by themselves. I knew she was right about Cleo, but she seemed happy at the fact I suffered from the words. She looked at both my clenched fists before laughing. "Is little Rosie going to hit me?" she asked in a mocking tone.

Something came over me. I don't know what it was, but everything suddenly slowed down and moved in slow motion. I didn't have to control a muscle in my body. My right fist flew straight at her face. She fell to the ground as blood started to pour out of her nose.

I could've beaten her up right then and there.

Taken all my anger accumulated over the years out on her. But I stopped myself.

I shook my head, and lowered my fist down. I wasn't violent. This wasn't me.

But it felt so good...

"You bitch!" she screamed. People around us were too drunk to notice, they just minded their own business. Not a single person glanced our way.

I was shocked at myself for actually hitting her.

"You worthless bitch!" she spat.

Without thinking, I crouched down and grabbed her throat with both hands. A boost of confidence came out of nowhere to save the day, or ruin it. That moment, no fucks were given.

"Say it, say it again."

She clawed at my hands. Blood was running out of her nose.

"You always have to ruin everything!" she said through the clenched teeth.

I squeezed tighter, but then something inside of me stopped me.

I shook my head again to clear the thoughts out of my head. This wasn't me. I wasn't a violent person. I hated violence. I refused to beat people the way Axel did.

I let go of her neck and stood up to stop myself from further hurting her.

But she deserves it.

"What did I ever ruin for you?!" I spat out. "You've been ruining *my* life since the day you walked in. On the first day of school, can't you remember? I happily introduced myself to you, and from that moment on, you hated me.

You've made every day of my life a living hell. What is it with you and hurting me? Or picking on those below you? You like to intimidate people to feel confident even though inside you're probably a shaking little brat trying to gain approval and popularity.

You got one of my best friends expelled from the damn school! You probably got your daddy to bribe the school-which is illegal by the way. I can see by how spoilt you are that he'd do anything to please his little princess." I glared down at her and said every single word in her face. I wasn't going to cower away like other times.

"Tell me! Tell me the exact reason why you hate me so much!" I yelled on the top of my lungs.

She broke down.

She started sobbing quietly while holding her face and bloody nose. Did she feel guilty? Of course she wouldn't feel guilty, she had no soul. I was sick and tired of her bullshit! It was my turn to give her what she deserved.

"You took her," she sobbed quietly.

"I took what?" I almost sounded as merciless as Axel.

"Her."

"Who the fuck did I take away from you?!" I grabbed her arm and shook her.

"My mom!" she screamed and sobbed at once, "my mom! You took her away from me!" She got up from the ground. "You've taken everything from me, what else do you want?!"

~*~

Chapter 38 SOB STORY

---Rose's P.O.V---

You've taken everything from me, what else do you want?

Layla's words kept spinning around in my head. I never thought I'd see the day where she'd break. The day where her perfect Greek goddess posture would come falling down.

If it were anyone else in my situation, they'd probably laugh in her face.

But this was me we were talking about, the softy who never did anything before a rebel walked into her life. Even though she made so many years of my life a living hell, I couldn't bear to do that to her. A part of me wanted her to pay for what she put me through, but the other part of me wanted to comfort her.

She was human after all.

My mom! You took her away from me!

Layla was sobbing hysterically in front of me with blood running freely down her face and neck and tears flooding her face. Her makeup was now smeared all over her face. She was a wreck.

"Who's your mom?" I asked her in a quiet voice.

She sniffed, "isn't it obvious?"

"My real mom?" I furrowed my eyebrows. That wasn't possible, my real mom was a deadbeat mom and she didn't have any kids before me.

"No, you might seem smart but you're really stupid." Of course she had to insult me no matter what. "Cleo, my mother is Cleo," she looked at me expectantly for some reason.

Everything froze that moment and something clicked in my mind.

Everything was starting to make sense. I put all the puzzle pieces together slowly.

In middle school, as soon as she heard my name she hated my guts, because my step mom was her real mom. Her mom left her to come marry my dad.

"January 13th, was the day I turned six," she sniffed, "she promised me she'd come to my birthday no matter what. She said even if she had to sail the seven seas she would still come. I invited all my friends from school and even dressed up as my favorite princess that day. Dad made sure to throw the biggest party," she wiped some tears away with the back of her hand, smearing even more makeup and blood on her face.

"I waited and waited. I promised her I wouldn't open the presents or cut the cake before she came home. All the guests arrived and enjoyed the party. That afternoon no cake was served, I wouldn't let anyone touch it until my mom came home.

Hours passed and guests left, maids cleaned up the whole place, but she still wasn't home. I told them to leave the cake on the table and the presents untouched because I wanted to wait for her to be here with me. I waited until it was midnight, four hours passed my bedtime.

Daddy came down to talk to me. He said she couldn't make it. I told him I didn't believe him and I sat there next to the window waiting all night. The maids all went to their rooms to sleep, and I was the only one left awake. I stayed up all night staring out the window, hoping she'd come home.

I didn't sleep a wink those two nights. The next day I insisted on waiting, but my dad told me to go shower in case my mom came home. I did what I was told and went to his office. I overheard him talking on the phone with my mom.

My mom said she had to take care of her boyfriend's daughter Rosaline, because she had a 'very important' dentist appointment that she couldn't miss." She looked up at me with watery eyes. "She couldn't miss her boyfriend's daughter dentist appointment, but she could miss her own daughter's birthday."

The amount of pain in her eyes physically affected me. I wanted to hug her.

She laughed bitterly. "Years and years passed, I spent learning about this girl Rosaline. The girl who made my world crumble down. The girl who was better than me, who my own biological mom was so in love with.

Turns out the girl wasn't as perfect as everyone made her out to be. She was fragile, shy and quiet. She was weak, so when my dad moved us back I could get revenge on the girl who turned my world upside down." She looked straight at me, "guess we're even then."

"No," I replied in a strong voice. "I never did anything to you in the first place."

Her lips formed a tight line. Her tears had stopped and her chocolate brown eyes were back to cold and cruel. "We're even, and that's final. Now get the hell away from me."

"How are we even when I didn't do anything to you in the first place?!"

"You took my own mom away from me-"

"No I didn't!" my hands flew out and grabbed her arms. "You just want to put the blame on me because you don't want to blame your own mother! You're in denial! You're just blaming me because you don't want to blame your own mother for leaving you!"

I grabbed her by her arms, "you've blamed me since the day she left you! Well guess what?! I'm not the one to blame. You want to get your revenge?! Go to your mommy dearest who left you!" I yelled in her face. "Not to mention, she's been sleeping around with Axel's step dad! Your mom's a slut! Let me spell that out for you, S-L-U-T, slut! She's as much of a mom to you as she was to me. She's tormented me too, can't you see? She's treated me as her puppet- even you said so!"

I didn't notice she was bleeding because of me until her blood seeped into my finger nails. I let go of her and got up. My white tank top now had fresh blood stains on them. I sighed and shook my head; I was going to have a lot of scrubbing to do...

My head whipped around when I heard clapping from behind me. Layla's best friend was clapping drunkenly. "And a point for the liar!" he threw his fist in the air. Layla stood up quickly before flinching. She rushed over to Matt's side and gave him a stern look. "What?" he threw both his hands up in the air. "Can't I have a little fun?" he pouted at her.

She shook her head. "I'm done with her, we're even now."

"Says the loser who got beat up," he laughed cruelly.

"You're drunk," she stated.

"And you're with Jaxon."

She cocked an eyebrow at him. "What?"

"I thought we were talking about things that wouldn't last."

"You're right, we didn't." She grabbed his arm. "Let's go."

He wouldn't budge. "Wait, that's past tense right? In meaning you already broke up?" he rubbed his eyes.

She nodded, trying to pull him away.

"What? When? Where? Why?!"

"We're not playing 21 questions here," she snapped, dragging him away. She suddenly stopped and turned around to face me. "Thank you," she said before dragging Matt away.

My mouth fell open in shock.

What the hell was that?

First she put me through hell for years because she blamed me for her mother leaving her, then after I blew up at her and punched her in the face... she thanked me? The girl had some serious issues...

"Ow! Why'd you do that for?" a familiar voice whined.

"Shut up! She'll hear us!" a voice hissed back.

I turned to where the voices were coming from. Sure enough, there were two crouched figures behind the bushes. I shook my head at the two morons. "You know I see you guys, right?"

"No you don't," one of the twins replied. I heard a loud smacking sound.

"You retard!" Axel hissed back.

I felt like a mom. "Get out of the bushes."

"There's no one behind the bushes." One of the twins replied. The twin spoke with some confidence, so I guessed it was Justin.

"Axel and Justin, get out of the bushes, now." I ordered. Axel bolted right up from the bushes almost immediately. Some leaves were sticking out of his messy blonde hair. He had a guilty expression his face. "What'd you do?"

"Nothing," he replied too quickly.

I rolled my eyes at him. "Justin, get out of the damn bushes."

"Justin isn't in there," Axel said.

"Sure he is. I saw two people crouched in the bushes."

"It's not Justin."

"You're being fooled," I shook my head at Axel. "Justin, get the hell out of the bushes."

"I'm not Justin," the guy who sounded exactly like Justin replied.

I called bullshit.

"It's Mr. Left Dimple."

"Dustin?" I was almost 100% sure that wasn't Dustin. "Dustin doesn't talk like that…"

"Maybe Dustin wanted to change," he slowly came out of the bushes.

His cheeks were flushed.

It could not have been Dustin...

The way he dressed had changed completely, his hair was messy like Justin's usual hairstyle, and the way he stood wasn't even Dustin-ish.

I furrowed my eyebrows in confusion.

But why would Dustin ever want to change? He was beyond adorable the way he was.

"Can you smile for me?" I asked.

The twin smiled sheepishly. Sure enough, he had a left dimple. Dustin had changed his style completely.

"Why?" I asked while walking over to him.

He just shrugged. "Maybe I'm tired of being the good guy all the time. Good guys are boring, right?"

I shook my head, "you shouldn't have changed."

Axel backed me up, "you look like a gay crack head version of Justin." He looked the twin up and down, "as if Justin doesn't look gay enough already."

I smacked Axel's arm and gave him a stern look before turning back to poor Dustin. "You're trying to impress Kasay, aren't you?"

Dustin bit his lip.

Axel leaned into me. "He's so whipped," he whispered in my ear.

"So are you," Dustin retorted.

Axel threw both his hands up into the air. "At least I'm admitting it."

"It's easy for you to say because the feeling you guys share is mutual." Dustin gestured to the both of us. "Kasay has no interest in me whatsoever. She likes Justin, who just happens to look exactly like me," he shook his head while running a hand through his hair.

"Are you a virgin?" Axel suddenly asked.

"What?"

"Just answer the damn question. Are you a virgin?"

Dustin looked incredibly uncomfortable. He tugged on the collar of his shirt as if he was asking for more air. "Do I really have to-?"

Axel shrugged, "depends on if you want my help or not."

Dustin glanced my way before clearing his throat. "Yes."

"Yes you're a virgin, or yes you're not a virgin?" Axel asked impatiently. Thank god all the people around us were wasted, otherwise we would've had a little crowd around us. I placed a hand on Axel's arm.

"I'm just trying to help him," he furrowed his eyebrows.

"I know, but you know you could help him without embarrassing him, right?"

He sighed while grabbing my hand which was on his arm.

"Yeah, but what fun would that be?" he smiled at me.

I rolled my eyes at *my* bad boy. "Fine, do whatever you want," I chuckled.

"Yes, I'm a virgin."

Axel didn't look surprised at all. " I knew that.," he waved his hand in the air. "We need to get you laid before anything."

"What? Why?" Dustin asked.

"You want to get that image don't you? The first step of getting that image is getting rid of your virginity," Axel replied with his signature smirk on his face.

I shot Axel a glare. "And when did you lose your virginity?"

Axel just shrugged. "When I was 9."

I gasped in shock. "What?!"

"I'm playing!" he laughed while throwing his hands up in the air.

"That's not funny," I frowned.

"It was to me."

I folded my arms across my chest and pouted. "You're mean!"

"Don't pout," he pouted back at me.

"Why?"

"Because I only want to do one thing to you when you're pouting."

"And what is that?" I teased.

HE pressed his lips against mine. I immediately brought my hands around his neck. One of his arms snaked around my waist, pressing me to him. His other hand was behind my neck, pressing my mouth to his.

Our lips moved in sync together. Mouth to mouth, chest to chest, my eyes fluttered closed. Everything around me didn't matter anymore, all that mattered was him. Every kiss left me wanting more. Our tongues gently twirled together.

One of my hands left his neck and ran through his silky hair. His hair was soft beyond imagine, what kind of shampoo did he use? Someone cleared their throat, interrupting us from our little make-out session. My cheeks were hot and flushed. I almost forgot Dustin was right there before he cleared his throat again.

"I don't actually remember asking you to teach me how to make out like a bad guy..." Dustin trailed off.

"It comes with the image," Axel winked with his arm still possessively around my waist.

"Nice to know," Dustin replied dryly. He turned to me. "So Cleo is Layla's mom?"

"I didn't know until she told me."

"The real lesson here is: Cleo's a whore and causes problems for everyone."

"I wander how many other kids she popped out," Dustin said.

"I think Layla's the only one." I didn't recall Cleo mentioning any names, well... she didn't even mention Layla's name to begin with.

"Who knows? She reminds me of a slot machine though."

"Why's that?" Dustin asked Axel.

"Because she-"

Axel covered my ears with both his hands not wanting me to hear what he had to say. I just rolled my eyes at him. I wasn't *that* innocent. I knew all about sex. Once he was done, he let his hands fall from my ears.

Dustin stood there with his mouth hanging open. Whatever Axel said to him was definitely dirty. "Take that as lesson one on being a bad boy." Axel nodded at Dustin. Dustin just stood there unmoving with his mouth hanging open. "Close your mouth or you'll catch fireflies," Axel turned to me after he said the inside joke.

I chuckled at his joke. "Says the bad boy who had me blow a firefly off his face-"

He quickly covered my mouth to prevent me from saying more.

"So let me get this straight, bad boys have to be afraid of fireflies?"

I snickered while Axel shook his head lazily. "Let's ditch this place," Axel waved his hand dismissively. "Fill me in on what happens."

"Sure will," Dustin nodded and smiled at the both of us. We both started walking away until Axel stopped and turned around.

"And Dustin!" he called out.

"What?" Dustin called back.

"Good luck getting laid," Axel grinned at poor Dustin whose face was as red as ketchup.

~*~

Never in a million years would I imagine Axel and me in a playground together.

But here we were… in a kid's playground/park together.

After we left the party (that didn't even have Halloween candy), Axel randomly drove us to an empty playground in the middle of nowhere because he needed to pee. I was now waiting in front of a portable bathroom because Axel didn't want me anywhere alone.

Taking me into the bathroom sounded too creepy, so he just told me to wait right in front of the bathroom. Even though there was no one here, he still didn't trust me to take care of myself. He was a bit *too* overprotective, almost as if someone was out to get him. So here I was waiting for Axel in front of a portable bathroom.

354

"You still there?" Axel asked for the 50th time from inside the bathroom.

"Yes, I'm still here." I might as well have recorded myself saying 'yes, I'm still here' and put it on replay every 5 seconds rather than standing there and confirming to him every 5 seconds that I was still there.

"Is this a recording?"

If he wasn't so damn hot I would've barged in and knocked all his pretty little teeth out and tell him to shut up. "No, this isn't a recording." I replied dryly.

"How can I be so sure that this isn't a recording?"

"Just shut up and finish pissing."

"Jesus, no need to get so pushy woman. Pissing takes time and concentration."

I scrunched up my face in disgust. "TMI!"

"How is that too much information?"

"It just is, now finish pissing."

I heard him sigh. "Like I said, pissing-"

"Takes time and concentration," I finished his sentence for him. "You done yet?"

"No, I'm still in here."

"You done?" I asked again, hoping for a different answer this time.

"No!" What was taking this Greek god so long to use the bathroom?

I asked him about five more times.

"You-"

"Jesus Christ! Yes, I'm done!" he announced. I heard the toilet flush before he barged out of the bathroom.

"Did you wash your hands?"

"Oops," he grinned sheepishly before stepping back into the bathroom.

I scrunched up my face in disgust.

He came back with clean hands. "That's what happens when you rush me, I forget to wash my hands!" he waved his hands in the air.

"You were taking way too long," I pointed out.

"And you were being impatient."

I huffed.

He put his arm around my shoulder, "it actually feels great to have someone wait for you."

What he said made me feel warm and fuzzy inside.

"Push me on the swings," I said, before stomping off to the swing set.

"Your wish is my command, Princess." He said, bowing down to me. The little gestures truly made me melt.

~*~

Chapter 39 EVERYONE'S INVITED

Turns out, Axel didn't take that long to pee. He was just taking his sweet time texting his mom and dad after doing his business.

Gross right?

A bathroom sink has about 100,000 germs per square inch, where the toilet seat has only about 100 germs per square inch. But, every time you flush the toilet you send an invisible six foot plume of bacteria which lands on exposed surfaces.

Not to mention about 7 million phone are dropped into the toilet each year! So why would anyone want to use their phone in the bathroom? When I told him that, he just patted me on the head and said, "Only you Princess, only you."

After half an hour of him pushing me on the swings, we both fell asleep on a bench under a naked autumn/winter tree. Luckily no kids were around because they were too busy trick or treating. It was a warm night, especially for the last day of October.

We used his jacket as a pillow. Somehow the bench was wide enough to fit us both. I didn't feel homeless though, I felt safe. I fell asleep in his arms while staring up at the sky through the naked branches.

I woke up to Axel poking my side trying to get to wake up. "I'm hungry," he stated.

"Then eat," I said trying to fall back to sleep, but he wouldn't let me.

"I'm hungry," he said, poking my side again.

"Leave me alone." I grumbled with my eyes closed.

"No, we're going to your place to shower then we're going out to breakfast." He said, poking my side once again. I tried swatting his hand away, but he pulled his hand away in time.

"Give me five more minutes," I mumbled, turning away from him.

"No can do Princess, you're getting up whether you like it or not. And just so you know, you really need to take a shower," he chuckled.

I bolted right up to a sitting position. "Are you saying I smell bad?" I narrowed my eyes at him.

"Maybe," he smirked at me before pushing himself off the ground. He held out a hand for me to take, and I gladly took it. He hoisted me off the bench and picked up his jacket from the bench. "Still smells like vanilla," he sniffed his shirt.

He was right, it still smelt amazing. But I pretended I was grossed out, "Do you know how many germs are on that?"

"No, and I don't want know." He walked us over to his motorbike, "hop on."
~*~

Luckily, Cleo wasn't home when we arrived. She left a small sticky note on the door that read:

ROSALINE, YOU ARE GROUNDED

When Axel saw it he snorted out loud before crumpling it and throwing it away. We took turns taking showers and decided on eating at my place.

"I need your opinion on something," Axel suddenly said. I nodded for him to continue because I had a mouthful of cereal in my mouth. "My step dad's hosting this anniversary dinner party next week and he's inviting pretty much everyone he knows to come."

I swallowed the cereal in my mouth and nodded for him to keep talking.

"They're going to show pictures from their wedding and photos of them traveling to everyone to brag about how good their life is, and then they're showing a clip from their shitty overpriced wedding. All for the public's eye of course, but Cleo will be there and I think your dad's going to be there too since he's one of my step dad's business partners-"

I almost choked on my cereal, "he is?!"

Axel nodded, "step dad trades in many industries."

He knew more about my father than I did. I nodded for him to continue.

"The question I was going to ask you is: how bad do you want to humiliate our stepparents?"

"How bad *can* we humiliate them?"

He smirked, "I like that answer. It all depends on what you'd like to do."

"I want Cleo to get what she deserves. For what she's done to my dad, what she's done to me, and what she's done to Layla."

"What she's done to Layla? The bitch has hurt you so much-"

I shrugged, "forgive and forget. She was hurt so much emotionally as a kid, and inside she's still a little girl who holds grudges."

He frowned, "but she hurt you. Least you could do was hurt her back."

"Axel, not everything in life is about revenge," I said gently. "I hurt her already just by being who I am, and not to mention I punched her and made her cry." He still didn't seem convinced. I sighed, "I just don't want to deal with her anymore."

He didn't look too happy, "it's up to you." He got up.

"Cleo on the other hand is going to get what she deserves," I said confidently while getting up with him.

That made his smirk reappear on his face. "Since when did you become so tough?"

"Since a little rebel walked into my life."

"I'd like to know who the rebel is," he tapped his chin, pretending to think.

"I don't know..." I replied, pretending to think just like him.

"Does this rebel have blonde hair?" He asked with an eyebrow raised.

"Yep."

"Is he... violent?" he asked, taking a step towards me.

"A bit too violent at times," I took a step back.

"How bad is he?" he took another step towards me.

I took a step back, "he's so bad... but so good to me."

"Does he scare you?" With every step he took forward, I took one back.

I looked down at his lips and swallowed down a lump I didn't know was in my throat, "sometimes, but he's also made me face my fears."

"Is he irresistibly attractive?" He took another step towards me.

"Most girls think so," I hid my smile.

"Do you?"

My red cheeks gave him the answer.

"Is he... soft?"

"Surprisingly, yes."

"Has he managed to persuade you he's not as bad as others make him out to be?"

I licked my lips, "he didn't have to. I realized it on my own."

"No pun intended with your initials spelling raw..." He was closing the little distance between us. "But does he hold your raw heart in his hand?

"Definitely," I replied, stepping back. My back hit the wall. I couldn't escape him, even if I wanted to.

He took a step forward, leaving about an inch of space between our bodies. "Tell me, who this 'rebel' is."

Our noses were almost touching and my heart was beating so fast I thought I was about to have a heart attack.

"I don't have to."

"Oh well that's where you're wrong Princess, you have to."

He leaned in so that our lips were brushing. All I could hear was the sound of my wild heart. If I died of a heart attack right at this very moment, he was going to pay for my funeral.

"You can't make me."

Instead of replying, he pressed his lips against mine making me freeze. It took a few seconds for me to actually kiss him back. He moved forward so that our bodies were pressed together and wrapped his arms tightly around my waist. He suddenly pulled away, leaving me wanting more.

"So now will you tell me?" he looked down at me hungrily.

"No, you'll have to keep trying to convince me."

Something flashed across his eyes before he leaned in and started to place small kisses up and down my neck. With every kiss, I felt myself grow hotter. My breath was caught in my throat when he lingered a little longer at one spot.

"W-what are you doing?" I asked in a shaky voice. It felt so good...

"Leaving a mark," he replied, tugging on the spot softly with his teeth.

I quickly pushed him off me quickly before trying to run away from him. But of course, me being the slow person I was I didn't even make it past him. He grabbed my waist and lifted me up in the air before placing me on the kitchen counter.

He placed both his hands beside my thighs and stood in between my legs. "Now you have no choice but to tell me who this guy is."

He was so damn close, I couldn't concentrate.

"Say his name." His voice was so silky. Fuck.

I just wanted him to kiss me so badly.

"Tell me his name, or I'm leaving another mark on you," he threatened.

If he wanted to tease me like this, I was going to get him back. "Dustin."

He jolted back, "the fuck?!"

Those emerald green eyes darkened, his eyebrows furrowed, and his jaw clenched. Though he probably looked threatening to others, he looked like a frustrated little puppy to me. I felt like giggling at his reaction. I couldn't hold in the laughter.

The moment I opened my mouth to laugh, he kissed me... hard.

I was about to wrap my arms around his neck, but he grabbed my hands and pinned them next to my thighs. He pulled away and stared at me those hauntingly beautiful eyes.

"Not funny. Take it back."

"Is someone jealous?" I teased. Instead of replying, he kissed me again, but this time even harder. The kiss was far hungrier than the first one. It was like he was trying to get something out of me. He bit my lip, making me weak. He pulled away from me, looking quite serious.

I frowned at his jealous reaction. "I was just playing around."

"Don't play like that if you don't want the guy killed."

I gulped at how scary he looked. It was a genuine threat. But somehow, it turned me on. Why was I attracted to such danger? "Sorry..."

"There's nothing to be sorry about," he chuckled after placing a small kiss on my nose. "Now let's plan a little anniversary surprise."

~*~

----*Layla's P.O.V*----

Even wasn't the word to use.

Rose and I definitely weren't even.

In fact, I owed her big time. But I knew my ego wouldn't allow myself to walk up to her house and apologize to her.

"You look frustrated," Matt commented taking a swing from the beer can in his hand.

"Maybe I am frustrated for once," I replied in a huff.

"Anything I can do to help?" he raised his eyebrows at me.

We were chilling at my place because I needed to blow some steam off. After the party I brought him back to my place because he wasn't sober enough to even stand. One thing I loved about Matt was that he was always there to help no matter how dirty the job was.

And no matter what, he was always on my side. He always followed me around like a lost puppy, because the truth was: he wasn't that smart. He was all muscle, no brain. He did whatever I told him to do because he trusted me. He was lucky to have found someone like me.

He wasn't smart enough to make his own decisions in life. Sure, he had his moments where he insulted me when he was drunk, but he had never hurt me. "You better not be thinking about that drama queen," he said.

"Jaxon's not a drama queen," I shot him a look of annoyance. He had never approved of the guy.

"Why are you defending him? He dumped you for the nerd."

I shot him a glare, making him throw his arms up into the air.

"I meant Rosaline, he dumped you for Rosaline."

I guess you could say I felt bad for what I put Rose through, so I made Matt call her by her actual name.

I sighed at him while shaking my head. "I don't blame him though."

"What do you mean you don't blame him? You have everything she doesn't have. You're hot, you're good to look at, you've got loyal friends, you've got the life babe," he gestured around my bedroom. My walls were covered in photos of friends.

I shook my head at him. "It's an image, Matt. Do you think I could smile and laugh without all this stuff?"

"No…" he furrowed his eyebrows together, not getting the point.

"Exactly. She can smile without the popularity, without the parties, without the countless friends." I gestured around me.

"She's genuinely happy with someone who likes her for who she is."

"I don't get it… but she's still not popular…" he trailed off.

I rolled my eyes at him. "Of course you wouldn't." He didn't get most things. "Anyways, my dad was invited to Axel's mom and step dad's anniversary dinner."

"And?" he cocked an eyebrow at me.

"My mommy dearest is going to be there," I grinned evilly at him.

An evil grin appeared on his face too. "Let's pay them a little visit."

~*~

Saturday, November 10th 2 P.M.

----*Jaxon's P.O.V*----

I sat on the edge of my bed with my head buried in my hands.

Why did I have to screw everything up? I had feelings for two girls, but I couldn't make up my mind which one I really wanted. And now, I lost them both. I should've just stuck with Rose from the start.

Maybe she wouldn't have gotten so close to Axel if I didn't get involved with Layla. The more I thought about it, the more I liked Rosie. But whenever I thought of Layla, I felt myself die a little inside. They were both incredibly beautiful in their own ways.

But now, I had no chance either of them.

"Honey! We need to talk to you!" my mom yelled from downstairs.

I sighed before getting up from my bed. My life was so fucked. Judging from the situation I was in, I assumed I'd probably grow old and die alone while watching Cinderella on replay. I made my way downstairs to find both my parents sitting on the loveseat waiting patiently for me.

I sat alone opposite from them on the couch.

"You've been down lately," my mother started after clearing her throat. "I haven't seen Rose in a while, so I'm guessing it's about her?"

It sucked having really observant parents sometimes. I nodded gloomily in reply to her question. They stared at me expecting me to expand on the topic, "Uh yeah, we kind of got in an argument." I scratched the back of my neck awkwardly.

"Well, don't you want to fix things between the two of you?" my mother asked.

"Of course, I'd do anything to fix things between us!" I replied quickly. She must've had something good in mind; my mom always had good ideas about things.

"The Spencer's are hosting an anniversary dinner, and I know Rose's parents are invited, so she'll probably be there too."

I shook my head at my mom. "Rose doesn't do social stuff."

"But she wasn't home all last night," my mom tilted her head to the side. "Cleo called me asking if I had seen Rosaline. I told her we hadn't seen her around recently. She just called me again to update me that Rosie was at a party!"

I was shocked. First things first. "You talked to Cleo?"

"Yes, just this morning. She grounded Rose for talking back, but Rose snuck out. I guess she's finally becoming a teenager, huh Jim?" my mom nudged my dad. "Just two weeks ago Rose started acting up!"

My dad nodded in agreement. "That girl has been good for too long," he chuckled. "Remember when she made herself throw up in elementary because she forgot her homework?"

That memory was still fresh in my mind. It made me crack a little smile.

We were in 3rd grade and the teenager assigned us a page of math homework. Rose forgot to do it so she forced herself to throw up so she would get sent home before math. She told me and my parents about it because she said she felt guilty.

"You like her, don't you?" my mom asked with a smile on her face.

"What? No," I denied a little too quickly. Grins appeared on my parent's faces.

"You do," they said at the same time.

"Mom, dad-"

"There's no point in denying it, it's so obvious!" my mom said before I could finish my sentence. "It's only natural. You've been best friends your entire lives."

"It's complicated," I ran a hand through my hair. I was starting to get a headache from the entire thing.

"How complicated could it be? You've been best friends since forever! All you have to do is tell her how you feel."

"Mom, it's a lot more complicated than that!" I groaned while throwing my head back.

"How? Tell us how? All you have to do is grow a pair and go up there and confront her."

"Did you just tell our son to grow a pair?" my dad asked.

"Yes, you've got a problem?" my mom snapped.

"No, not at all. I was about to agree with you!" My dad kissed my mom's ass.

"Mom, it's not just that-"

"Give me one good reason why you can't man up and go talk to her." My mom folded her arms over her chest.

"She's got a guy," I replied, staring her straight in the eye.

My mom's mouth formed an 'O' shape. She kept opening and closing her mouth like she was about to say something, but nothing came out. She looked like a fish out of the water. "Y-you didn't tell me."

"Well, I just did," I said getting up. "Now if you don't mind, I'm going back upstairs to re-think my life."

"Son, is there anyone else you may be interested in?"

"We found a used condom in the trash," my dad had to add.

I turned to my dad. "Could you be any more awkward?"

"Yes, if I were to ask you which gender you had intercourse with," my dad replied with a shrug. My parents were too open sometimes..."""Now answer my question, do you like anyone else besides from Rose. Don't forget, I once was a teenage guy. And when I was obsessed with someone, I always had a backup plan and someone on the side."

"She's not a backup plan, but yeah, I do kind of like someone else."

"She?" my mom turned to my dad, "he's not gay or bisexual?!"

Thankfully, dad ignored mom. "Why don't you ask her out?"

"Because I just broke up with her."

"Smooth move son, smooth move," my dad said sarcastically.

"Thanks," I replied with the same amount of sarcasm.

"Who's the other girl?"

I shrugged.

"Listen, pretty much everyone's invited to this dinner. So chances are both of the girls will be there. At least fix things with one of them." My dad gave me advice.

I sighed in defeat. He was right, "fine."

"Good, now go weep for the remaining hours," he shooed me away.

"And I thought I was better at this stuff," my mother smirked at my dad.

I got up quickly to get away from my parents. They were way too nosy for my liking.

~*~

----Dustin's P.O.V----

Trent's place was trashed Halloween night. Someone spray painted his family's piano which had been passed on generation after generation. He was so getting his butt whooped. Poor guy was screwed. At least scattered drunk people no longer decorated the place. Over a week later, we were still helping him repair the shit that was broken. What great friends we were.

"Yo Dustin! Someone's calling you!" Trent called from the kitchen.

I got up from picking up pieces of broken glass and ran to the kitchen. On the way, I tripped on Ricky who was attempting to take shirtless selfies on the ground. Trent handed me the phone. I was a little worried when I saw it was my mom. "Hey mom," I greeted.

"What color of ties do you and Justin want?" she asked, not bother to greet me.

"Blue and what are the ties for?"

"For Axel's step dad's anniversary dinner of course. I told you last month, did you forget?"

I face palmed myself. To be fair, a lot had happened within the last month. "Sorry, I've been a bit busy."

My mom sighed on the phone. "It's okay, just be home by five and tell your brother that. You don't want to be late." And with that, she hung up on me.

"What does mom want?" Justin asked, walking into the room.

It was clear why she preferred to deal with me, "she asked for tie colors."

"I hope you told her green."

I smirked.

"Fuck you, I look like shit in blue."

I nudged him, "we're identical twins, and I think we look pretty good in blue."

"Your fashion sense sucks."

I just shook my head.

"What are the ties for?"

"We're going to Axel's parent's anniversary dinner tonight, and we have to be home by five."

"Since when?"

"Apparently she told us last month."

That seemed to remind him. He swore, "I hate suits."

"At least we have that in common."

Suddenly, Trent's phone rang. He picked up and starting saying a lot of okay's. "Yeah dad, bye!" he hung up and looked up at us. "Me three, I guess we're all going tonight, huh?"

"I don't want to go! I don't give a fuck about Axel's parents!" Ricky yelled from outside of the kitchen. "I'm not going," he said in a firm voice. But a few seconds later he gave up. "Fine I'll go with you! Bye!" He came storming in the kitchen pissed off.

"So I guess everyone's invited, huh?" Justin nudged me in the ribs while laughing.

"I have a feeling shit's gonna' go down!" Trent said dramatically.

~*~

Chapter 40 BEFORE THE CLIMAX

----*Rose's P.O.V*----

"Laptop."

"Check," Axel replied.

"Thumb drive?"

"Check."

"Rope."

"Got that."

"Banana peels."

"Check."

"Rotten eggs."

"Tick that."

"Baking soda and vinegar."

"Double check."

"Camera, phone, blindfolds, and rotten pickles."

"Four yeses."

"Rotten food."

"Check, but why do we need so much rotten stuff?" he suddenly asked, looking up from all the expired food items. "We've got tomatoes, eggs, onions…" he scrunched up his face in disgust.

"So it'll smell," I replied. I looked down at the list again, "got all the paint?"

"Even purple, which I despise."

"Water balloons?"

He held the package up. The guy was pretty organized when it came to sabotaging.

"Extra clothes, trust me- we'll need extra clothes."

"All packed, even brought extra panties for you," he winked. I reached out and smacked his arm.

"We're trying to be serious here, remember? If we want to ruin this, we've got to take this seriously."

"But what's the fun in that? Plus, it's hard."

"That's what she said," one of the twins sang as he walked into my house.

I turned to Axel and narrowed my eyes at him. "Did you lock the door?"

He scratched the back of his head sheepishly. "Sorry, I forgot."

"You guys are planning something big, huh?" the twin stuck his nose in our business.

"Which thing are you, the goody two shoes, or the fuckboy?" Axel asked.

"Guess," he smiled showing his right dimple.

"Justin, what are you doing here?" I greeted.

He grunted, "Dustin shouldn't have told you." He threw his head back.

"Good job, Flower." Axel ruffled my hair, making me smack his hand away. "You're so adorable," he chuckled.

"God, I'm going to throw up!" Justin gagged.

"Shut up asshole, you're not supposed to be here anyway." Axel glared at the twin.

"So what are you doing here?"

"I came here to see what you two were up to," he shrugged in reply.

Axel narrowed his eyes at him making him throw his hands up in the air.

"Okay fine, maybe I also came here to talk."

"Talk about what?" Axel clearly didn't want him present.

"Her little friend Kasay who's been causing drama lately." he He turned to me and raised his eyebrows at me. "Heard Dustin likes her," he stated.

"No shit," Axel said.

"Shut up and let me talk to your girlfriend."

"Girlfriend?" I asked. The word felt foreign in my mouth.

"We're not exactly official… yet." Axel tugged at his shirt collar, obviously uncomfortable with the situation we were in.

"But you two were acting all lovey-dovey..." Justin trailed off looking confused.

"That's why I said the word yet, fucktard."

Justin turned to me. "Why is your bitch so rude?" he asked me innocently.

"He's not my-"

"I'm not her-"

"There's no point in denying it. You two are obviously in love with each other." He cut the both of us off mid sentence. We sat there in awkward silence for a while, before Axel decided to speak.

"Get out," he growled dangerously.

"Dude, I was just stating the truth-"

"Get out!" he growled a little louder this time.

"Fine! Be an asshole and don't admit it," Justin huffed before leaving.

I stayed silent, not knowing what to say.

Maybe he got mad because he hated being accused of loving a nerd.

I felt my heart drop.

Why would a sexy bad boy fall in love with a nerd?

Sure, maybe he could like a nerd like me, but he wouldn't fall in love with one.

Axel sighed, running a hand through his hair. "Now's not the right time to talk about that kind of stuff."

I stayed quiet, not wanting to end up saying something I would regret.

"Are you mad at me?" he asked in a quiet voice.

Was I mad at him?

I shook my head in reply, but he saw I wasn't okay.

"Can you at least reply so I know you're really not mad at me?"

I was mad, I was upset. "I'm not mad," I replied in a small voice.

Suddenly, he got up, walked over to me, and pulled me into a bone crushing hug. "I know exactly what you're thinking," he mumbled in my ear. "I don't want you to think that, because I do like you. It's just..." he was lost for words.

"Just what?"

He stayed quiet for a moment, before letting me go, "… it's soon to say it."

Was it? I was fully ready to admit it to it. "I-it's too soon?"

He was internally battling with himself. "Do you even know what love is?"

I was taken aback by the question. "Of course I do."

He waited for me to continue.

"Love is when you put someone first. It's when a smile on their face makes your day… it's when their presence calms and/or excites you… I could go on forever, but that's my idea of love."

He seemed to be digesting what I had just said. I couldn't see the emotion in his eyes. "Let's worry about that later," he looked up with a smirk, "we've got plans tonight."

How was he able to switch moods so quickly?

~*~

I wonder how my hair felt about getting switched back and forth from blonde to brunette.

"You done yet?" Axel banged on the door. The guy was pretty impatient.

"Almost," I replied, drying off my hair which was now dark brown.

I had decided it was best if I colored my hair to the dinner so that most people wouldn't recognize it, and so that my step mother would have trouble finding me. He hadn't even thought of that and called me clever for thinking of it.

"You take forever," he whined from the other side of the door.

"You shouldn't be the one to talk, Mr. I-Text-In-The-Bathroom!" I shot back.

"That was only one time…"

"And this is only a onetime thing. I usually don't take this long to get ready."

"Need any help in there? I'll happily come in to help you," he said in a suggestive tone.

Knowing that he probably had his ear on the other side of the door listening for my reaction, I smacked the door where I thought his ear would be making him groan out in pain on the other side of the door. I'd like to say I knew him pretty well.

"There's your answer, Prince Boner."

"Don't call me that."

"Well get used to it, I'm calling you that whenever you're being a pervert from now on."

"Comes naturally though, I can't help it."

"Well then it sucks to be you."

~*~

---*Dustin's P.O.V*---

'A tear slid down Summer's cheek as she stared into Damien's eyes lovingly.

"I love you Damien, I love you so much it hurts me every time I think about you not being with me."

Damien stood still, his eyes holding hers captive. "I love you too, my sweet Summer," he confessed, in barely a whisper. A single tear slid down his cheek as he rushed to her and held her in his arms. "I will never leave you again, I swear to be with you no matter what, I'll never give up on the love we have!" he promised her with his soul.'

I stopped reading the stupid romance novel and closed the book. I stared at the cover for a while. It was of a girl and a guy holding each other lovingly while staring into each other's eyes. The book was pure bullshit.

Things like that never happened in real life.

I decided to pick the book randomly out of my mom's shelf because I was waiting for Justin to get home. The guy just never knew when to come home.

I was always the best out of the both of us. I always behaved when my parents told me to, I did all my chores, I acted appropriately at family gatherings, but with him, he never did anything they told him to.

Yet, he still got more girls than I did.

He got the girl I wanted most. I meant to throw the book onto the ground, but I ended up tossing it instead because I was weak. I knew deep down inside, one of the reasons I wanted her was because I knew he had his sights on her for a while. I wanted to win a girl over him for once.

"Uncle Justin, is something wrong?" my niece asked me.

"It's Dustin June, it's Dustin," I snapped at her. I was starting to lose my cool.

"Sorry, I forgot," she apologized quickly while clutching onto her teddy bear. I looked at my niece, before feeling horrible. She was only five years old. She was missing her two front teeth and was wearing a little tiara on her head.

"No, I'm sorry Julia. Uncle Dustin is being a meanie." I tried smiling at her. She smiled back, showing her two missing front teeth.

"You're nicer than Uncle Justin because uncle Justin never says sorry," she stated. "Uncle Dustin is my favorite uncle!" she grinned.

I laughed while patting her little head.

Well, guess one girl was better than nothing.

~*~

---*Rose's P.O.V*---

I stood in front of a mirror and just stared at myself. I was wearing a long blue dress and clung on to all my curves. Axel had wanted to take me out dress shopping for the dinner, but I didn't feel like going out, so I decided to see what Cleo had in store. Thankfully we were about the same size.

My stepmother wasn't in the house either. Somehow I had managed to avoid her the entire time. Thankfully with Axel's sources, he knew exactly where she was in town so we had enough time to leave. He had connections I didn't know about.

She had some dresses she had convinced my dad to buy that she hadn't even worn yet! And one just happened to fit me like a glove. "You look hot in that," Axel complimented, grinning ear to ear. "You look hot in anything, but you look best in nothing."

Instead of smacking his arm, I decided to accept the compliment. "Which one's the best though?"

He shrugged, "they're all hot in my opinion."

"How am I supposed to choose?"

"Just go with this one. The blue really brings out your eyes."

"You're starting to sound like a girl," I giggled.

"Well, that's what happens when all your sweetness rubs off on me."

I scoffed at him. "Whatever, Mr. Bad Boy."

"So are you ready for me to do your makeup?" he raised his eyebrows at me with an evil grin on his face.

I started backing away from him. "You?! Doing my makeup? Is this a nightmare?!"

He threw both his hands up in the air. "Just kidding, Layla hit me up and volunteered to do it for you."

I held up my index finger. "Wait! I think my ears are playing tricks on me. Did you just say Layla?"

"Yup," he replied, popping the 'p'. "Layla, as in the psycho bitch who ruined your high school experience, yes, her."

"She called you and volunteered?" I furrowed my eyebrows together, not understanding why she would want to do such a thing.

"Shocked? You're not alone."

"Why?"

He shrugged, "I think she finally feels bad for everything she's done, and it's about god damn time she did. But personally, I think she deserves a few more punches thrown at her caked face-" Before Axel could finish his sentence, we were interrupted by the doorbell. "Well, that must be Satan."

"I'll get it," I got up to open the door.

"I'll be locked up in your bedroom going through your panties, if anything goes wrong, scream," he said before disappearing out the door.

"That's helpful," I mumbled before running downstairs. I opened the front door quickly, and was greeted with a bone crushing hug.

"Look, I know we're not on the best terms right now, but I'm trying..." Layla said, pulling away.

You could say I was left speechless. I didn't know what to do or say.

"I don't know how apologies work... but please take this as one. Now, let's get you prepped up."

~*~

Turns out, Layla was a lot gentler when it came to makeovers than Kasay.

Kasay didn't care about my well being, but Layla did. Layla was extra careful, with every little brush or tug of my hair, she'd ask if it hurt. She also gave me a mirror so I could see what she was doing to my face or hair.

"To gain your trust," she had said when she handed me the mirror. She applied makeup on my face lightly, not overdoing it.

"So, can I help with what you two are planning for tonight?" she asked me as she applied some mascara onto my eyelashes.

"How do you know we're planning something?"

"Your little friend Justin has a big mouth."

I had the urge to ask her why she was suddenly acting like the perfect friend, but I held my tongue. She treated me like an old friend she had known for years. It was... odd.

"Did you really like Jaxon?" The question slipped out of my mouth before I could even think.

She tensed up a little, but was still able to keep her cool. "I wouldn't use that word 'like'. I'd say I was physically attracted to him and I was kind of attracted to his personality."

"You still like him, don't you?" I pushed further.

I was afraid of her snapping, but thought she wouldn't be able to do anything to me in my own house, especially with Axel upstairs.

"He dumped me just over a week ago, what do you think?" she asked in a stone cold tone.

"That's all I wanted to know."

She relaxed a bit. "But if he were to ask for me back, I'd say no."

"Why?" I asked as she put her mascara away.

"He's made his decision, and his decision is to stick with you." She replied simply, "plus, there are plenty of fish in the sea... there's one in particular I have my eye on."

"Really? Who?" I asked, wanting to know who she had her sights on.

"Someone whose heart is actually dedicated to only one person," she smiled while getting up. "Well, I guess it's my queue to leave," she turned around to leave, but my hand reached out to grab her arm.

"Wait!" I said, making her turn around.

"Yes?" she raised both her eyebrows at me.

"Since Cleo is your mom... I'd like to ask you if you'd like to help with tonight's plans."

An evil grin stretched across her face. This time it wasn't actually as threatening, because I knew it wasn't directed towards me.

"I'd love to," she replied.

~*~

"This is a horrible idea," Axel groaned from the back seat, "should've ridden my baby."

"You have plenty of time for that in the future," Justin snickered, taking what Axel said sexually.

"Shut up and quit whining," Layla snapped at him. "We're going to get the twins whether you like it or not."

"But they annoy the fuck out of me." He turned to me, "Princess, please do something."

"No can do, Prince." I patted his head.

Layla snorted out loud. "Prince? That's a dog's name."

"At least I don't act one like you, bitch."

I rubbed both my temples before throwing my head back.

We were currently in Layla's pink convertible driving to the dinner. Layla and Axel had been arguing nonstop. Their personalities were too alike, they were both hard headed and confident in their way of life. A large weight got lifted off my shoulders when I discovered they couldn't get along if their lives depended on it.

Layla just flirted with him at school to get me jealous and pissed off. I should've known though. Sure she may have liked him at one point, but he'd never go for her.

They were both smart asses, loud, and both wouldn't take shit off one another.

"Quit being an ass! No wonder your name is Axel Storm Spencer, your initials spell 'ass'!" she turned to me. "Tell your boyfriend to quit being an ass."

"He's not my-"

"I'm not her-"

"There's no point in denying it. You two are obviously in love with each other." Layla rolled her eyes.

Déjà vu.

Axel was quiet for the rest of the ride to the twin's house. Layla and I were the only ones making small talk. She gossiped about half of the school population. Turns out, Ricky was caught French kissing a sophomore football player at the Halloween party.

"Those two were so wasted, you would think they were both thinking they were kissing women!" she laughed.

I glanced at Axel through the corner of my eye, but I noticed he was already staring at me with an unreadable expression. His emerald green eyes pierced through my soul, like they were searching for something.

"I told that junior skank she'd never be team captain even when I graduate!" Layla finished her other story. "Hey, are you listening?" she tapped my shoulder, making me turn around.

"Y-Yeah," I replied, turning away from Axel's intense gaze.

"We're here!" Layla announced, obnoxiously honking the car horn.

The two twins rushed out of the house all dressed up for the dinner. They were wearing matching blue ties and combed their hair to the same side so they looked identical.

"This is bullshit," Axel grumbled. "Now I have to sit in the back seat with two Dr. Seuss characters."

Both twins slipped into the seats next to Axel, so Axel was sitting in the middle. Both Justin and Dustin looked undeniably handsome.

"Jesus Christ! You have no idea how long we had to wait till you guys got here! Do you know how much torture it is having your grandmother question you about your sex life?!" one of the twins said.

No doubt it was Justin.

"You didn't have it as bad as me man; she gave me a whole lecture about *how* to get laid." Dustin shot back.

"Well, you do need to get laid though," Justin shrugged.

Axel spent the rest of the ride with his fingers plugged in his ears as the two twins bickered back and forth about what their grandmother put them through. Turns out, they had a niece named Julia who was only five. They had a sister in her early twenties who supposedly got knocked in high school.

"It was hilarious when she announced she was pregnant, mom fainted, grandma gave her a high five, and dad loaded his gun to go kill the poor guy!" Justin laughed.

"It was actually pretty scary," Dustin shivered. "Scary as fu-
"

"Dustin, if you try swearing again I will personally shove a handful of tampons in your mouth. Swearing doesn't suit you!" Layla shook her head.

Since when did we all become all buddy-buddy?

"Since Layla decided to pull that old stick out of her ass."

I didn't notice I said the question out loud until Justin decided to give me an answer.

Axel of course didn't acknowledge anything that was going on because of his plugged ears. He just sat there like a brick, not trying to get along with anyone. He was silently screaming 'I HATE LIFE'.

"Quit being a party pooper!" Justin ruffled Axel's hair, making Axel elbow him in the ribs.

"Don't. Ever. Touch. My. Hair." Axel growled, threatening him.

"Take a chill pill dude!" Justin threw both his hands in the air.

"I've got some Midol Teen in my purse if he needs any," Layla announced, throwing Justin her purse.

He caught it swiftly and started going through it. "Hmm... let me find it." That earned him another elbow in the ribs. "Quit being so violent! Jesus!"

"Maybe if you quit being an ass, he'd quit being so violent with you!" Dustin said.

"You know what Dustin? You're a dick, and you are what you eat." Justin insulted Dustin, making Dustin attempt to throw a punch at Justin, but Justin blocked it swiftly. "Nice try, little brother."

"Don't call me that! You're approximately 68 seconds older than me, that's nothing!"

"That's over a full minute, little brother!"

The two tried tackling each other with Axel sitting in the middle.

"Both of you stop it!" Layla scolded while driving.

Dustin tried throwing another punch at Justin, but Axel grabbed Dustin's fist before it could pass him. "Let me do it," Axel offered, throwing a punch at Justin's arm. Justin groaned out in pain.

"Rosie, seriously, calm your boyfriend down."

"I'm not her-"

"He's not my-" I cut myself off before I could finish the sentence. "You know what, I think I will." And I did something I never thought I'd do in a million years. I unbuckled my seatbelt, climbed onto the back seat, and pressed my lips against Axel's lips.

"Get a room!" Justin yelled.

"Keep it PG!" Dustin said.

"Not in my car!"

Never in a million years would I ever imagine making out with Axel Storm Spencer in Layla Cleo Star's pink convertible, with both Justin and Dustin on either side of us.

~*~

The dinner was held at a large fancy hotel. It was so big, even I was stunned at the appearance. His stepdad sure had money to burn.

Once we arrived, we all filed out of Layla's convertible and made our way to the main lobby. Axel's step father had booked the place and made sure the hotel was all theirs. People in fancy gowns, party dresses, suits, and tuxes decorated the main lobby.

Justin and Dustin grabbed all the equipment we needed and took it to a room near the dining room. No one suspected a thing because they thought they were just helping out with the dinner.

Axel grabbed my waist. "Have I told you how cute you look right now?" he asked in a whisper.

I turned around so that I was looking at him. "Just cute? I was kind of expecting something like 'beautiful' or 'extraordinary'." I teased.

His signature smirk appeared, "I'm not good at big words."

"Then get a dictionary, smart ass!" Layla said from behind us, making Axel glare at her.

"Can't I have a moment alone with Rose without being interrupted?"

A chorus of no's were heard from three extra voices. Trent stood there proudly with the twins behind Layla.

"What's up, Rosaline who gets the straight A's?" Was that necessary? "Sup, Axel, my man."

"I'm not your man, kid."

"Rosie! Rosie! Is that you?!" someone was pushing through people frantically to get to me. My eyes widened when I saw it was.

~*~

Chapter 41 SCREW EVERYONE

My eyes must've been playing tricks on me.

There was no way in hell that could be-

"Honey? Is that you?!" he pushed frantically through the crowd to get to me.

There was no way he could be here, no way. How was he here? Oh right, they invited pretty much everyone. Maybe I should've listened to what his secretary had to say...

Axel grabbed my hand and started pulling me away from him.

We squeezed passed people to get out of there. The twins and Trent followed behind us closely. We kept going until we could no longer see that patch of blonde hair following us. Once we got outside, Axel spun and quickly. His emerald green eyes were stone cold.

"They've gone too far!" he growled. It was clear he was talking about the fact they invited my-

"Who was that?" Trent asked, clearly confused.

"Isn't it obvious?" Dustin asked.

"He's old," Justin commented, "uglier than her."

"Of course, what do you expect?" Dustin scoffed. "It's her-"

"Why the fuck would they invite him?" Axel's eyes narrowed in slits. "It's like my step dad's testing us to see if we would really pull anything with everyone here."

"We're not canceling the plan no matter what," I found myself speaking. "Screw everyone; we're going on with the plan no matter what."

Axel turned to me with curiosity written all over his face. "You mean... you don't care if your dad sees what we're going to pull?"

"The more people here, the more humiliated Cleo and your stepdad will be."

"Hold up!" Trent interrupted our conversation. "That was your dad?"

"No, it was her mom" Axel replied sarcastically.

"Really?" Trent asked stupidly, making all of us throw our heads back and groan. "That's a really convincing transgender."

"Trent, you're an idiot," Dustin said.

"Good job bro, start with the little things. Insult people to build up to the bad boy image you're desperately trying to earn," Justin gave his twin a slap on the back, earning himself a glare from Dustin. But of course, Justin just ignored it. "But you've got to use harsher words. For example, the word 'retard' or the word 'dumbass'."

Layla appeared out of nowhere and squeezed through between both twins so that she was standing in between them. "Anyone wanna' get drunk?" she asked, raising both her eyebrows.

"Is that an invite to get into your pants?" Justin asked, wiggling his eyebrows suggestively at her.

"Only in your wildest dreams, peasant."

Just then, I felt an arm drape over my shoulder. I looked up at Axel and raised my eyes, questioning him.

"Want to play Cupid?" he questioned.

I pretended to think. "Hmm... maybe..."

Justin and Layla did look cute together. They were both experienced, pain in the asses, and popular... so they fit. Maybe Justin was the one Layla had her eye on...

I almost squealed out loud at the thought. If she did have her eyes set on him, it would be perfect though. Dustin could have Kasay, and Justin could have Layla.

What about Jaxon?

I scratched the back of my head at that question.

I had no idea who he would be a perfect match with.

You...

Who the hell said that?

I ignored the mysterious voice in my head. He was just a friend, we could never be together. My heart belonged to only one person, and that person was Axel.

"I bet you a make out session that Layla and Trent would make a cute couple," he said in my ear. I almost choked at his words. Layla and Trent?! I glanced at Trent and noticed he was staring at Layla, his eyes filled with adoration.

I wanted to turn to Axel and tell him how wrong he was, but the longer I stared at Trent, the more I noticed the dedication in his eyes. It was the exact same way Dustin stared at Kasay. I felt my heart flutter at the cute emotion. But Layla seemed closer to Justin...

When I turned to Axel and I saw the exact same emotion in his eyes. Except in Axel's eyes, there was a hint of something else too. I cocked my head to the side. "What are you thinking about?"

"Nothing," he replied a little too quickly before looking away. "So what do you say, Layla and Trent a couple? Or at least hooking up before graduation?" he asked, trying to change the subject. I let it slide and smiled.

"I was actually thinking Layla and Justin would make a cute couple."

"More like a disaster," he scoffed. "If those two paired they up would destroy the human race. Both hot tempered, loud, cocky-"

"Are you sure you're not describing yourself?" I interrupted him.

First he looked offended, but then his signature smirk appeared on his face, "good one."

Layla cleared her throat, interrupting our little conversation. "It's 7:00 p.m."

Axel checked his watch before nodding. "Let's head back inside."

He took my hand in his and led me back inside. I never thought someone like Axel was ever capable of wearing a suit and tie. "We need to get the thumb drive in the computer, and hook up all that shit. Then we'll double check on Layla's plan."

"It'll take us less time if we split up," I suggested.

"With your ex best friend, ex boyfriend, and evil stepmother lingering around here? I think not."

"Cleo's busy trash talking me and sucking my dad's asshole, Ricky's far too embarrassed about making out with that sophomore guy, and I know Jaxon- he won't try anything."

Axel seemed to agree on the others, except Jaxon, "You knew he was going to go behind your back and banging your enemy?" he asked. My mouth fell open, but before I could say anything he interrupted me. "I don't trust him, I'm afraid he's going to pull something."

"He won't," another voice cut through. We both turned around, so we were facing Layla. "I'll make sure of it," she promised.

Axel hesitated. "Last time I checked you were trying to make her life a living hell. Why are you suddenly acting all buddy-buddy with her?"

"It's called being guilty and trying to fix things, dumbass. I'm trying to set things right for once and make up for the shit I did," she replied. "You should try it sometime."

He ignored her snarky comment, "how do we know we can trust you?"

"Axel-"

"Rosaline," he said my full name seriously, "I don't trust her."

"You know I'm right here, right?"

"I don't care."

Layla rolled her eyes, "I was stupid, I was a bitch. Well, I still am, but that's not the point. I'm just trying to make things right, and you're not giving me a chance."

Axel hesitated, glancing at me. I nodded for him to give her a chance. He reluctantly gave in, "Fine, but make sure Jaxon stays at least a mile away from her at all times."

"Yes, dad." Layla rolled her eyes before grabbing my arm and dragging me away from him.

Once we were in the main entrance she turned to me with a grin stretched across her face. "You know the shit you prepared? Like the paint, rotten food and all that? It wasn't enough to fill up the entire place, so I brought extra stuff to replace what you brought." She gushed excitedly, "I made sure Trent got it all in his pickup!"

"And what exactly did you bring?" I asked as she dragged me through the halls.

"Just some... stuff; we're going to completely trash this place!" she giggled happily. "I can't wait to see that bitch's face!"

After a few minutes of giggling and dragging me through crowds of people, we finally stopped in the huge dinner room. "Looks like everything's set," she said while looking up at the ceiling.

My eyes found their way up to the ceiling too. A gasp escaped my mouth when I saw what was up there. Balloons hung all over the ceiling. There must've been at least five hundred of them because the dinner hall was huge.

"They're water balloons," she explained excitedly. "When the time comes, Justin will cut the strings, and all the balloons will fall on everyone. Not only that, will Trent be standing up there." She pointed at a balcony which looking down on the dinner room we were standing in. "He'll be dumping flour on all of the guests. Just imagine all of this on video!" she gushed out.

I had a feeling it would end up on YouTube. Kasay would get pissed how she wasn't involved. "How did you manage to get Kasay expelled anyway?" I asked without thinking.

388

"I didn't. I know you blamed me for it, but she was skipping school too much, and caught dealing drugs in the girl's bathrooms. She hasn't been fully charged yet, because they're still exploring the case. She was possessing weed and some hard drugs, like meth."

My mouth fell open in shock. There was no way Kasay could've been dealing behind my back... "Meth?!" I gasped, "no, Kasay's not that kind of person..."

"Hate to break it to you, but your two best friends were both doing things behind your back."

I didn't get it, why would Kasay even do that?

Axel was right when he said the two were keeping me in the dark.

"K-Kasay would never do drugs..." I spoke, attempting to sound confident.

"I don't exactly know if she did them, but she was in possession of the stuff, so... she was probably dealing. Heard they found connections between her and college guys too."

Layla spoke of it so normally, like she had been expecting it all along.

But for me, it was huge news. Never in my life could I ever imagine Kasay dealing drugs. I saw her as a different person now. What else was she doing behind my back?

"How do you know all this?"

"Everyone knows about it, it's been the talk of the school. You're just the only oblivious one around here."

I ran a hand through my hair. How could Kasay hide something like that from me? I guess everyone had their own secrets...

"So let's go over the plans again," she changed the subject.

I pushed the disappointment I felt about Kasay down and focused on sabotaging the anniversary dinner.

~*~

---Layla's P.O.V---

If you had told me I would be planning to get revenge on my own mother with Rosaline two weeks ago, I would've laughed in your face and reported you for taking drugs. But now, it all seemed to make sense. Hell, we even got along.

"I think you've gone a bit overboard..." Rose trailed off after I told her our entire plan.

How was I going overboard?

My mother was going to get exactly what she deserved, and so was the guy who was going along with her. They were both going to get what they deserved no matter what.

"I'm not going overboard. I'm just making sure they're going to get what they deserve."

"As long as Axel knows about it," she looked down and played with her fingers innocently. I observed her actions; she always did that when she was nervous.

"You're in love with him, aren't you?" I asked.

Her blue eyes looked up at me in shock. Her mouth fell open and her skin paled.

"W-what?" she stuttered.

"Are you in love with him?"

"W-who?" she asked innocently. She knew exactly who I was talking about.

"Axel Storm Spencer, the guy whose initials who spell 'ass'," I quoted.

She stuttered, "I-I-"

"It's so obvious. You two are obviously madly in love with each other."

She looked incredibly stunned by my statement. "W-we barely k-know each other," she managed to choke out.

"To be completely honest, I have seen you staring at each other for the past seven years," I admitted. "And I bet you every day after school you go and stalk each other's social media accounts too."

"W-we do not!" her cheeks flushed bright red.

I envied the way her pale cheeks could do that. My cheeks could barely turn light pink. She truly was a beautiful girl. Suddenly, my watch started to beep. It was time. My felt myself get a little giddy inside, but I kept all my excitement at ease.

"Let's go wait on the balcony," I said, grabbing her arm. She resisted and pulled back. "What about Axel?"

"What about him?"

"What if he isn't done yet?"

I sighed when I realized what she was trying to say. "Do we seriously have to go check on your boyfriend?"

"He's not my-"

"He's not her boyfriend," someone spoke from behind us. We both turned to the voice.

I felt myself die a little inside, but my posture remained the same. The red headed devil was wearing a suit with all the buttons buttoned up. Of course he was the only person to do that.

"Yes he is," I spoke icily. "Rose, go find your boyfriend."

"What about you-"

"Go," I dismissed her sharply.

"Since when were you two all buddy-buddy?" he asked, sounding curious. I avoided looking into his hazel at all costs.

"None of your business, Smith."

"Look," he ran a hand through his combed red hair, "I'm sorry-"

"I don't have time for this, nor am I interested," I interrupted him before trying to walk away, but he grabbed my arm.

"Please, I'm sorry, at least hear me out."

"You shouldn't be apologizing to me." I yanked my arm away from him. "You should be apologizing to your best friend." I said before walking away.

"What if she's not the one I want?" he called after me, making me freeze on my tracks. "What if you're the one I want?"

I turned around so that I was facing him. The people around us were chatting away, not paying attention to us at all. "Then it sucks to be you, Jaxon." I replied before flipping him the bird and slipping away from him.

As I slipped through bodies of people, a hand grabbed my arm. I spun around quickly and kicked the person's leg in a swift move. "Let me go-"

"It's just me!" Trent threw both his hands into the air. I sighed in relief, glad it wasn't Jaxon. His icy blue eyes very oddly reminded me of Rose's eyes. "Who did you think I was?" he questioned, leaning closer to me.

I took a step away from him. "No one," I lied, but he easily knew I was lying.

"You can't lie to me, I'm the master of lying!" he threw both his hands in the air dramatically. "Therefore, I know exactly when someone's lying to me."

I tilted my head to side. I liked the way he exaggerated things. "That's cute."

His pale face didn't blush, but his ears definitely turned bright red. "I-Is that a compliment?"
~*~
---*Rose's P.O.V*---

Axel's grades donkey butt, but he wasn't stupid at all.

He was in fact incredibly clever and knew how to push people's buttons. Just like the way he pushed the guy who was working behind the stage's buttons. "Can't find a proper job, huh?" Axel challenged the guy who was about to show an anniversary video.

"Get out of here before I call security, kid." The bald man threatened.

"You better call someone to fix that damn hairline before anything," Axel shot back.

The man reached for his walkie-talkie, but before he could reach it, he was knocked out cold. It was a bit mean, but to be fair, the guy looked pretty mean. "Moments like this, I'm glad I work out!" he said, staring at his clean fist.

"Is he dead?" I asked, poking the unconscious guy with my foot.

Axel just chuckled at my question.

He hooked his laptop up to the cords which lead to the giant screen. After a few minutes of him waiting for his laptop to finish connecting, something appeared on the screen.

"Password?! What password?!" he growled in frustration.

He randomly typed something in quickly, but '*Incorrect Password*' flashed on the screen. "Let's try this," he bit his lip, before typing in something else in. He ran his hand through his hair in frustration. "That's the password he uses on everything..." he said to himself, he clicked another button, "password hint... what the..."

I just bit my lip, not knowing what to do. The lights on the other side of the curtain faded and clapping was heard.

"Thank you for coming to our 10th wedding anniversary."

Tenth? Axel never told me they've been married for 10 years...

"First we would like to show all of you some slideshows and a little clip from our wedding," Axel's stepfather said on the microphone.

"No, no, no!" Axel hissed in frustration as he randomly typed in another password and got it wrong.

Murmurs were heard from the other side of the curtain. The shadow of the giant screen lowered down and the images started to project on the screen.

"What's the password hint?" I asked, crouching down next to him to look at the laptop screen.

$$v / c = (1 - t) / t = (2 - t) / (1 - t)$$

I almost laughed at the simple math equation before me. I reached over and typed in the answer which was '*2.41421*'.

How could he not solve something as simple as that? I pressed enter, and sure enough it let me in.

His mouth fell open in shock, "maybe I should start doing my math homework."

I gasped, "you don't do your homework?!"

"I've got that bad boy image I've got to keep, Princess." He flipped his hair before turning back to his laptop.

After a few more moments of him frantically clicking stuff on the computer, he got up and pumped his fist in the air.

Suddenly, the sound of music on the other side of the curtain was replaced by the sounds of moans. We both turned to each other with wide eyes. "Did we just put porn on display?" I chuckled nervously.

Gasps and yelling was heard on the other side of the curtain.

"You have no idea how great that feels," Axel breathed out, his emerald green eyes were glowing with something mysterious. "Their dirty secret is out."

People on the other side of the curtain were freaking out.

"Is that-"

"MRS. WINNEFRED!"

"To think she has articles on shaping the perfect family!"

"I can't believe I read her book!"

"Before anything, we've got to go up to the balcony, we were supposed to be up there 10 minutes ago, and we're running late!" I grabbed his hand, attempting to pull him up the stairs which were near the stage exit.

"Rosaline Arlene Winnefred!" a high pitched woman's voice yelled.

Both our heads snapped in Cleo's direction. Her eyes were narrow, and I swear I could see steam coming out of her ears. Her dark brown hair was pulled up in a professional bun and she was wearing a fancy black dress. If looks could kill, I'd be twelve feet under.

Axel didn't seem affected by my stepmother though, he just smirked at her. "Mad that everyone now knows your dirty little secret?"

"I helped you, Mr. Spencer!"

"You tried to get me shipped off to Military school, you spiteful bitch." Axel's arm tensed.

"I-I-I can explain!" Axel's stepdad said on the microphone on the other side of the curtain.

"Stay out of this, Axel!" she growled at him, before turning back to me. "All I never did was treat you kindly. I saw you as my own daughter because your mother had left you!" she said angrily. "And you repay me this way?!"

"I never asked you to leave your own daughter for me," I shot back. "All you did to my life was cage who I truly was. You wanted full control of everything I said and did. You wanted me to be *your* perfect daughter, you wanted me to be your lab rat that you could treat however you wanted. You treated me like your fucking puppet!

You left your own daughter hanging on her birthday! You knew it was her, didn't you? Every single time I told you about what happened, you would always press me into telling you who that perfect little girl at school bullying me was. My favorite color is blue, not pink. I asked for my room to be blue, not fucking pink!" I screamed at her.

"What kind of mother leaves her own daughter for someone else's daughter? Yes, my mother left, but all you did was the same thing my own mother did. You left your own daughter for a stranger's daughter!" I yelled.

"I helped you through hard times! And all I get is this for helping you?!" she asked incredulously.

"You call squeezing every detail about my terrible day helping?! You put me in the worst situations. You kept my in the dark my entire life, and refused to let me grow up. Maybe without you I would've been more confident on my own, maybe without you I would've learned to make better friends and learned to deal with things on my own! Maybe without you, I would've made my own choices in life instead of you making them for me!" I yelled, noticing everything was quiet around us.

The curtains were open and every single person was staring at us with their mouths wide open. I turned around, staring at all the attention we were getting. Axel was next to the curtain controls, smirking proudly.

"I-I-" Cleo stuttered, trying to find the right words. "But I love you."

"You don't know what love is," I said, everyone around us stayed quiet. "The boy you accused of having issues knows what love is better than you do."

"Ladies and gentlemen," Axel announced to the crowd staring at us, "introducing you to the truth." He gestured around him before bowing sarcastically.

Suddenly, water poured down on everyone not on the stage. I looked up at the balcony and saw Layla saying something to the twins and Trent. The water balloons hanging on the ceiling fell on random people, ruining their expensive gowns and suits. Balloons fell left and right, like it was raining water balloons.

Axel grabbed my hand and dragged me off the stage with him. Cleo followed us off stage with hatred filled in her chocolate brown eyes. Both Axel and I squeezed through people who were soaking wet and got hit by a few water balloons ourselves, but we didn't stop until we were halfway through the huge room.

"Rose?" someone called out. I turned around and found myself face to face with my dad. I barely recognized his face anymore. He had changed too much in the past few months. His icy blue eyes were crystallized. I felt a pang of hurt in my chest seeing my own father looking so heartbroken. "I-I'm sorry honey, I had no idea-"

"Dad..." He looked like a stranger to me.

"Sorry, no time for emotional moments, dad." Axel patted my father on the back. "Mind if I call you dad? You can call me soon-to-be-son-in-law or son," Axel said, giving my hand a little tug. "And sorry for touching your daughter, most dads would've probably shot me by now, but thanks for giving me a chance bro." With that, he pulled me away from my teary-eyed-dad.

We had no time to register anything. All I knew was something thick and powdery fell on us. When I opened my eyes, I started coughing. The whole room was literally white. Every single person was covered in flour.

"Looks like a cocaine factory," Axel snickered.

I coughed while shaking my head so some of the flour would come out of my sticky wet hair. Our fingers stayed laced together as he dragged me to the exit. Before we could leave, he turned to me, his green eyes glowing mysteriously.

"Okay, I'm going to make this as quickly as possible," he said, taking in a sharp breath. "This is the most cliché moment ever since we're both wet- wait- that sounds so wrong- okay my bad- sorry- let me just-" he held his index finger in the air trying to sort himself out before he took in a deep breath. "I'm horrible at this kind of stuff but will you- oh god I'm messing up again- wait I've got this- can you- ah fuck that sounds too cheesy-"

I placed my wet flour-covered finger on his lips. "Axel, will you be my boyfriend?" I asked, my voice sounding soft but confident.

His eyes widened, "That's my job! Take that back!" he grabbed both my hands into his warm wet hands. "Rose, Rosie, Rosaline Arlene Winnefred, will you be my girlfriend?"

"Yes!" I replied immediately.

"Then my answer is yes for you too," he replied. And with that, he pressed his lips against mine. Some people around us gasped at us, but I couldn't care less.

I was now Axel Storm Spencer's girlfriend.
Was I even awake?
And that was our cliché moment...

~*~

Chapter 42 ALL WE NEED

I was floating in cloud nine for the next months, except for the fact that Kasay avoided me at all costs before she was finally thrown in jail. Since she turned 18, they charged her as an adult.

Dustin was devastated when he heard about her, but with everyone's help, he eventually got over it.

Axel's mother wised up and dumped her husband's sorry ass.

Of course, Cleo and his stepdad hadn't looked at each other since. They both blamed getting caught on each other. The truth was they were both to blame. My father filed for a divorce right after the incidents that night, and she didn't get anything from him. He made sure of it.

Jaxon dropped off apology notes every single day. Each note was about different times we spent together. I made it seem like I never read them, but in all honestly, I read every single one of them. A few of them had dried tears on them, but I would never show them to anyone.

School was a lot better.

Everyone was making an effort and trying to be nice to me. Layla had changed my reputation instantly. She was trying extra hard to make it up to me. She even invited me and Axel to sit at her lunch table! But of course, we denied the offer. We didn't enjoy being watched by everyone while we ate.

Every lunch, he would take me outside, or to the school roof. But since it had gotten cold, we sat next to a large window on the top floor of the school which out looked the school's property. Thankfully, no one had classes up there during 5th and 6th period which were the periods before and after lunch. So we basically had the whole area to ourselves with no working video cameras watching us.

Jaxon had tried approaching us a few times, but Axel glared threateningly in his direction and Jaxon chickened out every time. I felt a bad inside sometimes. He had apologized countless times, but I wouldn't forgive him.

I stared up at my ceiling thinking about how much my drastically my life had changed. We'd all be going off to college soon and Axel still hasn't picked his college yet. His simple reply every time I bugged him about college was: *"I'll go anywhere you go"*.

The day my applications were due, I grabbed my files and applied to a few universities in Florida, ones with high acceptance rates and higher chances of me getting scholarships. Ivy League wasn't my dream, it was Cleo's dream. And now that she was gone, there was no point. I applied to multiple undergraduate programs. I was still exploring my options. I didn't plan on choosing till the summer when I'd be going.

Now I was lying on my bed on a Sunday night staring up at my dull ceiling. It was winter break and Christmas was coming up in a few days. My phone started to ring beside me. A picture of me and Axel flashed on the screen with the caller ID **'MY PRINCE'** in bold letters.

I knew it was incredibly cheesy, but I couldn't help myself when I changed the contact name on my phone. I answered the phone quickly.

"Why are you staring up at your ceiling like a possessed person?" Axel asked right when I answered.

"Well hello to you too," I rolled my eyes. "Should I start calling you Mr. Stalker now?"

"Nah, I prefer Mr. Bad Boy," he chuckled. "Or Mr. Sexy Bad Boy if you like. You should close your blinds though; anyone could be watching you right now."

I looked out my window onto the sidewalk below and sure enough, Axel stood there staring up at me.

A blanket of snow covered the pavement and my driveway. Bare naked trees and snow coated on their branches. It looked like a scene from a movie. "Someone's is watching me right now." I mumbled in the phone.

"Get dressed Princess, we're going out."

Every time he said something, a cloud of smoke came out of his mouth because of the cold.

"Has it ever crossed your mind that I might have other plans?" I asked him.

"Do you?" he replied to my question with another question.

"No," I replied.

"Good, now get dressed so I can take you out!" he grinned up at me.

"You didn't even say please," I huffed.

"Please?" His smile warmed me, even from far away.

I rolled my eyes at him. "Fine," I set my phone down on the bed, not bothering to end the call. I closed the blinds before changing into jeans and a long sleeve coat.

"You could've at least left the blinds open," Axel grumbled on the phone.

"Pervert!" I yelled back, trying to put on my winter boots.

"But you love it."

I couldn't help it when a smile appeared on my face. After putting on layered clothes, I skipped happily down the stairs. The walls were now decorated with photos of my dad and I, the evil stepmother was no longer in the picture.

"Rosie! Are you going somewhere?" my dad hollered from Cleo's old study, which he now transformed into his own.

"Yeah, out with Axel!" I hollered back.

Though my dad was hesitant about Axel, he supported my decision. My father had heard other parents talk about Axel, but I convinced him to give my guy a chance.

"Stay safe!"

I slipped out of the front door. Right when I shut the front door, I was embraced in a warm hug. Axel kept me in his embrace for a few minutes before letting go.

"I missed you," he grinned at me.

"We saw each other last night and talked on the phone until three a.m." I pointed out.

"Doesn't matter, I still missed you," he said before giving me a quick peck on my lips.

My heart fluttered and I felt the whole zoo in my stomach. Every single time he kissed me, even a peck, it never changed. My heart would always go crazy and my knees would always go weak.

He laced his fingers through mine and dragged me over to his new slick black car. Of course, he wouldn't let anyone call it a 'car'. His car was named after the couple name Layla gave us which was 'Raxel'.

Once we got settled in his car, he turned on some classical music, but of course he had to switch it to alternative. I didn't mind though. "So where are we going?" I asked.

"It's a surprise," he smirked.

"You're always filled with surprises."

"So you'll never get tired of me," he shot me a million dollar smile.

After a while of driving and normal chit-chat, we finally arrived at the destination. He shut off the car's engine and rushed out to open the passenger door for me.

"Where are we?" I asked, stepping out of the car.

"Guess."

The place was coated in snow. It didn't take me long to realize where we were. A gasp escaped my lips. "You brought me to a junk yard?"

"Not just any junk yard," he slung his arm over my shoulder, drawing me closer to his body. He kept me warm. "The one and only junkyard where we watched fireflies and drank tequila…"

"The junk yard where you started panicking because you had a firefly on your nose," I teased. "I still can't believe such a bad guy like you would be so scared of fireflies!" I laughed.

"I wasn't scared, I was…. Uncomfortable."

"Just blow it! Please!" I imitated him. "Yeah, not scared at all." I snickered sarcastically.

"Princess," he said in a warning tone.

"Prince," I said back with a smirk on my face.

His smirk appeared on his face after a few moments. "I'll get you back later. For now, let's climb that pile of junk." He pointed at the large pile of junk. The junkyard looked so different in the daylight.

Climbing the giant pile of junk was a lot harder this time, since it was all covered in snow and ice. I slipped multiple times, but Axel had managed to catch me every single time. Once we finally arrived to the couch on the top.

The first topic of discussion was university.

"I know you've always planned on going to an Ivy League school," he started. "And I fully support that."

I frowned, "but we won't be together."

"It's your future though, Rosie. I will support you no matter what," his eyes melted into mine.

"Axel…" I breathed out.

"I'll be fine as long as you're happy."

He was truly all I wanted.

"Axel…" I smiled, "I already chose where I'm going. I applied, and already heard back from them."

I had never seen him look that upset. He was completely shattered, but he still tried to look happy for me.

"I'm happy for you Rosie, I truly am."

I started laughing.

He sat there staring at me, utterly confused to why I was laughing.

"Axel, I didn't apply to any Ivy League schools."

He was pleasantly shocked.

"I applied to Florida…" I smiled. "I sent your application there too."

He started kissing me over and over again. "Rosie, you shouldn't have done that." Each short kiss was filled with passion. "You gave up your chances-"

"I didn't give up anything. Like I said, Ivy League has never been my dream. I just want to be happy."

I was overwhelmed with joy to see him happy. He looked like the luckiest guy alive. His eyes showed me how he truly felt about us being able to stay together and attend the same university.

We talked for hours and hours.

We talked about everything.

Parents. *My dad is considering getting back with my mom after all she's done to him.* School. *Is better with you there.* Teachers. *Sucks no matter what.* Grades. *I'm passing, so I couldn't care less.* Life. *Is wonderful with you in it.*

Friendships. *Always ended when people go off to college.* Playing Cupid. *Good luck, I'm still rooting for Trent and Layla.* Christmas. *I'm spending with you no matter what.* The Future. *With you in it.*

The sky. *The colors of your eyes.* Food. *Always a touchy subject since I hate peanut butter and you love it.* Graduation. *You'll be there with me.* Prom. *Can we just skip out?* Fireflies. *Please don't bring that up.*

Forgiving Jaxon. *I know you're planning to do that on New Year's Eve and I'm not going to stop you.* Children. *I want twins.* The Stars. *Shine in your eyes.* Music. *Your voice.* Being cheesy. *I can't help it Princess.* Fairytales. *Don't our lives seem like one?*

We talked while watching the sunset. Time passed so quickly when I was with him. We talked and talked, until the sky was dark and filled with stars, until the temperature dropped about ten degrees. Once it was completely dark, he lit the candles in the jars around the couch we were sitting on.

"Sadly, it's too cold for fireflies." He frowned at the lack of movement around us.

Heaps of snow decorated the whole junk yard. You could barely see any of the junk. He pulled out the same bottle of tequila from that night and handed it to me.

I accepted it and took a swing from it. The liquid burned down my throat, making me a little warmer from the cold around us. I handed it back to him so he could get his swing. He shook his head and put the bottle back under the couch.

"I'm driving," he shrugged.

"That didn't stop you last time," I chuckled.

"Habits change," he shrugged again. "Soon I'll become little Mr. Good Boy." He laughed. His laugh brought joy to my ears, I loved his laugh.

He leaned into me until our noses were touching. Before he could press his lips against mine, something glowed between our eyes. We both pulled back and stared at the firefly.

"It's impossible," I whispered, staring at the one and only firefly right in front of us.

There was no way the firefly could've been out in such cold weather like this.

"You thought lots of things were impossible, Princess." He whispered back, still staring at the firefly. The firefly started to flutter its wings like it was dying.

Axel held out his palm to catch the freezing firefly, but it refused to drop dead. He still kept his hand below the firefly though just in case. He stared at it like it was the most interesting thing ever. His emerald green eyes shone with curiosity and something else I couldn't point out.

"You thought me noticing you was impossible, you thought drinking for you was impossible, you thought Layla changing was impossible, you thought getting Cleo out of your life was impossible, you thought getting suspended was impossible, you thought skipping school was impossible, and you thought a lot of other things were impossible.

Flower, things are only impossible if you think they are. And I learned that when I met you. We've both had crushes on each other for years, but settled with other people because we thought *us* was impossible. But right now, we're sitting here, only the two of us on a pile of junk in a junkyard. That would've sounded impossible to us too if we thought about three months ago.

Now things are different. Things aren't impossible anymore. The sky is within our reach, and we should reach for the stars. Our lives have changed." He spoke, still staring at the fluttering firefly.

"I think that's the best speech I have ever heard," I admitted. "Did you make it up all on the spot?"

"I'm just that smart."

I raised my eyebrows at him, not believing him.

Finally he looked away from the firefly and sighed. "Fine, I actually wrote about half of it down. But it was different from what I said, I swear!" he threw both his gloved hands in the air. I couldn't help but smile.

He grinned sheepishly before grabbing my waist and pulling me so that I was straddling his lap.

"All we need are tequila and fireflies," he breathed into my ear. "That makes the perfect date."

"Correction, tequila and a firefly," I snickered.

"Not anymore," he said, making me look at the firefly.

The firefly was no longer alone. Another firefly was fluttering right next to it. I stared at the two fireflies in awe.

"Princess?" He called for my attention.

I gave him my full attention.

"You've got a firefly on your nose," he said, playfully flicking my nose.

I huffed, "liar."

"By the way."

"Huh?"

"I love you too." He grinned.

My breath got caught in my lungs as I stared into his truthful emerald green eyes.

"And I did not write that down."

~*~

Chapter 43 HAPPILY EVER AFTER

Graduation Day...

"We've all had difficulties we had to overcome." Dustin spoke confidently in the microphone. "For example, me trying to find someone who could actually tell me and my twin apart." He looked straight at me with those eyes as the audience chuckled.

"I must say, I'll miss high school," he admitted, earning a few groans from us seniors in the audience. "And I'm sure you will too once you get to college. I'll miss all the delicious school food," he said sarcastically.

Axel started gagging a few rows away from me. He turned around and caught me looking at him before sending me a wink. He looked hot in the red graduation robe he was wearing.

"I have to compliment the food; the lunch lady gave me extra cookies on November 1st. It was a treat, especially with the hangovers all of us had!" Dustin joked. "I'll miss the crowded halls, football with all the guys, and all the dances we've had. Even though I showed up at prom alone because I'm forever alone, I still enjoyed it," he grinned at all of us.

"I'll jack you off for twenty bucks!" a random girl yelled from the audience.

All of us seniors started laughing, but the adults glared at us in disapproval. "What an offer, but no thanks," he grinned sheepishly. "What made high school so great for me were sports and all my supportive friends. They've helped me through an experience of a lifetime."

"Says the virgin." Axel snorted out loud. I took my bracelet off and flung it at his head. Of course with my terrible aim, I missed and hit a person rows away from him. He noticed, and started laughing. However, he did keep his mouth shut.

Jaxon, who was seated right next to him, turned around and gave me thumbs up for what I did. I forgave him on New Year's Eve, since it was only fair to. Since then, he had been nothing but sweet to me. Axel still disliked him, but he didn't lay a finger on Jaxon, knowing I would get pissed if he did.

"Anyways, I'll surely miss high school. College is going to be a challenge for all of us, but I'm sure most of us will be able to overcome it. I want to thank all my friends, family, teachers, the Miami Hurricanes for giving me a full football scholarship and last but not least, the lunch lady for those extra cookies." Dustin finished his speech.

Everyone cheered and applauded for him.

The principal stepped up on the stand and cleared his throat. "Our graduation ceremony is a brief moment in our lives, but the memory of our time here at Jordan High will last forever. Congratulations class of 2013!"

Everyone stood up and threw their graduation hats in the air.

Deep down inside, I knew this was a moment we would never forget. I felt a pair of strong arms wrap around me before pulling me into a bone crushing hug. "I can't believe we graduated." Axel mumbled in the cusp of my hair.

"I'm actually surprised you graduated," I poked his chest.

He fake gasped in shock. "Are you calling me stupid?"

I grinned up at him. "You said it yourself, not me."

"Rosie!" Jaxon called out, rushing straight up to us. Axel still held onto me possessively, but he kept his mouth shut. "Congratulations!" he yelled while hugging both of us.

Axel didn't seem too happy about him interrupting our moment, but he didn't complain. "Congratulations to you too, and that scholarship you earned!" I grinned at him.

He scratched the back of his neck while looking down. "I wish we were attending the same university though…"

"Me too," I replied. He was going to a university in California while I was going to one in Florida.

"I don't," Alex looked down at Jaxon.

We just ignored him.

"At least you've got your boyfriend with you," he winked at me, but he didn't sound too genuine.

Axel had somehow managed to get into the same university I applied to. My dad seemed to think it was luck, but I knew he had stepped up his game in the past few months and really turned his grades around. His application was pretty impressive. Turns out, there was a lot of community work he did that I didn't know about.

Sure, I dropped my chance of going to an Ivy League school, but I was following my own path in life.

"You'll find someone... eventually," my boyfriend gave an awkward pat on the back to Jaxon.

"Love sick birds!" Layla shrieked as she sprinted towards us. She tackled me to the ground. "I'll miss you two!"

"We won't miss you." Axel grumbled.

"We'll miss you too," I replied. I wanted to add, 'only after October you'.

"What are you guys talking about?" Jaxon glared at Layla. "You'll be only three hours away from each other!"

"Shut up, Smith." Layla rolled her brown eyes.

"Well if it isn't the whole crew?" Justin and Dustin came walking into our little group. Dustin and Justin applied to the same university we were going to. Axel wasn't too happy when he heard about them, but he said it was better than Matt.

"I got news from Kasay!" Dustin announced, holding up a small post card. We all gathered around the postcard as he read it out loud.

Dear everyone,
First of all I have to apologize for hiding such a big secret from you. Especially you Rose, you were my best friend and I should've trusted you. I will be out in a few months because of my good behavior. #Swag
I'll miss you all, hope you all enjoy college. I don't know what

will come of my future, but I hope you all forgive me. I'm doing great here and I've got a girlfriend worth fighting for. You probably notice my grammar has improved. My girlfriend was an English major before she got arrested. Btw. Rose, say hi to your boyfriend for me. Dustin told me you and Axel are official now. CONGRATULATIONS!

Love,
Kasay

"I never would've guessed..." I trailed off. Kasay had a girlfriend. I was happy for her that she found someone.

"Really? I smelt it from a mile away," Axel smirked.

"Smart ass."

Dustin was surprisingly smiling at the letter too. "I'm glad she's found someone... I'm glad she's happy." he said, seeming a bit sad.

Trent appeared from behind Layla and kissed her on the cheek. "Happy graduation, babe."

Axel turned to me with a knowing grin. "You owe me a heavy make-out session, Flower."

I reciprocated the same face. "Remind me later."

"You've got to remember this moment, Princess." He leaned into me. "The moment we finally got out of this hell hole."

I looked around us.

People were congratulating each other everywhere. This was probably the last time we would see all of our classmates in the same place together. High school was over; done for good.

My eyes scanned over everyone's faces. Some people's eyes held joy, some held relief, and some held sadness. I turned to Axel and stared up at his emerald green eyes. The same eyes I'd been dying to look into for years.

He pressed his lips against mine, earning groans from our friends. I chuckled against his lips, knowing every moment with him would be a perfect moment like this.

And it all started from a little crush that never seemed to fade.

After all, it was just a ***Crush on Mr. Bad Boy***.

~*~

The End.

~*~

Crush on Mr. Bad Boy

LILLYCOOLEST1

"Firstly, I would like to thank you all for reading this book. It's been a wonderful ride, and I truly hope you all have enjoyed it. 'Crush on Mr. Bad Boy' has always been one of my personal favorites. I wrote it when I was quite young. In this version of the book, I was able to show more interactions between Axel and Rosaline and how their relationship blossomed fairly fast."

Will there be a sequel to Crush on Mr. Bad Boy?
"Currently, I am not planning on writing a sequel for Crush on Mr. Bad Boy; however I am writing a spin-off about Dustin and Justin, which Axel and Rose may make an appearance in."

Instagram: Lillycoolest1
Wattpad: Lillycoolest1
Radish: Lillycoolest1
Twitter: Lillycoolest1
Facebook: Lillycoolest1

Roadtrip Eclipse
LILLYCOOLEST1

Author's other works:
Seven Letters After You
How to Blackmail a Bad Boy
Roadtrip Eclipse
Damned Fate

PLAY CRUSH ON MR. BAD BOY ON EPISODE

414

Made in the USA
San Bernardino, CA
28 May 2019